Maura took one more bite of the cheese Danish and it was gone. You can't have more. You just can't.

There was something monstrous inside her this morning, a ravenousness that couldn't be satisfied. It was tough, sometimes, living with Larkin and Danielle, watching them in front of their mirrors, both so effortlessly beautiful.

Larkin could become a model just because of her looks. Danielle could work in a club. Things came so damn easily to both of them.

What did it feel like to be hired because everyone found you desirable, even irresistible?

Also by Janet Kotselas Clarke
Published by Ballantine Books:

CHASING FAME

NICE GIRLS

Janet Kotselas Clarke

BALLANTINE BOOKS • NEW YORK

Library of Congress Catalog Card Number: 89-90697

ISBN 0-345-34843-5

Manufactured in the United States of America

First Edition: July 1989

Book One

One

"You just shortchanged me," the woman said.

Danielle looked up at the woman, a real blond snob in a super-expensive fur coat. "Excuse me?"

"I gave you a twenty," the woman said. "You gave me back a dollar and change. You owe me another ten dollars."

Danielle looked at the cash register. Mrs. Myrowitz had said to always put the bill across the top. But yesterday when Danielle had done that, a ten-dollar bill had dropped right to the floor.

Anyway, she was sure the woman had given her a ten.

"I'm calling the manager."

"Wait!" Danielle practically screamed. It was only her second day, and it would look incredibly bad if they saw she was having more problems. "Look," she said. "I'm positive you gave me a ten. Maybe if you checked your wallet—"

The woman gave her a totally drop-dead look, turned on her heel, and walked straight over to the information counter.

Uh-oh.

Ivorsen & Shaw. One of the most important department stores in all of New York, and Danielle had thought maybe this would be her first real chance. She had gotten the job in the middle of the store's giant ad campaign, "1988: The Year of Living Luxuriously.'' And after ten thousand waitressing jobs in California, she had thought this would maybe be something different. The store was in the middle of changing from old-fashioned to modern, and maybe her life was going to change, too, since she was going to be twenty pretty soon. But now—

"Danielle!"

She turned around. Uh-oh. Mrs. Myrowitz standing with the customer.

"I understand there's some confusion about how much change Mrs. Parks was supposed to get."

"I'm not confused," Danielle said. "She gave me a ten."

Mrs. Myrowitz set her lips into a real thin line. She looked like ten million teachers Danielle had had in school in L.A., all saying, "Take this note to the principal's office."

Mrs. Myrowitz reached into the cash register, plucked out a ten, and handed it to the lady. "Please accept our apologies, Mrs. Parks. With some of our new help during the expansion—I'm sure you understand."

The woman, Mrs. Parks, looked Danielle right in the eyes, and right there Danielle could see she probably did this all the time to get some kind of weird kicks.

The woman left, and Mrs. Myrowitz came up real close to Danielle. She always stood much too close, and then you could smell this weird scent under her perfume, kind of an oldness even though she was maybe only in her fifties. "I don't think I need to tell you that ten will come out of your paycheck, Danielle."

"But—"

"You were told the proper procedure, and you ignored it. You've got to learn that mistakes can be expensive."

"But she was lying. We could check the register at the end of the day."

"Caroline Parks is one of the store's most important customers. I seriously doubt she was lying. And even if she were a stranger: you *must* follow procedures." Mrs. Myrowitz narrowed her eyes. "And I thought I told you to pull your hair back from your face."

"It didn't look good. I tried it and—"

"Danielle, you have one warning on your record already, and it's only your second day here. Look around. Do you see any of the other salesgirls with hair like yours?"

Danielle looked across the floor. There was Mrs. Kuzak in gloves, who had her hair cut super-short, and a girl named Misty Keyes, who had a ponytail. But they were different. Not to be conceited, but her hair was a lot nicer than theirs. Why couldn't she wear it long? It was blond and wavy, and people noticed it because it was pretty, not because it looked bad. Even strangers on the street. Even women. But this was the first floor, not like the third, which always had Bruce Springsteen and George Michael blaring from the speakers. This was the floor for old ladies.

"Okay," she said. "I'll fix it on my break."

Mrs. Myrowitz looked at her watch. "Fix it now," she said, "and be back by a quarter after, Danielle." Her lips got all thin again. "And let this be our last little incident."

"All right. I'll be back in a while."

"Not in a while, Danielle. Fifteen minutes exactly."

Danielle got her purse from under the cash register and got out of the store as fast as she could. Fifteen minutes. Putting her hair back. Getting yelled at in front of a rich, snotty woman. It wasn't what she had thought New York was going to be like.

But then, it was only her second day at the store. And she was always getting into trouble before things got good.

The main thing, anyway, was that soon her father would be back in New York from wherever he was working on his movie— London, he said—and then she knew things would be great.

"We'll make up for all those lost times," he had written when she was in California, and even though part of her had said, "Don't believe him. He's always lied before," she just had to. The other times she had been so young, anyway, coming to New York when she was ten and then fourteen. And sure it had seemed really bad that both those times he had suddenly had emergencies in Europe. "What kind of emergencies does a screenwriter have?" her mother had screamed.

But then, her mother was always talking against him, always saying to forget him and that he was no good. "He only wants to see someone when he can use them," she always said. "And I don't know how that man thinks he can use you, Danielle, but you can bet on it if he invited you to come to New York."

But who was her mother to talk? The great Victoria Austin, who hadn't acted in a movie in fifteen years but made promises as if she owned a studio or something. With those young guys she picked up on the beach, she'd say, "Oh yes, Cleve and I are still quite close even though we're divorced. Of *course* I'll send him your pictures."

Which she never did, not that it would've made any difference even if she did, because they *weren't* "quite close." They didn't even hardly speak to each other.

Plus why should she trust her mother about anything? At the end her mother hadn't even wanted her to live in the house anymore. "I don't want you around, Danielle," Victoria had said, "unless you're ready to say you're my sister." And she had actually done it, too. She had said, "This is my sister, Danielle," to this life-guard, and Danielle could see that the guy didn't believe her for one minute, necessarily. But then, it didn't mean he cared, either. Those guys never cared what Victoria said; they never had. And Danielle had to admit it was that her mother was extra sexy, she guessed. She had something that all those guys wanted. Even way in the past, she could remember one time when she was seven and Victoria had met a guy at a restaurant in the middle of nowhere. They drove to a motel, and Victoria said to Danielle, "Wait in the car." And it was about a thousand degrees out, so even the guy had said, "Are you sure?" But in the end he didn't care, because he wanted to be with her mother. And sometimes she felt it was why she had never fallen in love (her big secret). Maybe because her mother never seemed to love anybody; she just wanted as many cute guys as she could get.

But that was all in the past. Part One of Danielle's dream had already come true, just coming to New York. Parts Two and Three were the tough and secret parts—figuring out what she wanted to do "with her life," and then becoming rich and famous doing whatever it was she had decided. But you had to start somewhere.

The only sometimes weird part was at the apartment, living with her two roommates. They were both nice and everything, and she had to be grateful to Maura, who was kind of the more serious one, because Maura was the one, without even knowing her, who had said, "Do you want to come live with me and my friend Larkin?" And you had to admit that was a great thing to do, because they had only met that second, or maybe ten minutes before, in the waiting room of a job agency, and Danielle had been pretty upset because she had failed her typing test for the third time in a row, and Maura had said, "Don't worry," and then from there they had talked about everything under the sun. So she had to be grateful. But sometimes she just felt like such a third wheel or whatever it was. Because Maura and Larkin were like best friends, always laughing at things that had happened a super-long time ago. It was weird. But she guessed she'd get used to it. It was a place to sleep, anyway.

areas. Put your large bills *across* the register drawer, and try to smile at every customer."

"Okay." God, why didn't she just leave?

"Now, this gentleman who's coming over now—*no* strange looks even if he asks for panty hose in an extra-large size. That's *his* business, not yours."

But as soon as Mrs. Myrowitz left, the guy leaned on the counter and pulled out his card again. "Just take this card," he said. "Even if you don't want a job. You never know when it might come in handy to know someone important. Suppose you end up in jail?"

"I'm not going to any jail."

"All right. Whatever. Just take it."

She looked down at the card again. Raised lettering, which at least meant it was expensive. But so what? Practically anyone could afford even expensive cards. And what if he hadn't even had a whole lot made? Or what if he had a jillion different cards with different occupations on them, like Rockford used to? You just could never tell anything.

"Take it, put it away; I don't care what you do with it as long as you don't throw it away. And please—take some advice from someone who knows, Miss . . . What's your name?"

"Danielle," she said.

"Nice name. Okay. Danielle. Please: If I saw you, someone else could have seen you, too. So lay off with the sticky fingers."

"Good-bye," she said, and luckily a woman came up to the counter right then, and the guy must have figured there wouldn't be any point in hanging around anymore.

But it was weird. At first she had thought he was creepy, but now she didn't know. He seemed almost nice, the way he had given her advice like that. Not that she was going to call him or anything, but still—might as well keep the card.

And actually, he had given her some good advice, too. What had happened to her skills? She had obviously gotten rusty. He had seen the whole thing!

Well, it wasn't the end of the world. No one else had seen her, and she just had to "bide her time," as they said, till her father got back from London, and maybe by then her plans would also be more definite. Like her roommate Larkin. She wanted to be an actress so much; it was all she cared about in the entire world. And Danielle was almost jealous about it, the way Larkin could be so definite. But it seemed slavey to her, to be an actress, always waiting for this part or that part, waiting and waiting and waiting to be hired. It just wasn't enough.

She looked at all the panty hose around her, though—extra-large, support, all these stupid variations people asked about when she couldn't begin to understand why they never knew these things for themselves—and she realized this wasn't enough, either. She was going to last about two more days on this job before she went crazy.

Two

"I don't understand," Maura said, looking at the woman behind the desk. She had the longest fingernails Maura had ever seen. "The job was advertised for the first time yesterday—I've been reading the classifieds for two weeks now—so if it appeared for the first time, how can it already be filled?"

The woman stubbed out her cigarette and sighed. "Look. I've told you it's filled, all right? The job I'd *like* to send you out on *isn't* filled. It's in publishing, and it would be a *fabulous* foot in the door, Maura. *Really* fabulous."

"What kind of publishing?" Maura asked. She just wasn't going to get excited anymore; the agencies had all sent her to so many horrible job interviews, she didn't think anything decent could even exist at this point.

"Well, it's mailing lists, actually. So it's publishing *and* advertising you'd be breaking into. You'd have a foot in the door, and then you could take your pick."

"It isn't at AAA Mailing Lists, by any chance, is it?"

The woman blinked. "Did we already send you—?" She looked down at the index card with Maura's name at the top—*my torture card,* Maura thought. *All the nightmare appointments I've been on.*

"I was sent by another agency," Maura said, standing up. "And I can see why they haven't filled it yet. Do you know what the man at the company told me? I'd be organizing mailing lists on a computer, and I'd have to stay until I finished the work every night no matter how late, and there wasn't even going to be overtime. Ever."

She reached down and picked up the clipboard with all the agency's ads on it. Cosmetics, network, museum, advertising, fashion—they managed to include something for everyone, even for the idealistic with ads like "nonprofit but rewarding: *must like people*." "These are all fake, aren't they? I mean, that's the real truth, right?"

"Of *course* not. If certain jobs are filled, it's only because there's a delay, Maura. The ads don't come out the day we call them in to the *Times*, you know."

"Right. I'll bet. Look. Take me out of your files. I'm not interested in any of your crappy jobs."

The woman blinked. "Really. I—"

"Really. So shove your jobs, shove my so-called job card, and I hope you break every one of those hideous nails."

She turned and walked out, through the smoked-glass reception area with half a dozen pathetically hopeful new applicants. "The ads are fake!" she yelled. But all she got was blank looks, and she realized everyone probably thought she was crazy. She would have thought so, too, if she had been one of the people sitting on those stupid plush couches. (And she despised the word "plush" now, because half their fake ads used it—"Meet and greet clients in plush Park Ave office." Sure.)

Maybe I am *going crazy*, she thought as she got out onto the street. The agencies had to fill *some* jobs or they couldn't exist. And she guessed they did fill jobs, like the one at the mailing list company. But it was all so dishonest. When she had first registered and said she wanted to make four hundred dollars a week, they had said fine, absolutely, no problem. And then last Friday, Miss Long Nails, Margo Allison, had suddenly said, "Look, Maura, you're just out of college, you have no experience; three hundred is max, absolutely max."

"But what about four hundred?" Maura had stupidly said. "You told me—"

"We tried our best, okay? Now be realistic."

So now she was going to be realistic. Maura Cassidy, 1988 graduate of Scranton State College, was going to make three hundred dollars a week *if* she got a job, and then on that she was going to pay her share of the fifteen-hundred-a-month rent.

Which she could get used to if she could get a job. But she just didn't understand why it wasn't happening. She was smart—it was her father, not Yale, who had forced her to go back to Scranton after her summer session in New Haven. She had to lose some weight, but she was okay—dark-haired and plain, maybe, but clean, even corporate-looking when she went out on interviews.

So then, what was it?

"Your standards are too high," she could hear her father saying. "Always trying to be the big shot. Always turning away from what's right under your nose."

Which in her case had meant Patrick Delaney, her father's best friend's son, and she supposed everyone else in Scranton when it came down to it. When she had called that summer to say the counselor at Yale had said they wanted her as a full-time student, she had thought her father would be thrilled. What she had gotten was silence, and then: "You'll go to Scranton, Maura. What do you want to fool around with a place like Yale for?"

She knew that if her mother had been alive, she would have let her stay at Yale. Her mother would have been proud. But to her father it was just an expensive, unnecessary collection of buildings in a faraway city. What was the difference—Yale or Scranton? And if he knew she had turned down a job interview an employment agency wanted to send her on, he would have said the same thing. What's the difference, Maura? A job's a job.

She wasn't even asking for very much—just an interesting job at an interesting company. Something that could turn into a career or at least get her started. But that, apparently, was exactly what thousands of other new graduates wanted to do. And they all seemed to be from Harvard or Yale, and she couldn't exactly say, "Well, I *could* have gone, but my father said . . ." Suddenly she was nothing.

She was happy to be in New York, though. And rooming with Larkin and Danielle would probably work out, even though it seemed insane to be rooming with two of the most beautiful girls she had ever seen: Larkin, a perfect-looking redhead, someone any other woman would hate on sight, and Danielle, probably every East Coaster's picture of the typical California girl, blond and beautiful and . . . well, not really up there in the brain-power department.

But Maura loved Larkin—they had been an unlikely, mismatched pair of roommates that summer session at Yale: she had hated Larkin immediately, but they had ended up best friends and vowed to live together in New York after they each graduated. And miracle of miracles, they'd actually kept the vow, with help on the broker's fee from Larkin's extremely wealthy mother.

And Maura would never forget meeting Danielle—a sobbing,

young-looking blonde, crying in the reception area of an employment agency because the tester had told her she was "hopeless" as a secretarial candidate. "Don't even listen to her," Maura had said, grabbing Danielle's arm and leading her out of the agency—damned if she was going to stay for her own appointment. But those people were horrible—why did they want to reduce people to tears?

And she had ended up going out for coffee with Danielle and talking to her for hours—"Don't you see? They want you to lose all your confidence so you'll settle for a job nobody else in their right mind would take."

"Like what?" Danielle had asked. "I really need something super-quick, because I'm staying at this horrible hotel and I'm not even going to be able to *pay* pretty soon." And right then Maura had decided to ask Danielle to be their third roommate. The girl didn't know *anything*. How was she going to even survive?

Luckily, Larkin had agreed—Danielle took one bedroom, Maura took the other, and Larkin took the maid's room just to drive her mother crazy. "She'll die," Larkin had said with a smile. "Really. It will devastate her." And so far, it was working out. It was fun living with Larkin, and Danielle seemed sweet even if she *was* something of a ditz.

The only question was whether *any* of them would make enough money to pay the rent.

She walked into the Athena Coffee Shop, where there was a bathroom at the back and—last week, anyway—a broken phone booth that let you make long calls for a dime. Discovering it had been her one triumph in an otherwise failure-filled week.

"Pitch in on Fashion Design," she read as she unfolded the *Times* inside the booth. It had to be another lie. "Assist Baby Doctor"—*always* a lie, probably directed at girls who wanted to marry doctors. And what could be better than a baby doctor, with all those cute little patients? No old men falling down, or nasty old women leaving off stool samples.

She was obviously losing her mind.

"No Steno OK. Major network. Choose your fave: News, Soaps, Editorial. Network needs 15 new secys."

Amazing. Why had she ever believed any of it?

But on the other hand, someone did have to work in all those offices, didn't they?

And then she saw something: a tiny ad at the bottom of the page, so tiny it had to be real: "Admin Asst, interesting pos, entertainment biz. F/T, tough, hectic."

Well, it could be nothing. But at least it wasn't another agency ad.

She called the number, let it ring ten times, and was about to hang up when a man answered, "Yeah," clearly out of breath and in a hurry. She could hear phones ringing in the background.

"Hi, I'm calling about—"

"Yeah, yeah, the ad," he said, still out of breath. "Name—"

"Uh, Maura Cassidy. What kind of—"

"Hold on."

He clicked her on hold but came back a few seconds later. "So. Maura Cassidy. You can type? No bullshit?"

"Sixty at least."

"You interested in actingdancingsingingperforming?" he asked as if they were all one word.

"What? Uh, no. But why—"

"Beautiful. Shit. Hold on."

He put her back and forth on hold for the next few minutes, but eventually she managed to set up an appointment for the next day and find out what it was: a casting office.

A *casting* office. *That* could be interesting.

She could just hear her father: "Sure, casting office. More like casting *couch*. They want the beauties, Maura, those little . . . what do you call them? Bimbettes."

And she looked at herself in the glass of the booth: wavy brown hair, brown eyes, neither here nor there. A face the word "plump" was made for. Maybe he was right.

But she had an idea. It was chancy, and maybe it would backfire, maybe she'd be humiliated in a roomful of gorgeous blonds. Or bimbettes. Maybe the man would scream at her. But it was worth a try. Granted, it was the kind of thing Larkin was more meant to do than she was: Larkin had tricked and manipulated her way into everything she'd ever gotten, including several passing grades at Yale that otherwise would have been Fs. Larkin always used her looks. But there were other possibilities.

Fifteen minutes later she walked in through the already open door of Falcone Casting. The front room was tiny and—amazingly—empty: just a front desk with a phone, a couple of new-looking leather couches, gray carpeting, and dozens of cartons filled with files and papers.

The phone rang; she heard "Goddammit!" from behind a closed door, and then a muffled conversation.

Then the phone rang again, and again.

This was her chance; this was why she had come.

She walked over to the desk, pushed down the blinking button, and answered, "Falcone Casting; may I help you?"

"Yes," a female voice said. "I'm calling about your ad in the *Times*?"

"I'm sorry," Maura said, "the job has been filled."

She hung up, and the door to one of the inner offices flew open. A man who fit the voice—tall, burly, gray-haired, gruff-looking—was glaring at her. "Who the hell are *you*?"

The phone rang and she picked it up. "Falcone Casting."

"Hi, I'm calling about the ad?"

"Sorry," she said, glancing over at Mr. Falcone. "The job's been filled. But thanks for calling."

When she hung up, he walked over to the desk and leaned down so he was at her eye level. "The job's been filled," he said hoarsely. "Really. You mind telling me about it?"

"I spoke to you earlier," she said. "My name is Maura Cassidy? And we had an appointment for tomorrow, but I just thought—"

The phone rang again, and she went through the same routine. Mr. Falcone was still staring at her, but less menacingly this time, she felt.

"So you type?" he said when she hung up.

So he wasn't kicking her out! "Really well," she said. "And I'm a really good speller, I can take fast longhand if you talk pretty slowly, but I know I'll get better, I can work late—"

"How much do you want?" he asked.

She looked around. The office was an absolute mess—it looked as if a forklift had picked up the entire contents of another office and dumped it in the room—but underneath it all, it looked like good carpeting, and the two couches were leather. And *casting*—he had to be rich. "Four-fifty," she said.

He laughed. "Four-fifty what? I'll give you three seventy-five, no overtime, no tears if it doesn't work out. You clean up the goddamn mess out here, and if I see floor and carpeting and I can find where the hell you've filed all this shit, the job's yours."

Her heart skipped. A job! And a great one! She felt like hugging him. "That's *great*," she said. "So should I start now?"

He looked at his watch. "Yeah. Call in some lunch from the deli downstairs. And you know what to say when the girls call, right?"

Girls? "You mean the other applicants?"

"I mean the *clients*. They're a client, I talk to them—there's a list somewhere in one of those drawers. They're not a client, they send their eight-by-tens and a list of the clubs they've danced in.''

"Danced in—? Oh, you mean dancers?" She suddenly felt amazingly stupid.

"Dancers, yeah. Exotics." He turned and started walking back into his office, but then he turned around and faced her again. "What—you thought this was actors, shit like that?"

"No, no. I—"

He laughed, and she could hear him chuckling as he pulled out his chair and sat down in his office again.

Actors and shit like that. Well, yes.

"Hi, Dad. I got a job. . . . Uh-huh. Doing what? Well, uh . . ."

And then what was she going to say? "Booking strippers"?

Shit.

But a job was a job. And 375 was more than 300.

Hooray! Maybe.

She looked around the room, at the cartons sagging under the weight of years of files. It all suddenly looked seedier now that she knew the files weren't filled with eight-by-ten glossies of beautiful actresses and hunk actors.

But at least she was in New York. She wasn't in Scranton; and she wasn't going to have to marry Patrick Delaney. So that was all really good.

She guessed.

Three

"It doesn't fit," Larkin said, looking at her mother in the mirror.

"Darling, I think it looks divine. We'll get it for you in black and in silver."

"I don't want it," Larkin said, pulling the sweater off over her head. It fell on the floor, and Anne James bent down and picked it up.

"Have these wrapped and sent," Larkin heard her mother say outside the dressing room a few moments later.

Well, what the hell, Larkin thought. She could give them to her roommates.

"Darling, our reservations are for one o'clock," Anne James called in through the curtain. "Is there anything else you want to try on?"

"I told you no," Larkin said. Christ, she wanted to get out. But shopping and lunch with her mother were one of The Conditions. Yes, her father had left her wealthy. But with Conditions. And one of the conditions was that Larkin continue the rituals she had practiced with her mother for as long as she could remember: shopping and lunch on Saturdays, dinners with the "appropriate people" during the week, asking politely each week for the money that was rightfully hers as if it weren't.

But then, it had all been a trick of her father's, one of the convenient little deceits he had set up ever since he had discovered the truth about her and his brother.

"Larkin, it's nearly one o'clock."

"I'm coming," Larkin called out. She opened her purse and shook a Valium out of her pill bottle. "Be right there," she called out again, feeling better as soon as she tasted the bitterness. Fifteen or twenty minutes and she'd have a drink with lunch, too. *Then* she and her mother could talk about whatever her mother wanted to discuss.

"I'll have the sole," Anne James said, reading over the tops of her glasses.

"I'll have a vodka martini straight up," Larkin said.

She could feel her mother looking at her, but she continued to look at the waiter. He was cute, too, exotic-looking and muscular.

"Darling," Anne said. "What about to eat?"

Larkin smiled her fake smile. "I'm not hungry, thanks."

"But darling . . ."

Larkin handed the menu back to the waiter and extended her foot so that it rubbed his ankle.

He looked surprised and stepped back.

"Just bring me the drink," Larkin said. He gave her another questioning look and then walked off, and Larkin turned to watch: great ass, nice walk, really nice thighs.

"I wish you would eat something," Anne James said.

"I'm not hungry," Larkin said, searching in her purse for her cigarettes. She knew she'd be starved after lunch, but she could grab something at home. What she didn't want to do was share lunch with her mother.

"And your smoking is something we should discuss," Anne said.

Larkin looked across the table at her mother. "What's to discuss?"

Anne James looked down at her hands for a moment. "I can't say it was a condition of your father's will, because you know that it wasn't. But it was an element he would have included in his definition of suitability, whether you were living your life the way he'd want."

Christ. Larkin took another drag and put the cigarette down. "So you're saying what, Mother?" She sounded crude and she knew it—not like the daughter of Hamish James, not the one who had gone to Spence and then Yale. "Just spit it out, all right? Are you telling me I can't smoke? We *are* talking about the allowance, aren't we?"

Anne James sighed. "If he had wanted to make it a condition, he would have," she said. "But I think you should keep it in mind."

"Fine. I will," she said, and she took another drag.

But of course her mother didn't say anything more about it; that was what Larkin had finally learned about Anne after twenty-three years. She'd observe and she'd know things and she'd be unhappy and dissatisfied and judgmental, but she always stopped short of actually saying or doing anything definite. When Larkin's sister had spilled the details of their trip to Europe and all that she knew about Larkin's relationship with Geoffrey, even then her mother had never mentioned any of it directly to Larkin. All that her father said—although he was already in the hospital with lung cancer at the time—was, "I don't understand you. He's my *brother*." But then his real feelings had come out in the will: "To my daughter Larkin, who so obviously doesn't have the slightest concept of how to lead a good and decent life, I leave the sum of $350,000, to be held in trust by her mother until Larkin reaches the age of 40. Amounts deemed appropriate by Anne James may be distributed to Larkin before that time if, in the judgment of Anne James, Larkin is deserving of these monies, as reflected in her life-style, choice of career, and general demeanor."

Which, Larkin had discovered, covered just about everything.

"I'll be back in a second," she said, standing up. The Valium had hit, and she was feeling good. She loved wandering around in this kind of mood. And Café des Artistes was great for spotting interesting-looking men.

But the waiter was coming back, and she sat down, and she could feel her mother watching as she watched the waiter.

"What's your name?" Larkin asked the waiter.

Again, he looked surprised. Not a man who would go far. Didn't he know how good-looking he was? "Uh, Ramon," he said quietly.

"Where are you from, Ramon?"

He was actually blushing as he set down their drinks and then emptied the ashtray. "Ponce," he said—again, so quietly she could barely hear him.

"Ponce," Larkin said. "That's in Spain?"

"Puerto Rico," he said.

"Ah. Geography was never my best subject."

He gave a small smile. Not a man of a lot of words, either. But then, those were sometimes the best. . . .

"Thank you," Anne said loudly, and Ramon smiled again—but this time at Anne—and then moved off.

"St. Maarten is rather a long way off," Anne said to Larkin after Ramon had left.

"I'm well aware of that," Larkin said, sipping her martini and leaning back in her chair. St. Maarten had been absolutely great. A family trip, she had been sixteen, and she had spent every free moment in the hotel's staff quarters with one of the gardeners. They hadn't even been discovered until the day before the end, either. The bad part was that Gabriel had been fired, and he had a wife and two children, she'd later discovered from her sister. But it had been fun while it lasted.

"I'd like to know your plans for this fall, Larkin," Anne said. "You've told me nothing since you moved in with Maura and the other young woman."

"Danielle," Larkin said. "And I told you my plans: I got into the Kozloff Institute, which is incredibly hard to do. So I'll be studying improvisation and audition techniques."

"And what about the modeling?"

"I'm not going to do it," Larkin said. "We've been over it a dozen times."

"Your father felt it would be an excellent way for you to earn some money of your own."

"I'm not going to do it," Larkin said again. "It was easy for him to say he wanted me to, but I made it very clear to him when he was alive: I wasn't going to do it, and I'm not going to go back on my promise. And anyway, I'm too short. No one seems to realize that part, but it's true."

She started to light another cigarette and saw that her hand was shaking. So much for the Valium. But her mother didn't even know: it was Geoffrey she had promised, Geoffrey who had made her swear she'd never be a model. "I want you to be an actress," he had told her in Venice. "I know you can do it. But you won't do it if you become a model, and you won't do it unless you do it right away."

He had come to see her in productions at Yale even when her parents hadn't. He had never missed one. And when she was with him, she believed what he said: she believed she could do it. And she also believed that he knew what he was talking about, because he had gotten so sidetracked in his life, wanting to be an artist and ending up as what? A drinker, traveling around the world to the great museums because he could afford to without working, and knowing he had missed his chance. Ending up as a travel guide for his nieces' Grand Tour.

"Then what are your plans for making money?" Anne James asked.

Larkin took a deep breath. "I'm going to work part-time at whatever I can find," she said. She knew that sounded good and industrious and properly humble. Even though she'd barely have to work if she continued to get the allowance she had been getting. But there was no need to explain that to her mother. "And I assumed there would be the allowance."

There. She had said it delicately and evenly.

But her mother was looking off into the distance, and Larkin followed her gaze. Anne was looking at Ramon.

"Mother?"

Anne faced her. "Very well. I suppose . . . I suppose that what you've been getting would be reasonable."

She smiled and suddenly felt ravenous. "Actually, Mother, I think I'll have something to eat after all."

Because after all, she had gotten what she wanted one more time, and it had been easy, as usual.

Four

"So," Danielle said. She looked across the table at her father. It was just so much like a dream having him right here instead of a billion miles away talking on the phone. And he looked totally handsome, better even than when she had seen him in L.A. four years ago.

Except that he was still drinking. A vodka straight up now, and it was going pretty fast. And in his last letter he had said he had quit; so when had he started again?

And it was weird. In all her daydreams he was always the one doing the talking: "Tell me your plans, Danielle. Tell me your dreams. There's so much you can do here in New York. Where do you think you'll start?"

But now? Nothing. He still didn't even know what her job was.

The waiter brought their food—veal that right away kind of smelled like bad breath, and a couple of super-skimpy-looking salads.

"Thanks," Danielle said, and then she looked at her father. "So tell me about the screenplay you're working on with Colette. What's it about?"

"Ah. It's a great story. You've probably read about it—the family in Utah? The son who killed his brothers and father?"

She shrugged. "It sounds kind of horrible. You're making a movie about it? It's not a comedy or anything, is it?"

He laughed, and she realized she hadn't seen him smile in a super-long time. "Not exactly," he said. But then she felt like maybe she had said something dumb. And there was this huge silence again.

"So my job is okay," she finally said.

He looked up. "That's right," he said. "You're working."

She nodded. "At Ivorsen & Shaw. In, um, panty hose."

He looked disappointed.

"It's just—you know, till I get something more interesting. I mean I have to start somewhere, right?"

"Sure," he said. "Sure. But—panty hose? I thought you wanted to act."

"Me?" She stared at him. "I've *never* wanted to act. And I never will, either. I don't ever want to have to do all that pathetic waiting actresses always do, waiting for their agent to call, waiting for this, waiting to meet some stupid producer."

He smiled. "Like Victoria."

She shrugged. "Mom hardly even makes the effort anymore. But I can remember what it was like. And you'll never catch me doing that. Never."

"So then, what *do* you want? Not panty hose," he said.

"I have my own plans. They're a secret."

"And you're not going to tell me? Dear old Dad?"

She smiled. He didn't exactly look like a dear old Dad. But he was at least really interested. Finally.

"Well," she said, leaning in close to him. "It's kind of a secret, but I guess I can tell you: I mean, I've already done the first part, coming to New York. But the next part is figuring out what I'm going to do, like what I'm interested in. And then I'm going to get famous doing it."

"Uh-huh." He was looking around for a waiter. He signaled for another drink and then turned to Danielle. "Do you want another Coke?"

"Uh-uh."

He made another motion to the waiter and then turned back to Danielle. "So. Your plans."

"That's—that's what they are."

He looked surprised. "Oh. Well. That's good, honey. That sounds really good."

The smell of the veal was making her sick. "You know, I don't have a trust fund the way this girl, one of my roommates, does. I *have* to work, and so what if it's just panty hose? At least I pay my own way."

"I know that, Danielle. What are you getting upset about?"

"Nothing." She stood up. "I'll be back in a second."

She walked back through the restaurant, past a whole bunch of snotty-looking women who looked a lot like that Mrs. Parks at the store today. Past some snotty-looking waiters, too, into the ladies' room.

There was a black woman sitting there all in a uniform, black with a white apron, and Danielle just looked at her.

She had been planning—she didn't know what she had been planning, but it was going to be something bad. But now there was this lady; it was obvious *she'd* get in trouble if Danielle did something.

And anyway, she had never taken from a person, not ever. It was a rule. If someone reached over into the stall for *her* purse or something like that, she'd be super upset.

She looked at herself in the mirror. Her face was all red, and she felt like hitting someone. Her stupid father. Why couldn't he ever be what she wanted him to be?

Five

"You going to be okay? You know, it's late," George Falcone said. "It's almost seven."

"I'm fine," Maura said. "I'm leaving in five minutes. I just want to finish one thing."

"Suit yourself." He shook a key off a key chain and handed it to her. "You lock up when you leave, okay? I've got an extra key at home, so this one's yours."

"Okay. Thanks."

He winked. "You did good today."

She smiled. "Thanks. See you tomorrow."

She watched him leave, a tall man who moved slowly, as if moving was slightly painful and took more energy than he really wanted to expend.

And she realized he was as much of a mystery to her now as he had been at the beginning of the day. He had explained some of the mechanics of the business to her, but she still didn't know anything about him—how he had started, why he had started, how long he had been in business. She knew she liked him, though: there was an easy friendliness about him once you got past his occasional sarcasm, an obviously well-meaning heart buried somewhere in there.

And the business fascinated her already. She had thought it would be incredibly sleazy and depressing, with burned-out, aging hooker-type women dragging themselves into the office and doing weird stripteases to get work; her fantasies had been graphic and bizarre and totally inaccurate. The reality was that the three women she had met so far were all young, healthy-looking, and extremely pretty. One was a college student, one an aspiring actress, and one brought her three-year-old daughter in with her, whom Maura watched while the woman talked to George in his office.

And she had to admit she was also a little envious of the women. Maybe even more than a little envious. They were getting paid to show off their bodies, paid to excite men because they could do it. They got up there and danced and stripped, and were good enough that they were hired again.

And it made her wonder: What if she had to get up on a stage? "Ladies and gentlemen" (or just "gentlemen," she supposed), "Maura Cassidy. Maura the—" But she couldn't even think of a stage name. One of the women today, the young mother, was known as the Midnite Starr.

Ladies and gentlemen, Maura Cassidy.

If she took off her clothes, would they laugh?

She had looked at hundreds of pictures today, sorting through the mounds of files. A few of the women hadn't been that attractive, but most were so pretty. And the women in the office today, they were so easy with themselves and comfortable with their attractive-ness. She had imagined each one in her act, and it was easy: each would have looked good, with the audience cheering or watching in urgent silence—whatever it was that men did at places like the KitKat Club and the Junction.

And then she tried to picture herself.

Fat Maura Cassidy, ladies and gentlemen. You may not be able to see the waist, but there's enough woman here for all of you.

"You know, you're starting to get a little porky," was the way Patrick Delaney had put it so tactfully this summer after weeks of making love in the dark. "You could lose about ten pounds, Maura."

And now it was twenty. Which, if she lost two pounds a week, would take ten weeks, or two and a half months. Which felt like a year—so far away, it felt pointless.

She knew how Larkin felt about it; Larkin was willing to talk about it all day when she was in the mood. "If you only lost ten or fifteen *pounds*," she'd say. "It would be so *simple*." But even though she loved Larkin, she didn't want to talk about it. It was something Larkin couldn't understand at all—she had never had a problem with weight, ever, and she never would. Which was actually one of the first things Maura had hated most about her at the beginning.

It had been the summer session at Yale, and Maura had never been so excited about anything. A real school, a hard-to-get-into place that wanted her, a place that was far away from home. She loved the train up to New Haven, she loved the buildings, she even loved the person who told her how to find her room. And then she opened the door and saw Larkin: a thin, beautiful redhead, classic green eyes and perfect skin, lounging casually on the bed (the nicer one in the sunnier half of the room) with an enormous container of ice cream, and blasting jazz from the stereo.

Maura felt like a blimp as she dragged her huge, blimplike bags into the room. Larkin was watching her, but she didn't say a word. She sat there spooning ice cream into her mouth and watched.

"I guess you're Larkin James," Maura finally said.

Larkin nodded but didn't say anything.

Great, Maura thought. I hate her.

Her bed was in a dark corner, and she hated it. She looked over at Larkin, drenched in sunlight.

"Do you want this bed?" Larkin asked.

"Well," Maura said, "you already chose it."

Larkin shrugged. "It doesn't make any difference to me. I don't plan on sleeping here very much."

Great again. Maura hated her even more. And now, if she took the nicer bed, it would look as if she were planning to spend the entire summer in the room. "Don't move your things," she said, hefting one of her bags onto the dark, horrible bed. "I'll take this one. I don't plan on spending a lot of time here either."

Larkin smiled.

Bitch.

Maura started unpacking, but the music was getting unbearable. Loud, shapeless jazz with too much flute, and her head was killing her. The morning had started out as the best one of her life, and now it was awful.

"Do you mind if I turn that down a little?" she asked.

Larkin shrugged. "Do what you want. Why are you here, anyway?"

"Do you mean in this room?"

Larkin smiled, and Maura couldn't stand it—one of the most beautiful smiles she had ever seen.

"I mean here in school," Larkin said. "In the summer."

"Oh. It was a chance—I applied to transfer here, but my father—" Damn. She hadn't wanted to mention home. "It wasn't going to be possible for me to come year-round. But they said I could come for a summer."

"Why would you want to do that?"

"Oh—" She had been planning to say, "To study," but it would sound too corny. "I needed to get away for a while," she said, which was true, but not the way it sounded. She wasn't fleeing from anything dramatic—just a stultifying, limited life at home with a father who didn't think she could do anything right except—*maybe*—marry his best friend's son.

"Get away from what?" Larkin asked, and she grinned. "A jealous boyfriend?"

Fuck you, Maura felt like saying. Why was this person such a bitch?

"No, I mean it," Larkin said.

"Let's drop it, all right?"

Larkin shrugged and leaned over to her night table. "Want a drink?" she asked, pulling a bottle out of the drawer.

"What is that?"

"Vodka. Want some?"

"No, thanks."

Larkin stood up to get her cigarettes, and she swayed, and Maura realized that Larkin was drunk. Soused, as a matter of fact. She lit a cigarette, smoked it, and passed out, and that was all Maura saw of her for the first day.

For the next week they avoided each other, or Maura avoided Larkin—she didn't give Larkin a chance to do anything. And true to her word, Larkin spent only a couple of nights in the room. But Maura didn't want to ask for a change in roommates—it would be a chicken-shit, Scranton thing to do. "Sorry, but she's too pretty and she's a bitch. I can't handle her." She wasn't going to do it. And if she and Larkin avoided each other for the rest of the summer, great. All the better.

And then, sometime at the beginning of the second week, a girl from down the hall told Maura she had a phone call, and they'd been holding for fifteen minutes. Maura felt as if her stomach had dropped out. Something terrible had happened; her father had died.

"Hello?" she had said, filled with dread.

"Hi. It's Larkin," a voice said, sounding far away and almost underwater.

"Where are you?"

"Listen," she said. "You have to help me. I didn't have anyone else to call. Do you know where Bremmer Street is?"

Maura didn't, and Larkin explained where it was, on the outskirts of town. "I'm here. Or there. Can you come and get me?"

"What's the matter? Why can't you come here?"

"I'll tell you when I see you. Can you come? And bring some shoes?"

"Shoes?"

"Any of my shoes," Larkin said. "My running shoes if you can find them. And my sweatpants and a shirt."

Maura didn't ask any more questions. Larkin was obviously in trouble. She gave Maura the address, and Maura found Larkin's clothes in one of the huge piles at the foot of her bed and took off.

It was a horrible part of town, and at first Maura had thought, This can't be right, when the cab pulled up.

But then she saw Larkin, in a man's jacket and what looked like nothing else—she was barefoot—darting along next to the parked cars, slightly hunched over and picking her way so she didn't cut her feet. She opened the cab door, hopped in, and put her head back against the seat. "God. Thank you so much," she said, turning and looking into Maura's eyes. "I know you didn't have to come."

"That's okay," Maura said, and she told the driver to go back to campus. She gave Larkin the bag with her clothes in it, and Larkin crouched down and put them on. "Not a great place to go barefoot," she said. "Really, thanks."

"You don't have to tell me what happened," Maura said.

Larkin shook her head. "I met this man," she said, leaning back again and rubbing her temples. "I didn't think he was so great-looking at first, but something happened—suddenly I thought he was the sexiest man in the world—" she smiled "—meaning I had drunk enough, I guess, although I certainly didn't feel drunk." She sighed, and Maura couldn't get over how perfect Larkin looked even after a night like the one she was describing. "He mentioned his house, and we left, and I must have passed out—I don't know. I remember getting out of his truck and going into the house and thinking, 'This isn't very nice; there's something wrong.' But I must have—I think I had to lie down." She swallowed. "I was tired."

Maura couldn't believe it. She couldn't imagine going to a stranger's house, especially if she wasn't thinking clearly.

"Anyway," Larkin said, rummaging through her purse. "You don't have a cigarette—no, you don't smoke, do you?"

"Nope," Maura said, surprised that Larkin had noticed anything about her at all.

Larkin leaned forward and got a cigarette from the driver. "Anyway," she said, "luckily, I suppose, I don't remember a thing that happened after that. But when I woke up this morning, first I had no idea where I was or who I was with. I smelled something awful—I must have vomited during the night, because there it was on the floor—" she took a long drag of her cigarette "—on my side of the mattress. The man was horrible-looking—unshaven and huge—not someone I could have fought if I had wanted to. But luckily, he was sleeping. Snoring, as a matter of fact." She took a deep breath. "The room was filled with newspapers—probably years and years of them. And the shades were down, and I thought, 'I'll pull them up and find out where I am.' But I pulled them up, and the windows were painted over in black. And that's when I panicked. What kind of a person paints their windows black? Paints them over?"

"Larkin, I can't believe this."

She shuddered. "Neither can I. Anyway, I turned around to look for my clothes, and I looked at the man, and he opened one of his eyes. Really, I don't know why it was so horrible to me to see one of his eyes open—after a whole night, God knows what he did—but it was horrible, and I was terrified he would get up, even though he wasn't moving. I looked for my clothes, but all I could find was my purse, and I couldn't find *anything* else that belonged to me. Maybe my clothes are in his truck. Anyway, I took a jacket—*his* clothes were everywhere. Then I ran about ten blocks—I don't know. And then I called you."

Maura sighed. "You're lucky you got out of there," she said. "He sounds slightly crazy. Or maybe very crazy. You can't just go home with anyone, Larkin."

"I know," she said. "But it was always fine until last night. I'm usually really careful."

"Well, aside from getting hurt, you could also get very sick. Or pregnant. Are you even on anything?"

"Of course. I've taken the pill for years. And I'm not going to get sick. I'm careful."

"Last night you weren't. You don't even know what happened."

Larkin threw the cigarette out the window. "That's true," she said quietly. "I'm just glad I got out. I think he *was* someone I might have had trouble with." She looked into Maura's eyes. "So thanks. Really. After the way I've been, you didn't have to."

"Well." Maura didn't know what to say. "You've just seemed so unhappy."

"I *am* unhappy. I don't want to be here. They really should have kicked me out last year." She smiled. "But my father's money—and my grandfather's, too—has helped build an awful lot of class-rooms. Anyway, you've been nicer than you had to be. Every other roommate I've ever had has asked to be moved."

"Really? Why?"

Larkin shrugged. "They find me difficult, they've said."

"Difficult" turned out to be something of an understatement. At night Larkin begged Maura to wake her up in the morning, and then in the mornings needed ten separate wake-up pushes and ca-jolings to finally get up. In the afternoons she slept again, usually through her classes. It was no wonder she had failed so many courses. When she needed company she wouldn't take no for an answer, and three nights out of five, Maura was up till two, half-asleep but talking to Larkin, just being there, which was what Lar-kin seemed to need.

And Maura had thought, My God, she's a mess. She was rich and she was beautiful, but she went through money like water and went through men so quickly, Maura couldn't even keep track of their names. Half the time Larkin didn't even know what their names were. Was there any part of her life that was fun for her, or that she succeeded in?

And then Maura had seen her for the first time onstage. It was the only studying Maura had ever seen Larkin do—lines for plays and her acting classes—and Maura could finally see where all of her friend's energy and emotions had been going. It had been elec-trifying, Larkin had been transformed, and Maura could feel that the audience felt the same way. At intermission everyone was ask-ing the same thing: Who *was* that?

Larkin's parents hadn't come, and they never did come to any of the performances, even in the years after that summer, when Maura came up from Scranton to see Larkin act. "Family differences" was all Larkin would say. Her parents hadn't come up since freshman year. But that summer, Maura never missed one from the first, and it made her feel good. They were friends. She was Larkin's ally.

And they had done what they'd always promised each other,

moved to New York to start their "adult" lives. The only difference from the dream was that Maura had always assumed that by the time they actually did it, she'd know what she wanted to do with her life. But her college interests had had nothing to do with real life—she had majored in psychology, but she didn't want to become a psychologist. So what was she going to do? It made her nervous, at the back of her mind, that she was in one of those formless, unclassifiable areas. Where would working at an agency like Falcone lead? At least Larkin knew exactly what she wanted to do.

Maura looked around at the mess Mr. Falcone wanted her to clean up, and she wondered where she was going to begin. The phone rang, and she picked it up and looked at her watch at the same time. Ten after seven, and George said they usually closed at seven o'clock.

"Falcone Casting."

"Yeah," a male voice said. "I want to book a girl. One of them dancers."

This didn't sound legit. But she couldn't hang up until she knew for sure; a lot of the managers of these clubs, she had discovered, sounded like guys who had just been released from prison (which was probably true in at least a few of the cases). "Uh, what's the name of your club?" she asked.

"The Fantasy Lounge. George knows it."

George. Oh. So maybe it was a real call. "Well, we're closed at the moment. Do you want to call back in the morning?"

"*You're* not," the voice said.

"What?"

"*You're* not closed. You're still there. How about you?"

She didn't say anything.

"I like women with a little extra flesh. More to grab on to. More to love, they say. How about *you*? Why don't you tell me what you're wearing—"

She slammed down the phone.

God.

She looked up at the window. There were hundreds of offices across the street, some lit up and some dark. The person who had called—it wasn't just a random call: he knew who he was calling.

And what she looked like.

She stood up from the desk, walked over to the window, and closed the blinds. Then she walked back, picked up her purse and key, and moved to the door. It was definitely time to leave. It had obviously been unwise not to leave with George.

And suddenly she wondered—George. He had just left, only a few minutes earlier. Could it have been him?

But the voice had been totally different, not even a disguised voice. Just a voice she was sure she had never heard before.

But someone who knew her.

She opened the door, looked in both directions down the hall, shut the door, and locked it.

How about you? Why don't you tell me what you're wearing—

She had to be sick, or have something wrong with her. Because underneath the fear, the creepy thought that someone knew who she was, and was maybe even looking at her as he was talking with her, underneath the queasy fear, the idea was appealing.

Someone who was turned on. Maura Cassidy as temptress.

She had to be sick. She was supposed to be frightened, not turned on. But she was both.

Six

Andrew Morrissey, the man who had given her his card, was making Danielle laugh. He was trying again, saying, "I could get you the greatest job," and he was making things up: two hundred thousand dollars a year, three secretaries, crazy things.

"Stop," she said. "It's not true, what you're saying."

He smiled. "No, it's not. But you would have a good time, I can promise you that. You're exactly what Mr. King is looking for."

She shrugged. "I don't know."

He reached out and touched her hair. "Amazing," he said. She kind of felt like she was blushing, and she looked away, and the craziest thing: Her father was standing by the door, talking to the security guard, and the security guard was pointing at the cigarette Cleve was smoking. Then Cleve left, just like that, and came back a second later without the cigarette.

"Um, you'd better go," she said to Andrew Morrissey. "I have someone coming to see me."

Andrew Morrissey turned around. Cleve was coming toward the counter. "An old customer?" Andrew Morrissey asked.

"Um, my father."

Andrew Morrissey touched her hair one more time and said, "Don't forget. Call us. I mean it," and then he kind of almost vanished into thin air, blending into the crowd just like that.

"Hey, honey," Cleve said. He leaned across the counter to kiss her on the cheek, and she could smell vodka. "Who was that you were talking to? A boyfriend?"

"Uh-uh. Just a guy I met. What are you doing here?" It had come out kind of funny, but he knew what she meant, probably.

"I'm taking you to lunch," he said. "My treat."

"Um, lunch?" She couldn't think what to say. She was so shocked he was even here, especially since they had just had dinner. But that was what her mother said he always did: he'd pay a lot of attention to you, maybe even sometimes more than you wanted, and then he'd drop you like a hot potato.

"Name the place," he said.

She bit her lip. "Um, I can't," she said. "I don't get lunch till three-thirty."

He looked totally shocked. "Three-thirty? That's no time for anyone to have lunch."

She shrugged. "I'm the lowest one on the totem pole."

"Oh, they'll let you go, won't they? Just tell them your father's in town for one day and you have to see him. Tell them you have an appointment."

"I can't," she said. It was weird he didn't understand, but when you thought about it, it kind of made sense, because he had sure never worked in a department store in his whole life. "Um, why aren't you working? I mean writing?"

"Ah, we needed a break. It's not going as well as I had thought it would."

"You mean writing with Colette or just the writing?"

"Both," he said.

"When am I going to meet her, anyway?"

"Soon," he said. "Soon." And he looked super-sad. "You sure you can't come out just this once? Ask them to make an exception?"

"I can't. The supervisor hates me already. I'm practically on probation."

He coughed, and she could smell the vodka even stronger. "Daddy?" Whoops. She had meant to call him Cleve.

"Yeah, hon."

"What if—" She stopped. "What if . . . ? I mean, I thought—" She stopped again. She felt bad asking, but she had to.

"What if what?" he asked.

"What if . . . I thought . . . In your letter, I mean the last letter, you said you were jogging every day and all that. And now—" She stopped. "I mean, how do you know nothing's going to happen to you?"

"What, because I'm drinking a little bit?" He took her hands in his. "I'm fine," he said. "Don't even give it a thought."

"But—"

"I'm *fine*," he said, and he looked at his watch. "Hey, I've got to run. I'll call you later, okay?"

"Okay," she said. "I love you."

"Love you, too," he said, and he left.

But she felt bad. She wished she could've said yes. And she was feeling kind of lonesome, too, so it would have been nice to talk to him and tell him about some of the things in the apartment, like maybe he could give her some advice. Because it kept feeling like the harder she tried, the harder it was to fit in with Maura and Larkin.

Like this morning, when Maura and Larkin were drinking coffee, she had come in with the thing she had worked on till midnight, adding up the letters in their names to find out what kind of futures they had. She was really good at it—she guessed it was the one thing her mother had taught her, and she had thought they'd be super-impressed, especially because the numbers book said Larkin would be "involved in the arts" and Maura was good at organizing, which was probably true. But they just looked at each other like "What is she talking about?" and she felt bad. So it would have been nice to talk to her father and maybe get some advice. But she guessed another time, or maybe things would get better, too. She hoped, anyway.

Seven

"Fuck that shit!" George Falcone yelled from his office. "God-dammit, Mike, you give her the money or we never—I mean fuck-ing *never*—send you another girl. . . . Right. You got it, shitface. What the fuck are you jerking me around for *now*? You knew Cindy was a new one; what did you expect? . . . Ah, fuck it. Let me talk to her. . . . All right, but I get a report from her tomorrow morn-ing, so don't jerk me off. . . . Right. Right . . . Yeah." He slammed down the phone. "Motherfucker," he said more quietly.

The phone rang a second later, and George yelled, "If that's Mike Moscone, take a message!"

"Okay," Maura called out. "Falcone Casting," she said into the phone.

Silence.

"Hello?"

"Maura," a male voice said.

"Yes?"

"Maura."

It was the voice from last night.

"That's a real beautiful name, Maura. A beautiful name for a beautiful girl. And like I said—I don't *mind* the extra pounds. I like that. There's more to love."

She put the receiver down quietly.

"Who was it?" George called out.

"Um, a wrong number."

George came out of his office. "Listen. I should tell you," he said. "Some of these guys try to jerk the girls around on carfare, and when it happens you've got to give 'em hell. The older ones, they know what the situation is, but some of the new girls, we send them out to Lodi, Newark, places like that, and then they can't get home."

"I don't understand," Maura said. "Don't they get paid?"

"Through *us*," George said. "They get paid through us. And

34

meanwhile some of these bars are in the middle of fucking nowhere, and the girls panic. They don't even know how to call a cab, who to call; they get scared. So they call us—if they're smart—and then you've got to lay into the owner or the manager or whoever the fuck is in charge. Okay?''

Maura nodded.

George winked. "You're a good kid. You're learning fast. I like a kid I can use my French on." He looked at his watch, and she looked at the clock on the wall—seven o'clock, almost exactly the time she had gotten the other call last night.

Maura.

How did he know her name?

Eight

Danielle felt like a million dollars. Bloomingdale's at a super-rush time, right after work when there were nine jillion customers and tons of extra security. And she had just gotten the greatest present in the world for her father, a super-expensive brown cashmere scarf.

All day she had been feeling bad about how he had come all the way to the store, and then what? She hadn't even *asked* if she could maybe take lunch early. At least she could have asked. If the situations had been opposite, she knew she would have been upset, and he had looked kind of sad.

But this would be a great present. Plus she had decided she was definitely going to start calling him Cleve all the time. It was time to grow up. Especially if she was going to meet Colette. She didn't want to constantly be saying "Daddy this" and "Daddy that" like some kind of kid.

She pushed her way through the revolving doors and was just about to put on the scarf herself—it was incredibly cold all of a sudden—when she felt a super-strong hand on her arm.

"Excuse me," a male voice said. The hand hadn't even begun to let go. Uh-oh.

She turned around. It was a young guy, blondish, not in a uniform, but she could tell.

"Would you mind coming with me, ma'am?"

"I'm in a really big hurry," she said. "Sorry."

She turned to go, but he gripped her arm even tighter. "I'm afraid I have to insist," he said.

No answer. God. And they had said ten more minutes and then the police would be here.

She looked up at the blond guy, whose name was Matt, he said. "Um," she said. How could she call him Matt just like that? But he didn't turn around. "Um, Matt?"

Now he did.

"I still can't get my father."

He sighed and looked at his watch. "You'd better start calling some other numbers then, ma'am. When you get down to the police station, they're only going to give you one call."

Police station. She still couldn't believe it. But they were doing it, "prosecuting to the fullest extent of the law," the words that had burned into her mind.

"Okay," she said. She called the apartment for what seemed like the fifty-thousandth time, but there was still no answer.

"The thing is, I only know two numbers here. Can't I call L.A. ? I'll pay you back. I promise."

He held out his hands. "I've got rules," he said as if he were actually really sorry.

But now she was starting to panic. What if she still hadn't reached anybody by the time the police came? And why did he keep saying "police" as if there were going to be ten or something?

"Look," she said. "What if I—I mean why can't I just put it back? I *told* you it was that I just forgot. I was in a giant hurry and I went to one cash register and then another, and there were these really huge lines."

He sighed. "You'd better make your call," he said, looking at his watch.

Suddenly she remembered the card Andrew Morrissey had given her. "Suppose you end up in jail," he had said, as if he knew. But there was no way he could have known. This was Bloomingdale's that she had just wandered into. Not Ivorsen & Shaw, where he knew she worked.

She got out the card and dialed the number.

"Four thousand," a low male voice said. It didn't sound like Andrew Morrissey.

"Um, can I talk to Andrew, please?"

"Who's calling?" Totally expressionless.

"Danielle Austin. I met him—" But she had already been put on hold.

A few seconds later he came on. "Danielle," he said. "What a nice surprise."

She looked over at Matt. He was watching. "Um, listen," she said as quietly as she could. "You must be psychic or something, because I just . . . um, I just got arrested. . . . I mean, the police are on their way and everything, and—"

"Hold on and calm down, Danielle. Now, where are you? At Ivorsen & Shaw?"

"Nope. At Bloomingdale's."

"Shit," he said quietly. "You picked a rotten place, kid. Where are you now?"

"In the security office. But they've called the *police*, Andrew."

"All right, *don't* panic, Danielle, and don't say anything. Do you know what precinct?"

"I don't know anything. They said—"

"Let me talk to the person who's holding you."

"Okay. Hold on."

Matt was still looking at her. "Can you talk to this person?" she said. "I can't answer all his questions."

Matt came over and took the phone, but he just listened for a long time, and she didn't even hear any number, like "The third precinct" or anything like that. Just "Yes, I see." And "No, no, nothing like that." He was picking at a thread on his jacket, and then he pulled at it, which kind of shocked her, because what if the whole thing came apart? But he didn't seem to even know what he was doing: he was just nodding now, mostly, and saying, "I see."

Finally he hung up. "You'll be met at the seventeenth precinct by a lawyer," he said quietly. He looked at his watch. "I'll be back in a second," he said, and then he left and shut the door.

Danielle had no idea what was going on, but something had definitely changed. A few minutes later one policeman, not ten million cops the way she had thought, came in with Matt, and both were super-polite.

"Just come with me, Miss Austin," the cop said, and he told her to follow him outside, where there was a lady cop in the back-seat of a police car. For a second Danielle felt like an animal, and she wanted to run: was it a woman because they were going to search her? But she got in, and no one touched her or even said a word the whole ride over.

And at first when they pulled up to the police station, Danielle decided she wasn't scared: if it was so serious, they would have talked to her, right? But then they got inside, and it was all echoy with a million cops all over the place, and she wanted to run.

"Over here, Danielle," the cop who had come to Bloomingdale's said, and she was almost glad to sit down at the desk next to him, because at least he was a familiar face. But then he took out an ink pad and told her to press her hand down on it, and she thought, what if I never get out? All of a sudden it was so real. What if they fingerprinted her and threw her into jail and forgot all about her? And where was everybody she knew in the whole world?

"Now give me your address," he said when it was finished and he had slipped a sheet of stiff paper into the typewriter. He had typed out her name the way she typed, one letter and then about fifty billion years before the next.

"Um, I didn't think I was supposed to say anything," she said, looking around. Where was Andrew? Or whoever he was sending?

The cop stubbed out his cigarette and gave another cop a look, like *What now?*

Suddenly everyone in the room turned around, and Danielle turned to see what they were looking at: a man with white hair in a gray coat who was looking right at her as he came in.

"I'm Foster Bartlett," he said, shaking her hand.

And then it was just like TV: him asking what she had told, then they had to take the information she had refused to give before, like where she lived and all that. But Foster Bartlett was telling her the whole time what she could say, and it was obvious he was just a super-important lawyer.

They released her "on her own recognizance," and then Foster Bartlett took her by the arm, and she felt almost like Cinderella just walking out without anything really bad happening. What if she hadn't called Andrew? Would they have locked her up just like that?

"I'm so glad that you came," she said when they got into the cold outside. "Is Andrew coming or what?"

"We'll meet him on Fifty-eighth Street," Foster Bartlett said.

"Um, you mean now?"

Foster Bartlett nodded at a long white limo parked right out front. "I'll take you," he said.

"Actually, I think I should make some phone calls," she said. It seemed weird, just getting whisked away in a limo.

"Call from the car," he said, putting a hand on her shoulder.

And suddenly she had the feeling she didn't exactly have a choice.

Nine

"You call that *pain*?"

Larkin looked up at Arthur Kozloff, a small, white-haired man with black eyes.

"This is a scene of tremendous *pain*," he said, throwing up his hands. He paced to the edge of the stage and then turned back around to face her. "And what I get from you is placidity. Complacence. Where is the *tension*, Miss James? Where is the *fear*? You're supposed to have discovered that your great love, the great love of your life, is dead. Yet you're acting as if you've found there's no milk in the refrigerator."

A few people in the class chuckled horrid, complacent little laughs, and Larkin hated them.

"Have you ever had a close friend or relative die, Miss James?"

"Yes. Of course."

"And what was he or she to you? A friend? I mean someone close to you, Miss James, not a grandparent you barely knew when you were all of three years old."

"I have someone along the lines you're talking about," she said. God, she hated him. Why did he have to be one of the best acting teachers in New York?

"Then tell us," he said. "A relative, parent, friend? Who was it?"

"An uncle," she said.

"And you were close? Close enough to feel the kind of *pain* I'm trying to get you to feel?"

"We were very close," she said.

He narrowed his eyes. Beady little eyes. "Good," he said. "That's good. And when he died. You were where? You found out how, Miss James?"

"I—" She didn't see the point. "I was at college, and I read about it in the paper."

He was squinting. "You read about it? You didn't hear from your family?"

She looked up at him. She wanted a cigarette more than anything in the world, except to leave. "I don't understand how this has anything to do with the scene," she said.

He thrust his hands into his pockets and paced slowly across the stage, did a little pirouette, and paced back to where she sat. "I see," he said slowly. "You don't understand." He looked out at the class. "Would anyone care to tell Miss James why it's important? Why every *detail* is important? Every moment, every memory?" He whipped around to face her. "Or perhaps a better question would be why you feel these details *aren't* important. Why you reject your sense memories, your most intimate feelings, your unconscious thoughts at a time of deep pain. . . ."

Christ. How did *he* know what she had rejected?

"So now the question, once again, is how you felt, Miss James. You picked up the paper—a newspaper, I presume you mean?" She nodded even though she felt like spitting. "And you learned what? That he had died. Now, if you will go *back* to that moment, Miss James. Close your eyes. Go back to the room you were in; remember how it smelled, what the sounds were, whether it was hot or cold; were there children playing outside or was it—you were in college, you say?"

She hated him because he was bringing it back, the bastard. Picking up the newspaper because there was nothing else to read in the refectory and she was so late for breakfast that everyone else was gone. With a pounding headache and the nausea that came from a three-day hangover. Picking up the damn *Times* and seeing his picture. "Son of industrialist dead in Italy" it had read, with an absurdly young-looking, silly-looking Geoffrey staring out at her. Dead at age forty-four, in a hill town in Tuscany.

And what had her parents thought? That they'd never tell her? That it was their nasty little way of paying her back? She had stared and stared and stared at the picture, and the thought that she'd never see him again—

"Miss James. Now if you'll tell us: take yourself back and tell us the *details*. If you close your eyes—"

"I don't want to close my eyes," she said.

He was glaring at her. "I said if you'll close your eyes, Miss James."

"Sorry. Not possible," she said.

"What did you say?"

"I said no."

Someone in the audience dropped what sounded like an empty can onto the stone floor, and then it was dead quiet. And Arthur Kozloff looked furious.

"I didn't realize this was going to be a therapy session," Larkin said. "If you want me to 'get in touch' with pain, as you said—"

But he had walked away. He walked all the way across the stage and then half faced her and half faced the audience. He held out his hand. "A perfect example," he said to the audience. "She wants everything but the hard work, ladies and gentlemen. Well, Miss James, I suggest you go the route so many nongraduates of the Institute have taken: get your modeling career under way, and proceed from there with what no doubt will be great haste—I'm sure you'll have some rather brief spurt of fame on one of our venerable network television shows. Or perhaps a commercial for dishwashing liquid. You may pick up your refund at the front desk."

She stood up and looked out at the class, goddamn sheep who had drunk in every word. What if *they* had been up onstage? How would they have felt? She hated them all, every one of them. "You're all a bunch of sheep," she said.

But as she walked offstage and felt her knees buckle, she wondered if her voice had even been audible. And why would they listen to *her*? Who was to say she'd ever prove Kozloff wrong?

"You can get into another class," Richard said, stirring his coffee. "It will be easy."

He had a speck of bread or something at the corner of his mouth where he was growing a mustache and beard, which she already hated. He had sandy hair, but the beard was coming out red and wispy. Why didn't he shave it? And why was he so *relaxed* over what had happened? "You don't understand *anything*," she said. She finished her wine and poured out what was left in the bottle, but it wasn't much. "This isn't just *any* class; this isn't some pottery class for housewives, or some little neighborhood theater acting class you can take in your spare time. This was *Kozloff*."

"So Kozloff kicked you out. Find another."

"*God*, you can be infuriating. That's like saying, 'So you lost the chance at the partnership at the firm.' There's *one* best—Kozloff—and he kicked me out. And what a bunch of fucking *sheep* they were. I hate them all.''

He reached across the table and touched her arm, and his hand felt like rubber. "It'll be all right," he said. "I know it. You're too beautiful not to succeed."

She finished the wine and set the glass down. "You and Kozloff think alike, don't you? *You'd* like to see me in commercials. Or modeling, wouldn't you?"

"I'd like to see you in anything that would make you happy."

She wanted to throw something at him. "You can be very bland, did you know that?"

He blinked and just sat there, and immediately she felt horrible.

"I'm sorry," she said.

He wiped his mouth with a napkin, and the crumb fell away. "Maybe you're not," he said quietly. "If that's the way you really feel."

"It isn't, it isn't," she said. "I just feel so rotten about what happened. It's such a *fuck-up* on my part."

"But you did the right thing. You wouldn't have wanted to go on with the exercise."

"But maybe I should have; I don't know. It seemed so horrid at the time. And then when he said I should be a model and just *dismissed* me." She looked into his eyes. She did love him sometimes. "Anyway, I'm sorry I snapped. You just hit a nerve. Today when I left Kozloff's, I felt like shaving my head."

He was smiling. "You're kidding."

"I'm not kidding. I almost did it, I almost went into a barber shop that was right around the corner."

"But you're not going to do it."

She hesitated. "I'd like to. At least to chop it all off. Do something drastic to force people to take me more seriously. But the truth is . . . I couldn't do it."

He reached out and ran his fingers through her hair. "You'd be insane to do it," he said. "And I know you'll find another class—maybe not *the* class, but a good one. And this weekend you can relax in the fresh air—"

Shit. She had completely forgotten. They were supposed to go to Rhode Island to meet his parents. "Oh, Richard. I forgot. I can't."

"What do you mean, you can't? We planned this weeks ago."

"But I can't. I have things to do. I have to look into other classes.

And I'll be in a shitty mood. They won't even want to meet me in the mood I'll be in."

"Great. That's just great. You've canceled four times, Larkin. *Four* times. And don't think they haven't counted, because we all have. You can't do this."

She needed a cigarette.

"Where are you going?"

"To find a cigarette. I'm just getting my purse." She looked in her purse, but then she remembered: she had run out before dinner.

"I'll be right back," she said, getting her coat.

"You're going *out*?"

"I need cigarettes."

"We haven't finished discussing the weekend."

"I know, I know. But I'll be right back. I promise. I'm just going down to the corner."

He stood up. "It's late. I'll come with you."

"Don't be silly. I'm already gone." She slung on her coat and headed for the door.

She let it slam, and she took the stairs instead of the elevator. She didn't want Richard following her.

She couldn't face the discussion; she couldn't face Richard's disappointment. She needed to breathe a little bit, to be out from under his constant gaze. Was it that awful, what she was asking, not to go and spend an entire weekend with people she had never met?

She bought the cigarettes and started back for the building, and then she stopped, turned, and headed for the corner, where she could catch a cab. She was a bitch—she wouldn't argue with Richard later on about it—but she just couldn't go back.

Ten

Danielle couldn't believe it. The house she was in was like on "Dallas" or something, except in New York. She had definitely never seen anything so fancy in her life—real life, anyway—marble floors, a spiraling staircase, brocade-type wallpaper, and a billion chandeliers.

And here she was, about to meet the man who lived here.

Andrew Morrissey was supposed to come later—a man named Jake had told her that, who seemed super-nice. But the guy she was supposed to meet was named Joseph King. And at first she had kind of felt forced into the house, riding in that huge stretch limo with Foster Bartlett and not feeling like she even had a choice at all.

But it seemed great now, like one of her dreams come true: someone wanted to meet her, someone important.

"Miss Austin?"

It was Jake again, coming out from a room with sliding doors.

"Would you mind following me?"

"Sure. I mean no," she said, following him up the stairs. Red carpeting, just like for stars. And paintings on the walls in gold frames.

He opened another set of sliding doors, told her to go in and sit down, and shut the doors behind her.

It was a library-type room, with books everywhere and dark wood walls and lots of gold and maps and globes and things like that, that a really educated person would have. Plus a gigantic Oriental rug.

She sat down on a big leather couch, and a second later a man came in.

"Can I get you a drink?" he called over his shoulder.

She had hardly even gotten a look at him: he had dark hair and he moved fast. "A Coke would be great. I'm actually dying of thirst."

He opened a bar in the wall and came back with two drinks.

He was maybe in his late forties, really tan, with a dark suit on and really nice dark eyes. "It's a pleasure to finally meet you," he said when he gave her the drink. "May I call you Danielle?"

"Sure." She thought he was going to say she should call him "Joseph," but he didn't.

"Good. So. Danielle. Mr. Bartlett gave you his card and all the instructions you need?"

"You mean for the case?"

He nodded.

"He did, but I mean—" She had to ask. People always said she was super-naive, but she really wasn't when she thought hard about asking the right questions, and she had thought hard on the whole limo ride over. "I really appreciate what you and Mr. Bartlett have done. I mean, I don't know what I would've done. I still haven't even told anybody else, because I can't even *reach* anybody else. But this is the thing: I mean—" She stopped. She didn't know how to say it: How was she supposed to pay them back? Because if they thought she was going to suddenly turn into some kind of hooker or something, they were crazy.

"You're concerned because you don't want to feel that you're under any obligation," he said. "Is that it?"

"Exactly."

He smiled. "Let me put you at ease on that point right away. My associate, Andrew Morrissey, gave you his card for a reason. As it happened, his casual comment about your possible future needs came true. But that was a coincidence. He wanted you to call us because he knew I'd want to meet you."

She swallowed. This was the bad part, like when the assistant manager at Burger Bob's had said she had to give him a blow job. She just wasn't going to do it.

"I have a constant need for new faces and new talent," he said, "and my staff members, Andrew included, are always on the look-out." Uh-oh. So it *was* some kind of hooking operation. She took another sip of Coke. "For what should be obvious reasons, I wouldn't want to start you in certain areas of the business—handling money, for instance. But what I'd like you to do is look around— Jake will show you the third and fourth floors—and see if you'd find working here more interesting than working at—what was it? Bloomingdale's?"

She shook her head. "Ivorsen & Shaw. But actually . . . I appreciate the offer and everything, but—"

"You haven't even heard the offer," he said, smiling. But she couldn't tell what was under the smile: he seemed super-strong and like the kind of guy not a lot of people said no to. He looked into her eyes. "What is it that you think I want you to do?"

She shrugged. She wasn't going to say it. "I don't know," she said.

"Then let me show you." He stood up and pressed a button on his desk. "This is a private club, Danielle. A very private club. You'll see faces you know and faces of people you don't know only because they don't want to be known. It's by invitation only, revocable at any time. Do you know how to gamble?"

"Um, poker and blackjack."

He nodded. "We have everything here. Baccarat would suit you well, I think. But Jake will show you around. And I think I can assure you it would be far more interesting than working in a department store, Danielle. You'd meet many fascinating people.''

There was something super-odd about his face and the way he talked. She kept trying to listen to what he was saying—it did sound like more fun (definitely) than working at Ivorsen & Shaw. But there was something about his face that kept distracting her, something fake, like on a mannequin. And he talked like some kind of robot, not with an accent exactly, but as if he had memorized about a jillion phrases from a book.

The door opened and Jake came in.

"Show Danielle the fourth floor first," Joseph King said. "And then bring her back to me. And Danielle, all I ask is that after the tour, you protect the confidentiality of anyone you might recognize."

She had never been able to keep a secret in her life, but she said, "Okay." And suddenly she realized: she had the same feeling she thought she could only get from stealing—what Mr. Sackley had said was "adrenaline." So maybe this place—whatever it was— would be the start of a whole new life.

Eleven

Maura and Larkin started to laugh again, and Danielle felt bad. She had never seen anybody with so many private jokes, and the unfun part was that they kind of stayed private. Like nobody said, "The reason we're laughing is blah blah blah." Except once Maura did explain, and it made her feel even worse, because she didn't get the joke.

Plus she had to tell them the News. Otherwise she wouldn't even be hanging around the living room. But she didn't know how to start. Plus the TV was blaring, and they were kind of half watching, making fun of the guy who was telling the news.

"Um," she finally said, and Maura looked at her. Larkin seemed kind of out of it, like a little bit drunk even though they were only drinking beer. "I have something to tell you guys," Danielle said, and she took a sip of beer. But she hated the taste.

Now they were both looking at her. "Um, something happened to me, and I kind of feel . . ." God. She didn't know what to say. "I thought maybe you guys should know about it, that's all, since maybe . . . Well, I kind of got arrested yesterday—"

"What?" they both screamed out, and she almost had to laugh. They both looked so shocked.

"What happened?" Maura asked.

She shrugged. She hadn't even thought of it as such a giant deal. "I tried to take a scarf from Bloomingdale's, and someone saw me."

They were both staring like they still couldn't even believe it.

"You mean you were shoplifting?" Larkin asked. She had on kind of a weird smile—it was hard to tell what it meant. But Danielle felt her face getting red, and she wished she hadn't said anything. Except that she had kind of thought it was only fair to tell them, since maybe the police would come over or whatever.

She looked at Maura since Maura looked super-serious. "Are you guys thinking you want me to move out? I wouldn't take anything from either of you in a million years. I meant to tell you that part first but—"

"Don't be silly," Maura said. "Of course we don't want you to move out. Right, Larkin?"

"Of *course* not," Larkin said, putting down her beer bottle. Only it landed with a big *clunk* like she didn't know how heavy it was. "I think it's fascinating. Is this something you do all the time?"

She felt her face go all hot again. She didn't like the way Larkin had asked the question, like she was some kind of strange person for doing it.

"I don't know," she said. She shrugged. "Everyone did it in L.A." Which was a complete lie. But a lot of times when you said everyone in L.A. did something, people believed you no matter what. It was weird.

"But have you ever been arrested before?" Larkin had stood up, and she was looking down at her. "Have you ever gone to jail?"

"Definitely not. I was always good. I was never caught, even though—" She stopped. She had been about to say, "Even though I did it a million times," which was true. But it was probably better not to make such a big deal about how experienced she was at it. "Anyway, the great part is—"

"Wait a minute," Larkin said. "I don't want to miss anything."

Don't say anything until I come back. Is anybody else ready for a beer?''

Maura said she still had hers, and Danielle just said, ''Not yet.'' Even though she never would be. God, it was so bitter.

''You seem a little upset,'' Maura said. ''Is it about this or something else?''

Danielle didn't say anything. It would be dumb to say, ''I just wish I could fit in with you guys.'' Better not to say anything at all. And anyway, Larkin was coming back, rushing down the hall, so it would have been too late anyway.

''I haven't missed anything, have I?''

''Maybe Danielle doesn't want to tell the whole story,'' Maura said. ''It isn't a joke, you know.''

Larkin sighed and rolled her eyes. ''This is something you're going to have to get used to,'' she said to Danielle. ''Maura's very big on being serious, in case you haven't noticed. You can't take anything like this lightly. Ever.''

''Not everyone does,'' Maura said. She turned to Danielle. ''You really don't have to talk about it, you know. It was good that you told us, but that can be the end of it if you want.''

Danielle bit her lip. ''I guess—there really isn't anything giant to tell, actually, except the great part, which is that I got a job after.''

''After *what*?'' Larkin asked. ''After you went to jail? Don't listen to Maura—I want to hear the details.''

She figured she might as well, maybe, so she told them about Andrew Morrissey and Foster Bartlett and Mr. King.

Larkin was smiling. ''All because you couldn't reach any of us. Amazing.''

''Can you trust this King?'' Maura asked. ''It sounds great, but you don't think you'll be ripped off or anything—?''

She shrugged. ''I kind of don't think so, because how much am I even going to make? The place looked super-rich and fancy, so for someone like him to steal from me—I just don't see it.''

''I think it's wonderful,'' Larkin said, raising her bottle of beer. ''Congratulations.''

''Thanks,'' Danielle said.

Except that two seconds later it was all over, and Maura and Larkin were back to laughing and joking. She had the job, so that was great, and Mr. King had promised he'd get her off, but what about the rest of her life? She still hadn't even told her father, and it was a joke to think he'd even be more than a tiny bit interested.

He'd ask two questions and then he'd forget it had ever happened, the way Maura and Larkin didn't even hardly know she was in the same room with them.

But maybe the job would be great. She had to "look on the bright side," the way everyone said to.

Twelve

Maura took off her shoes and weighed herself again.

Damn.

The clothes had to weigh at least five pounds, but still—

As long as Terence didn't say anything; that was the main thing.

She still didn't know if it had been a mistake to call him or not. In college in sophomore year he had been her best friend—he was smart and gay and funny, and being friends with him had been like having a good girlfriend except without the competition. Then in junior year, Terence dropped out and "escaped" to New York and became a theatrical agent, and Maura had kept in touch with him only sporadically.

But tonight she had suddenly needed to be with someone— Danielle and Larkin were both gone—and she had called Terence since he was the only other person she knew in the city. They were meeting at the restaurant, and he was bringing his roommate— "straight and a lunatic, but the loft is his"—and they'd all have a bite to eat. But what worried her was the reserve she had heard in his voice, a distance that made her nervous—he was probably hurt that she hadn't even let him know she was in New York. And when he was hurt, he could be nasty.

"So," Terence said, sipping at his Heineken. "Tell us about your job. You're not *really* working for a man who books strippers."

"I *am* really. It's not exactly what I set out to do, but it was the first job offer I had."

"Maura's *always* filled with surprises," Terence said to Max.

"Like moving to the city and not even getting in touch with her old best friend."

"Well, everything's been happening really quickly," she said.

"I thought you said you had been looking for a job for ages," Terence said.

"Well, you know, it always feels like ages." She could feel Terence looking at her, and she looked down into her drink. Max moved forward in his chair. "I know what you mean," he said. "It took ages for me to find my first job, and that was a volunteer job."

"What kind of job?"

"Veterinary assistant," he said.

"So is that what you do now?"

Terence laughed. "Not quite. Max is a lawyer. Corporate deal making. Not exactly veterinary work unless you take the fact that he works with snakes into account. But he has an ancient dog, so I suppose he's still volunteering."

"What kind of dog?" Maura asked.

"A mutt. Former stray," Max said. He was turning his beer glass around in the water ring on the table, and Maura wondered how he could live with Terence, day in and day out.

He was interesting-looking—tall, thin, dark-haired, with a hawk nose and a slightly too large mouth, a face it would have been tough growing up with but that somehow looked good all grown-up. And Maura suddenly wondered: Was this some sort of fix-up?

"*So,*" Terence said, pouring out the rest of his Heineken. "Now that we're finished with Max's little life story—Maura: you're not really going to keep this job, are you? Aren't they all hookers anyway?"

"I don't know," she said. "I guess some of them have to be, but I know some of them aren't. Just today one of the girls got stuck in the middle of nowhere without carfare, so there are at least some who aren't." She shrugged. "It wouldn't bother me either way, though. It's sort of interesting, actually, to see the kinds of women who've gone into it."

Terence made a sound—a half laugh, half snort. "Maura's one of the all-time great bystanders, Max. It's such a perfect job for you, Maura, now that I think of it. You can spend the rest of your life just sitting back and watching."

"Terence," she said.

"What? I'm just telling the truth." He turned to Max. "What you have here is a girl who could have gone anywhere—Radcliffe,

Yale—they *wanted* her at Yale after the summer session. But she listens to Daddy and goes to college in Scranton, where I'm *literally* the only person on campus who even understands what the poor girl's talking about. And then the *boyfriend*. Another prize choice made by the great Mr. Cassidy. The *boyfriend* never knew what she was talking about. I think the last book he read was in high school, maybe a novelization of *Rocky* for a book report. But he didn't care that he didn't understand a word she ever said, because he got the Saturday nights in the backseat of his Ford.''

Max leaned forward. ''Terence, knock it off. What's the matter with you?''

Terence turned away and looked at Maura. His eyes were glistening in the half darkness. ''You've *never* had any idea what was good for you, who your friends were, what you could do with your life. This job. It's *grotesque*. I can't bear to see you do it.''

He stood up and pushed his chair back. ''Excuse me,'' he said, and walked to the back of the restaurant.

''Sorry about that,'' Max said.

She shook her head. ''It's not *your* fault.''

''I know. But you should know.'' He paused. ''He's really just hurt. That's what this is all about. When you called tonight he couldn't get over the fact that you had moved here without telling him. He considers you his best friend.''

''God. Really?''

''Really,'' Max said.

''That's awful.''

He nodded. ''He's had a hard time this past year. The business is brutal, you know. I don't know how he finds the strength against all the back-stabbings he's had to deal with. So if he seems wound up—that might be part of it, too.'' He paused. ''Anyway, he *is* crazy about you, if that helps at all.''

''It does. Thanks,'' she said. She looked up and saw Terence coming back across the room, a short, thin man who had made himself good-looking with the right haircut and the right clothes. And she could imagine how he had felt arriving in New York, comparing himself to so many perfect specimens. It had probably been much worse than her job-hunting experiences, when she had discovered she was suddenly one of millions.

''I just had a brilliant idea,'' Terence said, sitting down again. ''Max—don't you think Maura should come on Wednesday night?''

''What's Wednesday night?'' Maura asked.

Max wasn't saying anything.

"One of you guys want to clue me in to what I might or might not come to?" she asked.

"Come on," Terence said. "It'll be a foursome."

Max was half smiling. "It might be an odd evening," he said. "It's at a club called Benny's, and the singing will be . . . well, unusual. Inexperienced, I should say."

"It sounds interesting," she said. "Is it you?" The most interesting part was the foursome part. Did that mean she was going to sort of be with Max?

"It's Max's girlfriend," Terence said. "Vanessa Lyons, and remember that name, Maura. She's our client, and she's going to make it this year."

She nodded vaguely and looked at Max. Now, of course, she thought he was the greatest guy she had met in ages.

Thirteen

Anne James looked at her daughters and smiled. "This is so nice," she said. "It hasn't been the three of us in such an awfully long time."

Larkin looked away from her mother and Fernanda, at a man sitting at the other end of the restaurant. He had been staring since they'd come in. A businessman, from the way he dressed, and he reminded her of Richard, and she felt like shit.

She had been a bitch to him, no question about it. Saying what she had said, walking out on him like that. But what Maura had said at Yale once was true, that she didn't know how to be anything but a bitch when it came to having a relationship with a man. And she had apologized. No weekend in Rhode Island, but she had said she was sorry.

"So," Anne said. "I suppose we have more than one thing to celebrate." She looked at Larkin. "This is Fernanda's one-year anniversary with Merrill Lynch," Anne said to Larkin. "And Fernanda, Larkin has just been admitted to an excellent acting school."

Larkin hated this, the forced togetherness. Anne spoke as if they were strangers.

"One year isn't all that much," Fernanda said, "but what they've said is remarkable is how far I've come—to reach the sales level I've reached in only a year, especially in this market."

"Wonderful," Larkin said, draining her martini. "Where's the waiter, anyway?"

"I *don't* know," her mother sighed. "We're going to be terribly late if we're not served soon. We should have gone to the Palm Court."

"I couldn't make it that far uptown," Fernanda said. "I *told* you that, Mother."

"Well, you might have to leave early, dear, that's all." She turned to Larkin then. "But you don't have to leave, do you, Larkin? I had thought we could go shopping."

"No, I'm free," Larkin said.

"I don't know how you can stand it, not working," Fernanda said. "Don't you get bored?"

"I work," Larkin said. "Going to auditions and taking classes is work, Fernanda. Some people would say it's harder work, because you never know where you're going to be or how many times you're going to be rejected. All you know is that you're going to be rejected over and over again."

The man across the room was still staring.

"But that's the nature of the profession, being rejected," Fernanda said. "It isn't like being rejected for a normal job."

Larkin held up her hands. "Fine. Have it your way, all right? It's easy, and it's the easiest thing I've ever done."

"Darling, all Fernanda meant—"

"I don't care, all right?" Christ. She could barely look at her sister without remembering: "I can't *believe* you, Larkin. How *could* you? You must be out of your mind." Running out into the streets of Venice and not coming back for hours, and Larkin had had to explain to Geoffrey that Fernanda had walked in on them. And watching his face as he realized: everyone would know. His brother would know.

And she had never been able to find out why Fernanda had said anything to anyone.

The waiter came, and Larkin ordered another drink and ignored the look her mother and sister exchanged.

"Tell us about the class," Anne said when the waiter had gone. "How often does it meet?"

"Uh, four times a week, with the two classes," she said tonelessly. Did she want to tell them she had gotten kicked out or not? Wouldn't it be better to wait? At least till she was alone with her mother. Or why tell at all, now that she thought about it?

The waiter brought her drink, and a moment later the man who had been staring stood up.

Larkin watched him out of the corner of her eye as she sipped her drink and half listened to her mother and sister talking about clothes.

"Excuse me," a voice said.

Larkin had thought the man had passed, but he had come back, and now he was standing between her and her mother. "My name is John Harwood," he said, extending his hand. Larkin didn't take it. "I realize you three lovely ladies are in the middle of lunch, but I have to ask you," he said, looking down at Larkin. "Have you ever considered modeling?"

"You're bothering us," Larkin said.

"Larkin!" her mother said.

Larkin looked up at the man. "Get lost, all right?"

"Look," he said, not moving. "I'm sure you get questions like that all the time. But I'm a rep for—"

"I don't care who you're a rep for, I want you to leave us the fuck alone, all right?"

His mouth opened, but no words came out. Then he turned on his heel and walked out.

"Larkin, what on earth is the matter with you?" Anne said. "Everyone in the restaurant could hear you."

"So what? He was an asshole."

Her mother's eyes were wide. "I want you to stop that this instant," she said in a tight, thin voice. "Or Fernanda and I are going to leave."

"So *what*? Jesus *Christ*. You'd think I had just *murdered* someone." She looked at her sister. "And what are *you* staring at?"

Fernanda looked at their mother. "She's drunk," Fernanda said. "I think you should order her some coffee, Mother."

"Christ," Larkin said, rummaging in her purse for her cigarettes. "Drunk because I tell off someone who shouldn't even be *talking* to me? What's the matter with you two?" She was aware that she was talking much too loudly, that her voice had broken and cracked, that a woman at the next table was staring.

"What if you had an audition this afternoon?" Fernanda suddenly said.

Larkin looked at her sister. She had to squint to make the image one instead of two. "What audition?"

"What if you *had* one? What if you had all these martinis and then you got a call?"

"I'm not going to get a call *here*. At a restaurant? You think I'm going to get a *call*? I don't even get to go back to class, that's how good I am."

"What?" Anne said. "But—"

"You got kicked out?" Fernanda said.

"What if you stopped asking these idiotic questions?" Larkin said, hearing the anger in her voice as if it were from far away. "Just fuck off. Both of you."

On Madison Avenue, ten blocks away, she realized she had done exactly what Geoffrey used to do with her father. Get drunk, get into a fight, and leave in the middle of a meal. And it scared her. She had never blown up like that with her mother and sister, never so directly.

She walked all the way home, her head pounding, up through the park to 110th Street and then across. And then she tried to call her mother.

"Just a minute, miss; I'll see if she can talk," the new house-keeper said.

What seemed like half an hour later, her mother came on. "Yes, Larkin."

"Listen. I'm sorry. I don't know what happened. I was upset about class, and I took it out on you. And I guess I did drink too much."

"That's quite all right," Anne James said. "We all have our days."

Larkin couldn't believe it: We all have our days? But her mother seemed to have forgiven her.

"It's just that I really am upset," Larkin said. "Getting into the Kozloff Institute was a major coup, and now I don't know what to do."

"It seems clear to me," Anne said.

"Excuse me?" Larkin said. She didn't understand—

"It's quite clear to me and to Fernanda. What you need is to work, Larkin. If you'd like to be an actress in five or ten years, after you've earned something, that would be fine. But until then it seems quite clear to everyone."

Christ. "What are you saying, Mother? How much are you cutting me off?"

"I'm going to consolidate your trust in a mutual fund Fernanda is quite enthusiastic about. When you begin drawing on it, it should be substantially larger than it is now."

"You're telling me I'm going to get nothing?"

"At the *moment*," Anne said. "But when you're thirty, perhaps—we feel quite certain—"

"You can go to hell," Larkin said, and she slammed down the phone.

Fourteen

The door to Falcone Casting opened, and a tall, dark-haired man walked in.

For a second Maura thought she knew him from television. He looked like a cop, or an actor who would play a cop—thick hair, dark-eyed, not quite clean-shaven, and with clothes that would let him blend into a city street in seconds. Good-looking but in an unremarkable way.

"Hey," he said softly, coming up to her desk with a bounce in his walk. "You must be my dad's new assistant. Maura, right?"

She looked up at him. "Right," she said. George had mentioned a son, but Maura had imagined someone older.

"Vince Falcone," he said, nodding. "He in?" he asked, jerking his head at George Falcone's closed door.

"Not yet."

"Huh. He left before I did."

"Oh. You live with him?"

"Yeah, for now," he said, sitting on the edge of the desk. "I'll get my own place one of these days, but I'm never even home, you know? And Irene works nights."

"Oh, your sister?"

He jerked his head back and smiled. "You don't know a hell of a lot, do you? No, Irene. His girlfriend.'' He narrowed his eyes. ''You never saw her picture?''

''I don't—not that I know of.''

''Black chick? Used to work at the Fantasy Lounge?''

''Uh—I don't know,'' she said, not thinking. Because the way he had said ''Fantasy Lounge.'' It had sounded so much like the voice on the phone.

He jumped off the desk and went into his father's office.

''Here you go,'' he called out. He came back with an eight-by-ten and stood next to her as she looked at it.

She recognized the picture from George Falcone's wall, a very pretty black woman with shoulder-length, straightened hair and a crooked, knowing smile.

''Beautiful, huh?'' he said from over her shoulder. He took the picture and looked at it himself before taking it back into his father's office.

''You're probably wondering how he can do it, right?'' he said when he came out again. ''You know, knowing what she's doing in the clubs, all that shit.''

''I hadn't really thought about it,'' she said. ''I didn't even know—''

''I'm talking about *now*,'' he said, sitting down on the desk again. ''Now that you know.''

She shrugged. ''I don't know. I'm sure your father has worked it out,'' she said, looking away. Why was he asking her these things?

''I'll tell you how he does it,'' he said, pulling a pack of Camels out of his pocket. ''Smoke?''

''No, thanks.''

''You don't smoke?''

She shook her head.

He smiled. ''That's nice, Maura. I like that.''

And she knew, right then, the way he said, ''I like that.'' Just the way the man who called had said, ''I like that. There's more to love.''

''So I'll tell you,'' he said, slipping his lighter and cigarettes back into his pocket. ''He treats her like a fucking queen, that's how he does it. She does her act and that's it, you know? No hooking, nothing on the side; the only touching is when she collects the tips.'' He took a long drag on his cigarette. ''You know about the tips, right?'' He smiled. ''I can see in your eyes that you don't. How'd you get this job, anyway? My pop said you didn't even know what the hell it was.''

"I didn't."

"So now you know." He winked. "So you want to know about the tips? You should know all these things, Maura, or else—it's no good, you in here not knowing what's going on." He stood up. "So I'll tell you. They're dancing, right? Down to the wire, you might say. The bra goes, everything except the G-string—"

The front door opened, and George Falcone came in, his cheeks red from the cold. "Hey. Vince. Maura," he said, nodding. "What's up? Come on in. Any calls, Maura?"

"Just Deke from the Junction. He wants to know if Sherry can come back."

George Falcone laughed. "I'll bet. Tell him yeah. And call in some coffee, will you, Maura?"

He shut the door, and Maura could hear George and Vince talking, but not the words.

Maura. That's a beautiful name. I like that. There's more to love.

Maura called the deli downstairs and was in the middle of ordering when George's door opened and Vince came out.

"That's right," she said into the phone, "three coffees."

Vince made a sign for two.

"Make that two," she said. "And two Danish." Suddenly she was starved.

She hung up, and Vince smiled. "Two Danish," he said. "I like that. Not 'a couple of Danish,' not yeah this and yeah that. Where'd you grow up?"

"Scranton," she said.

"What? Upstate?"

"Pennsylvania."

"Huh. So look. You get off at what? Seven? Seven-thirty?"

"Usually seven," she said. "Maybe earlier today," she added, although it was a lie.

"Yeah?" He looked at his watch. "I've got some stuff to do, but I'm coming back later. Maybe you want to have a drink or something."

"I don't know," she said.

"What, one drink? Come on." He shrugged. "Whatever. See you around six-thirty, seven," he said, and walked out.

When she brought George his coffee, she thought of asking him if she could leave early, but something stopped her. She went back to her desk, ate both Danish, and pretended the morning hadn't even happened.

Fifteen

It was completely crazy to be nervous, Danielle knew. Christy was her cousin, someone she had known for sixteen whole years till Christy and her family had moved to New York. And now, so what if Christy was trying to be an investment banker, or whatever they called them? She had to be the same person inside.

But Danielle felt so sick to her stomach, and her fingers didn't even feel like they were hers. Plus it was freezing, which New York always seemed to be.

"Le Parc Parisienne," the canopy said. So this was the place. But did you sit down and wait, or wait outside? Christy had said she was going to make reservations in her name, so that probably meant wait inside. And maybe she was already there.

"Hi. I'm Danielle Austin?" *He doesn't care who you are, dummy.* "Um, I'm here to meet Christy Thorsen? We have reservations?"

She had definitely never worked at a restaurant this fancy, and she was glad. The maitre d' was hardly looking at her.

"Come this way," he finally said, and he led the way through the tiniest tables Danielle had ever seen. No wonder the restaurants made money, cramming so many people into a tiny little space like this.

"Thanks," Danielle said when he pulled out her chair. But he was gone a second later.

You haven't done anything wrong, and you're crazy to be nervous. What about all the games she and Christy had played together? Dressing up like hobos and going down to the tracks all the time, tricking people into giving them money, pretending they were lost or crazy or sometimes orphans—those had been the greatest times of Danielle's whole life, and Christy had definitely been like a sister. So there.

But she felt sick.

And Christy was engaged, she had said over the phone. So that was another thing. Everyone seemed to be living these giant lives—her father and Christy, anyway.

"Danielle?"

Danielle looked up. She never would have recognized Christy in a million years. She was blond, which she definitely never had been, and super put together like in a magazine, and in a suit with a bow tie and everything.

Danielle didn't know what to do. She had pictured her and Christy screaming when they saw each other, but you didn't scream in a place like this, plus Christy didn't look like the type that screamed anymore.

"Hi. God, you look so *different*," Danielle said, and Christy sat down, so that solved that. It had been five years, Danielle realized, since they had seen each other.

"Well, with a little help from Elizabeth Arden and a *lot* of help from Mario Videsti, I've managed. You look *wonderful*, Danielle."

"Thanks." She didn't know who Mario Videsti was, but he had to be a hairdresser or someone.

"Well. How do you like New York?" Christy asked. "Are you all settled in?"

"Almost," she said. "I'm sharing an apartment uptown with two girls who are really nice, so that's good, and I just got an incredible job."

"You're kidding. So soon? Wait a minute, here comes our waiter. It's impossible to get decent service here, so let's order now. Do you like *boeuf*—uh, beef stew? It's their specialty."

"Sure. Anything's—"

Christy ordered, but in French, and the waiter made a little bow and left.

"When did you learn French?"

"I always took French," Christy said with a weird half smile. "So. Tell me about this wonderful job you have."

"Well, I haven't even started. But it's at this private club, and you just wouldn't believe it. It's *so* fancy."

"What do you mean, a private club?"

"It's a club. You know—a casino, but people have to be members, and—"

"A casino? Danielle, gambling is illegal in New York."

"But this is private. People have to be *members*. They have to be *nominated* and accepted and all that."

"It's still illegal, Danielle. Where is this club?"

Don't tell her.

Danielle couldn't believe the voice inside that said not to trust Christy, but she knew she had to follow it.

"Danielle, start from the beginning. Where is this club, and how did you get this job? Where would you even *hear* about a place like that? And what are you *doing* for them?"

Danielle couldn't believe it. She sounded like a mother—not Danielle's mother, because her mother never cared where she went or what she did (it was the truth), but the kind of mother Danielle had sometimes thought it would be interesting to have. But that didn't mean she really wanted one, and the last thing she wanted was for *Christy* to act like her mother. What had happened to her, anyway?

"Look. Let's talk about something else, okay? I don't know why you're making such a gigantic thing out of it. I mean, we haven't seen each other in five years and you're acting like I'm a criminal or something."

"I'm *trying* to protect you, Danielle. God knows your father wouldn't do anything about it. Does he even know about your job?"

Danielle shook her head. "Don't tell him, okay? I want to surprise him."

"Oh, he'll be surprised, I'm sure. And impressed, knowing Cleve." She sighed. "Look. You really don't know anything about this city, Danielle—"

"I know enough to know I don't want to work in some crummy department store or at Burger King. This happens to be a great job. I didn't even go to college, you know."

"I know," Christy said quietly.

For a second Danielle could see the old Christy, the one who used to laugh so hard that the food would fall out of her mouth, the one who would scream she couldn't laugh anymore because her stomach hurt too much. They had spied on all those boys, too, building the ladder at the beach club so they could see into the cabanas, writing secret love notes to Scott Harmon and Tommy Wayne, all those silly things. . . .

"Tell me what you've been doing," Danielle said. "I mean, your job sounds really interesting."

"Do you know what an investment banker is, Danielle?"

God. "Um, well. Sure. I mean, everyone knows what investments are. And banking. Did you have to go to a special school for that?"

"I got my M.B.A. at Harvard. Remember? When I was in Boston?"

"That's right." When Christy had written once in three years.

"That's where I met Scott, as a matter of fact."

"Scott? You mean your fiancé's named Scott? God, that's such a coincidence."

Christy looked blank. "What do you mean?"

"Scott Harmon? At the beach club?" Christy still looked blank. "Come on. I can't *believe* you could forget that. He was the first guy we ever saw naked, Christy."

"Would you lower your voice, Danielle? The whole restaurant is staring at us."

Danielle looked around. Maybe one person, one guy, and he had been staring anyway. "You have to remember, Christy. Come on."

Christy took a deep breath. "That was a long time ago, Danielle."

"I know. God. But it's not like we committed some kind of *sin* or something."

"I know that. It's just . . . I'm rather a different person."

Rather. The old Christy would never have said "rather" like that, like she was in some English movie or something.

"So what's he like? What's his last name?"

"Jennings. He's with the U.S. attorney's office. He's an assistant prosecutor."

A prosecutor. Uh-oh. But they didn't deal with people like shoplifters. Danielle felt her face starting to go red, though. "Um, how did you meet him?"

"I told you. We were both up at Harvard." Christy looked at her watch. "The service here really is dreadful. I should have suggested another place. I have a two-thirty appointment, Danielle."

Danielle looked at her watch. It was already one-thirty. But Danielle was sure it was a lie. Why would Christy have made lunch for one o'clock if she had a two-thirty appointment? Plus at a restaurant where she said they were super-slow.

So it meant she wanted to end it, to get it over with.

Danielle looked at Christy, but Christy didn't look back. She was looking around the restaurant. As if she was eating lunch with a stranger or someone she didn't like. Wishing she was somewhere else.

It doesn't have to be true. It was so hard to believe, the cousin who had been her best friend. Who knew all her secrets. "Hey, remember when we told that guy we were investigators with the beach patrol? I think I was *twelve* that summer. Why did we think anyone would believe us?"

Christy smiled and shook her head. "It's all hard to believe. California seems like another world to me, though. And to tell you the truth, I have absolutely no desire to go back."

"But what about your parents?"

"Well, to see *them*, of course. But I would never live there again. No one is serious about anything. I'm so thankful I left when I did."

Danielle shrugged. "I just had to get away. Victoria was driving me crazy."

"I can imagine." She looked at her watch again. "But I *can't* imagine where our waiter is." She sighed. "Listen, Danielle. Would you think I was horribly rude if I rushed off? I can cancel my order and we can meet another time, when we have more time to talk. It's silly to pay for a lunch I won't have time to eat."

"Um, sure," Danielle said. She wished there was even some water, though, because her throat was suddenly so dry, it was aching. "But you'd better hurry and catch the waiter or it's going to be too late."

"I will," Christy said, standing up. "I'll be right back, Danielle."

But Danielle could already see the waiter coming with their food, and it was obvious it was theirs; he was looking right at them.

"Oh," Christy said as he came and set the plates down. She was still standing up. "Is it too late—? I've had an emergency, and I have to leave. Could you possibly cancel one of these orders?"

"Cancel it, madame?"

Christy had opened her wallet, and she put a bunch of bills down on the table. "For your trouble," she said.

"Very well." He picked up one of the plates, and Christy leaned down. "I'm awfully sorry," she said, kissing Danielle on the cheek. "I'll call you by the end of the week, all right? I just *can't* be late, and the appointment is all the way downtown."

"Go. Don't be late," Danielle said.

She watched Christy go, and she looked down at her food. A giant steaming plate of stew. And she wasn't even a little bit hungry.

An emergency appointment. God. What was wrong with her that she was so terrible to have lunch with?

And she knew—it wasn't that Christy hated her or anything like that. Christy probably thought they had "grown apart," the way people on soaps always said. But they were cousins, and they had been best friends. And now? Nothing.

The waiter walked past, and Danielle cleared her throat. "Um, can I have the check, please?" She couldn't really see eating in a place like this all by herself, plus the stew didn't smell all that great. Maybe Larkin would be home and they could go out for a pizza or something decent.

The waiter put the check down, and for a second Danielle thought there had to be a mistake. Seventeen dollars for one person? But there it was, in black and white. The most expensive meal she had ever eaten, and she hadn't even eaten it.

She was a bitch to leave like that; that's the truth, and that's all there is to it.

But it didn't feel like the truth. Maybe the truth was that there was something about her that she just didn't know that made people act like that, like even her father, the way he was embarrassed, practically, about the panty hose. As if her job was her whole life, her whole personality. Maybe Christy thought that was all she was, a nothing because she wasn't some investment banker or whatever.

God. She half felt like telling them both to go to hell, telling them she'd show them someday how she was the opposite of a nothing.

But suddenly, for the first time in her life, she wondered whether her secret dream would actually ever come true.

Sixteen

Maura looked at the clock on the wall and took another bite of her Milky Way. Six-fifteen, and George was gone.

Which meant she could go, too, if there were really a reason. She was supposed to stay till seven, but she knew George: he wouldn't be upset if she left early just this once.

So maybe she would go. Tell him tomorrow that she had had a headache. Today had been slow anyway.

She finished the Milky Way, put the cover on her typewriter, and was just getting her purse out of the bottom drawer of the desk when the door opened.

"Hey. *Caught* you," Vince Falcone said, letting the door slam shut. "So are you ready?"

"Oh, I can't leave yet," Maura said, forcing herself to look at the clock as if she were really concerned about the time. "And actually, I forgot: I told friends I'd meet them for drinks after work. And I told them to meet me here around a quarter of."

He moved forward, smiling. "You're afraid of me, aren't you? You know none of that stuff is true, friends meeting you." He pulled his cigarettes and lighter out of his pocket.

"I'm not lying," she said. "Why would I lie?"

He exhaled and then laughed. "I don't know." His smile disappeared. "You tell me."

God. *Think*.

All day she had thought about him, and all day she hadn't been able to decide: Was he the voice on the phone? And if he was, what did that mean?

On TV they always said the same thing: People who called and said odd things, people who wrote letters with words cut out of the newspaper, none of those people ever represented a real threat in person. They needed to keep their distance: distance was a prerequisite for their kicks.

But Vince Falcone wasn't a distance man. He was all too close, the kind of person who filled a room the minute he walked into it.

And there was something else, the thing that had been underneath the fear from the beginning (now that she could smell his sweat).

The fact that he was interested in her, that in person he wasn't at all bad-looking.

And all day she hadn't been able to get contrasting thoughts out of her mind.

Patrick Delaney insisting it had to be dark when they had sex: in the backseat of his car, at his father's house, at her father's house. Patrick Delaney's dry, unwilling kisses, the rough of his cheek when he'd turn away. And his one-two-three "lovemaking"—foreplay that took thirty seconds, then in, then out. And toward the end of the summer, his limp penis, which was like a joke to Maura because she felt like saying, "I didn't even really want you to *begin* with. You're just someone to be with, that's all." (And the only person she had ever been with.)

And all day she hadn't been able to stop thinking, just idly wondering (was wondering dangerous?), what Vince Falcone would be like.

"Just talk to me," he said, coming around to her side of the desk. He sat down facing her and took a long drag on his cigarette. "Talk to me, Maura."

"I have to go."

"I thought you said you couldn't leave yet. What are you, pulling my leg?" He laughed. "I tell myself I gotta be polite with you, Maura, you being so polite yourself. Like what I meant to say— Are you jerking me off?—that wouldn't be right, would it?"

She didn't say anything. She looked at the door, at the frosted glass that showed nothing on the other side—certainly not George Falcone coming back, and the girls always came to pick up their checks before the banks closed at three o'clock.

"What are you looking at?" he said, turning to look at the door. "No one's coming, so what's to look at?" He faced her again. "How about looking at me, Maura? Since you know me."

She looked up at him.

"You know me, right? You know what I'm talking about." He stubbed out his cigarette. "And you stayed."

"I have to go."

He hopped off the desk. "You have to stay, Maura." He held out his hands. "Don't you?"

"Listen, I really—"

He grabbed her wrists and pulled her up.

"Let me go."

He smiled. "You really want me to? I don't think you do."

She took a deep breath. "I do," she said, but her voice had come out breathy and weak. Her knees felt like water.

He was breathing hard. "You liked the calls, didn't you?"

She swallowed. "I don't know what you're talking about."

"The calls," he said. "I could hear you liked them. I knew you would, from what my father said. 'The shy type,' he said. But it's never that way underneath. I know you," he said. "You think you're not so pretty, you think you weigh too much. . . ." He rubbed her wrists with his thumbs. "I've been with girls like you before, girls who haven't been with a lot of guys," he said. He moved so he was pressing up against her. "You just need the right guy, Maura."

She jerked her wrists away from his hands and pushed him away. "Leave me alone," she said.

He looked stunned. "Hey," he said in a loud, new voice. "You don't have to *fight* me, Maura. You say no; the answer is no. Just don't think you're going to get all kinds of other guys, Maura. You want a guy, I'm it."

She turned away and walked out.

Seventeen

"Administrative assistant, hi pay. Must have pitch-in attitude, love teamwork, be willing to work late 3–4 nites per week."

"Secretary, type 60"—so that was out right there.

"Pediatrician's assistant, must love babies and anxious moms—"

Larkin put the paper down. Didn't they have any ads for people who couldn't type and *didn't* have a pitch-in attitude? She wanted to see an ad that said, "If you even hate the *idea* of working, here's the job for you." If she even hated the *wording* of the ads, how was she going to be able to *work* in any of these places?

"Anybody home?" Danielle called as the front door slammed shut.

"In here," Larkin called from the living room.

Danielle appeared in the doorway and looked slightly lost. "How was your lunch with your mother?" she asked.

"Don't ask," Larkin said. "What about yours? With your cousin, right?"

Danielle sat down across from Larkin on the couch. "I don't know," she said, looking down. "It was pretty bad, actually." She looked past Larkin for a second, and Larkin realized Danielle was holding her mouth in, as if she was trying to stop herself from crying.

"What's the matter?"

"Oh—" Danielle's lip was trembling. "God, I can't believe I'm so upset. It's so . . . so nothing."

"Danielle, what?"

"She just—she just—it was like I wasn't good enough or something, like . . . just because she went to school, I mean college and then Harvard, to graduate school, it was . . . she didn't even want to talk about the past, I mean not at all, and that would have been okay except . . . she talked to me as if I was stupid or something, saying *I just told you* when I asked where she had met her fiancé and she had already told me, and then . . . then she said she had to leave, I mean before our food even came, and she just left me there." Tears started to stream from her eyes. "And I mean, I wouldn't even *care* if I had just met her or something. I mean, the truth was I didn't even *like* her, today. But I've known her my whole life, and now I look back, and ever since she left California, she hasn't even wanted to know me. I mean, that's the truth. And it's so much like my father. They're both . . ." She stopped to wipe away her tears, and then she bit her lip, her chin jutting out like a child's.

"Both what?" Larkin asked, coming over to the bed.

Danielle closed her eyes for a moment. "I don't know what it is," she said in a hollow, soft voice. "I wrote to my father for a million years, and he never wrote to me—I mean hardly ever. And the same thing with Christy. And then I come here, and it's as if . . . it's as if no one even wants to know me, as if everyone wishes I had never even moved east. Which I could *take* except—" she sniffled "—it just isn't fair."

"But your father visited you at Ivorsen & Shaw, didn't he?"

"Well, but that's the way he is. That means he's going to ignore me for a really long time. He goes crazy over people and then he freezes them out. But now that Christy . . ." She looked into Larkin's eyes. "I want to ask you something, okay? And I really want the truth."

"All right," Larkin said.

"I just want you to tell me . . . I mean, is there something I don't know, some secret about how to act? Or is there something wrong with me I don't know about?"

"Danielle, not at *all*. How could you think that?"

"You would, too, if you . . ." She shook her head. "The thing is that I had such big plans. You know, coming to New York, becoming a giant success, making my father super-proud and getting to know him, starting a whole new life. And Christy wasn't even going to really be a part of it. But now—it's just—I feel like everyone's avoiding me."

"That's just silly," Larkin said. "Really, Danielle. If everyone's avoiding you—and by 'everyone' I mean your father and Christy—then that's their problem. I know it's easy for me to say, but maybe you just have unrealistic expectations of what your family is going to be like to you. Particularly because you haven't really *had* a family.''

"But yours—"

"I don't want to have anything to do with mine," Larkin said. "The only one I ever cared about is dead."

Danielle looked shocked.

"I mean it," Larkin said. "You have to learn to harden yourself a little bit, Danielle. What they think of you just doesn't matter all that damn much. I know it doesn't bother *me*. The only thing that bothered me about an otherwise awful lunch today was that my mother cut me off from my allowance."

"God. Really?" Danielle said. "But what are you going to do?"

"I don't know." She looked down at the ads again, and the room began to swim. She was *not* going to work for five dollars an hour, and she wasn't going to learn to type. And she wasn't going to give up acting, either.

"Hey, you know what? There's this new girl at the club, and she just left a job she loved that I bet you could do. She was a model at a showroom. You know, like a manufacturer? And they paid great, and she's about your height, so I don't even think you'd be too short. And she really liked it a lot. I know she made a ton of money."

"Really? Why did she leave?"

Danielle shrugged. "I guess she kind of got bored. She said she wanted to learn something new. Cici's the type that isn't going to stick to anything for a super-long time."

Cici. Larkin could just imagine. "Do you know what the name of the place is?"

Danielle bit her lip. "Um, R and something fashions, I think. But I could call her and find out for sure, or you could. She's really nice."

It sounded good. Promises or no promises, she had to make a living. And what Geoffrey had said made sense: models who made hundreds of thousands of dollars a year *did* get sidetracked. But this was probably a job she'd be able to turn away from quite easily. "Could you give me the number? It's at least worth a call."

"Just a sec." Danielle jumped off the bed and went running down the hall, and came back a few seconds later with a torn, ancient-looking address book.

"How long have you had that? It looks ancient."

"It is. Maybe ten years. Since I was ten. Cleve gave it to me when he came out to L.A. once. Except it was pathetic back then.

You wouldn't believe the addresses I wrote in it. The grocery store? Stuff like that. Anyway, here's Cici's number.''

Larkin wrote it down and thanked her. Maybe it would lead to something; at least it would probably pay well. And she had to make a living somehow.

Eighteen

"So how'd you hear of us?" Rochelle Lasky hadn't stopped chewing her gum once, and Larkin found it hard to believe that this woman was head of what Cici had painted as an empire.

"A friend of mine," Larkin said. "She has a friend who worked here."

"Name?"

"Cici."

Rochelle nodded her head and cracked her gum. "Nice girl," she said. She was obviously someone who had once been pretty, but she was wearing so much caked-on makeup and such thick false eyelashes, it was hard to tell what she really looked like at this point. "What'd you hear?" she asked.

"I heard that the hours are flexible, which would be great for me, and that it's not every day."

"It's not even every week," Rochelle said. "It's whenever the buyers come in. The buying days are when we need you. What else?"

What else? "Well, I heard you don't have to be five-eight."

Rochelle made a face. "Can you imagine, five-eight? Sixty percent of our line is petites. We don't need the five-eights, the five-nines. We need perfect size sevens, and you don't have to tell me: you've got the shape. So what else?"

"Well, that's really it." Larkin couldn't think of anything else. But she had the distinct impression there was more.

Rochelle snapped her gum. "Yeah, well, how do you feel about the buyers?"

"The buyers? What do you mean?"

"The buyers, the guys. You ever work on Seventh Avenue before?"

"No, I've never modeled."

Rochelle sighed. "You either love it or you hate it, that's all I can say. And let me say this: I don't force anyone to do anything, you understand? I want that straight now, and understood. I don't want you in here crying next week because you think it's some kind of requirement. The other places, they're like prisons, but not this place. You can ask any of the girls. I'm some kind of legend on Seventh Avenue, and you'll see why. You'll never see another one-woman operation, you understand?"

"But forced to do what?" Larkin asked, feeling naive for the first time in years.

Rochelle sighed. "All right, look. The buyers, they come in, they see a bunch of pretty girls, they pinch you, they give you a little feel, they want to take you out to dinner and have a good time. It's only natural, you know? So most of the girls, they go. There's a good dinner in it for them, and a hell of a bonus at the end, all right?"

"From the buyers?"

"Hell, yes, from the buyers. I'm not running an escort service here. But that's the way some of the girls think of it, if it helps you any. They could be working for an escort service and forced to go out with some guy, all they know about him is a voice on the phone—not even—or they can go out with guys they know, season after season. They do what they want, they have a good time, whatever."

"But we don't have to."

"Hell, no. I told you. It's up to the girls. Go talk to them if you want; I don't care; my life's an open book."

Larkin smiled. She liked Rochelle in an odd way. "That's all right. I believe you. And if you ask anyone who knows me, they'll tell you I'm not easily forced."

"Whatever," Rochelle said with a shrug. "It doesn't mean a thing to me. As long as you're nice to the guys while they're here. That part is a must. Hey, listen, are you free this afternoon?"

"Uh . . . it depends. For what?"

"Make a little extra money, okay? You're hired, obviously, so why not start today?"

"Really?"

"Sure. Why not jump right in, get the feel of it?"

Larkin couldn't really think of any reason why she shouldn't.

And it would be a quick enough way to discover whether she liked the atmosphere or not.

"Well, all right," she said. "But we should discuss my salary, I think—"

"Your salary's the same as all the other girls—two-fifty a show."

Amazing. That was what the other ads said she'd make in a week. "Sounds fine," she said.

Rochelle had stood up and was looking her over. "You take a shower today, Larkin?"

"What? Yes, of course."

Rochelle shook her head. "They're going to go wild over you," she said quietly. "I haven't had a redhead in years."

It wasn't at all what Larkin had expected. It was dirty, the back room where they all changed, and she had expected that; and hectic and noisy, which she had also expected. What she hadn't expected was the huge variety of girls, the huge range in looks. There were a few who were beautiful and could have been models anywhere if not for their height, but most were just pretty, some with bad skin, and a few had great bodies but nothing in the way of faces.

"Tough way to start," one girl said to her as they were getting undressed. She was one of the less attractive ones, but you could see why she had been hired: she had a dancer's body under her not so great skin, one of the most flawless bodies Larkin had ever seen.

"What do you mean?" Larkin asked.

"Well, lingerie," the girl said, and a few of them laughed. "You're not shy?"

"Don't I just have to walk out there and model?"

"With a little touchy-feely thrown in. It's later that gets tough."

"You mean if you go out with any of them."

"Yeah. Whatever."

"Does everybody go?"

"Are you kidding? I'm lucky my husband hasn't killed me just for *working* here. Ask Renee over there if you want to know about *dating* them."

The one named Renee just continued to get undressed. She had a sort of wounded, hurt-me look, one of those pretty girls who never really looked happy.

"Come on, Renee," the first girl said. "Tell how much the guy from Ohio, Iowa—whatever—how much he gave you."

But at that moment Rochelle came in with the clothes, and she was moving like a tornado. "You, the bra and panties set. You,

Renee—the baby doll. It'll look gorgeous with your hair. You, Larkin, the teddy and tap pants. There are nine thousand pairs of sandals in the other room; you make sure you find some that go. And that goes for *all* of you. I don't want any of that barefoot shit *ever* again, you understand?''

And Larkin felt as if she were being pushed out of an airplane with only half a parachute. She had barely gotten dressed before she was pushed into the hall and had to listen for her cue. ''And our newest model, Larkin,'' Rochelle said, and Larkin walked into the showroom.

She had expected an audience, a large group of people, men and women, in seats as if they were in a theater.

But there were nine, maybe ten men sitting around in folding chairs. It felt much more intimate, much more charged than she would have expected.

''. . . of acrylic,'' Rochelle was saying. ''Now, gentlemen, you're seeing Larkin on her virgin modeling turn, you might say. I hired her just this morning. So bear with her for just a few minutes. Larkin, each of these gentlemen would like a closer look at the outfit, so make your way slowly around the room.''

It felt odd, but she liked it, all eyes on her.

The first man just looked, but the second reached out and felt the material, then let his hand move up over the small of her back.

This part she wasn't sure about. He was fat and old and sweaty, and she moved away.

The next man just felt the edges of the material—the lace. Was he really interested in the fabric?

She made the mistake of looking at him, looking into his eyes, and his hand moved up inside the teddy.

She moved away—she might have even pulled away, she didn't know—and swallowed. Tough was right. This was a tough way to start.

But two-fifty a show. Wasn't this better than working at some horrid office for a week? She wasn't going to go out with any of *these* men; that was definite. But if an attractive one came along, well, that would be different. And in the meantime, two-fifty a show. She'd have to remember she was making two-fifty a show.

Nineteen

Maura took one more bite of the cheese Danish, and it was gone.

You can't have more. You just can't.

There was something monstrous inside her this morning, a ravenousness that couldn't be satisfied. It was tough sometimes, living with Larkin and Danielle, watching them in front of their mirrors, both so effortlessly beautiful. Larkin could become a model just because of her looks, Danielle could work at a club; things came so damn easily to both of them. What did it feel like to be hired because everyone found you desirable, even irresistible?

The phone rang, and she wiped her hands on a paper towel. "Falcone Casting."

"Yeah. George in?"

"Uh, not yet. Can I take a message?"

"Yeah, tell him Frank from the KitKat. I'll be in till eleven."

"Okay. I'll tell him, Frank," she said, and hung up.

One more. She had bought two, supposedly one for herself and one for George, but he wasn't in yet, and—

The phone rang again.

"Falcone Casting."

Silence.

"Hello?"

Silence. Then: "Hi." It was Vince.

"Hello," she said. Bastard.

"So. How's it going?"

"Fine."

"So listen," he said. "I didn't mean all that shit last night. You want to try again?"

"Nope."

"Hey, come on. Give a guy a second chance. I like you, Maura."

"I'm busy." Which she actually was—Max and Terence and Vanessa. But even if she weren't, there wasn't a chance she'd go out with Vince.

74

"So what about Friday?"

"Nope," she said. "I'm busy."

"So—what? You mean busy like what?"

"Listen," she said. "I have to go. One of the dancers just walked in." Which was true, a girl named Tammy.

"So what?" he said. "They can wait."

"No. I really have to go," she said, and she hung up.

"How're you doing?" Tammy said. She looked a lot like Danielle, blond with perfect skin, the kind of looks Maura had always dreamt of having. "He leave a check for me?"

"Right here," Maura said, getting it out from the drawer. "Here you go."

"Thanks," she said, smiling and giving a little wave as she left. Always cheerful, even with that job. A lot like Danielle in that way, too.

And she wondered. Was she going to turn bitter and awful because she was surrounded day and night by these women who were so great-looking? Why was it she could only attract people like Vince, or Patrick Delaney? She had come to New York, gotten an apartment with Larkin the way they had always planned. But when were the great parts going to begin?

The phone rang, and she answered it right away.

"Falcone Casting."

Silence.

Then, in a whisper: "I want to fuck you."

The door opened, and George Falcone came in.

"What's the matter?" he said, looking concerned.

She was still holding the phone.

The voice, in a whisper, said: "I want to eat you. I want to—"

"That for me?" he asked, heading for his office.

"Uh, wrong number," she said, and she slammed down the phone as hard as she could.

Twenty

"Filthy place," Terence said, wiping the rim of his glass. "One more year, maybe two, and Vanessa won't have to sing in places like this anymore. She won't have to sing at all unless she wants to."

"Why wouldn't she want to?" Maura asked.

"She wants to act," Terence said, looking around. "Where did Max go?" He smiled. "Probably in the bathroom. He gets more nervous than Vanessa does." He looked at Maura. "He's a great guy."

"He seems to be," she said.

"So are you seeing anyone these days? I assume Patrick's completely out of the picture."

"Not really," she said. "I mean yes, Patrick's completely out of the picture. But no, I'm not seeing anyone. What about you?"

He was blushing. It was the most amazing thing about Terence, and it was the first thing she had ever noticed about him—in a literature class, as a matter of fact. A man who blushed. "I was, but it's over. Another of my impossibles," he said with a smile. "Too good to be true, naturally."

"How long was it going on?"

He shrugged casually, but she could see he was uncomfortable. "It wasn't the length of time—we were only together once. But he was a client, and it was tough. New agency, new lover, I suppose."

"Does that happen a lot? With clients, I mean?"

He smiled again. "Oh, come on, Maura. Who are you talking to? Nothing like that ever happens 'a lot' with me. Don't you remember anything?"

She did, unfortunately. He had never been lucky. And it couldn't have been his looks. He was perfectly fine-looking, if not ravingly handsome, certainly articulate enough, well-read and all that. And she had often wondered what kept him from ever having any long-term relationships with anybody.

"However," he said. "Enough about the unlucky adventures of Terence White. I have something important I want to talk to you about." He looked at his watch. "I had thought I'd wait for Alexandra, but she's *chronically* late—it's gotten absurd—so I'll tell you myself." He picked up a fork and began wiping it with his napkin. "As you know, Alexandra and I have a small agency. It's the two of us and an assistant, and we do quite well. But our assistant has just given us rather abrupt notice, and we need to replace her. And naturally, I thought of you."

She didn't know what to say.

"Now, before you start making all sorts of objections, let me tell you what the job would be, all right? As I said, it's a small agency, but we have about twenty regular clients, and several clients we represent on a project-by-project basis. People who are free agents, I suppose you'd say, but will use us as agents if we find them work. Maura, it would be so much more interesting than what you're doing at that absurd place. Do you know at all how an agency works?"

"Your kind of agency? Not really."

"All right. The most important part of the day—for you—is mid-morning every day, when the breakdowns come in. Every agency—every legit agency, anyway—subscribes to something called the breakdown service. It lists every new play, movie, any kind of project that's going into production. Casting directors and producers list what they're looking for. Let's say it's a feature film. They'll give a paragraph about the movie, what it's about, and then a breakdown, a few lines, of what they want for each character—male lead in his thirties, handsome, Ted Danson type, that sort of thing. We might get one or ten of these each day, and we take each one and try to fit them to our clients. So for the young male lead, we might submit five of our clients. And what that means is getting together the right picture for each client, the one that will fit the part, putting his résumé with it, making a list of all the clients we're submitting for that part, and sending it to the casting director. That would be what you would do, but for each part. But your job would be much more than that—it would be making sure each client knows about the auditions they're going on, confirming all sorts of appointments, meeting an awful lot of interesting people, fielding calls . . . let's see. What else?"

"It sounds like a lot right there. What kind of hours do you work?"

"Alexandra and I generally don't come in until midmorning. Nothing important ever happens until around eleven. But we like to have the assistant in by nine-thirty or ten. The middle of the day is the crunch when the breakdowns come in, though. So what do you think?''

"I don't know. I'd have to think about it."

"Have you seen Tony Rinaldi in *Last Chance*?"

"Sure."

"He's our client, and we placed him in that picture. What about *For or Against*?"

She shook her head. The only play she had ever seen in her life, aside from ones Larkin had been in at Yale, was *The King and I* when it came to Scranton.

"All right, what about *Obvious Differences*?"

"I've heard of it," she said.

"You've heard of it. When did you last go to the theater, Maura?"

"I just moved here, Terence. Come on."

"Then it's *time*. What did you come to New York for? To work in some grimy back-office sleaze chamber or to meet some interesting people? If you *tried* to get a job like this, you'd have to wait *years*."

She looked past him and saw Max making his way between the tables. "Here comes Max," she said.

Terence turned. "Max. *You* convince Maura to take the job."

He slid in next to her on the banquette. "Say no to anything Terence suggests."

She smiled. "I probably should. You know about the offer?" She turned to Terence. "What about money, by the way?"

"We'll pay you two-seventy-five a week. Which is more than other agencies. A lot of agencies just hire college kids as interns. But we feel this is too important a position for a college kid. We'll pay because we want to find someone who takes it seriously."

Maura looked at Max. "So what do you think? *You* know the guy better than I do at the moment. Is it on the up and up?"

Max was fiddling with his empty beer mug. "It's on the up and up," he said. "But a more important question is whether it's what you would want to do with your time."

"Thank you *so much*, Max Epstein," Terence said, "for making the job sound irresistible."

"It's a great job," Max said. "But not everybody would want it. That part seems to be more important than whether the job is good or not. Is it what Maura wants to do?" He looked at Maura. "*Is* it what you want to do?"

"I don't know. Let me think about it, all right, Terence? Uh-oh, he has that peeved-Terence look on," she said, laughing.

Max laughed, too. "Maybe we'd better leave now, do you think?"

"Neither one of you is taking this offer very seriously," Terence said. "And I haven't made it simply for my sake, or Alexandra's. It would be a fabulous step for you, Maura. Why aren't you *thinking* about that? What could this stripper thing possibly lead to?"

"Well, that is a point."

"It's more than a point. I refuse to sit back and see you waste your time in New York the way you wasted your time in college. Who was it who told you to go to Yale that summer? I did. And who was it who talked you out of—*Lord*—spending the rest of your life with Patrick Delaney?"

"I never would have married him," she said.

"Don't you be so sure."

He did have a point. He had opened up her life, in ways she never would have done on her own. And what *was* the Falcone job going to lead to? How could it lead to anything?

"Just one more thing," Terence said.

"Yes?"

"Please don't turn it down because you think you wouldn't be right. *I* know you haven't been in New York a long time, and *I* know you haven't ever been involved in the theater or films. But don't turn it down just because it's new or strange or uncomfortable. Of course, something like what you're doing now is more comfortable—no one's going to test you, no one's going to say, 'Oh. Scranton.' " He paused. "You know what I'm talking about."

She did. She was afraid of being humiliated. Someone would mention a play she hadn't heard of, and it would turn out to be the most famous modern play of all time. Or an actor.

But he was right. When was she going to start living Real Life, or adult life? It *was* a job that was probably impossible to get.

"I'll do it," she said.

"Beautiful. How much notice do you have to give to your boss?"

Damn. She had completely forgotten it would mean quitting Falcone. Well, she'd give George enough time to find someone else, maybe even help him with the search.

"There *is* one thing," Terence said. "Alexandra has to agree, too. But I know she will if she ever *gets* here."

He looked toward the entrance and waved. "Well. Speaking of you know who. Here she comes now."

Maura turned. An enormously fat woman was coming through,

but she was having a hard time because the tables were so close together.

Maura looked away. Was she on her way to getting that fat? What a nightmare. And it was another case of "such a pretty face." Alexandra had an almost beautiful face—almondy, uptilted eyes, a really exotic look, long, dark hair with a white streak on one side. But who would notice?

Terence introduced them, and Alexandra shook her hand. "Nice to meet you," she said in a low, cigarette-and-whiskey voice, and immediately turned to Max. "How's Vanessa?"

"She seems pretty relaxed. She was worried about the crowd, but it's filled up a little."

Alexandra looked around. "Goddamn Jerry Osman. I *told* him to advertise in the *Voice*." She sat down and looked around again. "So who do I have to fuck to get a drink around here? Did you talk to her about the job?" She was obviously talking to Terence, although she was so constantly moving, it was hard to tell.

"She said she'll take it," Terence said.

"Good. Waiter!" she yelled.

Maura glanced at Max.

"Congratulations," he whispered.

And for a few minutes she was excited: it was a dream job.

But then the lights went low, and Vanessa came out onstage, tall and blond and thin, and the minute she began to sing, Maura's heart sank. Of *course* someone like Max would go out with someone like Vanessa. This was New York, where people were thin and beautiful and successful. And if you were like Max, just okay-looking in a kind of offbeat way but smart as hell, you chose the thinnest and the most beautiful, and they went for you because you were smart. It was a fast track, and everybody knew it. What was she even doing here?

She looked over at Terence, and he turned and smiled, but she didn't trust the smile. She didn't belong, at all.

Twenty-one

Danielle looked into the mirror and frowned. "Hi. My name's Danielle, and I'm your hostess. Is there a particular game you're interested in playing?"

It sounded so dumb, she couldn't even believe it. When Ingrid, the woman who trained all the new girls, had made her say it yesterday, it had sounded fine. "Hi, I'm Danielle." Just totally normal. But now—especially the part about the game. What if they all said, "Yeah, I'd like to play with you" or something like that? It seemed kind of obvious. Plus would all these men even think of the gambling as a game? It seemed pretty serious, from what she had seen yesterday. A bunch of men and a couple of women, and they didn't even look like they were having a good time.

The bell rang—it sounded like in an airplane when they said to fasten your seat belts—and that meant it was "first call," five minutes left, for the morning shift to get going. Half the girls had already left the dressing room, but there was still one—she could hear rustling—and Danielle got up and went into the other room.

A girl named Petra was in the middle of changing, and Danielle couldn't help staring. She had just taken off her underpants, and there was no hair there at all.

Petra glanced at her in the mirror and started squeezing into her outfit, the same as Danielle's, only blue instead of red.

"Hi," Danielle said. "This is my second day. You're Petra, right?"

"Right," Petra said without looking at her.

"Hi. I'm Danielle. Um, can I ask you a question?"

"What is it?"

"Do you like working here? I haven't really had a chance to talk to anyone yet."

Petra shrugged. "It's okay. Nothing special."

"Are you kidding? Really? It looks so great."

Petra shrugged again. "It's a job like any other job." She clumped a giant makeup bag onto the dressing table and sat down. "The money's great if the players do well, but beyond that . . . it's just a job, Danielle." She looked at Danielle in the mirror. "Are you new to New York?"

"Uh-huh."

"And are you planning to work on the side?"

"On the side?"

"You know. Hooking."

Danielle just stared. And then she realized she had to be totally naive not to have known. In a place like this, with all these super-skimpy outfits . . . "Um, I don't plan to," she said, trying to sound cool.

"Smart girl," Petra said. "Girls who try to cut King out are very sorry afterward."

"Sorry?"

"They lose their jobs, for one thing. And it's just not a smart thing to do. You go through King or you don't do it at all."

"But—he didn't even *mention* that to me. I mean, when I met him, I even *asked*, and he said no."

Petra shrugged. "He doesn't care. There are enough girls who want to do it that he doesn't have to ask anyone. Most girls here do—it's that much more money—but you wouldn't catch me doing it in a million years."

"God," Danielle said. "I guess I should have known. But where—"

"Fifth floor," Petra said.

The airplane-type bell rang again, and Petra put her mascara back in her bag. "You'd better get going," she said. "You're going to be late."

"Okay. Thanks for the advice," Danielle said.

"Anytime," Petra said, edging some lipstick off her mouth with an unbelievably long fingernail.

Danielle looked in the mirror one more time. "Hi, I'm Danielle." And a hooker if we both agree. She knew it was super-naive, but she still couldn't believe it.

"Hi, I'm Danielle. Is there a particular game you're interested in playing?"

It was two Chinese or Japanese men—was it true you couldn't tell the difference unless you knew?—and they both looked nervous.

"Ah, blackjack, blackjack," one of them said, and she was so relieved, she almost kissed them. Easy enough to show them to the blackjack tables. But what if they had said they wanted *her*? And how come Ingrid hadn't warned her?

She got them drinks even though it was only eleven in the morning, but that was what they wanted, and then she went back to her "station," a red-velvety area at the front of the casino.

It was weird, all these people playing blackjack and craps and roulette so early in the morning. But there they were, and according to Ingrid, some of them came practically every day. The trick, everyone said, was to be in the right place at the right time, so that if people won, you could get really big tips. Winners were almost crazy, everybody said. Except that not too many people won.

The thing was, though, you were never supposed to let anyone just sit there—that was the main thing. If there was a guy standing against a wall or sitting on one of the couches or something, you were supposed to get him playing or at least ordering something expensive to drink, like champagne, or if you were really good, both. And she saw a man right then, sitting on a couch just the way they weren't supposed to, looking down like he was really depressed or something.

She saw someone else heading for him, a girl she hated, and she sped up. She wanted to try it. She wanted to be great at this.

"Hi, I'm Danielle," she said.

He looked up. "Allan Greshner," he said. He was cute—older, like maybe forty-five or something, and maybe not the kind of guy that would ever be an actor or a model, but he had a nice face. Super-nice blue eyes and dark, curly hair.

He was smiling. "Something I can do for you?" he asked.

"Oh. *I'm* supposed to say that. Or something like it. They want us to say, 'Is there something you'd like to play?' but I think it sounds really dumb, don't you?"

He was still smiling. "Depends on who's saying it and what they mean."

She shrugged. "I guess. But, um, *is* there something I can do for you? Like would you like a drink, or would you like me to explain any of the games?"

Now he was laughing. "Can you really explain every game in the casino?"

"Well, enough to give somebody the idea of whether they'd be interested in playing or not."

"What would you say about craps?"

She bit her lip. That was the one no one wanted to talk about.

"Um, well, it's a game with dice, and you can either bet with the shooter, the one that has the dice, or against him. Um, if you bet with him, it means you hope he gets a seven or an eleven."

"Very good. End of explanation?"

Uh-oh. "Almost. Is there a lot more?"

"A lot. But it's okay. I know how to play."

"Oh. Do you come here a lot? Whoops. Never mind."

"What's the matter?"

"That's like almost the main question we're never supposed to ask anyone. Like what if they're embarrassed or something?"

"I'm not sure that's right," he said. "Anyone who came here that often wouldn't be embarrassed, I don't think—and anyone who didn't . . . well, whatever. I've only been coming here for a few weeks, and I'm certainly not embarrassed."

"Oh. Good. How did you come, anyway? I mean, how would a person hear about it?"

"Friends, probably. That's how I came here, through a friend. Never gambled in my life till then."

"God. Really?"

"Really."

"But now you really like it?"

He stood up. "Come watch. I have the feeling you'll be lucky for me, and if they see me playing after talking to you, maybe I'll be lucky for you, Danielle."

She liked the way he had remembered her name. Most people didn't even care.

She followed him to one of the craps tables, twenty-dollar minimum, which was a super lot. She could never believe how fast the games went, and with that kind of minimum, you could lose thousands in a second. Or win thousands. In a few seconds Allan Greshner had laid out some money and one of the dealers had given him what looked like a billion and one chips, which he put into the little groove in front of where he was standing.

She looked over at the pit boss, this guy Nick Dotson, and he was giving her a totally weird look. She could never tell with him—what did he mean? He was cute, but only if you didn't pay attention to the look in his eyes. Kind of like Michael J. Fox, but crazy-looking. Super-young to be a pit boss, though, or that was what everyone said. But now he was staring at Allan Greshner, kind of in a weird, intense way.

But Allan probably didn't even notice, because someone was in the middle of throwing—or shooting, she guessed you said—and then the dice landed, and everyone started screaming and yelling, including Allan. The dealer yelled, "Eleven!" and Allan turned around. His face was all red, and he put his finger to his lips like he was saying, "Don't talk, but stay."

The guy rolled again, and everyone started screaming and yelling again, and it seemed to go on forever—again he rolled and won, and again and again, and everyone, including Allan, was throwing bills and chips on the table as fast as they could, and even if you didn't know anything about the game, you'd be able to tell it was a super-good roll, because all kinds of people had come to the table, and people who wanted to play couldn't even do it, because everyone was pressing in and yelling and screaming, and there just wasn't enough room.

But there was a ton of chips on the table, and Allan had a zillion and finally, when the guy lost, people groaned, including Allan, but it didn't seem too serious because he and everyone else really had won gigantic amounts.

Finally he looked at her and let out a deep breath. "Glad I met you, kid," he said, and he picked up a bunch of his chips. "Here." He took her hand and pressed the chips into it.

"Allan, wait," she said. Because really, there had to be six or maybe even seven chips. Which meant six or seven hundred dollars.

"Take it," he said. "I'll see you later, all right?" He looked like he had been running or wrestling or something.

She took it and said, "Are you sure? Really?"

"Go," he said, super-seriously, and he seemed to want her gone. Which was something she had heard about people at casinos: they were extra-superstitious, and you weren't supposed to argue.

But it was weird. Because a lot of the times, the girls also said the men weren't too nice, that all they were interested in was gambling or sex, never talking. And she felt like, well, why shouldn't they be? That's what they're here for. But Allan Greshner seemed nice. Easy to be with.

She waited for a while and served some customers, and then went back to see if he was still at the table and how he was doing. But he was gone.

"Looking for Greshner?"

She turned around. It was Nick Dotson, the pit boss who had been on the shift, except his shift was ending.

"Um, I was just wondering if he was still here."

He had a weird look on. "What do you want to hang around with losers like that for?"

"He didn't lose. He won a ton."

"Hah." He laughed in this really mean way. "You should've stuck around. Some winner."

Which made her feel bad. He had given her seven hundred dollars; she had counted. But maybe she'd see him again sometime. She hoped, anyway. He was the first new person she had liked in a long time.

Twenty-two

"You don't have a choice," Maura said into the phone. She looked up at George Falcone, and he winked. "No, wait a minute. You don't pay and you *never* get another girl from us, do you understand? Right. I can't make it any clearer than that. Right. Nope. Today by noon or else. Is *that* clear? Good-bye."

She slammed down the phone and George gave her the okay sign. "You did good," he said. "Real good, Maura."

"Thanks. It was fun. I think we'll get our check, too."

"Yeah, yeah. You did real good." He nodded and looked at his watch. "You had your Danish yet? Call down for a couple of Danish and a couple of coffees, and take it out of petty cash, okay? They're on me."

"Thanks."

"Hey, you're doing great," he said, and walked back into his office.

She hated the idea of quitting on him. He really was a sweet man, and she loved the way he obviously cared about the girls, how he made sure every one of them got every cent she was owed. How many people could you say that about?

And would it be true of Terence and Alexandra? Granted, maybe in the world of "legit" show business, you didn't need a heavy like George to get paid. But it was obvious he would have gone out of his way for the girls, no matter what. And he would probably go out of his way for Maura if she asked.

But she was going to quit on him. The idea made her sick.

Scranton, an inner voice said. You don't care about hurting George's feelings, you're just scared of the new job.

Which was true, the scared part. Theater. Actors. What was she going to say to any of them?

When the coffee and Danish came, she took them in to George's office and set them down on his desk. "I have to talk to you."

"Shoot," he said, opening the bags and taking out the coffees.

She couldn't bear to look at him. "I . . . a friend . . . I, uh, I have to leave this job," she said.

He looked into her eyes. "When?"

"Monday."

He nodded slowly. "It sure as hell better be a good job for you to dump me like this, Maura. What is it?"

"I'd be—I mean, I *will* be—the assistant at an agency. It's a real chance. The pay isn't even that great, but it just seemed . . ." She stopped. She didn't want to say "better." She didn't even feel that was true. "It just seemed like something that would lead to a lot of other things."

"Hey, you don't have to explain to me. I knew you weren't going to spend thirty years in the business. I just thought it was going to be longer than this." He took a bite of his Danish. "But what the hell—it's an opportunity; you have to take it. As long as you promise me something."

"What?"

"You don't like it, you come right back. All right?"

"You're sweet."

"Hey, I'm not trying to be sweet. I'm trying to run a business."

"Well, you're sweet, too," she said, and she had more doubts than ever about leaving. She was comfortable at Falcone; she liked the girls and she liked George. She didn't know anything about Alexandra Fielding, on the other hand, except that she was Terence's friend and she looked like a bitter and unhappy person. And as for Terence—she already knew *he* was bitter and unhappy. But it was a chance, and she knew it.

Twenty-three

"So you're an actress," he said.

Larkin finished her Scotch and set the glass on the table. She felt just the way she wanted to, hazy around the edges, perfect for the afternoon. "What else?" she said. "Isn't that what they all say at Rochelle's? I'm an actress? Or a singer?"

She was enjoying this. The first good-looking man who had walked through the door, and afterward Rochelle had said he wanted to take her out to lunch. "Do I need to tell you you get the afternoon off if you go?" Rochelle had said, and Larkin had thought, Why the hell not do it? Life with Richard had been boring; something had to give.

"Tell me what you've been in," he said, signaling across the room for another round of drinks.

"Nothing yet," she said, lighting a cigarette. "But I just graduated from college."

"What school?"

She blew out a long stream of smoke and said, "Yale."

He looked impressed. They always did. "Beauty and brains. Quite a combination. So what are you doing working at Rochelle's?"

"What's a nice girl like me doing in a place like that? Making money, obviously. And don't get the wrong impression about Yale. I slept with half my professors to get through."

He was looking at her intently. "I'm impressed," he said.

"You should be."

The waiter came and set the drinks down on the table and left. She liked this—a hotel, the anonymity of it all. Was the restaurant always filled with out-of-town buyers and girls like her? Did the waiter know what she was doing?

"Now, don't drink too much of that stuff," the man—what was his name? Stuart Marsh—said.

She took a sip and then another sip. It was with Geoffrey that

88

she had discovered that perfect level, the way to maintain it. "It's just enough," she said, taking another sip.

He put a hand on her knee. "I like my women conscious."

It felt good. The hand of a stranger. She touched his thigh and he flinched, as if he hadn't expected it. "Mm," he said. "Don't get me started."

"Why not?"

"Christ. Not here—"

She laughed. It was so easy to control him.

He stood up, red-faced. "I happen to have a room upstairs—"

"What a surprise," she said.

"Are you ready, then?"

"Stuart, I've been ready since I first saw you."

She felt awful. She sat up and lit a cigarette and closed her eyes. At least with Richard he was someone she could stand to look at afterward.

"Mm," he said, and he reached out for her. "What a woman. Unbelievable."

She moved down the bed. She didn't even want him to touch her anymore.

"I have to go," she said.

"Jeez—so soon?"

"Yes, so soon. Is that all right with you?"

"What are you getting itchy at *me* for? What did I do? Anyway, I thought Rochelle gave you the day off."

She looked him square in the eyes. "Does that have anything to do with you?"

He held up his palms. "Hey—I had a good time, you had a good time; what's to get pissed about? Here, let me give you something."

He got off the bed and went to his wallet, and her heart started to skip. This was it: what separated certain kinds of women from certain other kinds of women.

"For an amazing afternoon," he said. "Really amazing."

She counted the bills. Fifty dollars? She looked up at him. "Are you serious?"

"What?"

"This is fifty dollars."

"Hey. A good time was had by all, right? I didn't hear any complaints. It isn't an escort service. You do what you want."

She had heard it before, of course, from Rochelle herself. So was that what that had meant? If you do it, it's because you want to, so no one's going to pay you very much?

She started gathering up her things, but her hands were shaking. "You make me sick," she said. She wanted a drink. "You're ripping me off, and you know it."

He was smiling. "Call the police, *Larkin*." He said her name with contempt. "Or complain to Rochelle. See what she has to say."

She didn't even want to look at him; she just wanted to get out.

"You *did* have a good time," he said. "I could tell."

"Go to hell." She picked up her purse, walked out, and slammed the door.

Twenty-four

Maura felt wildly protective. The girls who had responded to the ad for Falcone were such ditzes. Had she seemed that scatter-brained? Or the ones who weren't ditzes were so tight, so straight-laced. Why had they even come?

Poor George. She felt awful about the whole thing. But on the other hand, if she was going to go, she wanted to go.

Finally the light on his phone went out, and his door opened. "So I guess this is it," he said.

"I guess so," she said, standing up.

"You call me, okay? No matter what, you hear?"

She nodded.

"Okay. So I'll see you, Maura." He hesitated and then leaned forward and gave her a kiss on the cheek.

"I'll see you," she said.

When she went to the door, she felt her heart sink. So this was it. She looked around the office at the pictures of the girls and thought, Well, shit, Scranton, who would have thought you'd work in a place like this? But it had been fun.

Except for Vince, of course. He had called today—George had told him she was leaving—and when she had told him about the new job, he was contemptuous. "They'll eat you alive," he said. "You oughta stick with my pop, Maura. They'll fucking eat you alive." And she didn't know why he seemed to know so much about her, how he knew how to play on her fears. The truth was that the changes did make her nervous. Living in New York—something she and Larkin had always planned, but she'd never thought would actually happen. Living with these two beautiful women. Suddenly having one of the "glamour jobs" she had come to think didn't even exist. It felt wrong.

"Larkin?" she called. She had heard a crash when the door had slammed shut, but now there was nothing. "Larkin?"

"I'm in the kitchen," Larkin called.

Maura didn't know what the smell was at first—it smelled like a doctor's office. But when she got to the kitchen, Larkin was on her knees with some paper towels, and Maura saw the broken bottle: vodka and glass all over the floor.

"What happened?"

Larkin waved a hand. "Losing all my coordination," she said. "I'd offer you a drink, but you're looking at what's left."

Maura glanced at her watch. Six o'clock, which was early to be that drunk. She had certainly seen Larkin at her worst at Yale, but the drinking had been wildly inconsistent—Larkin had gone on binges but then not drunk for weeks at a time. And here at the apartment, she hadn't drunk anything but beer.

She knelt down to help Larkin clean up the glass. "What's going on?"

Larkin gave an odd laugh. "Oh, another day of wasted talent, missed opportunities, that sort of thing."

"You mean at the showroom?"

"If you can call it that. Ow!"

Blood started to pour from Larkin's hand, and Maura stood up. But Larkin was just staring at it.

"Larkin, what are you doing?"

She stood up slowly, still looking at her hand. Blood was dripping all over the floor. "It looks like *Psycho*, doesn't it?"

Maura took Larkin's arm and led her to the sink. "Come on. You have to get that wrapped up." She turned the water on and put Larkin's hand under it and went to get some gauze from the bathroom. When she came back, Larkin hadn't moved. Maura gave her the gauze and made her sit down. "Now, tell me what's going on."

Larkin sighed. "Oh, it's so—I don't know why I'm even upset. Honestly. It's so silly."

"What's so silly? Tell me."

Larkin took another deep breath, and Maura suddenly had the feeling she was trying not to cry—something she had never seen Larkin do. "Oh—" she said again. "It's so ridiculous. I went to a hotel with one of the men from the showroom, and it turned out to be awful. Just—afterward I didn't want him to touch me, even to look at me." She took another deep breath. "And after all that, after we were together and I had—well, given him a very good time, he gave me fifty dollars. Can you imagine?"

Maura sighed. "When are you going to realize you can't go around sleeping with these men you don't know?"

Larkin shrugged. "I don't know. It seemed like an appealing idea until it was over. But you might be right. It was pretty awful."

"Then stop," Maura said. "Or at least don't go out with any more of them. You said that wasn't a condition, right?"

"Right," Larkin said, but she seemed distracted, as if she wasn't really listening. She looked down at her hand again, and Maura did, too, and the blood had come through the bandage. "The worst part was talking to Richard this afternoon. He was his usual sweet self, absolutely sincere, wanting to know all about my day. Completely unsuspecting."

Maura looked down at Larkin's hand. "You'd better run that under some more water," she said, standing up. "Come on."

Larkin followed her to the sink, and Maura turned the water on. "Why don't you try being sincere with Richard, then? You're over the fight about Rhode Island, so *be* with him—not with strangers who are awful to you. Or do you need them to make you feel comfortable with Richard?"

"I need the money," Larkin said.

"That's not an answer."

"You know how much acting classes cost."

"Uh-uh," Maura said, shaking her head. "First of all, you're not even *taking* any classes at the moment. And I thought you said Rochelle was paying you two-fifty a show, no matter what you do with the men."

"It's not enough."

Maura looked into Larkin's eyes. "All right, then do it. Go ahead. But you're the one who's drunk at six in the evening because you're unhappy."

"I'm not drunk."

"Hi, you guys."

Maura turned around. Danielle was standing in the kitchen door. "Oh. Hello. We didn't even hear you come in."

Danielle bit her lip. "I guess not." She hesitated. "So how was the showroom, Larkin?"

"Rotten."

Danielle came up to where they were standing at the sink. "God, what happened?" she said.

"I cut my hand," Larkin snapped. "What the hell does it look like?"

Danielle looked at Maura. "Um, I guess I'll see you guys later," she said quietly, and she walked out.

"That was nice," Maura said.

"Look. She asked an obvious question, all right? I've had enough questions for one afternoon."

"Fine," Maura said. "I'm going to talk to Danielle. Come join us if you feel like being civil."

Danielle's door was closed, but she called, "Come in," when Maura knocked.

"Sorry about before," Maura said. "Can I come in?"

"Sure."

Maura sat down on the bed. "Larkin can be a little touchy, obviously. It can take a while to get used to." Danielle didn't say anything. "I hated her when we first met at Yale."

"Really?"

"Of course. She was beautiful, she was rich, she was at Yale even though she didn't seem at all smart. And she was a bitch at the beginning."

"So what happened?"

"Well . . ." Maura paused. "She needed me for something. She's incredibly insecure and needy underneath it all. And we got to be friends. It just takes a little time, if you can stand it."

Danielle shrugged. "She was so nice to me the other day, I thought—I don't know—I thought we were friends. I don't like it when people snap like that." She shrugged again. "But if you say we'll be friends after a while—"

"I know you will be."

"Okay. Then I guess I feel better."

"Good."

"And guess what, Maura? I met the greatest guy at the casino last night, and he seemed to kind of like me."

"Really? Tell me about him," Maura said. Tell me about him.

Tell me about your problems. She felt as if it was all she ever said, all she ever did. She listened to Larkin and Danielle, she helped them, and it came naturally and she liked it. But things were always happening to them and for them. What if nothing ever happened for her?

Twenty-five

"Why can't you help me? You said you had more money than you knew what to do with."

Fernanda stirred her coffee. "That doesn't mean I would feel comfortable simply giving it away, Larkin."

"I told you it would be a loan. I don't expect you to *give* me all that money." Not that it was that much—just enough for her to have a few months to get started. Take some lessons and find a job.

"And anyway," Fernanda said. "It's not as if I would be giving—or lending, if you say—money to someone who would be going into some reliable profession. It's not as if you'd be finishing law school in three years. You have no way of knowing—at all—whether you'll *ever* make money as an actress."

Christ. Where was the waiter, anyway? She had finished her drink ages ago.

"What are you looking for?" Fernanda asked. "The waiter is right over there."

"Oh." She signaled, but he didn't see her.

"Don't tell me you're having another drink."

"All right. I won't." God, she was feeling obnoxious. But she couldn't help it. Why was Fernanda being such a bitch?

The waiter finally deigned to come over, and Larkin ordered another drink.

"I don't know how you can think anyone would give you anything," Fernanda said. "What are you doing with your life? As far as anyone can see, it's a combination of drinking and sleeping. Not exactly inspiring."

"Ah. I see. If I were inspiring, you'd lend me the money. Hm. What about the reviews?"

"What reviews?"

"From Yale. Mother has them all—somewhere—at home. You read them or were forced to hear them at the time. What about those?"

"They were very nice. But that was at Yale, where you had some sort of structure. This is different."

The waiter brought the drink, and Larkin took a long sip. "How come you never came?"

Fernanda was picking at her salad. "I was busy with school. I couldn't just take off." She looked away, past Larkin, and Larkin took another sip of her drink. She was beginning to feel rotten. She had gone over the edge, that level that felt good and not out of control, and now she was feeling drunk and reckless, and she didn't want to feel that way with Fernanda. She didn't know why, but there were still occasional vestiges of good feelings; they were still sisters, and she could remember the wonderful times so clearly: teaching Fernanda to draw, hiding from the maid, learning to swim. The easy part was that their roles had been clear—she was the older one; Fernanda was younger and the baby. The new arrangement felt wrong, but it had somehow shifted forever.

"Listen," she said. *You're going to regret this.* But she was starting to feel desperate. "I want to be completely honest with you so you'll understand. And I'm not asking you to lend me money— you're obviously not willing to do that. But just to talk to Mother. Explain why I need it."

"She's made it clear—"

"I haven't *told* you yet. And I'm not going to tell Mother, but I want to tell you. I told you about the modeling I was doing."

"The job you're going to quit."

"Right. I might quit. I hope to, but obviously I can't if you don't talk to Mother. Do you know what part of the job is? It's not just walking around and turning on a runway. It's not on a runway—it's in a sweaty little room they *call* a showroom, but it's just a horrible little back room. The men pinch you, they touch you in places you wouldn't want anyone but your lover to touch you—"

"Are you serious?"

"Very. They also expect you to go out with the men afterward."

"Go out with? You mean for dinner, or—"

"The 'or' part, Fernanda. You have to sleep with them. They

give you some money, but it isn't much. The man I was with gave me fifty dollars.''

"You *slept* with him?''

"Fernanda, it was my only choice. It's part of the job.''

"But that's prostitution!''

When was her sister going to grow up? "It's Seventh Avenue. That's what the garment business is all about.''

"Larkin, I can't believe you did that.''

Fernanda really did look shocked. Shaken, really.

"You could have walked out. You didn't *have* to do it.'' Her eyes changed. "Or did you want to?''

"Don't be ridiculous. I need the money, Fernanda. I need acting lessons, singing lessons, dancing lessons, if I'm going to be serious. And I'm not going to be able to afford that on a receptionist's salary. Not to mention the fact that I wouldn't even have *time* for any of those things if I were working nine to five.''

Fernanda still looked stunned; she had actually lost some color from her cheeks. "All right,'' she said quietly. "I'll talk to Mother. I'll tell her you're trying hard, that you've gotten very serious about it all. But then you have to promise you will be.''

"Of course,'' Larkin said.

"And you'll quit that job, obviously.''

"Of course.''

Fernanda sighed. "I'm glad you called me. It was important. And I think Mother will be responsive if I talk to her.''

Larkin nodded. It was unbelievably aggravating that all it was going to take was Fernanda's word. But if it was going to work, it was worth it. Now maybe she could be serious about the acting.

Book Two

Twenty-six

The phone rang, and Maura picked it up on the first ring.

"Fielding-White," Maura said.

"Um, hi," a hesitant female voice said. "I was wondering if I could come in and talk to Miss Fielding?"

"Have you worked with her before?"

"Um, no. But—"

"Then send us your picture and résumé, please."

"But will she look at it? I—"

"We'll look at it," Maura said.

"Okay, what's your address?"

"315 West Fifty-seventh," Maura said.

"Can I send two? I mean, will it help if—"

"Just one, all right? Good-bye." And she hung up, even though the girl was still talking.

"That took much too long," Alexandra called from inside her office. "You know what you're supposed to say, Maura: 'Don't call and don't come in.' Is that so difficult to remember?"

Maura didn't say anything. In the week and a half she had been working there, she had gotten along with Alexandra once or twice. And she didn't know why there was such a problem, exactly, except that Alexandra seemed to have a problem with a lot of women:

actors she loved; actresses she seemed to be able to do without. And Terence, unfortunately, hadn't been in the office all that much—he was out of town all week this week—so she and Alexandra had been thrown together more than either had wanted.

"Are you there?" Alexandra called.

"Yes. I heard you," Maura said. She didn't even have to raise her voice, because the office was small. Alexandra and Terence shared an inner, large office, and she sat in the small entry room, which was crammed with filing cabinets and stacks of pictures everywhere.

And at first she had thought it was glamorous: the eight-by-tens on the walls weren't of strippers, they were of actors and actresses she recognized. On the backs of the pictures, their résumés were all incredibly impressive—rundowns of careers that were obviously the heart of all of these people's lives. And now that she knew what they all had to go through, it was even more impressive that any of them had found any work at all. Now she knew how completely humiliating, dehumanizing, and hopeless the business was. There were so many *thousands* of people who wanted to be actors. Every day, dozens of eight-by-tens arrived in the mail, and Alexandra and Terence didn't even look at them. They claimed to, and occasionally they did, but most of the time they just gave them to her to file away, where you were immediately classified by age and by looks.

Maura had read a couple of books on the "business" of acting in the past week, and so much of the advice they gave was just painfully wrong. "Drop all the casting directors on your list a note every week, letting them know what you're doing," the books said. "Even better, make up a postcard-sized picture of yourself and send that with a note on the back. Monthly or even weekly contact will keep your name and face in their minds."

Which was a joke. The postcards came in by the sack every day, and Alexandra and Terence didn't even make a *pretense* of looking at them. Maura filed them the same way she filed the pictures, and so much for those monthly or even weekly contacts. Actors dropped off their pictures and résumés in an envelope taped to the wall outside the office, and they accepted the ignominy of not even being allowed inside because it was just another of the thousand awful rules. Now she understood Larkin's terror of auditions; now she understood why just because Larkin was beautiful, it didn't mean *anything*, because there were hundreds of equally beautiful young actresses in New York.

Which reminded her. She had forced Larkin to make up a

package—pictures and résumé—for Alexandra at the beginning of the week, and Alexandra hadn't said anything about them. It was a dead time of the afternoon, so she walked to the doorway of Alexandra's office and knocked.

"Yes?" Alexandra hadn't looked up from her paper.

"I was wondering if you had looked at my roommate's picture."

"Mm," Alexandra said, smoothing out the paper. "What about it?"

"Well, I was just wondering . . ." She should have waited for Terence to come back; it was so obvious. But it was too late now. "You seem to want to see certain people based on their pictures, or their résumés. I thought—"

"She doesn't have enough experience," Alexandra said. She finally looked up. "She's your roommate, right? You were in college together, right?"

"Yes, but—"

"So what does she have? Almost nothing. And her picture doesn't say anything to me at all."

"Well, I'll see what Terence thinks when he comes back," Maura said. She walked over to Alexandra's desk and started going through the piles of pictures and manila envelopes on the floor. Generally, she tried to file the pictures every day so they didn't build up too much, but she hadn't had a chance this week, and—

She found the pictures of Larkin. They were still in the sealed envelope Maura had addressed herself, sealed herself so they wouldn't drop out onto the street.

She looked up at Alexandra. "I see you really studied this," she said.

Alexandra set down the paper. "Look. I'm a busy woman, all right? If I looked at every goddamn roommate of every goddamn assistant in this office, I wouldn't have time to do anything else."

"Fine. I understand that. But you lied."

"Sue me, all right? And order up some coffee. I'm getting a splitting headache. And see if you can find Terence in L.A. He was supposed to call me an hour ago."

Maura walked back to her office and looked at the door. It was so tempting, the idea of just walking out. But Terence would be back soon, and that would probably change things. She had to give it much more of a chance.

Twenty-seven

Danielle wanted to get off the phone, but she had only been on two seconds. Still, she didn't have anything to say to her mother. Plus she was in a giant hurry to get to the lawyer's.

"What's wrong?" Victoria asked. Super-sweet and concerned-sounding, which of course was a lie.

"Nothing," Danielle said. She looked in the mirror and looked away. She had put on too much makeup. "I'm in a hurry to leave, though, so I can't stay on."

"Where are you going?"

"Out," she said. And then, even though she knew it was a totally giant mistake: "I'm having breakfast with Cleve."

Her mother didn't say anything, and Danielle could just picture her, in her little white shorts and halter top, with her feet up in the window, the sun coming through like crazy. She could laze away mornings and whole days in Venice Beach like no one Danielle had ever seen. Thinking about the sun made Danielle miss Venice, though, even if it was where her mother was. "Have you been seeing a lot of him?" Victoria finally said.

Seeing a lot. As if Cleve was some kind of date. "A real lot," Danielle said. "Almost every day." Which of course was a total lie. She hadn't seen him in weeks, since he came to the store that day.

"That will change," her mother said, as if she was some kind of judge. *Thirty years in jail*, or whatever. "I hope you realize that, Danielle. I don't want to see you get hurt the way I was hurt. The way he hurts everyone. You know he's just using you."

"How can he be using me? And for what? You always say that, and you don't even half know what you're talking about."

"Danielle—"

"I have to go, okay?"

"Is Cleve—"

"I've got to go. 'Bye," Danielle said, and she hung up before

102

her mother could say another word, because also she knew what her mother was going to say: Is Cleve drinking?

And Danielle hated to answer the question because it always changed everything, and that wasn't right. Sure it was bad that he was drinking, but that didn't mean everything was going to turn into one gigantic disaster. Plenty of people drank and had jobs and families and everything. Even good jobs, and happy families. So maybe he could be like one of those people. It was possible, anyway.

And the main thing was that she would finally be getting a chance to talk to him "face-to-face" about her new job and the arrest and everything, how a lot had changed since even a couple of weeks ago, that she wasn't selling panty hose anymore. A "heart-to-heart" talk the way the kids used to have on "Eight is Enough" with Dick Van Patten.

She double-checked the way she looked in the mirror again: she was wearing by far the most serious clothes she had, a navy blue skirt she had stolen from the May Company in L.A. (but who would know?) and a shirt she had actually bought from a store on Melrose.

And then she got ready (mentally, the way that L.A. preacher on TV said to do) to go down into the subway. Just go down and pretend it's another part of Venice Beach, she said to herself. The L.A. preacher said to "visualize, visualize," by keeping your eyes closed and imagining "the best." But the subway station was too loud. And she knew there would be all kinds of people she was afraid of when she opened her eyes, and she was right. Plus could it be smart to keep your eyes shut in a subway station? It seemed like a really bad idea.

But she got through the ride, even though it felt like nine hundred people were pressing up against her, and when she went up into the street with the sun blazing and tons of smog (but not like L.A. smog, because there wasn't even a beach to go with it), she began to wonder if it had been a smart thing to move to New York. It seemed so horrible. Not even a single tiny palm tree.

And the neighborhood this lawyer's office was in. Joseph King had told her she wouldn't be going to Foster Bartlett for the actual case, because it wasn't necessary. Plus she had said she wanted to pay Joseph King back, so he was taking the money out of her paycheck, and she didn't want it to be ten million dollars, which it practically would be if Foster Bartlett handled the case. But the neighborhood this new lawyer was in looked super-scary.

On TV lawyers were always in shiny high-rise buildings, with a beautiful receptionist, tons of carpeting, and a million plants. But this office was in the west Forties, what seemed to be a really bad part, and you had to walk up a flight of stairs, because there wasn't even one single elevator.

And the receptionist was a chain-smoking old lady with whitish-blue hair. "Yes?" A demand right there, like Danielle had already done something wrong. And Danielle never knew how to act around old people. She had never really known any, and she was always positive she was about to say the super-wrong thing, or that they'd drop dead right in front of her eyes.

"I have an appointment, but I'm also meeting someone here."

"Danielle Austin?"

"Uh-huh."

"Go right in."

"But I can't. I'm meeting my father. It isn't eleven yet anyway," she said, looking at a clock on the wall. It had a long, hairy dust ball hanging from the bottom of the circle.

The lady sighed. "Five minutes," she said. "If he's not here by then, go in, and I'll send him in when he gets here."

Danielle flipped through the magazines, but there wasn't anything to read—just something called *The American Lawyer* plus about nine million old newspapers. And she couldn't help wondering: What kind of law firm had newspapers on their coffee table? It seemed weird. On "L.A. Law" they sure didn't.

Plus where was Cleve?

Maybe he was the kind of person they called "chronically late."

She picked up an old *Daily News*. "Riot on the A-Train," it said, and she put it down. They were always talking about violence in New York, nine hundred times a day. Maybe things happened in California, too—especially in L.A. and all the other cities—but they didn't *talk* about it so much. They talked about the weather tons more.

"You can go in now," the receptionist suddenly said.

"But my father—"

"I said I'd send him in. Your appointment is for eleven, and it's eleven o'clock."

Danielle wanted to argue some more, but she didn't know what to say and she didn't want to get in trouble, so she went in.

The lawyer was a guy in maybe his sixties, short with white hair and smoking a cigar, with a face that looked all skinny and withered even though he was an overweight man. As if maybe he was sick or even dying.

And Danielle didn't like the way he was looking her up and

down, staring at her chest. She had worn that really nice blouse from Melrose because she wanted to look nice, but now she was sorry. It was too tight. And he was staring, staring, staring, sucking at his cigar as if he was sucking at her.

And more than ever she wished Cleve would come.

"I hear you've been a busy girl," he said, licking his lips.

"Well." She looked down at her hands.

"Don't you know girls like you can go to jail for doing bad things like that?"

She looked past him, out the window. "This is New York," she said. "I really can't believe that would happen."

"Oh, but it could," he said. "The stores are cracking down. Bloomingdale's more than any of the others. They might want to set an example. You made a bad choice."

She shrugged. She didn't know what to say, and she didn't want to look at him.

"Have you ever been in prison, Danielle?"

She looked up at him. "You're supposed to know the answer to that if you're my lawyer," she said. "Didn't Mr. King tell you anything?"

"He told me to take care of a case for a girl, that he'd pay my salary and you'd what? What's he doing? Docking your pay?"

She nodded. "Every week."

He shook his head and looked at her for a long time. "You wouldn't last long, you know, a girl like you. They'd be all over you in a minute. Some of those women have been cooped up in there for years." He was breathing kind of weirdly, and she didn't want to be there. "You'd be a changed woman when you got out, Danielle."

She swallowed. How could she get him to change the subject? "I thought Mr. King said you could keep me out," she said, but her voice had come out all breathy and weird.

He leaned forward. "I'll try, of course," he said, stubbing out his cigar. He licked his lips. "But it's going to be a tough case, the way that guard caught you outside of the store. That's why they wait, you know, so you can't say you were looking for a cash register." He looked into her eyes. "So keep that in mind for the future."

"I don't plan on being arrested again," she said.

"Oh, you'll do it again. All my clients do. It's like a disease—like drinking, hives, whatever." He leaned back in his chair. "I had one girl, she couldn't keep her hands off the jewelry. Whenever she went into a store, it was like a trance came over her. She didn't even know she was taking them—earrings, necklaces, whatever—till she was out the door. Sometimes she didn't know till she was home and looked into her purse." He shook his head. "Bailed her out five times. She's up at Dannemora now. Maximum security."

Danielle stared. "Are you kidding?"

"They don't like repeaters," he said. "You're going to have to learn to control yourself, Danielle. But you have trouble with that, don't you?"

She didn't say anything. It sounded like a dirty question.

"Theresa did, too, the girl I was telling about. I'll show you a picture of her," he said, and he reached into his desk drawer and pulled out a folder. "Here are some pictures of her and her friends."

She reached for them without thinking, and then she didn't know what to do. The top picture was of a blond woman who maybe had been pretty a while ago, like ten years ago, with a flip and pretty good teeth. But then the next picture: two ladies naked, and Theresa was one of them, and the other was black.

Danielle looked up at Mr. Minsky. His face was all red. "They'd eat you alive," he said in a weird, husky voice. "Those black bitches would fight over you like cats and dogs. Bitches in heat. One look—" He moved his knees against hers.

"Don't," she said, but it had come out too quietly.

"You're crazy to owe King, Danielle. *One* time," he said. He started to unzip his pants. "Just *one* time, Danielle, and I won't charge you a thing."

She stood up. She felt sick and dizzy.

"Hey," he said, grabbing her wrist.

She looked down at him. His eyes were all narrow and mean-looking. "What is it? You think you're too good for me, Danielle? When those black bitches are all over you, you'll wish you had said yes."

"I have to go," she said, and she ran out of his office and out past the old lady as fast as she could.

Work was one big blur: "Hi, can I get you a drink?", nine jillion guys looking at her chest, licking their lips, sometimes brushing against her—especially the foreign ones, which she couldn't even begin to figure out. Was it because they didn't understand the language that they thought she couldn't feel their hands on her? Or was it that it was okay to be that way in those countries? She just didn't know because she had never been.

But anyway, she didn't pay much attention, just getting through the day trying not to think what she'd have to tell Joseph King whenever he got back from wherever he was—would she tell him the truth or what? She didn't want to have Mr. Minsky as her lawyer, that was for sure.

Plus Cleve. He had truly let her down. For a second she wondered if maybe she was trying to "force" things too much with him, like maybe she didn't even really love him as much as she went around saying (even to herself) that she did.

But then she did her test. She thought of him getting killed, all mangled or sliced super-suddenly away from life, dead just like that. And she felt a wind at the back of her thighs: fear. Which meant he had passed the test, that she did love him.

Which in a way made her feel worse when she was leaving and the night shift had come on. She had thought maybe she'd even show him the casino now that he knew about it. But was he interested? No, because it was her life.

"Hello there!"

She had just been let out by the club's secret doorman, and her eyes hadn't adjusted to the night yet.

"Don't you remember me?"

It was the man who had given her the gigantic tip the first day, and then she had never seen him again. "Hi," she said.

"Are you leaving?" he asked. He had one foot on the top step and one on the bottom step, like he had been frozen in a statue game.

"Um, yes. My shift just ended."

"Are you all right?"

She didn't say anything. She just looked into his eyes, super-blue in the moonlight. He looked a little bit like Richard Burton in one of those Shakespeare movies the teachers had forced them to watch in school.

"Come," he said, holding out an arm and turning back down the steps. "Whatever's wrong, you look like you could use a drink."

It was funny, because they didn't even talk all the way to the restaurant. She just held on to his arm, and he held on to her hand, and they walked and walked, and only when they went to the back of this real dark, pretty fancy place did he say something, sitting next to her on the banquette.

"So? What would you like? Vodka? Scotch?"

"I don't drink," she said. "A Coke would be fine."

"Then a Coke it is," he said. He ordered a Scotch and soda and a Coke, and then he leaned back and touched her chin. "Last time I saw you, you were on cloud nine. Now you look like you just lost your best friend. Do you want to tell me about it?"

Her lips started to tremble, and she realized she was about to cry, which felt incredibly dumb. But he was the first person who wanted to know something about her.

She took a sip of Coke and then told him the whole story, how today her father hadn't shown up and also the whole other story, how she had been caught at Bloomingdale's. "Joseph King bailed me out," she said. "And this super-expensive lawyer came to get me and spring me, I guess you say. But today the guy I went to was completely different, a totally skeevy—"

"Skeevy?"

She shrugged. "You know, like . . . I guess you say 'seedy.' My friends and I always used to say skeevy. But anyway, he was pretty gross, and he wanted me to do all this stuff, and he was showing me pictures—"

"What kind of pictures?"

She could feel her face getting hot. "You know, pretty dirty pictures; I mean, I only saw one, but if you had seen his face—"

"You're going to see a friend of mine tomorrow," he said in this super-mad voice. "And you're never going to go back to this Mr. Minsky, do you understand?"

"Look, it's fine with me. I ran out of there, and I don't ever want to go back. But what about my case?" She paused. "Are you a lawyer?"

He shook his head.

"Is it a secret, what you do?"

He laughed. "It's no secret; it's just not very interesting, that's all. I'm business manager at an apparel manufacturer. The rag trade."

"God. Fashion? It must be fascinating."

He smiled. "Not my end of it. But tell me something. Are you hungry? Would you like to get a bite to eat somewhere?"

She bit her lip. She hadn't eaten anything all day.

"Or would you like to call home? Have you tried calling your father? Maybe he's worried about you."

"He's not worried." She hesitated. "But maybe he did call. Maybe he even showed up late, since I ran out so fast. Maybe I could check—"

"Go ahead and call," he said. "Do you have money?"

"Yup. I'll be right back."

* * *

He watched as she walked across the room. And every man in the room watched, too.

She seemed like a damn sweet kid. A little mixed up, but then, what kid wasn't these days?

"She's a kid, you asshole," he could hear his friends saying. And his ex-wife. Oh, would *she* have a lot to say.

But he liked her. A lot. Maybe she was young, and a little naive. No question about it—the word "airhead" came to mind. But she was so uncomplicated. And he liked helping her out. He felt alive; it was different from the rest of his life, numbers and ledgers, accounts and orders. She was beautiful and friendly and affectionate.

So why is she with you?

He wasn't going to question it. Stranger things had happened, hadn't they?

She came in from the back of the restaurant, and once again heads began to turn.

"My roommate said I didn't get any calls," she said, avoiding his eyes as she sat down again. Then she sipped her Coke and began looking around—down at her hands, to the left, to the right, everywhere but into his eyes.

"What's the matter?" he asked.

She looked like a scared rabbit. "Do you live around here?" she asked.

"Sixty-first and First," he said.

"That's close, right?"

"Five blocks over."

Danielle bit her lips and looked into his eyes. "How about ordering something in at your house, okay?"

She waited. If he said no, it would all be over. Everybody in the whole world had said no to her.

"Let's go," he said, standing up and holding out his arm.

"I want you," she whispered.

She was like a wild animal. He hadn't been with anyone quite so voracious since his honeymoon. And Christ—Gail hadn't been like *that* again for the next eighteen years.

And she was gorgeous, Danielle, a pinup come to life, all blond hair and smooth skin and wet lips.

"Take me," she whispered, biting his ear. She moved on top of him and then rolled over, pulling him on top of her, and he suddenly realized, reaching inside of her—

—it was all an act.

"Take me, Allan," she cried.

He rolled off onto an elbow, and she opened her eyes.

"What's the matter?" she asked.

"What are you doing?" He wiped the sweat from his eyes.

"What do you mean?"

"Acting like this. Why the act?"

She bit her lip. "I'm not acting."

"Danielle, why?"

Her face twisted into a frown. "I'm not acting," she said, this time more quietly. She looked past him, up at the ceiling. Her eyes were glistening with tears.

He reached out and touched one, and a tear rolled onto his thumb. It was warm, and it broke his heart. "Tell me," he said softly.

"Nobody loves me," she said.

He took her more tightly into his arms and held her.

Twenty-eight

"Hi, Dad," Maura said into the phone, talking too loudly. But her father was slightly deaf, and more so on the phone, she had discovered.

"Hello?" he yelled.

"It's me."

"Maura? Is that you? What are you calling for at ten in the morning? You lose your job?"

"No. I thought I'd call from here. From the job. One of my bosses said to go ahead. Is everything all right?"

"Yeah, yeah. Sure. How about you?"

She swallowed. "Everything's great," she said, missing him. How could she miss Scranton? But she did. "And the new job's good, too."

"New job?"

"You know, with the agent. I told you."

"Oh. Yeah, that's right. I told Patrick about it last week."

"What did he say?"

"He said a cousin of his friend, one of his friends at the factory. She's already an actress, and maybe she could help you. She was in a play, something at some church. So with you just starting out and all, maybe she can show you the ropes."

Maura sighed. "It doesn't work that way," she said. "*They* need *us*. You never get an actor to help you."

"What?"

She hadn't said it loud enough. But she didn't want to yell. "Never mind," she said. "How's Patrick?"

"He misses you, that's how he is. When are you coming down for a visit?"

"I don't know. I've been pretty busy."

"What—lots of parties? You got a lot of friends up there?"

"Sure, sure," she yelled. Sure. A million.

Silence. What else was there to say?

"Listen," her father suddenly said. "I don't know how to tell you this, Maura."

Oh God. "Tell me what?"

"About Patrick." Another silence.

"What? Is he sick?"

"Sick? Nah, he's strong as an ox. Nah. Something worse. You know Charlie Shane, down at O'Malley's."

"The bartender?"

"Yeah, yeah. He's got a daughter." Silence. "Patrick's been out with her two, maybe five times."

Maura smiled. "Two, maybe five? How'd you come up with a figure like that?"

"Hey, it isn't funny. You're losing him, Maura."

"Dad, I've *lost* him. I mean he's lost me. I don't *want* him."

"Hey. He was good to you."

In the backseat of his Ford, Maura thought. Always in the dark, even in the house, always as fast as he could, almost as if he were getting it over with.

"And you're my baby, but even *I* gotta say: there aren't a million guys out there, Maur."

"You mean for me," she said, swallowing against a dry throat that suddenly hurt. Where was the goddamn coffee she had ordered?

"He always liked you, Maur."

"He's not good enough for me, Daddy, hard as that might be for you to believe. I have to go now, okay?"

"Sure, sure. So you want this actress girl to call you?"

"No. I *told* you." But of course he hadn't heard. "Just tell Patrick to forget it, okay?"

"Sure. I'll tell him to forget it and you miss him, okay, honey?"

What was the use? She said good-bye and hung up and sighed. She knew her father wasn't right; there was no way she was going to spend the rest of her life with Patrick Delaney or anyone like him, anyone who hated the way she looked and treated her the way he did. But when your own father . . .

It made her miss her mother and all the times they hadn't gotten to share, all the discussions they could have had. And that was one of the worst things about her dying, aside from the death itself. It was the silence that had suddenly come over the house, a silence between a ten-year-old girl and a father who had never really spoken to each other much at all. He didn't know how to cook, how to talk to her, how to act, and she hated him and felt guilty for hating him. Where was the person who was supposed to root for her?

And the little things that other girls' mothers did. She could still remember the day she had found a drawing on the floor of the fifth grade classroom, picking it up because she had seen her name on it. A note? Maybe from a boy? Valentine's Day was in a week, so was it a valentine?

But it wasn't a note or a valentine. It was a drawing with her name under it, of a girl—fat, round, dark-haired. And at her chest, two stick-figure-style breasts, with nipples like targets.

And on top of feeling humiliated, she had wanted to say, "I know I should be wearing a bra, but do you expect my *father* to take me to the store?" What money was she supposed to use? She wanted her mother to take her, but her mother was dead.

Well, it was ridiculous to get maudlin about it now. Calling her father always brought back memories, but that was silly: she hadn't cried once in thirteen years, and she had tried never to look back.

There was a knock at the door, and she called, "Come in."

The door opened, and a tall—Christ, he was like an ad for Greek God cologne or something ridiculous like that; just a perfect-looking guy was standing there. Smiling, with a manila envelope that obviously had his eight-by-tens in it. With a silly-looking silver pin near the neck of his sweater, a coat that had probably cost more than a month's rent, an outfit that had obviously been studied and considered for hours. Weren't there any men in New York who didn't spend all morning wondering what to wear?

Maura held up a palm. "Sorry," she said. "Thought you were the coffee shop. You're supposed to leave your eight-by-tens in the envelope out there. Isn't it out there?"

He laid the envelope down on her desk. "I'll save you the walk, okay? Are you Alexandra Fielding?"

"Nope. They're both gone for at least the morning, so don't even bother."

He was frowning. "Bother?"

"Trying your act. Whatever. I'm just an assistant here, so don't waste your breath."

"Hey. Did I do something wrong?"

"As a matter of fact, you did. The sign out there is about two feet tall, and you can't miss it."

He was looking around at the walls, at all the eight-by-tens of the actors and actresses Alexandra handled. "So these are their people, huh?"

"Yup."

He turned his eyes on her. They were the brightest green she had ever seen. Contacts, probably. "Do you know how hard this is? Making the rounds? I can't even get in to *see* anyone."

She spread her hands. "You've seen me," she said. "And surprise. That and a token."

"You don't make this easy," he said.

"You hit me on the wrong day, all right?"

He sat down and pulled a chair forward. "Anything special?"

She shook her head. The door opened, and the man from the coffee shop came in. The actor jumped up and paid him and handed Maura the bag.

"How much did you give him?" Maura asked.

"Hey, it's on me."

"Don't be silly."

"Forget it," he said, sitting down again. "This is worth it, getting to talk to you."

"Listen, I told you: I *don't* have any power here. It doesn't get you anywhere."

"So this will be my morning break. Just talk to me," he said. "How'd you get into this? Did you want to act?"

"Nope. It was one of those fluke things. I didn't even know I'd like it. A friend, that sort of thing."

"Interesting," he said, nodding his head slowly. "Listen. Do you go out much?"

"What?"

"I mean are you seeing anyone? Would you like to have dinner sometime?"

She stared. "You're kidding, I assume."

"Why would I kid? Not at all. I'm new to the city, and I'm trying to meet as many people as I can."

"Oh, *give* me a break. Look. You've given me your pictures, so you can leave now, all right?"

"I don't understand," he said, feigning innocence. He wasn't that great an actor anyway. "What did I say?"

"Just leave, all right? I mean it: now."

He stood up. "I still don't understand," he said.

"Then maybe there aren't any brains behind that pretty face. The door is right behind you." She looked down at some sheets of paper in front of her—she couldn't even see what they were—and stared until she heard the door shut.

Twenty-nine

"I missed you," Danielle said, wrapping her arms around Allan. She loved him so much, she couldn't even believe it.

Love. She had never even thought, and here he was, an actual man, and she actually loved him.

Plus she even loved sleeping with him. Or "making love." All the time when her friends used to see guys on the beach and say, "Ooh, he's so cute. Can you imagine what he's like in bed?" she used to have to pretend, because to tell the truth, she had never felt anything. She always did it anyway because it was fun to go out, and the end part was what they expected, plus she couldn't say it was the worst thing in the whole world. *One* time was, on the beach, when Rick Sarkman got sand up inside of her and kept going anyway, but except for that, most times were okay.

But with Allan it was the greatest thing in the world, and she felt so relieved to finally know what everyone was talking about.

Plus he had taken care of everything on the case. Her new lawyer was the greatest, and Mr. King didn't seem to mind she had gotten a new one, and the lawyer, Jason Brackman, said he'd get her off, no question, because it wouldn't even go to trial. It was just a matter of making some kind of deal. So ninety-nine percent of the time, she wasn't scared. And when the 1 percent happened, Allan promised it would all be okay.

And it made a super-giant difference, too, when it came to Cleve. When he called to say he was sorry he had missed the appointment (he had forgotten all about it; could you believe it?), normally she would have just said, "Forget it; I don't want to even speak to you ever again." Because it had bothered her a lot, the way he hadn't showed up and she didn't even know why. But Allan had said, "Just play it by ear; don't decide anything in advance," and it turned out it was good advice, because they had made up, kind of, and she hadn't "burned any bridges," which was probably good.

"Did you miss me?" she asked. She loved running her hands through his hair, just the way all the books said to do.

"Mm." He was almost asleep.

That was the one thing she didn't think was the greatest thing in the world, that sometimes he fell asleep the second after they had finished. That was the time she liked to talk and know that Allan was awake, too, and maybe thinking about things. But she guessed it wasn't the worst thing in the world.

Suddenly Allan jerked awake and opened his eyes. "What time is it?"

"It's only seven-fifteen," she said. "You've got plenty of time to get to work." Which was another great thing. In the mornings when she stayed over, he had to go to work super-early and she got to laze around his apartment, which was pretty fancy, especially compared to her and Larkin and Maura's apartment, and take showers and things like that. Watch color TV. So she almost didn't mind when he left for work.

"Shit," he said, sitting up and rubbing his eyes. He stumbled out of bed and put a robe on and said, "Be back in a second," so quietly she almost didn't hear him.

She got out of bed and got washed up and put a robe on (he had even given her one last week, to keep at his apartment) and went toward the kitchen.

But she heard Allan talking, and she stopped in the hallway to listen.

"Yeah," he was saying. "No . . . I said no, Marty, and I meant it." Silence, and then he slammed down the phone.

Danielle counted to three and then made a lot of noise when she walked into the kitchen. She had the definite feeling it wasn't a conversation she was supposed to hear.

"Coffee?" she said.

"What?" His face was super-white. "Yeah, sure, help yourself."

"I meant do you want some."

"What? Oh, sure. Yeah. Help yourself."

"Allan, what's the matter?"

"What?"

She reached her arms up and wrapped them around his neck. "You can tell me."

He shook his head. "You don't want to know," he said quietly.

"But I do want to know. I really do."

He rubbed his eyes and sat down real hard in the chair. He sounded like a sack of potatoes.

"I'll make some coffee," she said. "And you can tell me everything."

He was looking up at the ceiling.

She said to herself, Don't pressure him, because he almost didn't want to tell. But that was what love was, wasn't it? Helping each other work things out. Or part of what love was, anyway.

She made the coffee black and extra-strong, just the way he liked it, and sat down next to him. "So what was that call?"

He sipped the coffee and leaned his head back. "A guy I've known for years, done business with for years. Suddenly he wants to change the way we do business. I don't want to do that."

"What does he want to change?" she asked, looking into Allan's eyes. She loved talking about his work and his problems. It felt so adult.

"He wants a kickback, basically. And Christ—it's the garment business. There's give and take, little things here and there you do for people. But that isn't what he's talking about."

"But why was he calling you at home? That seems weird."

He stroked her hair. "He thinks he can pressure me."

"But he can't, right? I mean, you're too strong for that, right?"

He smiled. "Come here," he said, kissing her. He was looking super-seriously into her eyes. "You know what?"

She shook her head.

"I love you," he said.

She couldn't believe it. He had never said it before. And the truth was no one ever had, except maybe her mother when she was high. "I love you, too," she said.

It almost sounded fake, but she meant it. It was just that she had never said it, and the words felt funny. She had meant to say, "Allan," but it hadn't come out.

"Until I met you—" he said, but then he stopped and shook his head.

"Allan, what?"

He smiled. "Gail had me believing I'd never meet anyone else. And I had always thought she was right. She was it, I lost her, it was over."

"But Allan?"

"Hm."

"Why did she want to get divorced?" She had never asked the question, but now she felt it was okay.

He tucked her hair behind her ear and looked super-sad. "She said she didn't love me anymore," he said real quietly.

"God. Really?"

"Really," he said.

"I can't believe it."

He smiled. "That's nice to hear. But it's true."

They drank their coffee for a while, not even saying anything, and it was nice. But suddenly he looked at his watch and jumped up. "Christ, I'm going to be late."

She jumped up, too. "Do you want something to eat?"

"Nah, I've got to get going."

She followed him back to the bedroom, and he asked, "Will you be on the floor or in class today?"

"Um, dealers' class in the morning and on the floor in the afternoon. Are you going to come to the club?"

He shook his head. "Meetings all day."

But the funny thing was that later on, when she got to work, they changed dealers' class from the morning to the afternoon, so Danielle had to work the floor in the morning. And she was right in the middle of serving a vodka tonic to a Japanese man at one of the poker tables when she looked over at the craps table, and there was Allan.

At first she was going to go over and say hi, but he looked like he was losing, and suddenly she had the feeling she wasn't even supposed to have seen him there, otherwise he would have come over and said hi, the way he always had. Once a week, like clockwork, he came to the club, so this wasn't his "schedule." But so what? What difference did it make?

"Miss!"

A man was touching her arm. The Japanese businessman's friend. "Another drink? Vodka tonic?"

"Sure," she said. "Just one sec."

She turned to look at Allan one more time, but he was gone.

Thirty

Allan stepped out into the sunlight and squinted. It was the kind of day his father had said was a day to live for when they were up in the Catskills. "A May sky," he'd say. "You'll never see anything like a May sky in the mountains as long as you live."

Only now what?

He didn't know what had been happening lately. How many weeks had he been coming to Joseph King's? Six, maybe seven. Since Oscar Green had brought him here, which was when the fall line had come in, so that was seven weeks. And for seven weeks he had been winning. Betting a little here, a little there, once a week and then twice, three times, so that wasn't too many times. But almost always he was a winner. Then last night he went down by nine hundred, today by almost twenty-four hundred dollars.

Just the numbers made him sweat. But the twenty-four hundred made him want to cry, because twenty-four hundred was the down payment his father had put on their house in the Catskills. "Twenty-four hundred down, and look what we have: a blue sky, some green grass; what more could anybody want?"

"Twenty-four hundred back," was the obvious answer. "Plus the nine hundred I lost the other night."

He'd stop. That was the answer. He was still ahead, by eleven hundred dollars. He had gone in to Joseph King's club and gotten eleven hundred dollars. Wasn't that enough? Quit while you're ahead, and he could do it: just quit. Plus he had other pressures, like Marty Bliss wanting that kickback. But he had never cheated his boss—never.

He was going to quit the club, quit talking to people like Marty Bliss, get it all over with.

He turned the corner and looked back down the street. Of course he'd have to hear about the club from Danielle, but couldn't he quit? Shit, yes. What had he done before? He'd never gambled in his life, except the usual craps games in the army. The *idea* of it hadn't even interested him till Oscar Green had brought him into that room with all that money and yelling and all those girls. And all that money coming his way. That was what had turned his head.

But it was time. He had loved it, but his life had been empty then. He hadn't felt anything—he hadn't felt alive—for years. That adrenaline when the dice were flying through the air, when they pushed the chips your way, all the yelling and smoke and action— he had needed it.

But now he had Danielle. And Christ, if he hadn't fallen in love with her. From that first night at his apartment, when she had cried and he had realized—well, it sounded so corny—but he had realized he had forgotten how to feel. No one had given herself to him that way, not for years—and he had shut down, cut himself off from people.

So he didn't need the gambling anymore. And if Danielle asked about it, why he wasn't coming to the club anymore, he'd tell her the truth: it didn't interest him anymore.

Thirty-one

Danielle shut the oven door and wiped her hands on her jeans. She was so nervous, she couldn't even hardly breathe. And she still didn't know if she had made some kind of crazy mistake, inviting Cleve and Colette for dinner. The thing was, it had just kind of slipped out, the invitation. She had been mad at Cleve, but he had turned everything around, somehow. And she didn't want to think about what her mother would say—"That's his *specialty*, turning things around that way"—she could just hear her saying it, because she had said it a thousand and one times. Right now, if Victoria knew they were coming over for dinner, she'd say the same thing—"When are you going to *learn*, Danielle? *Forget* him!" But it was crazy. How could she? He was her father, and she had come all the way east.

The doorbell rang, and she swallowed, but her throat was completely dry. Parched. God. So this was it.

She opened the door and said "Hi" and kissed her father and looked at Colette. She was kind of what Danielle had pictured, skinny with black hair, or almost black, super-pretty. Smelling like perfume. And he smelled like himself, smoky and vodka-y. "Come on in," she said, backing up to let them in. Suddenly the hall felt totally cramped. "I feel like I already know you," she said to Colette, which was a lie, but it was what people always said, wasn't it?

Colette smiled and stepped past her.

"Um, do you guys want to see the apartment or should we just go into the living room? I think it's going to just be us unless my roommates get home early. So do you want drinks or to look around or what?" She was talking much too quickly, but she couldn't slow down.

"A drink would be fine," Colette said, stepping into the living room.

"Okay, I have iced tea and soda and probably anything else you can think of."

"Iced tea would be fine," Colette said, sitting down on the couch.

"Iced tea sounds great," Cleve said, and Danielle felt good. So he wasn't going to drink tonight. She felt like calling up her mother and saying, "So there."

When she came back, Cleve was sitting in the butterfly chair, and she couldn't help thinking Uh-oh, because everyone fell down in that chair even when they weren't even drunk. But he wasn't drinking, so she guessed it was okay.

She put the tray of iced tea down and handed Colette her glass. "I feel like I already know you," she said, and then she realized Whoops, because she had said it before. "I guess I already said that," she said.

"It doesn't matter," Cleve said quickly. "Iced tea's great," he said, holding up his glass.

"Good. I made it from scratch. And for dinner we're going to have cold chicken and macaroni and cheese. I hope that's okay. I wanted stuff I could cook in advance.''

"Sounds great," Cleve said.

And then nobody said a word. Danielle could feel her face get hot and that she was getting all nervous again, and she knew if she got too nervous, she wouldn't even be able to think of a single thing. But Colette was so quiet. Danielle couldn't think.

"So," Cleve said, leaning back in the chair. It tilted, but then it was okay. "How's the new job?"

"It's so great I can't believe it," Danielle said. She looked at Colette. "Did Cleve tell you where I'm working? At a private club?"

"Yes. It sounds very interesting," Colette said.

"It's fantastic," Danielle said. "I've met some great people, and in one day I made more money than I did the whole time working at Ivorsen & Shaw. Plus I'm going to be starting dealers' class soon."

"Really," Colette said. She sounded super-surprised. "Do they know about your record?"

Danielle shrugged. "They really know, 'cause that's when they hired me. I didn't even meet any of them till I was arrested." She looked into Colette's eyes. "It isn't the biggest thing in the world, you know. Plenty of people have been arrested for shoplifting. And some of the people at the club think I'd be really good." She looked at Cleve out of the corner of her eye, and he was smiling, and she felt good.

"What about your case?" Cleve asked. "Have you met the new lawyer?"

"Uh-huh, and he's totally confident. He told me just what Allan told me, which is that in New York I'm the last person who'd ever go to jail. So—" she shrugged again "—I'm not worried anymore."

Cleve nodded, and she suddenly saw he was sweating. "Um, is it too hot in here?" she asked. "I can try to turn the radiators off."

"It's okay," he said. He stood up. "I just need some water. Where's the kitchen?"

Danielle stood up. "Right down the hall on the right. I'll come with you."

"No. Sit," he said, like he meant it, so she guessed it was a signal, like he wanted her to stay and talk to Colette. Or he wanted a drink, and she wondered if he'd find it. She had felt bad, because it meant she didn't trust him a hundred percent, but she had put the bottles of liquor way high on the top shelf of one of the cabinets. And she had thought when she was doing it, This will mean a lot if he finds them. But maybe he won't. So it was a question. She'd just have to see.

Colette was looking out the window. "Nice view," she said. She had some kind of snooty accent. Swiss, Cleve had said.

"Thanks," Danielle said. And suddenly she didn't feel like being polite. If Colette wasn't going to hardly even try, why should she? And she didn't want to test Cleve anymore. She didn't want him to screw it up. "Um, I'll be right back," she said.

He was drinking when she came around to the door, and she could tell he hadn't heard her, because he was pouring more into the glass.

"Dad?" she said, and he jumped and turned around. "Are you okay?" she asked.

"Fine, fine," he said. He put the bottle down, and she knew she could say something about it, but what was there to say? She had said it already, at the store that day.

"I don't think it's going too well in there," she said.

He waved a hand. "Ah, don't worry about it. Colette always takes time to warm up to people. It doesn't have anything to do with you."

"Every time I say anything, I feel so dumb when I look at her face. She always looks like everything I say is just stupid."

"Come here," he said, holding out his arms.

She came to him and he hugged her.

"Nothing you say is stupid, do you understand?" he said. He stroked her hair, and she looked up into his eyes.

"I guess we'd better go back in there," she said.

He nodded. "I'll be in in a second."

Now she couldn't help it. "Okay, but don't have a lot, okay? It was so great that you started out with iced tea."

"I'll be fine," he said. "Go on. I'll be out in a minute."

The dinner was the most giant disaster she had ever given. Not that she had ever made dinner for anybody ever, but she knew this wasn't what it was supposed to be like.

For one thing, Colette was spooning the macaroni and cheese into her mouth in the tiniest bites Danielle had ever seen, as if she couldn't even stand to eat any of it. And at first Danielle had thought, Uh-oh, something's wrong with it, but there wasn't anything wrong, so what did that mean? No one had eaten any of the hors d'oeuvres (cheese and olives on crackers, right out of an ad) except for maybe a few, and now they were both picking at their chicken as if it was something they had never seen before.

Plus Cleve was smashed. You didn't have to even know him well or be a genius to see that. He wasn't even focusing his eyes right.

And Danielle wished she had maybe invited Allan, or that Maura or Larkin was here. At least to have a friend instead of two people who felt like strangers.

And they left super-early. She had thought, like at the back of her mind, that maybe they'd stay real late and everyone would be talking and having a great time, and Larkin would come home and maybe Cleve would even give her some advice, like about acting and movies, except the truth was they left at eight-thirty. When she heard the front door slam, she felt like not even saying hi to whoever was home. Everything was a failure, and what was the point?

"Danielle?" It was Larkin.

Danielle put the dishes in the sink—there were a million of them, plus a million and one pots and pans. "I'm in here," she called.

"Hey. How'd it go?"

Danielle turned the water on super-hot. "It was horrible," she said. "They left like at eight-thirty. Probably some kind of giant record for the earliest that anyone ever left in the history of dinner parties."

Larkin was frowning. "Do you need some help?"

"Nope. I just want to get all this cleaned up and forget about it."

Larkin sat down at the table and lit a cigarette. "Maybe you shouldn't try so hard," she said. "Maybe you're expecting too much from your father. You came east and you expected certain things to happen, but maybe now you need to set those hopes aside."

Danielle shrugged. "I don't have to set anything aside, because I don't have anything—I mean any hopes. I give up."

"Listen," Larkin said. "Don't get bitter about it. Just get a little more realistic. You can't count on anyone but your very best friends. Your family—well, in my case, anyway—they are not your friends, and it's silly to count on them for anything but minimal support. My sister came through for me today and got my allowance back—"

"You're kidding. That's great."

Larkin nodded. "It meant I could quit the job at Rochelle's, which I did right away. Fernanda does rise to the occasion from time to time. But only from time to time, and that's what's important to remember. Expect nothing except from your best friends."

Danielle didn't say anything. What best friends?

"So how does that sound?" Larkin asked.

She shrugged.

"That means me and Maura, Danielle. We should all have some sort of pact, maybe. No matter what happens to any of us, we always stick together, look out for each other, that sort of thing."

"Do you mean it?"

"Of course I mean it. Maura does that anyway, but we'll have to work at it—" she smiled "—all right?"

"God, that sounds great." And she felt great. Maybe Larkin was right, that she had been expecting too much, knocking her head against the wall. But now she had friends, finally. And she could say, "So there" to her father. She didn't need him anyway. So there.

Thirty-two

"Okay," Danielle said, crossing her legs Indian-style on Maura's bed. Maura was dying to go to sleep, but Larkin and Danielle were wide awake and "ready to have fun," as Danielle put it. And it was great for Danielle and Larkin—neither one had to get up before nine—but Maura was exhausted. "Okay, is everybody ready?" Danielle asked, smoothing out the magazine. "First question. 'When you first see a man, you look at his A, eyes. B, derriere.' They always use that word, don't they? 'C, mouth.' "

"That's it?" Larkin asked. "Just three choices?"

Danielle nodded, and Maura laughed. "Not enough for Larkin, obviously."

"Not even 'other'?" Larkin asked.

"Uh-uh."

Larkin nudged Maura. "Remember Brian Thomason?"

"Oh, stop," Maura said. "Come on. I have to go to sleep." But she was already laughing.

"Remember for the rest of the semester? 'I'll have a large pepperoni to go'?"

"Stop," Maura said.

"What are you two talking about?" Danielle asked.

"Oh, a guy at Yale the summer I was there," Maura said. "Larkin always talked about him and kind of had her eye on him. He was—well, he looked—ridiculousy and suspiciously well-endowed, and we used to joke about him. Then during some parade—some August thing—he was hit by a car, and a couple of kids went with him in the ambulance. And as the medics—whatever you call them, the EMS people—undressed him, the truth came out—"

"In the form of a pepperoni," Larkin said, laughing. "He actually stuffed his pants with one every day. Can you imagine?"

Danielle looked stunned. "God," she said. "But what a dumb idea, because what if you went out on a date? And didn't he always smell like a pizza?"

Maura laughed. "I don't know. I never got close enough. Larkin?"

"Luckily, neither did I."

Danielle shrugged. "I don't know. I really do look at a guy's eyes. To me they mean everything. I mean, Allan's eyes are just the greatest in the world."

"But you want to be *involved*," Larkin said. "You want someone wonderful. That's different."

"Then what do you want? I don't get it," Danielle said.

"I want to have a good time."

"But you *can't*," Danielle said. "It's so crazy. I mean, even in L.A., super-young girls don't even sleep around anymore. At least not like they used to."

"Oh, I'm careful," Larkin said. "Anyway, the only person I sleep with these days is Richard, unfortunately."

"But don't you love him?"

She sighed. "I'm very fond of him."

Maura was thinking about food. One of the best things about sleeping, she always felt, was that you got to dream about food, eat all you wanted in your dreams and wake up having had nothing. But this—it was almost midnight, and she was suddenly ravenous. It was lucky Larkin and Danielle were around, because if she were alone, she'd be raiding the refrigerator, starting with Danielle's strawberry ice cream and working down from there. But what she *didn't* want was to be awake.

"Listen, you guys—"

"But *wait*!" Danielle said. "We were just getting to *you*."

"Getting to me about what?"

"Your ideal *guy*," Danielle said. "We've figured out ours, and now we're figuring out yours."

"Well, when you *find* him—forget about this figuring out—wake me up, all right?"

"Come on," Danielle said. "We're serious. Mine is Allan. But if I had to describe him, like if Allan didn't exist, I'd say someone great, who really cares about me, who likes to give me flowers even if Larkin thinks it's corny. Someone who can love me."

Maura smiled. "And what's Larkin's? I'm almost afraid to ask."

"You shouldn't *have* to ask," Larkin said. "You should know by now, Maura. Great-looking, great in bed, someone who doesn't smother me with affection. But yours is the interesting one."

"Why is that?" Maura asked.

Larkin smiled. "Because even I'm interested. Smart is number one. Not necessarily great-looking, but he has to be distinctive in some way—"

"Smart-looking," Danielle said. "That's what we agreed before, Larkin."

"That's right," she said. "So he's smart and he looks smart. Completely principled, Mr. Wonderful in terms of being right, doing the right thing, that sort of thing. Someone you can always count on—"

"He'll be super-concerned about other people's problems," Danielle said. "He's not selfish or anything like that."

Larkin laughed. "So we realized. It's a male you."

"Great," Maura said. "My interest just dropped to zero. You take him and I'll take yours, Larkin."

Danielle was frowning. "How come I'm the only one that wants Allan?"

"Because he's right for you," Maura said, "and you're right for him. It's just one of those things." She looked at her watch. "You have to get out of here, you two. I have got to go to sleep."

Danielle stood up. "Okay. But I won't see you guys tomorrow 'cause Allan and I are going to Atlantic City; can you believe it? I'm so excited."

"You don't have to work?" Maura asked.

Danielle shook her head. "I've got my days off, two in a row. This is my first trip with a guy, ever. I just can't believe it."

Maura smiled. "Have fun. So *good night*, you two."

They left and went down the hall, and Maura listened until they each went into their room. Then she got out of bed, went into the kitchen, and opened the refrigerator door.

A male her indeed. They were ridiculous, those two. And she was starved. Time to get down to some serious eating.

Thirty-three

"Honey, you're gonna love this," Allan said, looking away from the road for a second to look at Danielle.

But he didn't have to convince her of anything. She had loved the drive so far—they were on the road to Atlantic City on a Saturday morning that was almost as beautiful as a sunset at Venice Beach.

And Allan was like someone from out of a dream, except that she had never even known enough about men to know *how* to dream. When she was in a bad mood, like usually about Cleve, Allan was ready to talk about it no matter what kind of mood he was in, and that was totally unusual in a man, she had heard. Like in "Dear Abby," where the women always said the men never wanted to talk.

Plus he was super-encouraging about her dealers' classes. The truth was that she didn't know if she could do it. She liked the people at the club, even the ones who ran it and even Joseph King, but especially the customers, so she knew she'd be a good dealer in that way, which was more than you could say about a lot of the other girls in class, plus a lot of the guys. So many of them were "just in it for the money," and it wasn't true of her at all. And the numbers she kind of liked. She had almost a photographic memory for all the odds and things like that, and it was kind of like a giant puzzle. Craps so far was her favorite, because so many people needed the dealers' help, even at a club like Joseph King's, where you'd think everyone knew how to play every game in the world. But it wasn't true at all, especially with the women. And it would be super-fun to give them help and everything. But she had the feeling she wasn't even sure she'd ever get to actually deal. So many of the other cocktail waitresses wanted to do it, too.

"Honey," Allan said, "reach into the glove compartment and see if there's some gum?"

She couldn't believe it. Someone calling her "honey."

"Um, fruit-flavored or mint, Allan?" She still hadn't called him "honey" yet.

"Give me a mint and then close your eyes," he said.

She slid one out and gave it to him and leaned back and closed her eyes. He loved surprising her with little things, like last week a bunch of blouses from his company. Super-expensive, too.

"All right. Now," he said.

She opened her eyes and she couldn't believe it. They had been driving along flat, flat land, first peanut fields, Allan said, and then super-piney-type forests, and now suddenly there was a whole sparkling, gleaming city of tall hotels, and you could just tell the ocean was right past them. It looked like Oz.

"God. I didn't know there were so many."

Allan was smiling. "Which one do you want to go to first? We can leave our bags in the trunk and check in later at the motel."

"I don't know. Which is the best? Where do you like to play?" He had said he had been a few times with friends, but he couldn't remember where they had gone.

"The Golden Nugget's nice," he said, and he signaled for a right at Atlantic Avenue. She couldn't believe the names of the streets—Connecticut, Vermont, just like in "Monopoly."

The Golden Nugget was much fancier than Danielle had thought it would be, but the great thing was that you didn't have to be dressed up, and almost everybody was dressed the way she and Allan were, in pants and shirts, nothing special.

Allan was smiling. "Want to practice your craft?"

She looked over at the roulette tables. They were pretty crowded except for certain ones that were roped off, and then one over in the corner that had only two people at it. They were nice, fancy tables, mostly with a five-dollar minimum. But she didn't feel like playing.

"Can I just hang around with you first?"

"Busman's holiday, huh?" he said, taking her by the arm and leading her toward the craps tables.

"What does that mean?"

He explained what it meant—she had never heard of it before, but there weren't that many buses in California—and then he led her over to one of the craps tables that only had about six people at it. He bought a ton of chips—five hundred dollars' worth, and it was a two-dollar minimum table—and then he gave her half. "Play with these," he said.

"I don't really feel like playing yet," she said.

He shrugged. "So hold them for me, then." And he played his bet, fifty dollars on the pass line, which meant if a seven or an eleven came up, he'd win fifty dollars and if the person with the dice threw craps, two or three or twelve, Allan would lose.

Danielle had a bad feeling, and the shooter, a woman with bleached blond hair, maybe fifty-five, threw the dice, and they came up twelve. "Craps!" the dealer yelled, and one of the stickmen (which seemed like a great job) pulled away Allan's chips with a thing that looked like a hockey stick.

And Danielle didn't want to admit it, but she could tell even from that one throw and the way Allan was sweating at his temples (already!) that he was going to lose all his chips in about two seconds. It was the weirdest thing, the way you could sometimes tell, but Danielle had already noticed it a whole bunch of times at Joseph King's club. You didn't see it in class too much, because in class people weren't playing with their own money, and she had the feeling that that was the key: was the person desperate?

"Craps!" the dealer yelled.

Uh-oh. Two in a row. It could be a streak, even though a lot of people didn't believe in streaks. But she had seen a jillion of them even in the few weeks she had been paying attention, where guys made a ton or *lost* a ton because something came up again and again and again.

"Bet against her," she said, but it was too late. Allan had put a hundred dollars on the pass line, and two seconds later, the blond lady threw a three and the stickman was hockey-sticking away Allan's money.

Allan didn't say anything. He just took the pile of chips he had given her to hold and slid them down the slot to in front of him.

"I'll be back," she said, and she walked away.

She didn't want to watch him lose. He was her hero, the greatest man in the whole world except her father. When she thought of him dying, he passed the "love test," too, a wind against the back of her thighs and her stomach dropping out.

But he was sweating like a loser, and she didn't want to see it.

She walked through the casino to one of the lounges, where a guy was singing and nobody except one old lady was listening. Everybody was just blabbing, blabbing, and you could see in the singer's eyes that he was hurt and totally discouraged.

"Thank you thank you thank you," he said when he finished a song. But no one was clapping, and Danielle realized if she clapped, it would sound worse than no one clapping. It had to be a nightmare for the guy.

He sang a few more songs, and they started to make her sad. It was super-glamorous, the casino and the lounge and everything, plus her job at Joseph King's: she still couldn't believe she had found something so exciting so quickly. But clubs were just one tiny part of her life. What if that wasn't true with Allan?

She had never really thought of it before, because it *did* seem to be a tiny part of his life, because he didn't hardly even come to Joseph King's anymore. But he had come to Atlantic City a couple (at least!) of times before, maybe tons more, and what if he gambled all the time? What if it meant everything to him?

The singer finished another song, and the old lady clapped, so Danielle clapped, too, and she watched the guy walk across the stage—he wiped his face and gave one last look at the audience, and suddenly he looked about twelve, a kid who had lost his dog, even though he was maybe twenty-five or twenty-six.

Then he hopped down off the stage and came right over to Danielle. "Hey there," he said.

She smiled. "Hi. That was a good set. You have a great voice." Maybe "great" wasn't the word she would have used if she was telling the truth, but he probably needed all the encouragement he could get.

"Thanks. Mind if I sit down?"

"Sure. Have a seat." He was wearing super-tight clothes—shiny, satiny pants and a fringey-type shirt—and it looked maybe a little out of date, more like a few years ago, at least out in California. But how could she tell him? Plus she guessed it wasn't necessarily any of her business.

"So are you here alone?" he asked. "What's a pretty girl et cetera et cetera?" he said.

"I'm here with my boyfriend."

"And he's at the tables, right?"

"Uh-huh."

The guy—the sign on the stage said his name was Randy Shandell—was shaking his head. "Crazy guy. When he could be here with you?"

She shrugged.

"So you're not into the tables much yourself, are you?" he said. "You like the slots?"

"Slots are for suckers," she said, and he looked a little shocked. Maybe she had said it too loud, but it was true. "Plus I'm a dealer at a private club in New York, so this is kind of a busman's holiday for me.''

He was nodding, so she guessed she had used the expression the right way. "You're a dealer, huh?"

"Well, I'm *training*. I'm a cocktail waitress right now, but pretty soon I'll be a real dealer."

"And she'll be a great one," a voice said.

Danielle turned around. Allan had come up behind and put his hands on her shoulders.

"Hi, honey," she said. "Um, sit down. Allan, this is Randy Shandell. Randy, Allan Greshner."

Randy shook Allan's hand. "Nice to meet you, Allan. How's the action over at the tables?"

"Good, good," Allan said. He wasn't sitting down. "Danielle, can I talk to you for a minute?"

"Sure," she said, and she stood up, and he led her away a few feet. "What's the matter?"

He had a weird look on his face.

"Allan, what is it?"

"Instead of staying at the motel, how'd you like to stay here at the hotel? In one of the suites."

"What? But how?"

"Just tell me. Would you like to? The show's included, too. Andy Williams."

"Allan, you're kidding!"

"So we're on?"

"Sure. God, Allan."

"Great. Then I've got to let them know. I'll see you in a while," he said, and he kissed her on the cheek.

"Okay."

And he was gone. She walked back to the table, and Randy was standing up. "Are you leaving?" she asked.

"Yeah, I've got to get ready for my next set. You gonna stick around?"

"Yup. It turns out we're going to spend the night here."

He was giving her kind of a funny look. "In a high rollers' suite?"

"In a what?"

"A high rollers' suite. For high-stakes players. The hotels put 'em up, treat 'em to some shows, the whole bit. They lay it on thick, and they get back every penny and more."

"Oh." She shrugged. "We're just staying here because Allan feels like it."

"Good. You don't want to get involved in any kind of junket-type shit, Danielle. They *always* make their money back. But then, you probably know that if you work at a private club."

"Of course," she said. Randy went backstage to get ready for his next set, and she drifted out of the lounge back to the casino. She felt super-bad all of a sudden, since Randy had said that. Allan wasn't a sucker and he wasn't a loser. She looked around at all the people playing slots, with the bells ringing and the lights going crazy, mostly old women screaming about dimes and quarters. *They* were the suckers. Allan wasn't.

"Oh my God," Danielle said. Allan was tipping the guy who had showed them to their room, but Danielle had even forgotten anyone else was even there, because the room was the most incredible thing she had ever seen, like a dream come true or out of a super-old movie that took place in the desert. The bed was like a tent, practically, with giant hanging pieces of cloth and four giant pole-type things, and everything else looked like it was in the desert: two giant straw couches, or maybe rattan, and rugs that looked like they had been made by millions of natives. And gold and brass everywhere, like lamps and everything.

When the door shut and the bellhop had left, Allan came across the room to where Danielle was standing and took her in his arms. "So you like it?" he asked.

"Allan, it's beautiful. It's the most beautiful room I've ever seen in my life. I feel like I'm in a movie."

He kissed her, and she felt like it was magic, that with every kiss he was taking every bad thought away: Why was the casino paying for the room? What about what Randy Shandell had said? What if they ended up losing a ton of money?

But Allan was a business manager at a super-successful firm; money was his business, and he knew all about it.

Plus the truth was she had always, her whole life, wanted to stay in this fancy a place, and now it was finally coming true.

Thirty-four

Danielle let her head sink into the pillows one last time. They were going to finally leave this afternoon, Sunday. And it was weird. They said, "Time flies when you're having fun," but this weekend had been the greatest weekend of her life, and it felt like maybe a year. Or a month at least.

She just couldn't believe Allan and how fancy everything was. They had lived like a king and queen for two days. And when Randy Shandell had said all those things about how the hotels only gave weekends to high rollers, she had gotten a little scared. But it had turned out fine. Allan had won over two thousand dollars, so how could anyone criticize?

Plus she finally knew what people meant when they said things like, "It was like our second honeymoon." Even though they had never even had a single one, it felt like a second one, with Allan super-affectionate the whole time. And the way Randy had made it sound, she had thought maybe Allan would spend the whole time at the tables. But it wasn't true at all.

But then the biggest thing had happened when she was asleep, in her dreams, or really just one great dream, the greatest dream she had ever had. In it were she and Allan at a country house, a beach place, so maybe it was right near Atlantic City in real life, or California. And the new part was that they had a baby, a little boy. And Danielle, when she had woken up this morning, it was all she could think about.

A baby. It would be the greatest. And who would have thought, since she had never even been in love?

So now the plan was to make Allan want one, too. They had never even talked about getting married. He was just divorced, so she figured the subject would make him kind of nervous. The last time they had talked about it, he had said Gail "didn't get such a great deal" when she had married him.

But Danielle didn't think that was true. Allan would be the number one great husband in the world.

"Honey?" Allan called from the bathroom. "What time do you have?"

"Um, quarter to four." She sat up. "What happened to your watch?"

"I must have lost it," he said, coming out of the bathroom and tucking in his shirt. "It's the weirdest thing. How do you lose a watch?"

She shrugged. "I used to lose them all the time on the beach."

He got on the bed and took her in his arms. "But we didn't *go* to the beach, silly." He rubbed his nose against hers. "And you *are* silly, you know that? The way you talked to that old woman on the boardwalk today. How do you know she wasn't trying to pick your pocket? Or take my watch, come to think of it?"

"Because she wasn't. And someone needed to talk to her."

He rolled onto his back and moved her on top of him. "Well, you're sweet," he said, tucking her hair behind her ears. "Silly, but sweet. And I love you."

Her heart jumped. It jumped every time he said those words. She still couldn't get used to it at all. How did people ever fall out of love once they were in it? "I love you, too," she said, resting her cheek against his. She loved to feel his five o'clock shadow at the end of the day. "Allan?"

"Mm, honey." He was rubbing her back super-slowly.

"I was thinking."

"Mm?"

She lifted her head so she could look down into his eyes. "Um, wouldn't it be the greatest thing if we had a baby ?"

"A baby?"

She had to laugh even though she didn't mean to. The way he had said it, it was like he had never even heard the word before.

"Danielle, are you serious? You're only what? Twenty, right?"

"So? Plenty of girls back home had them when they were in high school, even. It wasn't such a big deal. They just *did* it."

"It is a big deal," he said. He brushed her cheek with the back of his hand. "It's a very big deal. Lifetime, as a matter of fact."

She bit her lip. She had to, because she didn't like the look in his eyes or what he was saying. "So, um, are you saying you don't . . . What are you saying? You don't want—"

He brought her head down so he was kissing her, and he brushed his lips against hers and then looked into her eyes. "Don't," he said softly. "I can't stand to see that look in your eyes."

She had to try not to cry. That was super-important, she knew.

"I'm not the right guy for that, honey. I'm just not." She could feel the tears start, and she tried to wipe one away, but he did it for her. "Don't cry," he said. "Please. You're so young. You don't need *me*. You need someone your age—"

"I don't want someone my age. I want you."

"You're too young to know what you want," he said. "And I know that's hard for you to understand now, but it's true. You don't want *me*."

She put her face against his chest so he wouldn't see her crying. He was probably just making it up, the part about him being the wrong person. He probably just didn't want to have a "lifetime" with her.

"Honey, please," he said, stroking her back. "Don't cry."

She raised her head and wiped the tears away, but right away more came.

"You look like a seal," he said, wiping her eyes for her. "A brokenhearted seal." He kissed one eye, a bunch of tears, she guessed, and then the other eye. "Tell me what you're thinking."

She shrugged. "What's the point? You don't want me, and you've said it."

"Danielle, I want *you*. Don't ever think I don't want you. I love you. But I'm not the right guy for you if you want a house and a car and three kids in the suburbs."

"I don't want to live in the suburbs."

He sighed. "I'm too old to start, and I'm not the right person. But you should have all of that and more if that's what you want."

"I just said one baby. I didn't even say anything about a house. Or the suburbs. You don't even know what I want." She felt like she was talking to her father all of a sudden, except that she had never even talked to him that way. It was always letters—"You didn't even call on my birthday." "How did you like the shirt I sent you? Let me know if it doesn't fit." "How was your trip? Were you in L.A. ? I thought I saw you at the Santa Monica Pier, only I was in a car."

So maybe that was the truth, that they (men) just never really wanted you.

Allan was stroking her back super-softly, and it felt so sweet and great, she started to cry again, because even though the truth was probably that he didn't want to have a baby with her, she just couldn't give it up. Why did people think you could when it was impossible? How could Dear Abby say, "Don't you see that man's never going to come around?" Or all those radio talk-show ladies (doctors). "He's made it clear, Alison. He doesn't want children. And that *is* his right. He's telling you going in." But what were you supposed to do? Just pretend you didn't care?

Allan shifted his weight so Danielle's elbow wasn't jutting quite so sharply into his hip. He knew she was still crying, and also that she didn't want him to know she was. She was tensed up like an animal, but her shoulders were shaking and he could feel slow tears against his chest.

And he felt awful.

He had never met anyone like her, anyone even close to her in terms of straightforwardness. He had never once heard her question someone else's motives or assume they were lying. She never started sentences with the words, "But if he were telling the truth—" or "Don't you see what he *meant* by that?" To her, whatever you said you meant, and whatever she said she meant.

And he knew he had hurt her.

All day, when they had taken breaks to walk along the beach or eat, he had been thinking, "This is the life." A beautiful girl, who was smart, too, once you got to know her: she could remember a string of eighteen numbers at a roulette wheel and every shoot in a craps game. Smart, beautiful, happy, easy. But he wasn't for her; he wasn't the one. He had thought he'd quit the gambling, and he hadn't. And it didn't worry him—he had won today; he was ahead by thirty-eight hundred. But he still wasn't the one for her. He wasn't good enough.

He tried to picture himself with Danielle in a year, with a baby. But he couldn't do it. He tried the mountains, the Beaverkill Dam, where he had spent the greatest times of his life with his father.

And then he saw it, himself and Danielle and a carriage. (Did people bring carriages to the country? He didn't even know.)

Danielle sniffled and wiped her cheek against his shoulder. "So then let's forget it," she said. "Do you, um, can we still see each other?"

"Of course," he said, kissing the top of her head.

"Okay, so we'll just, you know, forget it."

"No," he suddenly said, heard himself say. "I think we should do it."

Her eyes were huge, and he wondered what he was doing. But

the words had come out, and they were still—"It could be fun," he said. "It could be great."

"Allan, do you mean it? God, really? You're not just saying it?"

"I'm not just saying it. Really."

She hugged him, and he knew why he had done it. He wanted to want it, and he wanted to make her happy. And if he wanted that rosy, Danielle-optimistic future enough, maybe it would actually happen. "Let's just not rush into it, though. There's a lot to think about."

"I know, I know," she said, excited already. "I mean, I'm still on the pill, so I have to get off of it, and then my dealer training, like with all the smoke and everything? I want to finish it out. But then, okay?"

He kissed the top of her head. God, he loved her. "Okay," he said.

She looked into his eyes. "You've made me the happiest person in the whole world," she said.

The awful part was that he knew it was true.

Thirty-five

"Darling, *no*," Alexandra said into the phone. "No, no, a thousand times no."

Maura looked across the room at Alexandra. How superficial and theatrical could a person get? She didn't know how much more she could stand—although it apparently didn't bother Terence in the least.

And why should it? she had to ask herself. This was an agency. For actors. Everyone who came in was theatrical. *She* was the odd man out.

Alexandra laughed her loud laugh, the false one that meant she was nervous. "Don't be silly. Damian, honestly. That's disgusting."

Another phone line rang, and Maura answered it. "Fielding-White Agency."

"Hi. Yeah. Alexandra, please," said a male voice.

"She's on another line. Who's calling, please?"

"Victor Jarosch."

Hm. A name she had never heard of. And that was part of the problem. She still didn't know who was important.

Another burst of laughter from Alexandra's office. "Uh, is Miss Fielding expecting your call?" Maura asked.

"Yeah. Tell her I'll call back," he said, and he hung up.

Maura put down the receiver just as Terence came through the front door.

"Any calls?" he asked.

"Good morning to you, too."

He didn't smile.

"Just a call for Alexandra," she said.

Alexandra appeared in the doorway. "What happened to that call?" she asked.

"He said he'd call back."

"Who's 'he'?"

"Victor Jarosch."

Alexandra glanced at Terence and then glared at Maura. "What happened? Why didn't you buzz me?"

"You were on another line."

Alexandra threw up her hands. "That's beautiful. *Just* beautiful, Maura. The call I've been waiting for for a week."

"He said he'd call back. If he said—"

"He is a *nut* case," Alexandra screamed. "He's in another fucking *universe* half the time, and if he said he'd call back, the one thing you know is that he *won't* call back. That's *just* beautiful."

She turned and went back to her office, and Maura heard her punching out a number on the phone.

She looked at Terence. "I guess it's just beautiful," she said.

He rested his palms on the desk and leaned forward. "You're going to have to be more careful," he said softly. "These calls are important. Jarosch is an actor we'd really like to handle, but he's an actor *everyone* would really like to handle. Alexandra's been cultivating him, and one wrong move could send it all down the drain."

"Then *tell* me about it," Maura said. "And not *after* the fact, Terence, because if you do it then, it doesn't do me any good. All I've heard since I started here is 'Screen the calls, screen the calls. Everyone will pretend we're expecting their call, and you've got to screen them out.' *Tell* me you're expecting these calls if they're so important."

"All right, you have a point," Terence said. He was wearing too much after-shave, and she had the feeling she was going to become allergic to it. "Until you get the hang of things and get to know who we know, if they're on the client list—"

"I know the client list," Maura said. "I have it right here, and I know it, Terence."

"I was going to *say*, if you'd let me finish—if they're on the client list, you already know them. If they're obviously actors running down everybody in *Ross Reports*, you know what to tell them— don't call, don't visit, et cetera et cetera. And if they seem to fall somewhere in between, check with one of us."

"All right. Do you want anything from downstairs? I'm ordering up some iced coffee."

He didn't say anything. Then: "Maura, you don't seem very concerned."

"Jesus Christ, Terence, what do you want me to do? Commit suicide? I understand what you said. And I'll do it. Now, do you want anything or not?"

"Uh, no, no." He looked into her eyes and then walked into his office. A second later he put his head around the corner. "Hey. Sorry. Wrong side of the bed and all that."

"Apology accepted," she said.

But she wondered if it *was* going to be all right. When was the fun part going to begin?

The phone rang again, and she answered it on the first ring. "Fielding-White Agency."

"Hello, I'd like to speak with Alexandra, please," a woman's voice said.

Maura could hear Alexandra on the phone in the other room. "Who's calling, please?"

"Alana Kennedy."

Not a client.

"Uh, may I ask what this is in reference to?"

"Yes. Jack Frantzen suggested I call."

Well, Jack was a client.

"Uh, hold on, please. I'll check and see if she's available yet."

She buzzed Alexandra and got nothing.

She buzzed again.

"What is it?" the voice said through the intercom.

"There's an Alana Kennedy on the line. She said Jack Frantzen suggested she call."

"What does she want?"

Great. "I don't know."

"Christ," Alexandra said. "All right, I'll take the call." A few seconds later the door slammed shut, and Maura could hear raised voices, Terence's and Alexandra's.

The front door opened and the coffee arrived, along with a great-looking guy Maura recognized from one of the eight-by-tens that had come in last week: Keefe Scott, Alexandra's eleven o'clock appointment.

"Hi, is she in?"

Alexandra's voice came through the door loud and clear: "Goddammit, Terence, not again—"

"I guess so," he said, raising an eyebrow.

"You might as well sit down," Maura said.

He sat down across from her and stretched out his long, blue-jeaned legs. "Whew. What a day. It's crazy out there. You born-and-bred New Yorkers have no idea what the subway does to us out-of-towners."

"I'm not exactly born and bred," she said.

"Really? You look it. Where are you from?"

"Pennsylvania."

"No shit. Me, too. Whereabouts?"

"Scranton."

He laughed. "Then you know Smitty's."

"Ten miles away," she said. "Right? And Velma Ann's? And the Valley Drive-In?"

He clapped and let out a whoop. "What a trip. What's your name?"

"Maura Cassidy."

"Keefe Scott. Nice to meet you. How'd you end up working here?"

"*Why* did I end up working here might be a better question," she said. "Actually, Terence is a friend of mine, and they needed a new assistant, so—"

The office door flew open, and Terence came out with some papers in his hand. He glanced at Keefe and then sat down next to Maura. "Problems," he said, laying the papers on the desk. They were letters she had typed the day before.

"First of all, that call. You should have taken her name and number—"

"Now, wait a minute," Maura said. "You just went through a whole song and dance about whether someone was a client or not and what I was supposed to do in the middle ground. You *know* that, Terence."

He gave a look toward the inner office. "I know," he said quietly. "But it was a call Alexandra didn't want to take, as it turned out."

"Then just what do you suggest, Terence? I'm not a goddamn *mind* reader. And if I were going to read anyone's mind, it wouldn't be Alexandra's."

"Calm down," he said.

"Why should I? You tell me one thing, and I do it, and then—"

Keefe Scott was gesturing with his hands, palms down, mouthing the word "shh."

"All right," she said. "I'll try to ask more questions, okay? I *will* try." Keefe made the "okay" sign with his thumb and forefinger. "But you have to realize no one is going to know exactly who everyone is until they've been here awhile."

"I realize that," Terence said. "As long as you try. Now about these letters . . ."

She looked down, and her breath caught. He was flipping through them, and every single one had large red circles on them—circles around mistakes, presumably.

"Alexandra has rather a particular way of doing things," he said. "In this one, for example. You've spelled et cetera e-t-c-period. She likes it spelled out all the way."

Maura couldn't stop looking at the huge red circle in ink. It was a two-page, single-spaced letter.

"So she wants me to do it over," she said. Her voice had come out hoarse and hollow.

"Right," Terence said quickly. "And on this contract. Where it says—"

He went on and on, and Maura's head was swimming. She had never known how it felt to be so angry she couldn't see, but now she knew: she wanted to rip up everything she had typed over the past two days, leave, and never come back.

While Terence was going on with what felt like an hour-long speech, Alexandra called Keefe in, and it was awful to half listen to *their* conversation. Keefe was as sycophantic as any of the actors who had ever come in looking for representation, and Maura wished they would close the door.

Terence went back into the office, and Maura looked at the stack of letters and contracts she had to retype. There had to be fifteen pages, and there was no way to get out of it unless she quit.

"Dear Mr. Haskell," she typed. "Our client, Hal Luening, has agreed to accept the part you've offered in 'Another Day.' We have several stipulations, though . . ."

"How's it going?"

Maura looked up at Keefe. "Well, I've done half," she said. "Which is more than—"

The phone rang, and she turned to answer it, and as she turned—she saw it in slow motion even as it was happening—her elbow hit the cup of iced coffee and it tipped over, spilled, and spread slowly and then so quickly she couldn't believe it, all over the stack of new letters.

"Fuck."

"Hello?" the voice said from the phone receiver.

"Oh. I'm sorry. Fielding-White. Uh, may I help you?"

"Yeah. Terence, please."

She put him on hold and buzzed Terence.

"Yes, Maura."

"You've got a call," she said.

"Who is it?"

Fuck again. "Oh. Christ. Terence, listen. I don't know, because I just spilled coffee over everything I retyped. Do you want me to find out?"

"That's okay. I'll take it."

She hung up. Keefe was blotting up the coffee with a handkerchief.

"Thanks," Maura said. "But I think it's hopeless."

"This page is," he said, holding up a sodden, brownish contract. "But I think I saved the rest."

"You're a lifesaver," Maura said. "Really. I haven't seen anyone with a handkerchief in years."

"I guess it's my hick half," he said with a grin that *was* a little hickish. "But it comes in handy. Listen. Do you get a lunch hour?"

"I usually order in and eat at my desk. One of the perks of the job."

He was shaking his head. "I sure hope you love it. Would you want to get together after work sometime, then?"

"After work?"

"To go out. Get a bite to eat. Talk about Luby's and the A-Q Drive-In."

She was suddenly acutely aware of a silence in the office, the first silence all day.

Well, fuck 'em if they wanted to listen. "Sure," she said, even though she didn't believe for one minute that he would actually call. "You can call me here anytime."

"Give me your home phone, too, okay? I'm usually running around all day. And I'll write mine down for you."

He wrote his number on a memo pad and underneath wrote: "Go Scranton!" and she laughed.

"So I'll call you," he said. "And you call me."

"Okay. See you, then," she said, and he left, a too-good-looking guy to have asked her out.

A few seconds later, Alexandra came into the room. "When do you suppose you'll have the Luening contract retyped?"

Luckily, that one had been rescued by Keefe. "It's already done," Maura said, pulling it out from the bottom of the pile.

"Ah. Good. Rescued by your hero?"

"I beg your pardon?"

"You ought to be warned," Alexandra said, sitting down next to Maura's desk. "The first few times, you don't realize it's happening, but if someone warns you, it's easier."

"I don't know what you're talking about," Maura said, sounding as unfriendly as she felt.

"This *job*," Alexandra said. "It happens to everybody, and usually quite quickly. And of course it happens more often to me and to Terence. But don't you be fooled. You will have men, women, gays, straights, everyone who's ever read a copy of *Backstage* or *Variety* asking you out."

Maura hated her. "And?"

"And you should realize what it means. I even once had the woman who was giving me a *bikini wax* whip out an eight-by-ten."

"I hope it didn't hurt," Maura said.

"What?"

"Look. I don't need, want, or appreciate any lectures about my social life, all right? I'm not you," she said. And please don't ever let me get as fat as you are, either.

Although she was coming close, with all the pizza she had been eating.

Alexandra stood up, picked up the contract, and looked down at Maura. "Don't say you haven't been warned."

"I wouldn't dream of it," Maura said.

But she looked around at the walls that were plastered with eight-by-tens of people who were all great-looking or talented or both.

And she felt more Scranton than ever.

Book Three

Thirty-six

"Thirty-five!" Danielle called out. "The number is thirty-five, folks. Thirty-five." Oops. She wasn't supposed to say "folks," and the teacher had warned her a million times. "Thirty-five, everyone," she said, but luckily the pit boss who was "on the job," Nick, was someone who seemed to like her a lot. He was a little bit young, especially compared to Allan: like, for instance, he didn't even know how to end a conversation—he kind of just stood there and "faded out." Plus he had a super-hot temper and really screamed at people, meaning the staff and never the customers, when he got upset. Which seemed a little weird considering that he was a pit boss in a super-fancy casino and practically in charge of the whole place, from what she had heard.

But anyway, he kind of had the habit of "looking the other way" when she said the wrong thing, like "folks," which was lucky, because this had to be the greatest job she had ever had in her entire life. So far she was still a trainee, which meant she only got to deal one or maybe sometimes two times a week, and the rest of the time she had to be a cocktail waitress, which was a little bit weird, because then the regulars, who would've seen her dealing the night before, at first some of them thought she had been demoted to being a cocktail waitress again, as if she had done something wrong, so she had to do a lot of explaining.

"Six!" she called out. She loved the way you first saw where the ball went into the little slot, almost in a race with the customers. You had to be first and yell it fast or you looked really bad. "The number is six, ladies and gentlemen."

Which was great, because a new guy, a man she had never seen before, was a winner, plus a lady had a quarter of her chip on the six, so she got nine chips. And this was the best part, *chink, chink,* stacking up the winning chips and letting them run through her fingers, having everybody look and be totally impressed over the way she knew as fast as anyone how many there were just by the feel and the rhythm.

It had taken her a million hours to learn, or at least it felt that way, but Allan and Nick were both impressed, they said, and Nick said she had "a real knack," better than any trainee he had ever seen, for the payoffs, including the math.

Which was one thing that really *wasn't* a surprise to her, for once. Even when she had cut nine million math classes, she always got A's, even in her super-worst periods of school, when she was failing everything else. It was just something she knew, the way some people could tell you all kinds of dates and other people could spell, or even name all the fifty states. You either "had it" or you didn't, and for once, people weren't saying, "if only she could spell." They were saying she had a knack.

The only bad part was a certain thing that was going on with Allan, and she couldn't even swear she knew what it was. It was just that ever since he had said yes to the baby idea, he had been kind of different. All the time they were together, he said he loved her, and he seemed proud and happy to be with her, so she didn't think it was that he was sick of her. But there were certain times . . . well, the truth was that when they were in bed together, sometimes he didn't want to make love, and even when they did do it, it wasn't exactly as great as it had been before. Sometimes he didn't even feel like finishing. She had never even heard of anything like it before: Sure, sometimes guys didn't want to make love— everyone knew that. But didn't they get sick if they didn't finish?

And that was what scared her. Maybe he was sick. He looked pale and worried, and at first she had thought, Uh-oh, maybe that singer Randy Shandell was right, and Allan was a sucker-type gambler, one of the ones who lost a ton of money at the casinos.

But it wasn't true. He swore it (because she even came right out and asked him). The truth was that he had been maybe $175 behind, but then he had made it up. And at Atlantic City he was still ahead.

So that was the thing. She had the horrible feeling he was sick. And she had already decided: tonight she was going to ask him point-blank what was wrong, just like that.

"You don't understand," Allan said into the phone. His hand was so sweaty, the receiver was soaked.

"No, *you* don't understand. You got till tomorrow, Greshner; otherwise we call your boss." Then a dial tone.

You got till tomorrow. Allan swallowed and leaned back in his chair.

It all felt so unreal. Thirteen thousand dollars. Five hundred tomorrow. Another thousand next week. By the time he paid it off, it would be a hundred thousand. How had it happened?

He had been on a streak for weeks. The Giants had beaten the point spread, Atlantic City was like the Atlantic City National Bank and Trust—he had won thirty-eight hundred when he was there, so no wonder they kept trying to get him to come back. And for a while, he had been doing great at King's place. The craps tables there—he couldn't explain it, exactly, but they gave you the feeling you couldn't ever lose. The girls brought the drinks, the dealers were fast, everything was go go go. He had been up $315. Then $4,000, when he had moved to a table with higher stakes. And then somehow . . .

The problem was the credit. He hadn't kept track; he hadn't written it down. I'm a business manager, he had told himself. My head is filled with figures every day; it's what I do.

But he knew the figures were right, because he had questioned them last week, and they had handed him the credit slips he had signed for the pit boss. Two thousand here, fifteen hundred there, twenty-two fifty here, and on and on. Not to thirteen, but in a week the interest had made it thirteen. And then yesterday, Nick, the pit boss he had been dealing with most of the time, saying, "Sorry, Mr. Greshner, you're at your limit."

So he couldn't even go back and win it back, even though he *knew* he could do it. The losing streak had to end somewhere.

There was always Atlantic City, of course, and there was always the Giants game on Sunday. But the game was days away, and you only doubled your money, and where was he going to get sixty-five hundred to even lay down?

He knew exactly what he had in his checking account: $75.39.

Savings, zip. Paycheck that was coming on Friday, well, that had to go to pay the rent.

And Danielle's birthday was on Sunday.

The sweat was making him stink. Goddamn office windows that didn't even open.

His intercom buzzed, and he jumped. "Yes, Patty."

"Mr. Kates wants to change the meeting to three. That okay with you?"

"Uh, yeah. Sure, sure," he said.

But he wasn't thinking. He was looking down at the key to the petty cash drawer as he hung up the phone.

Something he wasn't supposed to be doing.

Something he hadn't let himself think about, ever.

But it would be temporary. Five hundred to pay the club the first payment tomorrow, and two thousand to put on the Giants, which were a sure thing with the point spread the club was quoting. It would be a start, anyway. Keep the club off his back.

"I have to talk to you," Danielle said, looking into his eyes. "And it's about something super-serious."

His heart skipped. She was breaking up with him; she was seeing someone else; she had decided he was too old.

She bit her lip. "Um, I've been trying to figure this out," she said, sipping her wine. She still winced whenever she drank the good stuff he gave her, the stuff he liked. But she had insisted she'd learn to like it. "And I think—I mean, I really have to know, that's all, even if you don't want to tell me."

"Danielle, what is it? Tell you what?"

She took a deep breath and tore her napkin slowly down the center. "When we started seeing each other, everything was super lovey-dovey." She shrugged. "I mean, it wasn't something I ever had before, and it was great. But now . . ." She bit her lip again, looked into his eyes for half a second, and then looked down at the table. "I want to know if it's me or something worse." Her eyes were filling with tears.

"Danielle, it's nothing. Really. I've just been tired." Christ. "Come here," he said, and he took her in his arms. "Any man would be crazy not to want you all the time, and I never would have thought I could be that crazy. But sometimes I'm just too damn tired." He forced a smile as he looked into her eyes. "That's what you get for going out with an old codger like me."

She was frowning. "I don't know what a codger is, but this is the thing: Are you sure there isn't anything else?"

"Anything else like what?"

"Like—" She stopped and took a deep breath. "You're not sick and not telling me, are you?"

"Not unless it's something I don't know about."

"Are you sure?"

"Positive," he said.

She looked up at him. "Do you think we need to go to somebody, then? I mean, like, you know."

He didn't know what she meant. A marriage counselor? Couples therapy? "You mean a therapist?"

She shrugged. "That's what they always say."

He kissed her long and hard, and he could feel her responding, slowly at first and then more passionately.

He started to feel something, and then he remembered that voice—"You want us to call your boss, Greshner?"

Danielle pulled away and sighed, looking down at her hands. "Then it's me."

"Honey, it's not."

"Maybe we should stop seeing each other. I mean, if that's what you want."

He pulled her closer. "Danielle, that's the last thing in the world I want. Really."

"Well, okay," she said. But he could see in her eyes that she didn't believe him—she still thought *some*thing was wrong.

And he guessed there was. He'd have to clear the damn thing up one way or another. He had taken the cash, and it had been shockingly easy. Twenty-five hundred dollars that would have gone to hiring some girls for the buyers next week, but there was still enough. The worst part was when he had thought about Marty Bliss—how many weeks ago had he called, asking Allan for money? And Allan had felt it was unthinkable: taking money from the company. Imagine.

And then the part he couldn't think about at all. His father. His boss's best friend. It would have killed him to know.

But he wouldn't think about it. He had done it, and it was over. The purpose was clear—to get out of debt. He'd make the first payment, make the money on the Giants game, and then get out of the rest of the debt and be clear forever. Somehow.

Thirty-seven

Danielle looked at herself in the mirror and felt like screaming. She looked like she hadn't slept in about nineteen days, which was almost the truth. It had been a dumb idea, the party, when she had thought of it, and it was even a dumber idea now, because she was so nervous, she was ready to die.

Her birthday. Except she had told everybody not to bring presents, because it sounded more adult that way. And she guessed they'd probably listen, except maybe one person wouldn't, which would be nice (like her father or Allan).

But God. Why had she even thought of the idea in the first place? It seemed like kind of a great idea since she had just found out about her case: dropped, just like that. Or maybe not just like that, but the cops had dropped it because, just like Allan had said, there were millions more super-serious crimes going on in New York every single second, and they'd be crazy to put her in jail or even on probation for trying to take a scarf. So that was the great news, and so far no one even knew it. She guessed she'd make some kind of announcement, and then it would be like a double celebration, her birthday and no jail.

Only now, God—she totally dreaded it. What if Cleve forgot to show up? What if Colette was a bitch? What if nobody had any fun? And the weird part was that when she had decided to have the party, and buy all the stuff herself and everything, a voice had said, Don't do it, because you know your birthday's always a disaster, a hundred percent. Which was true. Even when she had been almost nothing, like maybe five or something, the parties were terrible. Like at one when everybody complained about the food and then her father threw up all over the table. Or when nobody except two girls showed up the next year. She had felt so bad.

But life was different now. She had a man she loved, so that would probably make a giant difference, or maybe make a little bit of a difference, anyway. And Maura said she'd come with this guy who she had never said was a boyfriend, but Danielle had the feeling he was, just because of the way Maura started to blush whenever she said his name. Keefe. So that was good. And Larkin had said she'd try if she didn't have to meet her mother, since they had had another fight and she had to make up with her. Which Danielle could definitely understand. Her mother sounded like a supersnooty bitch. Anyway, maybe things would be different from when she had been little.

She took another last look in the mirror and then went to the kitchen to start taking the food out: egg salad and tuna salad and potato salad—she had made them all herself—and bread and potato chips and tons of stuff to drink on trays. It was time for everyone to come, and no one had rung the doorbell yet or even called, but she wasn't going to think about that.

She heard a key in the door, and her heart jumped. She hadn't wanted to admit it before, but she had been hoping like crazy that Maura or Larkin would come first, before the others (even Allan). Either one of them would make her feel a hundred times more relaxed.

It was Maura coming—she could tell by the walk—and then she stuck her head in the kitchen doorway. "Hey, happy birthday." She came over and gave Danielle a kiss on the cheek. "What's the matter?"

"God, I'm dying of fear. Does it show?"

Maura smiled. "A little. What are you worried about?"

"Oh, everything. The food, my father, Allan, if anyone will even show up—"

"Everyone will show up except Larkin, who promised she'd try. But everyone else will, and everyone will have a good time."

"Is your friend coming?"

Maura blushed. "He said he would."

"See? You're not sure either. Maybe we'll be the only ones here."

"We *won't* be. Now, stop it. Come on. I'll help you take this stuff out to the living room. That's where you want it, right?"

Danielle nodded, and they each took a tray. "Um, can I ask you something?" she said to Maura.

"Sure," Maura said, putting the tray of glasses on the orange crate next to the couch.

"Is it serious with this guy Keefe? I mean your relationship?"

Maura blushed again. "Oh, I don't think so. I mean no, of course not."

"Why of course not?"

"Because it isn't."

"Oh." It was obvious Maura didn't want to talk about it. And it was weird: She was always so ready to talk about everyone else's lives, and not in a bad way. In a really good way. But she was super-private about her own life, and sometimes Danielle wondered: Was she happy? It was hard to tell, but sometimes it seemed like Maura never really was.

"And then he walked up to Terence's desk and said, 'I think you're a scumbag,' spat on his papers, and turned around and left."

"You're kidding!" Keefe said.

Maura shook her head. "It was unbelievable."

Danielle didn't want to admit it, but she couldn't help it. The only two people at the whole entire party who were having a good time were Maura and Keefe.

And God, she had to say she was happy for Maura. You could just tell that Keefe was really nice, plus he seemed like a boyfriend instead of just a friend. And he was super good-looking. Maybe a little bit on the quiet side, but that wasn't necessarily something you had to criticize, as long as the person was friendly.

But Cleve was drunk out of his mind. She just couldn't believe it. The only good thing was that he hadn't come with Colette. She had made some lame excuse, and he didn't even act like he expected anyone to believe it. "A terrible headache" or something. Danielle couldn't even hardly remember. Because the main thing was that from the second he had kissed her hello and happy birthday, you could tell he was super-smashed, and he had bumped into the wall on the way in and almost fallen over in the hallway. And the dumb part was that she had thought, I'm not going to put any vodka in the living room, like that would solve something. When the truth was that first thing, he had drunk one of the beers really fast, and then he just went into the kitchen and found a whole new bottle of vodka. So it had been a joke, thinking he maybe wouldn't be drinking.

Plus Allan was jumpy and nervous, like some kind of cat or something. And she had felt, at first, Well, he's nervous about meeting Cleve. Which would have been easy to understand and even would have made her feel good, like he cared and was tense. But he and Cleve hadn't hardly said two words to each other, so that probably wasn't even it.

"You're pretty," Cleve suddenly said.

Danielle looked up. Cleve was leaning back in the butterfly chair so far he was almost lying down, and he was looking across at Maura.

"Thank you," Maura said. But she looked nervous.

"Don't look so surprised," he said.

Maura didn't say anything, but she looked super-uncomfortable.

"You're not so overweight, you know."

Now her face was bright red. "Did I say I was?"

Cleve turned to Danielle. "She's not so overweight."

"Dad—"

Cleve stood up. "Look at her. She's got a beautiful face. Did you ever see such a beautiful face?" He leaned down to put his cigarette out, but suddenly he looked like he was tipping over, almost like one of those movies where you see the western men cutting trees, and the trees fall super-slowly at first, except that he crashed into the table, and it sounded like he hit his head really hard. But right away he got up, like nothing had even happened.

Danielle looked at Allan. He was looking at his watch, and for that second, she hated him. Why was he wondering what time it was? And it made her feel bad because when they had found it in Atlantic City (under the bed), they had been all lovey-dovey. But now it was like he was in another world.

Cleve was moving toward the doorway. "Anybody for some ice?"

Nobody said anything. The party had turned bad.

When he was gone, Danielle looked at Allan. "What do you think I should do?"

"Don't worry about it, to begin with," he said. "Everyone here is your friend."

"But what about *him*?"

"He can take care of himself."

She heard a door slam shut, and she looked at Maura. "That was the front door, right?"

Maura nodded. "Maybe Larkin's home."

Danielle stood up. She knew it wasn't Larkin. Her father had gone. It was the kind of thing he had always done, and it always drove her mother crazy; he'd leave just like that.

She walked down the hall and looked in the kitchen. His coat, where he had flopped it onto the chair, was gone. So he had gone, just like that. And the bottle of vodka—it had been new, she knew, because Larkin had bought it just last night, and it was hers, actually. But it was empty.

She went back to the living room, but just Maura and Keefe were there.

"Where's Allan?" she asked, feeling a little flip in her stomach. Even though he couldn't've gone, too, but where was he?

"I don't know," Maura said. "Maybe in the bathroom."

She had a bad, flip-type feeling, and she went to see. The bathroom was empty, but then she heard voices, like a TV, coming from Larkin's room, and she opened the door, half-open.

Allan was sitting on the bed, right in front of the TV, with the remote in his hand.

"What are you doing?" she asked.

He turned around real suddenly. "Oh. Hi, honey. I just wanted to check on something."

"What are you checking?" Her voice had come out super-quietly. It didn't even sound like hers.

He was looking at the screen, and he said something about "the game," but she couldn't hear him.

"My father left," she said.

He didn't say anything.

"Did you hear me?"

"Just a second," he said.

She turned and walked out, and she felt like she was caving in or her mind was about to burst. What was the matter with Allan? What was the matter with everybody? How come he hadn't even brought her a present, and Cleve hadn't either? How come they didn't know it was "just a saying" to say "no presents"?

She looked into the living room, and Maura and Keefe were talking like two lovebirds, their heads real close together, and she didn't feel like going in.

" 'Bye," she suddenly said.

Maura looked up. "What? What's the matter?"

"If Allan wants to know where I am, just tell him I'm gone, okay?"

Maura stood up. "Danielle, what's going on?"

"Nothing. Just tell him, okay?"

She marched out—she felt like some kind of soldier—and then she burst into tears when she got out into the hallway. She didn't even know what had made her feel so crazy, except that the party hadn't turned out the way she had thought it would. Even though she had said to herself, "They're always disasters," secretly she had hoped: "This one will be different, because I have Allan." But he had let her down.

* * *

Allan looked everywhere for Danielle, but he didn't know where to look. Where did someone like Danielle go? Everyone she knew in New York was in the apartment. He had screwed up, and he knew it—he wasn't paying attention; he hadn't even realized Cleve had gone until he had gone out to the living room and Maura had said. So naturally Danielle had been upset. But he hadn't *known*.

He walked down Broadway, past mostly closed stores, and then as he passed a bar, he heard a cheer, and he stopped.

The Giants.

He turned around and went in. Two TVs on the wall.

His heart was beating so fast, he didn't know if his voice would even come out.

"Giant's win?" he called out.

"Yeah, yeah," a guy at the bar said.

But there was a goddamn commercial, so no score.

"So what was the score?" he asked. Casually. Make it happen. Please please please.

"Twenty-one fourteen. Incredible game."

So he had lost. They had won, but he had lost.

"You sure?" he managed to ask. "Twenty-one?"

The guy looked at him with fishy eyes. "Yeah, twenty-one. You want to argue? Who asked who?"

Allan held up his hands. "Forget it," he said, and he walked out.

He was in deep, deep shit.

Thirty-eight

"Hi there," Terence said. "How's the party?"

"Over," Maura said, cradling the receiver against her neck.

"Is Keefe still there?"

"Keefe? Sure. Do you want to talk to him?"

"Yes. And get to the office early tomorrow, all right, Maura? Alexandra will be in at nine."

That'll be the day, she said to herself, and went into the living room to get Keefe. They were the only two left after the party—Allan had gone right after Danielle.

"It's Terence on the phone," she said. He was watching "60 Minutes." "You can take it in here."

"Thanks. *Hi*," he said into the phone. "What's up? . . . Uh-huh. *Really* . . . Okay. We'll be there. Or I'll be there. . . . Right." He hung up and looked up at Maura. "How'd you like to go over to Terence's?"

"Now?"

"Yeah. He just got a script from a director—some friend of his—and he wants me to read a part."

"I thought you were Alexandra's client."

He shrugged. "Terence has been more responsive. Does it make a difference?"

"Of course it does. You're either a client of one or the other. If they split—"

He was standing up. "I don't know about that. All I know is that he has a part that sounds great. Do you want to come?"

She didn't know what she wanted. Of course she wanted to go, and they left the apartment. But as they stood together on the subway and it was too loud to talk, she tried to look at Keefe as if through someone else's eyes.

He was *so* good-looking. And he was nice and funny and generous, everything she would want in a man except for two things. He wasn't all that smart, and he had never laid a hand on her.

Well, that wasn't quite true. He had kissed her several times in the two weeks since they'd first met, and they weren't brother-sister pecks on the cheek. But they weren't anything special, either—a brush against the lips, a hesitant hand at the waist, and that was it.

And she had tried not to think of the obvious: Alexandra was right and he was "using" her, and/or he couldn't stand to go any further because she wasn't attractive to him.

"Remind me to make a call when we leave Terence's," he said. "I've got someone staying with me—a friend from Pennsylvania—he's been staying on my floor while he's been looking for work. You don't know anyone who needs a piano tuner, do you?"

"Nope. That's what he is?"

He nodded, but he looked distracted.

"What's the matter?" she asked.

He was hesitating. Finally he said: "Tell me the truth, Maura.

Do you think Alexandra and Terence are good agents? I mean, are they legit and all that?''

"Of course. Why?''

"I don't know. I guess because they're the only agents who have taken any interest in me at all. I mean at *all*. And you'd think—'' He stopped.

"You'd think if you were good that someone else would be interested, too?''

"Well, yes.''

They climbed the steps to the entryway of Terence and Max's place and rang the buzzer. "Forget it,'' Maura said. "It doesn't work that way.'' She pushed open the door at the sound of the buzzer, and they started up the three flights of stairs. "Sure, once someone's *famous*, and sure in a few cases even at the beginning, but just because no one else is interested in you doesn't mean Alexandra and Terence aren't legit.'' She smiled. "Got it?''

"I think.''

"Which isn't to say there aren't a lot of really unscrupulous agents in this town. But Alexandra and Terence are for real. They're doing well. So stop worrying.''

They were in front of Terence and Max's door, and Maura rang the bell.

"I don't know what I'd do without you,'' Keefe said, and he kissed her—another brush on the lips—just as the door opened.

"Ah. Lovers in a world of their own,'' Terence said. "Come in, come in.''

Keefe walked in first, and Terence gave Maura an amazed smile, eyes wide, as she followed.

"So,'' Terence said, putting his hands together. "Wine? Beer? None for you,'' he said to Keefe. "You've got work to do. Coffee? Tea?''

"Coffee's fine for me,'' Maura said.

"Same. Hey, this is a great place. Can I look around?''

"Sure,'' Terence called from the kitchen, gesturing for Maura to come over. When Keefe was at the other end of the loft, Terence leaned forward confidentially. "So, Maura. Tell. Tell.''

"Tell what?'' she asked, knowing full well what he was talking about.

"Oh, come on. The meeting of two souls. The fateful kiss at the doorsteps. How long has this been going on, and why haven't you told me about it?''

"There's nothing to tell. Really.''

"Have you slept with him?"

"Terence." She turned and walked away, something you just had to do with Terence every so often.

Keefe was standing in front of a painting, very modern, something a friend of Terence's had done. "You like this?" Keefe asked, standing back and tilting his head.

"Nope. Do you?" she asked.

"I don't get it. But I don't know anything about art like this."

"Don't say that. If you don't get it, it means it isn't that good. You like some modern art, right?"

"Sure. I guess."

"So it isn't necessarily you."

Terence was coming down the length of the loft. "Isn't necessarily you what?"

"Nothing," Keefe said quickly.

"Neither of us can stand the painting," Maura said. "And I was just telling Keefe—if he doesn't 'get' something, it isn't his fault. If it's good, you'll get it."

"I didn't say I couldn't stand it," Keefe said.

"It's my favorite painting," Terence said.

Maura could practically see the wheels turning in Keefe's head. It was going to be a test.

"Yeah, well, it kind of grows on you." He shrugged.

"Really?" Maura said. She couldn't resist: "So what does it say now?"

Keefe grinned and put a hand across his chest. "Hey, come on. You're asking a guy from Scranton?"

"That's right."

"Well, shit. I don't know. It says: 'This is your agent's painting. Don't you *kind* of like it?' "

Terence laughed and looked at Maura. "Touché," he said. "And the coffee is ready."

They went over and sat down in the middle, living-room area of the loft, and Terence was just starting to tell Keefe about the part when the door opened and Max came in with his dog, a white and brown hound with a gray muzzle that had obviously once been brown.

"Hi, everybody." Max gave Sophie a scratch behind the ears and she lumbered over to the kitchen to her water bowl.

"Our resident major drinker," Terence said. "She won't stay off the sauce no matter *how* much Max talks to her. How was the vet?" he asked, swiveling around in his chair to face Max.

A cloud passed over Max's face. "Fine," he said, not sounding at all as if he meant it. He walked over to the kitchen and gave Sophie another scratch behind the ear, as if he didn't want to leave her alone.

"What did he say about the moles on her face?"

"Leave them alone," Max said, so quietly Maura almost hadn't heard him.

"What?" Terence asked.

"He said to leave them alone."

Terence was shaking his head. "What a shame."

"What are you talking about?" Maura asked.

"The dog has this gorgeous face—really, she could have been in commercials if I had met her when she was younger—but she has these *moles* growing on her face now. And *I* thought they should be taken off."

"Why?"

"Because they're awful to look at," he said with a shrug of his shoulders. But he must have seen the look in her eyes, because he added, and quickly: "And because they might be cancerous, obviously."

"Bullshit," Maura said. "You just said that because you know how it sounds. Criticizing a dog's looks? Why not give her a nose job?" Out of the corner of her eye she saw Max crouching on the floor, feeding Sophie and patting her. You could tell from the sway of her back that she was old. "Why don't you have Max dye her hair? She's getting a little gray around the muzzle."

"You don't believe anything I say these days, do you?" Terence said, picking up his coffee. "I'm genuinely concerned, Maura."

"Right. Why don't we drop it?"

"Fine with me." He smiled artificially at Keefe. "Don't pay attention to our little spats, Keefe. We've been having them for years."

Keefe just shrugged his shoulders.

"Well," Terence said, putting his hands together. "Enough about dogs and lifelong spats. How would you like to read for Dorian Christopher?"

"You're kidding."

"I never kid," Terence said.

"Dorian Christopher? You know him?"

"Certainly. And I told him about you, and he'd like to meet you."

"You're kidding."

"Please, Keefe. You're beginning to sound incredibly one-noted. I'm not kidding about any of this."

"Well, shit. When did you meet him? I mean when did you tell him about me?"

"Last night at a party. Anyway, long story. But he *would* like to meet you, and I told him you'd be well prepared."

Maura stood up and started to walk across the loft.

"Where are you going?" Terence called out.

"I thought you'd want to talk privately. And I want to talk to Max."

"I want you to learn. If you're going to become an agent, you have to *learn*, Maura."

"Read the script," she said. "Write a bio of the character—his past, his hopes, et cetera et cetera. What he wears, hates, eats, loves. Get a good night's sleep. Call you—or me, actually—before the audition to confirm time and place. Learn the scene backwards and forwards. Uh, let's see—"

"Go talk to Max."

Max was finishing the last of the coffee. "You sound a little fed up," he said, leaning back against the counter. "I thought it would be an interesting job for you."

"It is, it is. It's just that at times . . . well, you live with Terence and you know Alexandra, so you'll know what I'm talking about when I say they're not exactly easy to get along with. I know it's a great job. It's just that they drive me up the wall."

"He thinks you're doing a terrific job; I know that, Maura. He talks about you all the time."

"Really?"

Max nodded. "He's talked about making you an agent in a year or so, also. Although now that I've said it, I probably shouldn't have told you."

"I won't say anything. I'm amazed, though."

"He's *always* talked about you." He looked across the loft to where Terence and Keefe were talking, heads together, voices lowered. "He *is* good at it."

"I know. He really is. And he does seem to care about the people he represents. I didn't know he had even noticed Keefe."

Max didn't say anything. Then: "You want some more coffee?"

But the phone rang, and he picked it up at the end of the kitchen counter. At first he was talking so quietly, Maura couldn't understand what he was saying—she was crouched on the floor patting Sophie, who had lain down after eating only a few bites of her food.

"Oh. Great," Max said, suddenly more loudly. "No, I don't understand. We . . . Right." He turned his back, and Maura stood up to give him some room, but he turned around and waved her back, and then gestured at Sophie as if to say, "Keep patting her." "Uh, no," he said. "I didn't have time. We had a vet appointment, remember? . . . Well, just okay. She needs some tests. . . . A blood test, an X-ray they couldn't do today—" He got down on his knees and stroked the dog along her muzzle. "I think so," he said quietly. "No, don't. It's not your fault. . . . Okay, talk to you later."

He stood up and hung up the phone, and Maura stood up, too.

"So," she said, half wishing she hadn't overheard the conversation.

"So," he said, looking a little doubtful. "Where were we?"

"It doesn't matter. Is she okay? Sophie, I mean? I couldn't help overhearing. When does she have to have those tests?"

"Starting tomorrow. I couldn't get enough time away from the office today. We're preparing a huge case against the city, and as it is, I can't even always get home to walk her in the middle of the day."

"You come home to walk Sophie?"

"Sure. The office is only eight blocks away. Why? You think I'm crazy, don't you."

"No, I think it's magnificent. You work for this yuppie law firm, and everyone else is probably going to the health club or meeting with their broker or their analyst, and you're taking your dog out."

She knelt down and gave Sophie another scratch. "But then, I would, too, if I had a dog like you, silly."

"Hey! Scranton!" Terence called across the loft. "Come get your boyfriend. Make him go home and rehearse all night. I'll give you flowers in the morning if he gets to the audition on time."

Boyfriend indeed, she felt like saying. A few unexciting kisses.

Keefe came across the loft with the script in his hand, and she didn't think she had ever seen him look so happy. "You're not going to believe this script, Maura. You're just not going to believe it." He turned to Max. "Have you seen this?"

"It's for your eyes only, I think."

"What?"

"I don't think it's for general circulation. But Terence said it was really good."

Keefe looked at Maura. "Will you help me with my lines?"

"Sure. But we'd better get started."

"Let's go. See you, Max. And Terence, I'll call you tomorrow."

They left after a bunch of good-byes, a slurpy one from Sophie, and went back to Keefe's apartment. The piano tuner friend wasn't there, and they had the place to themselves—a small bedroom, a living room/kitchen, a half bath, all dingier than anyplace Maura had ever seen except in the movies.

But suddenly the evening was beginning to feel romantic. Keefe had had his arm around her on the walk all the way across town, and he was opening a bottle of wine, another good sign.

And then flashes of Patrick and Vince: "You really oughta lose some weight, Maura." "Just don't think you're going to get all kinds of other guys, Maura." And a voice inside said, "Are you *crazy*? Keefe is gorgeous. Why would he have anything to do with *you*?"

But she had lost some weight—

And he liked her—

And—

"Let's have a toast," he said, bringing in some glasses and setting the wine down on the table. "In a year I'll be a star, you'll be my agent, and we'll be on the beach somewhere, soaking up the sun and celebrating my first big contract."

"Sounds great."

"And until then—" He paused. "I have a surprise." For a second, he almost looked as if he were blushing. "I never seem to get you alone," he said. "And I thought—if you wanted—that we could go up to a friend of mine's cabin this weekend. If you wanted to. And if you aren't busy."

"Keefe, I'd love to. Where is it?"

"Upstate in the mountains. It's supposed to be really nice, really private."

"It sounds great."

"Good, good." He sipped his wine.

"Keefe?"

"Mm," he said.

"We're alone now."

He was a great kisser once he got started, and Maura couldn't believe how good it felt, how much she had wanted to feel this way again, to have someone touching her.

She heard a sound and then another sound: the front door slamming shut. Keefe jerked and then moved away from her. "Tim, hi!" he called out—too loudly, she felt, more like a teenager who'd been walked in on by his parents.

A tall blond guy walked in, all arms and skinny legs. He *looked* like a piano tuner, though, oddly enough. Half-scientific, half weird-musical. "Hey," he said.

"Maura's helping me with some lines," Keefe said. "Oh— Maura, Tim. Tim, Maura. My agent got me an unbelievable audition for tomorrow."

Tim was looking at Maura rather than at Keefe, and she had an odd feeling, as if she were being too carefully observed. "That's great," he said, taking a beer out of the refrigerator. "I'll leave you two alone," he said, and walked into the bedroom and shut the door.

Keefe wasn't looking at her.

"Have I missed something?" she asked.

"No. Let's read the script, okay?"

She moved closer to him and read the cue, and he started reading his lines. But he sounded completely wooden and detached. Something was bothering him—and she didn't know what it was.

Thirty-nine

The club was totally crowded, but Danielle didn't even feel nervous. She was a good dealer—no one even had to tell her that—and she would be able to handle the crowd. And if they didn't let her deal tonight, she'd just do the waitressing. She didn't even care. Just as long as she didn't have to think about the party.

Nick was being pit boss over by the roulette, which was good, because another pit boss definitely wouldn't open up a new table just because a dealer felt like dealing an extra shift. But Nick liked her. So maybe he'd say yes.

She walked up to the ropes, but his back was turned.

"Hi, Nick."

He turned around, and his whole face kind of lit up. "Hey, Danielle." He frowned. "This is your day off."

"I know. But I felt like working. Um, is there a chance?"

He laughed. "That's a new one, someone wanting to work extra days.'' He looked at his watch. ''Give me a few minutes, and Pete can take over for me.''

''Okay.''

A girl she hated was doing the dealing at the next table. What a snob. Which was weird, because one of the best things about dealing was that you didn't meet a billion snobs, even with the players. Everyone was super down-to-earth.

Except for this one, Suzette. It was even a fake name, Danielle had discovered. And everyone hated her. Why didn't she work on the fifth floor, where the girls were hookers? It was sure what ''Suzette'' sounded like. Except that Danielle had met a few of them, and they had seemed super-nice. It was just that she acted so superior. Who did she think she was?

''Thirty-three,'' Suzette called out. ''The number is thirty-three.''

She didn't even have any expression in her voice. Where was the excitement? It was supposed to be a game and fun, not an announcement at a funeral.

''Let's go,'' Nick said, putting a hand on her back.

''Um, can I work?''

''We can talk about it,'' he said. ''Come with me.''

They walked past the roulette tables and the craps tables and through the doors to one of her favorite parts of the club, the velvety stairs. They weren't really covered in actual velvet, but the carpeting was maroonish purple and super-soft, and the walls were covered with a silky maroon and gold-type material. Really like a dream.

''Let's go upstairs,'' he said.

That meant to the fifth floor, where she had never been except to look around.

''Um—''

''I want to talk to you,'' he said.

They got upstairs, and it was fancier than she had remembered— more gold walls, but with furniture right out of ''Dynasty'' or one of those TV movies about rich people.

''We can go in here,'' he said, opening a creamy white and gold door.

She had heard all the rooms were different. There was a western-type room with antlers on the walls and things like that, and a French provincial, which was an architectural style, and a super-modern.

This was one of the more normal ones, she guessed, kind of like a den in someone's house.

Nick sat down on this big leather couch and patted the cushion next to where he was sitting. "Have a seat."

A voice went off in her head, the one that always warned her: "Something's about to happen."

But it was also a dare, kind of an invitation to see. She almost never turned back when the warning went off.

She sat down next to him and crossed her legs.

"So," he said. "What's all this about working an extra night?"

She shrugged. "I just feel like it. That's all."

"You like it that much, huh?"

"Uh-huh."

He put a finger under her chin. "You like me?"

"Sure." She felt her face getting red. "Of course."

"Come here," he said.

He pulled her close and kissed her, and for a second she thought: Allan. The man she loved. But she didn't feel like she loved him right now. He just flew out of her mind, and she started kissing Nick back.

"Mm. I knew you'd be a great kisser," he said, laying her back on the couch. "You know, I've wanted to do this from the first time I saw you," he said, kissing her lips and then moving down to her neck.

Something about him felt great, the way he was moving against her. *Allan*, she thought again when Nick undid her blouse and touched her. But suddenly she didn't care. She just wanted to have a good time and forget.

"Mm, mm," he said, nibbling at her ear. "More fun than working, huh?"

She felt horrible, worse than she could say, even.

For one thing, she had forgotten to use anything. Not that she had ever gotten pregnant in her whole life even though she had forgotten a million times. But she had stopped taking the pill with Allan, and then with Nick—

Allan.

That was the worst part.

She was still mad at him, but it didn't mean she had to cheat on him.

"So what do you say?" Nick said. His breath felt too hot in her ear all of a sudden.

"Um, I have to go."

"How can you have to go? If I'd've put you to work, you'd still be working."

"I know. But I forgot something."

"What'd you forget? What could you need that you don't have right here?"

Allan, she said to herself. She had been super-upset, and now she had cheated, and she felt worse than ever.

Forty

"You'd be *perfect*," Alexandra gushed from the other room. "Gloria, I *promise* you."

This was the worst. This was definitely the worst interview—or whatever you called them—that Maura had ever heard.

Gloria Stone wasn't a client of Fielding-White. She was an independent, which meant that Fielding-White represented her for certain projects, mostly plays. But she was free to—and did—work through other agencies, too.

Which meant that not only was Alexandra being her usual hypocritical self; she was also nervous and trying too hard.

A burst of laughter—theatrical and female and low-pitched—came from the inner office, and a second later, Gloria and Alexandra came into the reception area.

"Maura, be a darling and call Gloria a cab."

"Oh, that's all right," Gloria said. "I can get one over on Sixth."

"Don't be silly. That's what we pay her for. Maura?"

Maura picked up the phone. "You might want to sit down," she said to Gloria. "It sometimes takes a while." Bitch, she added silently.

"I really must run," Gloria said to Alexandra. "Would you do me another favor, Maura, and call this number—" She said the last few words as if she were speaking to a child. Then, slowly, "Five, five, five, nine three, five three. Do you have that?"

"Yes," Maura said.

"Would you read it back to me?"

Maura sighed. "Five, five, five, nine three, five three. Right?"

"It's a Maurice Hartell you'll be speaking to. Do you have that? Maurice—"

"Hartell," Maura said.

"Good. Please tell him that Gloria Stone will be a *few* minutes late, but that I *have* the tickets. All right?"

"Few minutes late, have tickets. I think I can remember that."

"Good." She kissed Alexandra on the cheek and left in a cloud of perfume.

"Take care of that call right away," Alexandra called over her shoulder as she went into her office. But then she came back out. "And when you're finished, I need you to run some errands for me." She had a shopping bag in one hand.

"Yes?"

"These sweaters need to be taken to the cleaners. The French cleaners on Sixth and Fifty-third. The top one needs to have the elbows rewoven. The *red* one, all right? And then these"—she set a manila envelope on Maura's desk—"have to go to Dorian Christopher's apartment."

"What about a messenger?"

"It's six blocks from the cleaners. You can be there and back in twenty minutes."

"All right. I'll do it after I finish the contracts."

"Do it after the phone call, Maura. Dorian needs the pictures right away—he's in the middle of the auditions."

"At his apartment?"

"It's a loft, actually, and it's his office, too. You'll see when you go there, and I'd like you to get there before noon."

"All right."

Maura made the phone call, gathered what she had to take on the errands, and left. Try not to despise this job as much as you do, she told herself.

But why was it that even the job with George Falcone had been more glamorous than this one had turned out to be?

Dorian Christopher's loft was in an industrial, probably fashion-related building on Seventh Avenue, one of those places Maura had recently learned always looked awful and dingy on the outside and amazing on the inside.

When she got up to the twelfth floor, the top, and rang, there was no answer, and she thought of just slipping the envelope under the door. But she could just imagine when she got back to the agency: Alexandra's annoyed, condescending questions: "You *what*? Why didn't you wait? He was sending me something back." Or: "You *what*? Don't you know you have to make sure these people actually *get* the pictures? Do you know how much *mail* these people get?"

So she knocked again, then tried the door. It was open.

It was an enormous place—once a factory, she guessed. Obviously there were rooms she couldn't see, because there was a hallway that began about fifty feet from where she was standing. But the main room itself was five times—at least—as big as the apartment uptown. And its vastness was emphasized by the stark decor, all low tables and couches, almost everything either black or white.

"Hello?" she called out.

Nothing.

But *someone* had to be here; they wouldn't have just left the door to this enormous place unlocked.

"Hello?" she said more loudly.

She heard a sound and she followed it. It had come from the direction of the hallway, and she went through the doorway to the hall and started down it.

She passed a room, and something registered under the surface, and she kept going and then stopped.

People.

She turned and went back and stopped dead.

They had heard her, clearly, but they were as paralyzed as she was—two men in bed: Keefe and Dorian Christopher. And suddenly her thoughts turned weirdly scientific and unemotional: how odd it looked, two men together, two sets of large shoulders and flat chests, masculine legs.

"Excuse *us*," Dorian Christopher said, and he leaned off the bed to flick the door with his hand, and it slammed shut in Maura's face.

She didn't know what she did with the envelope—she didn't even remember leaving. All she knew was that after a while she was out on the street and her heart was pounding and she was walking as fast as she could.

When she got back to the office, everything was the same. Why had she expected it to be different?

But she had. So much had changed. Christ, what a fool.

"Did you see Dorian?" Alexandra asked.

"Uh-huh." Alexandra couldn't have set it up, could she have?

It was impossible. But might she have suspected, wanted to take a chance? Have a little fun? Prove her point? ("Don't say you haven't been warned," she had said.)

But Keefe had been different; she was sure. He was so *nice*.

But he had had secrets, too. What about his houseguest's poutiness? Tim hadn't acted like the usual friend grateful for a floor to sleep on. He had acted like Keefe's lover.

She closed her eyes and thought about his offer of a weekend, and then the way he had looked in bed with Dorian Christopher.

God, what a fool she had been.

Forty-one

Allan walked into the bank, turned around, and walked out.

Christ, he had to get a hold of himself. What if one of the account officers had seen him? A sweating middle-aged man, as suspicious-looking as they came. And why? Why would a man who was opening an account be sweating like a pig?

He took a deep breath and walked back in. He had the briefcase in his hand, he had the right suit, he had the papers—*some* of the papers—so he was all set.

There was a long line, of course. But that was good. It meant the officer would be in a hurry—maybe, if he was lucky. And not too interested in the fact he didn't have the d/b/a papers.

"Yes?"

He turned to where the voice had come from, a black woman coming from a desk way down at the end behind the counter. She was looking straight at him.

"I believe these people are ahead of me," he said, gesturing.

"They're being helped."

Great. The first time in the history of banking that he had jumped to the front of the line.

"Well, uh . . ." Christ, *say* it. "I'd like to open a business account. I've got most of the papers you'll need right here," he said, snapping open his briefcase.

"Most?" she asked loudly, and he jumped; he hadn't expected her to pounce on the word like that. But he hadn't wanted to say "all," or he'd look like he didn't know what he was doing.

"Yeah, well, the corporation's splitting up," he said, "and the city screwed up on the d/b/a papers. Lost in the system, they said. You know, when you go down there on a day when the computer's down, you might as well save your time and turn right around and go home. I've done it a thousand times, and it's always the same." While he talked, he handed her one piece of paper after another so at least it would seem as if he had most of it.

At first she didn't say anything.

Then: "We'll need the d/b/a papers within thirty days."

"Fine," he said. In thirty days he could make back the money and close the account easy.

"Do you have any deposits?"

"Just one." Now his heart was pounding.

He pulled out his wallet and looked at the check, made out to B&Z Velvets, and he saw an odd look come into the woman's eyes. *Wrong move, you turkey.* Why had he put the check in his *wallet*? He should have been carrying it with the papers.

Don't say anything. An excuse will make you look even more suspicious.

He handed it to her, and she took the check and some of the papers and walked to the back, and he let out his breath.

Thirteen G's. He was going to pay back the whole debt, wash his hands of Joseph King, and—

"Mr. Greshner."

The woman was back at the counter, and she didn't look happy.

"Yes?" You're under arrest for embezzlement. We called the number you gave, and the company doesn't exist. We—

"You didn't endorse the check," she said.

He let out another breath and hoped she hadn't noticed he had been holding it. "Here you go," he said, signing. "How soon will I be able to draw on this, by the way?"

She glanced at the check. "Three business days."

He nodded. He had planned on three to five. He could give King the whole amount plus the interest in three days. "Fine," he said. "Do you need me for anything else, then? I have an appointment across town, and traffic—"

"You can go," she said. "We'll send you your documents this afternoon."

He smiled and beat it out of there as fast as he could.

Christ. He had done it. It had been easy. It didn't even feel like stealing—just moving money from one line to the other. But he couldn't forget it *was* stealing, that he had to put it back—and soon—or else.

For now, though, he felt great. He had the first payment, and he'd have the rest in a few days. He had done good, as his father used to say. Allan, you did good.

It had definitely been weird at the club tonight, Danielle felt. Nick—it wasn't like he was some huge super-jealous type. He was the type of guy who felt he was too cool for that. But he was different to her, definitely different. Kind of questioning, super-confident as usual, but with a question in his eyes.

Which was okay, she guessed, as long as she didn't have to answer The Question. She never wanted to be with him again, that was for sure. And the thing that disgusted her most was that she realized it was exactly the kind of thing her mother had always done, getting really upset about something and then just kind of going on the fritz. Once in Venice they had been talking on the beach, and Victoria saw this guy she really liked, one of the million young guys she hung around with at the cafés. Except that he was with another girl, or maybe you should say "a girl," since Victoria wasn't exactly young at that point. But anyway, she just went crazy and picked up practically the first guy she saw, a super-tan, super-hairy guy at Muscle Beach who was working out. And she said to Danielle, "Come home in about four hours."

Or another time, also over a guy, when he had stood her up, and she had said to Danielle, "Let's go for a drive," and they had ended up going all the way to Montana. "I heard the men were normal here," Victoria had said.

And the thing was, when Cleve had disappeared like that, and then Allan watching TV, she had snapped just the way Victoria would have. Not enough attention, she guessed, even though the feeling had been: My life is over. She couldn't even explain why, it just felt totally dramatic and she had hated Allan more than anyone, and then, like a bunch of dominoes, she had hated everyone in the whole world, even Maura, who hadn't done a thing.

But the Nick part made her realize she was acting crazy, and she didn't want to be that way. Her father—well, he had called this morning to say "Hi" and that he was sorry, he had just kind of "drifted out," and she felt bad, and it made her realize there were more important things than her stupid birthday party. Like was he going to stop drinking and would he be okay? Things like that. He still passed the "love test" in her mind.

But Allan. She didn't know what to think. He couldn't've called her today at the club, so she couldn't complain, but what about tonight? She felt he'd better call or else, just to say—she didn't really know. But maybe to apologize because he hadn't really been all that great. So there.

She signed out at the front desk and left the club, and she felt a lump in her throat just thinking about that first night with Allan, how he had been so nice, the first person in the longest time who wanted to know how she felt and all that.

And now—

"There you are."

She turned around and there was Allan, coming down the street with flowers in his hand. "Hey, kid," he said. "You like roses?"

She looked inside. It looked like there were a million. Then she looked into his eyes.

"I owe you," he said. "I'm sorry."

She bit her lip. She had thought maybe she'd make some big speech, but it was hard, looking into the eyes she loved. And she didn't want to sound like a baby, talking about her "party" like it was the most giant thing in the world. "Well," she said.

"I didn't even realize Cleve had left," he said.

"That's because you were watching the stupid TV."

"I know. And I'm sorry." He kissed her and took her in his arms, and right then she looked across the street; she didn't know why. And Nick was walking down the sidewalk, right opposite from where they were, and she swore he had seen them and stared. Which wouldn't be that weird, but he seemed to kind of be lingering.

"Forgive me?" Allan said.

She shrugged. "Of course I forgive you. I just—it wasn't the greatest day for me."

He sighed. He felt like a piece of shit. He had meant every word: he wished he could take back the whole afternoon; he wished he could have been a hero. Instead he had what? Spent that night worrying about money and the next day lying to get his hands on more.

But it had nothing to do with Danielle, and he meant every word now: he really was sorry.

"How about trying again?" he said. "Have our own birthday celebration, just the two of us."

For a moment she hesitated. But then she said, "Um, let's get Chinese, okay?" and she took his arm.

"Anything you want," he said.

God, he loved her. And it *would* work out.

Forty-two

"I feel so bad," Danielle said.

Maura sighed. Danielle was always so extremely happy or extremely upset. She didn't go into depressions the way Larkin did, and she certainly didn't drink to drown her sorrows. But they both had such extreme mood swings. "I can see why you feel you made a mistake sleeping with Nick, but it's over. You won't sleep with him again, and just try not to have that much to do with him."

Danielle was biting her lip.

"What is it?" Maura asked. "Is there something else?" She realized she sounded impatient, but she was: She had to talk to Larkin about something important, and it was important that she talk to her alone. And Danielle was taking all morning to eat breakfast, and Larkin wasn't even up yet.

"I don't know," Danielle said with a sigh. "It's so hard to think about things ever working out with anybody a hundred percent, you know? I mean, don't you wonder about you and Keefe, like how it can always stay really good? You guys seemed to get along so well at the party, but don't you sometimes wonder?"

"Keefe and I aren't going out together," Maura said. "We were just friends."

"What do you mean, 'were'? Like you're not anymore?"

Maura took a deep breath. "We had a falling out." She looked at her watch. "Do you have nine-twenty?"

"Uh-huh."

"Have you heard anything coming from Larkin's room?"

Danielle shook her head. "I don't think she's up yet. I didn't hear anything."

Maura stood up. "I'll be right back." But as she headed down the hall, she heard water in the bathroom, and she went back to the kitchen.

"Did you wake her up?" Danielle asked.

"Nope. She's up. Which is just as well. She always hates to be woken up. At Yale she used to tell outright lies in her sleep to try to convince me she didn't have to get up."

"But why does she have to even get up? Now, I mean?"

"She has an audition," Maura said. "Something I heard about at work."

"God. That's great. That you can do that, I mean. She must be so excited."

"Well, in her own way. It's tough for her."

"You mean the auditions, or what?"

"I think all of it," Maura said. "At Yale she amazed everybody with her performances, but it scared her. She never took the route she could have taken."

"What kind of route?"

"Well, most people make really great connections there, for one thing. They go right into classes or productions with people they've met there, but she didn't want to do that. She purposely screwed things up so that certain people refused to work with her—"

"They refused?"

Maura nodded. "She committed all kinds of what they considered to be cardinal sins. Showing up drunk for a rehearsal, which absolutely crossed her off the list of someone really important who had seen her as his next discovery."

"God. She must have been totally upset."

"She was and she wasn't. She had planned the whole thing. Trying to seduce the husband of one of her acting professors was another brilliant move. Things like that over and over again. So that by the time she came to New York, she had cut off what could have been amazing ties."

"Oh *God*," Larkin said, coming in and rubbing her eyes. "Someone tell me my clock's wrong and I have four more hours to sleep."

"You don't even have four minutes," Maura said. She stood up and put the water on to boil again as Larkin sank into a chair. "Don't let her put her head down," she said to Danielle.

Danielle smiled. "Are you kidding?"

"She'll fall asleep at the wheel of a car at this hour."

"Cigarette," Larkin said, looking around.

"On the counter," Maura called. "How are you feeling?"

"Like hell." Larkin put her head in her hands. "I think I'll skip this one, Maura."

Maura put an extra half teaspoon of coffee in Larkin's cup and brought it to her. "Decide after you wake up."

"Did you put in extra coffee?"

"Of course," she said. She winked at Danielle. "One of the tricks I learned at Yale."

Larkin smiled. "So I missed half my classes instead of all of them. They should have given Maura my diploma at the end."

"God," Danielle said.

"Not really," Maura said, finding she was almost annoyed at Danielle's naïveté this morning. But what she had to talk to Larkin about made her nervous.

Finally Danielle got up—Maura wasn't saying anything, and Larkin was half-asleep—and Maura girded herself. She didn't know why she was so nervous about this—Larkin was her best friend. But she couldn't find the words.

She got herself another cup of coffee and brought it over to the table. "Listen," she said. "I've been thinking. What if I wanted to be your agent?"

"You're kidding."

"Really. What about it? You'd have every actor's dream, being your agent's only client."

"What about Keefe?"

Maura took a sip of coffee. She hadn't told Larkin what had happened. "Not that it was ever anything other than in my own mind, but whatever it was is over. I found Keefe in bed with Dorian Christopher when I went to drop off some pictures."

"Oh *no*. You're *kidding*."

"Is it that amazing? I was surprised, too, but I felt I shouldn't have been. Just another unrealistic fantasy on my part."

"Well, you're lucky you found out sooner rather than later."

"There wouldn't have ever been a later. And you're not answering my question. How would you feel about having me as your agent? If I asked Terence and Alexandra, obviously. I haven't asked them yet, but I don't want to unless I know your answer."

"You must be crazy to even ask me," Larkin said.

Shit. "What do you mean?"

"You dope, of *course* the answer is yes. Come on. How could you ever think I'd say no? Of course, of course, of course!"

* * *

"No, no, no," Terence said, shaking his head. "Can't allow it. Sorry, Maura."

"Why not?"

"It's too soon. Much too soon."

"According to whose standards? If Larkin's willing, why can't you be, too? It's *her* career I'd be affecting. I'm not asking you for clients. I have a client."

"You'd be working under our aegis. Larkin would be going out as one of our clients. She'd be using our name."

"Come on. You saw her at Yale. You admitted she was great. You said, and I think I'm quoting you here, that it was 'the finest piece of acting' you had ever seen by anyone that young."

He was shaking his head. "It won't work."

She stood up. "Then I'm going to look for another job, Terence. If I want to suffer from nine to five or eleven to seven or whatever, I might as well get a decent salary while I'm suffering."

She started to walk out.

"Wait," he said, and she stopped and turned to face him. "Would you really quit?"

"This hasn't been a lot of fun for me," she said. "I see why you're good at your job and even why Alexandra is good at hers. Max told me you think I'm good at mine. I know I'm asking something outrageous, but then again, I don't have a lot to lose, do I?"

He was fiddling with a pencil. "I'd have to talk to Alexandra," he said.

"Does that mean you say yes?"

"Anyone else, Maura, and I'd kick them out just for asking." He paused. "She'll probably say no, though, I have to warn you."

Maura thought about the setup with Keefe. Or even if it wasn't a setup. She shrugged. "Then I'll say good-bye and good luck. Talk to her, okay?"

Maura watched as Alexandra put on her coat and left the office. Not one word. Just out the door and that was it.

"Maura?" Terence called from the inner office. "Come on in for a minute."

So it was bad news. Well, why had she expected anything else? She picked up her coffee and brought it in to Terence's office.

"Sit down," he said.

She felt as if she were applying for college or something equally awful. Because she didn't want to quit; she didn't want to go out and have to pound the pavements *again*.

"So," he said, steepling his fingers. "I discussed your idea with Alexandra."

"And the answer is obviously no," she said.

He smiled. "You think you're so damn smart, don't you?"

"You've always told me I was. Speaking ironically, of course."

"Of course," he said. "Because you're wrong, for once. Alexandra agreed, provided you agree to certain conditions."

"Terence, she didn't even *speak* to me when she left."

"She's in a rotten mood," he said. "And she didn't want to talk to you until I spoke with you first." He paused. "You might not like it."

"You might be right. Tell me."

"All right. To begin with, she was more receptive than you would have thought. More receptive than *I* would have thought. *I* know she thinks you're good at the job, despite the way she might talk to you. Let's just say she has faith in my judgment and a rotten office manner. She's a pig as a boss, and she knows it. But she brought up an important point almost immediately: She and I are partners in the business. We have our financial necks on the line, and every month we have to come up with a substantial overhead. We work for the business and for ourselves. If you came in, what risk would you be taking?"

Maura hadn't even thought about it. "Well, that is a point."

"It's an important point, and it's the key to the offer. We still need an assistant. You'd like to become an agent. You couldn't go anywhere else in the city and get this independence, Maura. So this is what Alexandra proposed, and I agreed to. You continue as our assistant, but you'll also grow more involved in the business. You can bring clients in if we agree to them. You'll get a share—not ten percent, but we'll work it out—of your clients' earnings. And you'll take a large cut in your salary—again, we'll work that out, but it will have to be about a sixty percent cut, we figured—to offset the differences."

"What differences?"

"In the contributions you're making, in your risk and our risk. We'll work it out; don't worry."

"What if you don't agree to any of my choices? Then it'll all be bullshit."

"Maura, we want to do this. We've been talking about bringing in another agent for over a year now, and we had always assumed it would be someone with experience. But we both agree it could work. And if it doesn't, you can quit or go back to what you were doing, or we can try something different. I think we'll know soon enough if it's working, don't you?''

The phone rang, and Maura picked it up on the first ring. "Fielding-White Associates."

"Ah. Maura," he said.

Right, shithead; you never even called me after that day. "Hello, Keefe. How's it going?"

"Oh, pretty well."

"*Pretty* well? Are you kidding? I heard you got the part."

"Yeah, yeah. I'm pretty happy about it."

She glanced at Terence. He was watching her with a half smile. "Would you like to talk to Terence? Alexandra isn't here."

"Terence? Sure. And, uh, about the weekend—"

"What are you, kidding? Here's Terence."

They spoke for half a minute, and then Terence hung up and looked at her. "Trouble in paradise?"

"The paradise was all in your puny little feverish brain," she said.

"Was it?" he asked.

"You were saying."

He shrugged. "I'm finished. Take it, leave it, or think about it. But remember—if you take it, it's going to be rough."

"It already *is* rough," she said. "You're on."

Book Four

Forty-three

Larkin took a deep breath and then another deep breath. "You bastard," she said. He was probably the most handsome man she had seen all year—certainly the most handsome she had been this close to in a year—and so far, he had fed her the lines perfectly. "You told me to go to Whispers just so I'd see you with Laurette, didn't you—"

"Don't be silly," he said, grabbing her by the waist. "Serena, you have to believe me."

"Get out of my sight," she said, pushing him away.

She pushed him too hard, and he fell back against one of the lights. A grip caught the light, and Larkin held her breath. Had she screwed up?

"Thank you very much," she heard, and her heart sank. Another rejection. And Maura had said the agency was submitting eleven people for the part, and ridiculous as it was, she had had the fantasy she'd be able to go back to Maura and say, "Guess what? I got the part." And Maura would look great at the agency, something she absolutely didn't look at the moment with such a fuck-up as her only client.

Shit. She looked at the producer, a woman named Felicia Crawford—someone who had seemed tough and competent and smart—

183

but the woman didn't even look at her. They were already calling the next person.

"So that's five in a row for you," Larkin said. "Five fuck-up auditions. I'm sure you're thrilled you're my agent."

"Don't be ridiculous," Maura said, stacking up eight-by-tens while she talked. She hadn't stopped moving since Larkin had come in: Even when she was answering the phone, she was also organizing her desk or sorting through eight-by-tens. It was the only way she could get everything done in a day, she had said, and it made Larkin feel even worse. "You've always known what it would take," Maura said. "You don't get the first part you audition for, and I'm the last person who'd expect that."

The phone rang, and she picked it up on the first ring, and Larkin stood up and got the key to the ladies' room. Although she hated using it—it was down a horrible dark hall, the kind of bathroom that really needed a lock. Why were so many agencies in such dingy, run-down buildings? It wasn't just Fielding-White, at all. When she had made the rounds before Maura had decided to take her on, they had almost all been like this. Or worse.

When she got back, Maura was off the phone and, for the first time since Larkin had come in, doing nothing—absolutely nothing. And she had the oddest look on her face, not quite a smile but almost. "I have some interesting news."

The door to Terence and Alexandra's office was closed, but Larkin could hear Alexandra screaming.

"Aren't you going to ask me what it is?" Maura asked. Now she was leaning back in her chair with her arms crossed. Smiling.

"What's the news?" Larkin asked.

"Oh, you're to report to Studio E at CTC tomorrow morning."

"For a callback?"

Now Maura was grinning. "Congratulations, Serena," she said. Larkin didn't believe it. "Are you kidding?"

"I would never kid about a part. You *got* it, Larkin. Congratulations."

"I don't believe it."

Maura laughed, and the door to the inner office opened.

"Maura, I need you to write up a contract."

Larkin turned around. Alexandra looked the way Maura had described—overweight, pretty face, dark, wavy hair down to her shoulders. But Maura had never said she was that overweight, that enormous. "I just spoke to Terence in L.A., and Hayes Atwood agreed to our changes. I need it in triplicate, and I need it now.'' She handed Maura some papers.

Larkin couldn't stand Alexandra's tone of voice. How could Maura bear it? But all Maura did was take the papers and say, ''I'll start them in ten minutes.''

Alexandra sighed. ''What did I just say?''

''*I* said I'll start them in ten minutes,'' Maura said.

''She's with a client,'' Larkin said, standing up. She held out her hand. ''Larkin James.''

Alexandra shook her hand unenthusiastically. ''Nice to meet you and all that, but Maura has to prioritize her time as an agent *and* an assistant, not necessarily in that order. And we have working clients—''

''Including me,'' Larkin said. ''Although I should really say *Maura* has a working client, since I'm hers rather than yours. I just got the part of Serena Blake on 'Coronado.' ''

Alexandra's jaw dropped, and Larkin had to smile. What a fucking bitch. She wasn't even pleased. Probably just pissed off it wasn't one of her pets who had gotten the part. ''Well,'' Alexandra said. ''Congratulations.''

Larkin looked at Maura. ''How much will I be making?''

''Three thousand a week,'' Maura said.

''Then I think you can prioritize a little more time for me, don't you think?''

She could tell Maura was trying not to laugh. She told Alexandra she'd get to the contracts soon, and Alexandra stormed back into her office.

''Nice move,'' Maura said.

''What a bitch. God. How can anyone stand to have her as their agent?''

''She's very good,'' Maura said.

''You should have some sort of palace revolution. Steal her clients and form your own agency.''

''First things first,'' Maura said. ''Like thinking about tomorrow. They'll fit you for wardrobe, work out your makeup, give you the bible of the show and your script, and I'll iron out all the details of the contract this afternoon. But you're pleased, right? That's more important than anything else.''

''I'm thrilled,'' Larkin said. ''It makes you look good, right?''

Maura smiled. ''It makes me look great.''

''Then I'm thrilled.''

''But for yourself, too, right? That's much more important.''

"Of course I'm thrilled. Don't be silly."

But after she left and got out on the street, she was suddenly filled with panic. She had seen some of the scripts at the audition. Pages and pages of lines. You had to get up at four in the morning. They gave you last-minute changes every day, five days a week, and you had to learn them on the set. Be great every day. So yes, of course she was thrilled. But what if she screwed up? And why did she feel as if it was completely inevitable that she would?

"God, I'm *so* excited," Danielle said, balancing the cake on the bag of groceries and ringing for the elevator. "I just can't *believe* it, that I'm going to know someone on TV. I can't *believe* it."

Maura smiled. "That's what Larkin kept saying. She really was shocked. I don't think she had any idea how good the audition was. Anyway, this is nice, that we can surprise her."

Danielle bit her lip. "You think she'll really be surprised?"

"Of course. She couldn't possibly know that we met downtown to go shopping, that we got all these things."

"God. It's so great. I hope something this great happens to every one of us, you know? Wouldn't that be the best?"

Maura laughed, and they dragged the bags into the elevator. They had spent much too much money and bought much too much food, but if anything was worth celebrating. . .

The apartment was dark when they opened the door, but the TV was blaring from the living room—much too loudly for someone to be watching it. "Larkin?" she called.

"I thought we were going to surprise her," Danielle whispered.

"Something's wrong," Maura said, going down the hall.

There was no one in the living room, and she flicked off the set. But something else was still blaring—from Larkin's room?—and she went to see.

The door was half-open, and she opened it all the way. Larkin was lying on the bed asleep. There was food on the bed—potato chips and dip—and a half-empty bottle of vodka on the floor. Her own celebration, Maura thought, and she wished they had told her what they were planning.

But why was she asleep?

"Larkin?"

Nothing but regular breathing. But it sounded wrong.

"Larkin?"

Danielle came into the room. "Is she okay?"

"She's asleep."

"With that noise?" Danielle turned the TV off. "You'd better wake her up," she said. "She's out like a light."

"But you think I should wake her?"

Danielle reached down and pushed Larkin's shoulder. "She could be sick," she said. "It happened to my father once when I was real little, but I can remember. They said you can't let someone like that sleep, like what if they took something else?" She was shaking Larkin's shoulder, but nothing was happening.

"Larkin!" Maura yelled. What was wrong?

Larkin opened her eyes and groaned. "Oh God," she said. "Have I overslept? Am I late?"

"Late for what?" Maura said, sitting down. "Are you all right?"

Larkin rubbed her eyes. "Big headache," she murmured. "But I'm okay."

"Did you drink all that *vodka*?" Danielle suddenly asked, her voice piping up like a kid's.

"Of course not," Larkin said, sitting up and rubbing her eyes again. She looked into Maura's eyes. "So I didn't miss tomorrow. It's still tonight."

"It's still tonight," Maura said. "Do you really think I'd let you oversleep tomorrow?"

She had said it with a smile, but Larkin wasn't smiling.

"We were going to have a giant party for you," Danielle said. "We got every kind of food they make in the entire world. But you don't look too hungry."

"I'm not," she said, swinging her legs to the floor. "But I'll eat with you guys. That was nice of you."

Danielle was already halfway out the door. "We got *everything*," she was saying.

"Are you really okay?" Maura asked.

"I'm fine. I just needed a couple of drinks and then a nap, that's all."

"What about the TVs? What was that all about?"

"Research, of course," she said, standing up. She looked unsteady, but she walked to the door and then turned to face Maura. "I'm fine. Really. And Danielle obviously wants to have a celebration, so let's go help her out. And no more questions. I'm fine."

Forty-four

"Yeah," Nick said, putting his feet up on the desk. "Mr. Soames."

"May I ask who's calling?"

Yeah, fucking Santa Claus. "Mr. Dotson," he said.

"One moment, please."

Goddamn hold buttons. That was the fucking worst part, being put on fucking hold. But it was worth it.

"Mr. Dotson? Mr. Soames is in a meeting. May I take a message?"

Could she take a message? Yeah, suck this. "Listen," he said. "Tell him I can't wait more than an hour. If he doesn't call me back, I'm calling Mr. Roe."

"Would you like to speak with Mr. Roe now?"

"Nope. Just give Soames the message," he said. "I'm sure he'll get back to me." He hung up. Yeah, give him the message, sweetie, and watch your boss sweat. That was one thing he sometimes thought about, cozying up to some of those secretaries. Kind of a double whammy, hitting these guys where they worked. Maybe banging the typists on the side. Taunting them, maybe. Yeah, Soames, I've got your boss's name and I've tasted your secretary's twat, and I know every fucking thing there is to know about you, asshole.

That was the amazing part, all the fucking information these guys gave when they wanted the credit. You tried to talk to them before that, zip. But when they needed something, they were ready to put their fucking mothers out on the street. "Place of business" made some of them shut up for a few seconds. "What do you want to know that for?" the assholes asked. Like it wasn't important. "It's the main fucking thing I have to know," he always said, except not exactly in those words. King was a fucking stickler on that point. And some of the wise guys said, "Well, as long as you don't ever call me there," and he'd say, "Oh, of *course* not. We just need the information for our files.'' Right. And Santa Claus was going to visit them in a fucking month.

But the thing that amazed him most was that these guys—who the fuck did they think they were?—when they lost, all of a sudden it was some big fucking surprise that they had to pay the money back. And that was the part that made the shit-work parts of the job worthwhile, watching these guys sweat, listening to them shit at the other end of the line. Fucking ''executives,'' thought they'd never have to pay it back. And they scared so easily, it was pathetic: ''Do you want me to call your boss?'' And they'd sell the fucking house to pay him back.

The only bad part was another of King's rules. No guns, no rough stuff. It was a way to stay out of trouble, no question. Nobody went whining to the cops about anyone shooting off their kneecaps. And the executive types were more piss-scared of their bosses than of a fucking gun anyway. But shit—when he had done it with one of the lowlifes some asshole had let into the club, a fucking mechanic who didn't even have a fucking boss, what a thrill. One look at the gun and he had shat. And paid up, so there.

And what a beauty the gun was, what a waste not to use it, just to flash it. He slid it out from the back of his waistband and held it out. ''Last wish, brother,'' he said. He had made up the words himself. They said it all.

And fuck. King was a great guy, a genius if you thought about it. He had had his whole face redone—plastic surgery—and he *looked* like a fucking king. But what the fuck were all these rules about? They didn't make sense. They made everyone feel crimped, whatever. Like his rule about ''fraternization,'' too, which meant you weren't supposed to fuck any of the girls. What was he, kidding? Some of the ones on the fifth floor he could do without. Fucking pros. No feeling. But Danielle, shit. He wasn't going to give her up just because of some fucking rule. And Greshner—who did he think he was, planking somebody like Danielle? He was a nothing, a nobody. So *fuck* King's rules. He'd ''fraternize'' with whoever the fuck he wanted. And he was going to branch out, too, lend some money of his own. Fuck the rules. It was time to have some fun.

''Last wish, brother.'' It gave him a hard-on just to say the words. He put the gun down and unzipped his fly.

Forty-five

Danielle felt bad. Cleve had called early in the morning to say he and Colette were going to Paris for a while, just like that, out of the blue. And she had thought, Maybe for two weeks, something like that. Like a normal vacation for normal people. And then he had told her: maybe six months, maybe even a year; they were trying to finish the stupid screenplay they were working on. And she couldn't believe it. She had just come east, and now what? Her dumb father had to move even more east than her. Plus he couldn't even get together for a "good-bye," because they were leaving right away. Or that was what he said. Sometimes she didn't even know if it was crazy to even believe him.

So the club. It didn't even feel like fun right now. She hadn't even started, and already she felt like leaving.

"Hey. How're you doin'?" Nick asked, coming up out of the blue from who knew where. He had a way of bouncing on his heels or toes or something, that Danielle didn't like too much, now that she had slept with him. Which she still couldn't believe! How could she have been so dumb?! Maybe he was kind of good-looking, plus she had been mad at Allan, but still!!!

"I'm okay," she said. She pulled at her outfit and then wished she hadn't, because he was looking right where her hands were, where the leotard-type thing met with her tights. "Um, I'd better get to my shift, though."

"That's okay," he said softly. "You've got ten minutes. Almost fifteen."

"Well—" She couldn't think of an excuse. "The thing is, I like to look at how it's going before I start working."

"You're just waitressing today."

She shrugged. "I know, but—"

"Come on," he said, putting his hands at her waist. "We'll go up to the fifth floor."

She bit her lip. "Um, I don't think that's such a great idea."

He didn't say anything. He just looked mad. Then: "You're still seeing Greshner, huh?"

She had wondered when he'd say it, but now that he had, it felt like a surprise. "Sure. What if I am?"

He smiled, but it was kind of a mean smile. "What if you are? I'll tell you what if you are. Are you serious about him or something?"

She felt like telling the truth. "Super-serious," she said.

"Then you're super-serious about someone with a big problem, Danielle. He was into us for thirteen G's till just last week."

Her stomach flipped, and she didn't know what to say. Thirteen G's. Thirteen thousand dollars. "You're making that up," she finally said.

"You want to see his credit slips?"

"I don't have to. Actually, I knew all about it. I just didn't think *you* knew."

"I authorized the credit. And tell me this, if you know so much: How does a guy who sinks into a thirteen-thousand-dollar hole get out of it in three days?"

She felt sick. "I don't think I should tell you that," she said. "It's personal."

He laughed. "Personal? You've got some imagination, Danielle. You don't know a thing. You didn't even know about the thirteen G's. But I'll tell you something: If you find out, you let me know, okay?"

"Why would I?"

"We like to know these things. Greshner's obviously got more money than we thought. Which means we can extend more credit the next time he comes back. *Capisce?*"

"I have to go," she said.

And this time he let her go. But the whole club was a giant blur. Thirteen thousand dollars. Why hadn't Allan told her any of it?

"Hey, honey," he said when he opened the door. He kissed her and followed her in. "How was your day?"

She shrugged. "Not so great. Cleve is going to Paris for a super-long time, and I feel kind of bad." She couldn't face the money part yet.

His face fell. "Oh, honey," he said, taking her in his arms. "You have to stop expecting so much from him." He put her head against his shoulder. "Live your own life. Remember? You have so much going for you. You're a brilliant, beautiful young woman." She loved it when he said brilliant. But he said she really was, the first person who ever said that, too. "Cleve has problems he may never get over, and you're going to have to realize that." He paused. "Everyone has their problems, things they do, sometimes too much of, that they wish they could stop. But he may never stop."

She nodded, but she was already thinking about him, and the worst part of the whole day. The money. "Um," she said. "Something else." She looked into his eyes and got ready; it was just like diving into super-cold water: "Nick Dotson told me you owed the club thirteen thousand dollars," she said. The words felt unreal, but she had said them. Allan looked totally shocked.

"How do you—? Oh, Dotson," he said quietly. "He has some nerve telling you about it."

"But Allan, how did it happen?"

"I got in over my head. I lost track," he said. It sounded like his voice had cracked when he said "track," like his throat was extra-dry.

"But, Allan, it's just what you said with Cleve. Something maybe you do too much of. I mean, is it?"

"Not at all," he said, stroking her hair. "It doesn't interfere with our relationship, does it?"

She shrugged. "I guess not."

"Well, that's what they say. If it starts affecting the other parts of your life—"

"But how did you get the money to pay the loan *back*? That's what Nick wanted to know."

"Then let him ask me about it."

"Allan." She felt totally adult all of a sudden. Because what was a relationship if the people in it didn't tell the truth? "The truth," she said.

He sighed and leaned back against the couch. "The truth," he said quietly, rubbing his eyes. "The truth, Danielle, is that I took an unofficial loan from the company. I shouldn't even be telling you this, but I'm too tired to lie. And it doesn't matter anyway. I'll pay them back before anyone knows it's gone."

"Are you kidding?" Her voice had come out like a screech. "Are you crazy, Allan? If you get caught, you'll go to jail for years. *Years!*"

"It'll be all right," he said. "I promise." He kissed her and looked into her eyes. "End of discussion, okay?"

But she couldn't stand it. Embezzlement, they called it. What if he got into trouble?

Forty-six

SERENA: You're Tom List, aren't you?
TOM: And you?
SERENA: Serena Blake. I've just moved to Coronado.

The lines were simple enough—they made sense; nothing too dramatic for Serena's first scene. And Larkin was sure she had the first page down cold. But there were five pages.

She set down the script and looked around the set. It was what she had expected in the way of looks—broken-up rooms, mostly of a town house, with areas set aside for makeup and wardrobe and for the writers. So in that sense, it was what she had expected. But she had thought more would be made of her first day, somehow, that there would be—well, not a *ceremony* or anything, but some sort of announcement, some sort of greeting.

But it was too crazy and hectic, she supposed. A couple of the actors had come up and said hello, certainly Peter, the man she'd be doing most of her scenes with. And then everyone had rushed off with the same apology—"Sorry, have to study lines"—and she could see why. Everyone not only had pages of lines, but pages of changes, so that half of whatever they had learned the night before was worthless. "It's the crazy writers," Peter had said, and she was grateful at least for that, that they wouldn't, as far as she knew, make any changes in her script for today. She was new; what was there to change?

"Larkin?"

She turned around. It was Monica Morgan, the director. Ex-model, ex-producer, ex-leading lady of two major soaps.

"Darling, Wyeth is going to be bringing you some changes; he's that fellow over there, the young man who thinks he looks like a young Dennis Hopper."

Larkin looked where Monica was pointing, to the stage set that looked like Whispers, a local Coronado disco, and she didn't see anyone who looked like Dennis Hopper, but she wasn't looking too carefully. She couldn't even think. *Changes?* "Uh, will there be a lot?"

Monica smiled. "Not at all. Everyone knows this is your first day, darling."

"Good. Because I had trouble just learning these."

Monica was frowning. "Really?"

Christ. "Well, not *really*, but it was a little tough." A little tough. Having Maura feed her the lines over and over and over until they were both about to scream.

"You're going to have to get used to it, you know."

"Oh, I know," Larkin said quickly. "And I plan to. Really."

Monica smiled. "Good. We see a long future for you here on 'Coronado.' Here's Wyeth now," she said as she left.

Larkin couldn't imagine why he thought he looked like Dennis Hopper. He was just a snipey, skinny, unhappy-looking guy with extremely expensive clothes. "For you," he said with a little bow. "Enjoy them. Although I won't say get used to them, since you'll probably have more."

"What does that mean?"

He blinked. "It means there will be more. Was that so difficult to understand?"

"Well, yes. You made it sound as if these would be made obsolete."

"They *might* be," he said, throwing up his hands. "If they knew, then they wouldn't have written these, would they have?" He sighed petulantly and stormed off, and Larkin looked down at the pages.

"SERENA: You must be Tom List. I'd know those eyes anywhere."

Oh no. That meant they had changed all her lines from the *beginning*.

She looked away from the script—she had to—and Peter Alther was coming toward her. He seemed friendly, and he was certainly great-looking, the kind of leading man every soap had ten of, from what she could tell. But he seemed so gay, she couldn't imagine viewers believed him in his role. Maybe he was a great actor or maybe they didn't care.

"How's it going?" he asked, sitting down. "You look as if you've seen a ghost."

"These changes," she said. "I had just learned the first version."

"Get used to it, honey. Happens every day. AFTRA's been trying to get some rulings on this for years, but we haven't been able to yet, and *I* personally don't think we ever will. Soap writers have always worked this way, and they always will. Do you need some help?''

"God, *I* don't know." What she needed was a Valium. She was too nervous to concentrate on anything. "I'll be back in a second," she said, standing up.

"We've only got fifteen minutes," he called. "When are you going to learn your lines?"

"I'll manage," she said.

She couldn't get to the bathroom fast enough. She locked a stall and pulled out the bottle of pills, shook them out . . . and only one came out. Christ. She had forgotten. The other night she had taken her second to last, and then she had gotten distracted when Maura and Danielle had come home. She hadn't called Dr. Weinstein to get more, she hadn't set up any kind of appointment, and now she had *one*?

She popped it into her mouth and chewed it up and closed her eyes. *You can do it,* she told herself. You can do it, at least for Maura's sake. How would it look if Maura's only client lost her job on her first day?

She went back to the set, sat in a corner that was supposed to be Coronado's local beauty shop, and started to read. She could do it if she really tried.

Forty-seven

"So God, Larkin, tell us everything!" Danielle said. "Was it scary?"

Maura couldn't stop looking at the pizza. Danielle and Larkin were taking forever to eat it, and she had eaten her container of cottage cheese in five seconds.

"I really thought I would die," Larkin said, letting the crust of her third piece drop to the plate. So there were three crusts, all uneaten, and about nine pieces of pepperoni. "I've never had to memorize so much so quickly in my life."

"But you did it!" Danielle said. "God, it's so great. And you get to ride in a limo. Maura, aren't you the proudest?"

"Of course," she said. "My discovery. But I always knew she could. And it sounds corny, but this really is just the beginning."

Larkin was smiling, but uncertainly—almost vaguely.

"What's the matter?" Maura asked.

Larkin picked at a crust and put it down again. "Just . . . what if I can't do it?"

"You can do it," Maura said, "so don't start worrying about things that aren't going to happen. This *really* is just the beginning. And don't think you're going to stop going to auditions, because you're not. We'll drop this as soon as something better comes along. But it's great training and great exposure."

Larkin swallowed. "But it won't be great exposure if I screw it up—"

"You won't screw it up." Maura couldn't stand it anymore. "Listen, are you guys going to eat that last piece or not? Because I'm starved."

"I'm stuffed," Danielle said. "Go ahead."

"Larkin?"

"Go ahead," she said, pushing the box away. "I'm just glad you're more interested in the pizza than in my problems. It gives me that perspective I obviously need."

"Oh, come on. I'd be worried if there were something to worry about. *You can do it.* I know it. So knock off the self-indulgent-actress bit. It's not going to fit with your career."

"I thought you wanted the pizza," Larkin said, pushing it toward her.

"I do." Maura felt as if she were reaching for it in slow motion, and her mouth was already watering. How long had it been? Months. And she had been so good until the other night when she and Danielle had bought all the junk food. But it was so discouraging. Months of cottage cheese and gallons of water, and how much had she lost? Three pounds. Even Alexandra was losing weight these days, hardly eating anything—ever—at the office.

She bit into it, into a piece of pepperoni that was incredibly salty and greasy and wonderful, and she realized it was hopeless. How could she ever give things like this up?

"I think Maura's right," Danielle said. "You're going to be a giant star, and it's crazy to worry. *We* know you can do it."

Larkin stood up and threw down her napkin. "Great," she said. "I'm glad everyone is so confident. See you all later."

"Where are you going?" Danielle asked.

"To study my lines."

"But we can help," Danielle called.

"Forget it."

"Let her go," Maura said when Larkin was gone. "We can help her later if she wants us to."

"But what's the *matter* with her? Is she just scared?"

Maura nodded. "And it's better to leave her alone, I think. She really does want this; she just has to get used to the idea. She hasn't even told Richard she got the part—"

"Are you kidding? God, why not?"

"Because she's letting it sink in, she said."

"God, I could never do that. It's weird, don't you think? I think secrets like that are the worst thing in the world." Her face started getting red. "Maura?"

"What is it?"

"Do you believe in streaks? Like that everything could be going totally well for all of us and then right away everything could be really terrible?"

"What do you mean? Did something terrible happen to you?"

Danielle was hesitating. "It's not terrible, exactly, but I was just thinking . . . like with Larkin, everything seemed so great, and now she's so scared about everything, and with me and Allan." She bit her lip.

"Did something happen with you and Allan?"

"It's not me and Allan, exactly; I mean everything's still great. But I found out—this guy at the club told me that Allan is in a super-lot of debt. I mean really a lot."

"Do you know how much?"

She shrugged. "A lot. I don't even want to say. But thousands. And it was a secret. I mean, he wouldn't've told me except that this other guy did."

"Danielle, that's very serious."

She shrugged again. "I guess. I mean, I was pretty upset. So I was wondering. Like . . . ." She stopped and looked into Maura's eyes. "I mean, I was worried. But then when I hear you say, 'That's very serious,' I say to myself, It's true, but you love him so much. So I guess you just have to take the bad with the good, like they say. I mean, when you love someone that much, you can forget about anything, you know?"

Maura didn't say anything. No, she didn't know, and it depressed her. Danielle was in love, Larkin had just gotten a great part, and it felt like high school again, just what she had dreaded and known would happen if she moved in with these two gorgeous women. No, she didn't know what it felt like to love someone that much.

Danielle went off to her room, and Maura began to eat the rest of the pizza—first the pepperoni that had dropped off Larkin's slices, then the crusts she had left. And then she was starved.

Not much exciting in the refrigerator, but there was some cheese and bologna (Danielle didn't know a thing about nitrates) and some old Stouffer's dinners, and she ate till she felt sick. Yes, she had a great job, and yes, she looked good for having gotten Larkin the role. But nothing had changed. She didn't feel any better about anything.

"Maura?" It was Danielle calling from down the hall. "You've got a phone call!"

She took the last English muffin from the refrigerator, called to Danielle that she'd take it in the hall, and picked up.

"Maura," the voice said.

It was Vince.

"So how're you doing?" he said.

"What is it?" Her voice sounded dead. The way she wanted it to.

"It's my dad. He's in the hospital. He wanted me to call you."

"Oh God. George? What happened? Is he all right?"

"They don't know. He had some kind of heart attack or something. Like a stroke, maybe. I don't know exactly; they're talking at me from nine different directions."

"When did it happen? What hospital is he in?"

"Saint Clare's Roosevelt. Over on Ninth? He went in . . . let's see . . . last week, I guess."

"Why didn't you *call* me? He's been in there for a week?"

"Yeah, well. Whatever."

"Can I visit him? What are the hours?"

"To nine every night," he said, "now he's out of intensive care. You should go see him. He'd get a big kick out of it, Maura."

"I will, I will. I'll go tonight." Immediately she wished she hadn't said it. Of course Vince would have known she'd go, but she hadn't had to pin it down like that.

"Yeah, well, maybe I'll see you there. So how're you doin' otherwise? Everything going okay at the new job?"

"It's fine," she said. "Listen, I have to go, Vince. But I really appreciate your calling. Tell George I'll be there."

"I will, Maura. I will," he said, and he hung up.

* * *

George was in a roomful of men—Maura realized after a few seconds that it was only four altogether, but with all the noise from the televisions and the coughing and the visitors, it sounded like a stadium.

He looked weak and pale and thin, but he smiled when she said hello, and he seemed happy she had come.

She hated the feeling, being the only person there. Not that she wanted Vince to be there, too, but where was George's girlfriend? Where were his friends, and some of the girls?

She sat down and took his hand. "So how's it going, old friend?"

He smiled crookedly. "Ah, what can I tell you? I want to get out of here," he said. His words were slurred, but he was speaking more quickly than she had expected from looking at him. "I don't want one of those angel-of-death nurses coming at me and giving me the old heave-ho. Remember that shit? 'I'm going to make you feel better,' one of them said." He shivered. "You're at their mercy in a place like this, that's all I can say."

One of the patients across the room was staring, and Maura wanted to change the subject. "Well, what happened, exactly? Is it a stroke or a heart attack?"

"They say a stroke, but who knows, Maura? I felt dizzy, I got a big headache, boom down I went, the girl—the one who took over for you, name's Rana, something crazy like that. I wake up, she's shaking me, she calls the ambulance, and here I am." He shrugged. "No big deal."

"No big deal," Vince said, coming through the door. Maura turned. He looked the same, but he had cut his hair: a tall, dark-haired, good-looking guy. His eyes met hers and she looked away. "No big deal," he said again. "You know the *therapy* this guy's going to have to go through? Seven days a week, two hundred dollars a pop, no one but me taking care of him—"

"Vince," George said in a warning voice.

Maura looked at George. "Where's Irene?"

He smiled. "Irene said good night." He laughed. "Get it?"

She smiled, too, but she could see his eyes were sad. "When did that happen?"

He waved a hand and looked away, and Maura glanced at Vince. He put his index finger to his lips.

"Dad's like me," Vince said. "Love 'em and leave 'em."

For the first time, George's eyes lit up. "Don't you listen to him," he said, looking at Maura. "So, Vince, leave us alone for a minute, okay?"

Vince made the "okay" sign and left—too quickly, Maura felt. Something was up.

George moved as if he was trying to make himself more comfortable, but he was wincing.

"Can I help you?" Maura asked.

"Nah. Thanks," he said, settling back. "So, Maura," he said.

"So, George." She wanted to keep it light, but she had the feeling she wasn't going to have a choice.

"I gotta talk to you about Vince," he said.

Great. "What about Vince?"

"He told me you almost went out with him once but it didn't work out."

"No, it didn't."

"He's having some problems," George said. "I'm worried about him, Maura."

"What kind of problems? What do you mean?"

"I don't know, exactly. He doesn't sleep. I hear him in the apartment, all hours, pacing, pacing, like some kind of animal."

"Is that why Irene left?" She had made a wild guess, spur of the moment. But from George's eyes, it looked like she had guessed right.

"I don't know," he said. "Who can say with a woman, no offense, Maura. But Irene, she was kind of like a cat. That woman was happy in one place in the whole world, and that was onstage. So who can say? I sure can't."

"You must miss her."

"I want you to do me a favor," George said.

"I'm not going to go out with him, George."

"Did I ask you that?"

"I think you were going to."

He was shaking his head. "Still a smart-ass, aren't you?"

"What's the favor?"

"I'm going to be going home soon," he said. "It's no good, me and a nurse and Vince; it's not the same. Now, I know you're busy, I know—how's the job?"

"It's a nightmare ninety percent of the time and magnificent the other ten percent."

"That's nice," he said. "I guess. I know you don't have a lot of time, but I'm not asking for a lot. Just—once, twice a week come by, say hello, bring some life to the house."

"Jesus Christ, George, 'bring some life to the house'? What are you going to tell me next? That you have a little orphan girl you want me to adopt? Come on. What do you want, exactly?"

His face looked thinner all of a sudden, more drawn. "Forget it," he said quietly, looking at the window. "Tell Vince he can come back in."

"George, come on. We're not finished."

He looked into her eyes. "Sure we are."

"What is it, George? You want me to stop by? I'm here now, aren't I? What makes you think I wouldn't visit you when you get home?"

"I said forget it," he said quietly.

"All right, I will." As if on cue, he turned to look at her, and she smiled. "I'll forget you asked, okay? Of course I'll visit you. Just don't ask me to go out with Vince. It didn't work out."

"But I'll see you, then," he said. "I can count on it—?"

"You can count on it," she said.

"So tell Vince he can come back in," he said.

She went out into the hall, where Vince was pacing. "What'd he say?" Vince asked.

"Nothing that you need to know about."

He looked into her eyes. "So how've you been?"

"Fine."

She turned and went back into the room. George asked her more about the new job, and as she answered him, she could feel Vince watching her. "It's pretty hectic," she said, "and people do try to use you. I had always heard that, but it's true."

"So you got clients?" George asked. "You got 'em working or you just send them out on auditions so far?"

"Well, the amazing thing is that I have a client—my roommate Larkin, who's my only client so far. And she got a job last week, on a soap. On 'Coronado.' "

George looked impressed. "Not bad. What about some of the girls at Falcone? Think you could use them?"

"Actually, I had been thinking about that. It depends. Maybe Cindy. She seemed to be the most serious."

"What are you, kidding?" Vince said, jumping off the radiator he'd been sitting on. "Maura's got real clients, Dad. They're not *strippers*. She's in a different world."

"It isn't that different," Maura said. "It's just as awful. Worse, actually. Really." She looked at Vince and immediately wished she hadn't. His eyes were suddenly filled with triumph.

"What?" he said. "What are you looking at me like I'm supposed to be surprised or something. That's what I meant, different. They don't accept just anyone. They'll take a look at you, a good look at you, and throw you right back."

"Ah, don't listen to him," George said. "You'll do great, Maura."

But Maura was still looking at Vince. Why did he know every one of her fears?

When Maura got home, Danielle's light was out—she seemed to need enormous amounts of sleep every day—and Larkin was in the kitchen studying her lines.

"How's it going?" Maura asked.

"Much better. And sorry about before. I seem to be panicking easily over these lines, but it's not as bad as I thought. Danielle helped me."

"Good."

"She also told me about George. How did that go? It was the son who called you?"

It was odd—she always forgot she had never talked about Vince. But she told Larkin a little about the visit without mentioning the past. "The son is kind of weird," she said, crossing her legs underneath her on the bed. "He's always . . . it's as if he knows all my insecurities and wants to . . . I don't know. Make me feel rotten."

"How well do you know him?" Larkin asked. "I mean, when else has he done this?"

"I don't know. At the office. Different times. But tonight—I suddenly looked around at the hospital room, at George and Vince, and I might as well have been back in Scranton with my father and Patrick Delaney, in the kitchen with them playing cards and me making coffee and cake. It was just like my father saying I'll never become anything."

"Then don't go back," Larkin said. "Why have anything to do with people like that?"

"George was great to me," Maura said. "And he's not like that. He's really encouraging."

Larkin flipped back a lock of her hair. "I don't see it that way. They sound the same to me. Why ask for punishment? You should spend time with people who believe in you."

Maura knew she was right. But who really believed in her, other than Danielle and Larkin? She wanted a relationship so much. And so far what had she had? Patrick and Keefe.

Face it, Maura. But she couldn't. She wanted someone, she wanted to be part of a couple, she wanted a great guy.

Face it, Maura. You're asking for too much.

Forty-eight

"Too late," Danielle said, picking off the lady's chip from the board, from the line between six and seven. She threw it back and started the wheel, and she heard a weird sound, like something in a pond. The chip had fallen into the lady's drink. Whoops.

But the ball landed on six. Shit. "The number is six," Danielle called out, not looking at the woman. "Number six, *número* six, ladies and gentlemen."

"I want the name of your supervisor," the lady said. She was blond and had a ton of makeup on, and was probably about three thousand years old if you scraped off all the layers.

"My supervisor is named Nick Dotson," Danielle said. The best part was not breaking up her rhythm—two people had had a quarter or half of a chip on six plus on black, and she was paying them off one, two, three, just like the best dealers at the club. She loved the way they could talk and work at the same time, and now she was doing it, too. "If you have a complaint, take it to him."

"I certainly will," the woman said, and she gathered up her chips and her drink (with the chip still in it) and left in a huff.

"Okay, ladies and gentlemen, time to make your bets. *Faites vos jeux*," she said. Speaking French. It was so much fun.

"Are you going to be in some trouble?" a man named Al-Sadir or something—she could never get it right except all she knew was that he was an Arab and that they got killed in their homeland if they gambled—asked. He played almost every day, but mostly at the more expensive tables.

She shrugged. "I don't see why I should," she said, starting the wheel. "I have rules, and most people understand them. You can't just throw down a chip whenever you feel like it."

The ball popped up into the air—she loved that part, when it was kind of deciding where to go—and landed in the Arab man's number, number nine, which he played every single time.

"Number nine," she called out. *"Número neuf, nueve, nòve."*

She paid off the smaller bets, the ones who had red and one to twelve and things like that, and then Al-Sadir's or whatever his name was, $350.

But out of the corner of her eye she could see Nick coming, with the blond, ancient bitch.

"This one," the woman said, "and she couldn't have been ruder."

Nick made a little bow to the players. "My apologies, ladies and gentlemen; this will only take a few minutes." He held up the glass and looked at Danielle. "Not the club's policy," he said.

"It was a mistake. I couldn't help it if it landed in her glass. She played the chip way after I had said they could."

"That's absurd," the woman said. "And to be as rude as she was—"

"I wasn't rude," Danielle said. But Nick had that angry, faraway look he always had now that she had said no to him about a million and one times.

"May I intrude," Al-Sadir suddenly said, going over to where Nick stood. "I was a witness to the incident, and there was no rudeness except from the customer. The call had been made. It was unfortunate that the chip landed in the glass, but it was a mistake. The bet was not valid."

The woman looked furious. "You're going to listen to *him*? *I'm* the one it happened to, and I demand an apology. And seventeen dollars."

Nick looked at Danielle. "Danielle?"

"It was a mistake," she said. "Really, Nick."

"An apology," he said. "I'm sure these customers would all like to get on with the game."

She looked around, and they all did look pretty restless. "Okay, I'm sorry I missed and that the chip landed in the glass. But the bet was late. We don't pay off on bets that are late."

Nick was holding out his hand. "Your tips," he said.

"Why? I'm not giving her the money. The bet was too late."

Al-Sadir slid his pile of chips—the $350—across the table to Danielle. "Here is *my* tip to you, Danielle," he said, and he turned to Nick. "But I must request—I would like to continue my play without a disturbance from rude customers such as this lady. You seem to honor the customer, Nick."

Nick looked furious. "Of course," he said. He picked out $17 worth of chips, which looked tiny compared to the $350. Then he handed them to the lady, and she looked furious, too, because as Nick led her away, a few people at the table clapped and cheered.

"Thank you, everyone," Danielle said. "And thank you, too, Al-Sadir."

He bowed. "A pleasure, as usual."

But the truth was that she didn't feel any giant feelings of victory or anything like that. Because it wasn't fair: People like Al-Sadir were rich and just got richer. They had all the luck. But Allan . . . She just couldn't stop worrying. What was he going to do? And the thing was, at the beginning she had thought, Uh-oh, if he's a super-serious gambler, it'll be bad and I'll have to break up with him. But now it had come and gone, and she loved him, just like she had said to Maura. She didn't care about the gambling. She just wanted him not to get into trouble. Plus what was the difference? What about the ladies who were married to guys who played the stock market? What was the giant difference? She just didn't see it.

"*Faites vos jeux*, ladies and gentlemen," she said. But it didn't have the same ring to it that it had had before.

"And then I came here, to this country," Al-Sadir was saying. It was way past the time she usually went home, but Al-Sadir had asked her to have a drink, and since he had stuck up for her today, she kind of felt obligated, plus the $350 . . . "And my children, naturally they love the conveniences, the sports and all the diversions."

"How many kids do you have?"

"Six," he said. "With another on the way."

"*Six?*" She laughed. She hadn't really been paying any attention to what he was saying, but now she was interested. "How old is your wife?"

"Twenty-six."

"God. How old was she when you got married?"

"Seventeen. I was thirty-seven. It is traditional in my country. But then, I have broken with many traditions."

"Is it true you'd be killed if they caught you gambling? I mean in your own country?"

He gave her a super-mysterious smile. "Where do you hear things like these?"

"Everywhere. On TV, plus in magazines." She shrugged. "Everywhere."

He held up his glass. "They frown on drinking and gambling and many of the vices I enjoy," he said, and he moved closer to her on the banquette. "Which is one of the reasons I come to this country."

He was sitting too close, and his thigh was pressing against hers, and you didn't have to be a genius to figure out what he was getting at.

"You are a very beautiful woman," he said, and his voice had gotten all husky. "So young." He touched her arm and ran his fingers along her skin. "Like a ripe fruit, so ready to be picked. So delicious."

"Um, actually, I kind of have to get going," she said.

"Not yet," he said. "You have not touched your drink."

"Um, actually, I don't drink much."

"Not even champagne?"

"Nope."

He shook his head. "It is a shame for you to miss any of life's pleasures, Danielle." He put a hand on her knee. "I could show you so much. Give you so much. I have an apartment fully set up, with everything you could wish for, all the clothes, all the jewels, gifts you could not even imagine." He paused. "I love more than anything to drape my women in jewels. To put the jewels everywhere."

She bit her lip. What did he mean, everywhere?

"Um, I really kind of have to go, Al-Sadir." She stood up, and he stood, too.

"I am not an easy man to take no for an answer," he said.

"Well, I'll think about it, okay?"

He took both her hands and squeezed them, and looked super-deeply into her eyes. He *was* kind of good-looking, kind of like Omar Sharif in one of those movies that took place in the dunes. But she just wasn't interested. "I am counting on it," he said, and he let her go.

She walked out—right past Nick, who just looked at her from behind the ropes and didn't say a word—and into the changing room. And she did kind of have an idea. What if she could get the money from Al-Sadir? It was kind of a horrible idea, but weren't you supposed to do anything in the whole world to save the person you loved? Plus Allan was the only real true person in her life—not Cleve, not her mother. Maura and Larkin, maybe, but Allan most of all. He was the one.

So she was going to do it. If she could.

Forty-nine

"Long time no see," Nick said, rocking back and forth on his heels. "Where've you been?"

"Here and there," Allan said. But he wanted Nick gone; Nick was going to ruin his luck.

"So you need anything?"

"Nope."

"You don't need credit?"

"Nope. I'm fine." Allan moved away, into the crowd. No good starting when you were thinking about something else. One wrong look from the wrong person and you could lose all your concentration. And he was sweating like a pig anyway. It was Danielle's night off, so that was good. But there was too much pressure. He was losing the feeling that had made him come tonight in the first place.

There was one table where the dealer looked like Danielle, so that was out; it would distract him—and one where the guy was a nasty bastard, a snipey little asshole, and Allan started to sweat even more. What if he couldn't even find a table?

But then he saw Charlie, one of the old ones, the nice ones, a guy who could be a bartender or a bus driver, who wasn't in it for the "contacts" or any other bullshit reason.

"How're you doing?" Allan said, and he laid down a thousand dollars. *Take your time, take your time,* he told himself. There was no hurry; he was here for a long, leisurely win, the kind he had had at the beginning. Nothing quick about it, but sure and easy.

And there were two ways of looking at it, he knew; he couldn't fool himself, he couldn't lie to himself. He had written out another check, this time for ten grand, and he had the money with him.

And he knew some people would say it was crazy, that he owed enough already, so what was he doing taking another ten out? But he could win it back—he knew it—he just needed a big enough stake to play with. You couldn't go in with five hundred dollars and expect to win ten thousand just like that. One bad streak and you'd be out, and it wouldn't even be your fault.

He laid out his chips—four of them, a hundred dollars' worth—on the pass line. Nice and slow. Slow and easy. The shooter was a guy about his age, relaxed, looked like he had a few miles on him but not too many. He threw the dice, and Allan closed his eyes for half a second. This was going to be a streak one way or another; he could feel it.

He opened his eyes. Seven. Beautiful.

He kept the two hundred on the pass line and waited.

Eleven. Beautiful again.

So four hundred. Not bad for a minute's work. Four hundred on the pass line, look around the room, relax—

"Eight! The point is eight."

So that was good. You couldn't ask for a better point than six or eight, as long as the guy didn't crap out—

Do it; this is going to be good.

He put five hundred dollars in chips on the pass line and looked away.

"Eleven!"

So he had won nine hundred dollars. He had *known* it was going to be a streak; he had known it.

"A hundred for the crew," he said, throwing some chips onto the pass line for the guys. Good luck bred good luck. He slid ten hundred-dollar chips onto the pass line and made some come bets, two hundred dollars each, and looked around the room again. Casual. Nothing special.

"Yo'leven," the dealer called out, and Allan's heart started to pound. The guy couldn't lose. He had seen it a dozen times, he had read about it, and it was happening when he had the cash to ride the wave.

The numbers came up like a dream, and he had them all covered, and the table had gone crazy. And when the guy finally crapped out, Allan stopped to count his money—bad luck, but he had to know.

And he almost laughed. Nineteen thousand two hundred dollars. He had made back almost all the money he had borrowed.

"Can I get you a drink?"

He turned around. One of the cocktail waitresses he had never seen before. And he felt like celebrating. "Yeah, a Scotch on the rocks."

She smiled. "Right away, sir," she said, glancing down at his winnings.

Well, she'd get a big tip. Hell, *everyone* deserved a big tip tonight.

Nick watched Celia move through the crowd, and he grabbed her as she turned to go to the bar. "What'd he order?"

He didn't like her. Snotty college girl, thought she was better than everybody else.

"What did who order?" she asked.

"Mr. Moneybags. The one you're creaming over. What'd he order?"

"Scotch on the rocks."

He snapped his fingers for Raoul. "Make it a triple," he said to Raoul. "And keep them coming," he said to Celia.

She was giving him her fishy, snotty-nosed, I'm-better-than-you-are look. "Are these comps?" she asked.

"Of course they're comps. What the fuck do you think they are?"

She didn't say anything. She just took the fucking drinks for Allan and whatever other assholes had ordered and went back to the table.

And he watched. The asshole gave her a pile of chips—what did he think? She was going to spread her legs for him, too? Did he think it was some kind of rule, you won a lot and then you got to fuck a cocktail waitress for free?

But shit—it was *great* that assholes like Greshner believed that shit, that they thought they were getting some kind of a fucking free ride when they got comped. What did they think, they were ripping the place off? That was the beauty of it, the great beauty of comps, and it worked almost every fucking time. You gave the guy a few free drinks, maybe got him hot with one of the waitress's tits brushing against him, took his mind off the game thinking about some dipstick waitress's snatch, and then you watched.

Nick crossed his arms and leaned back against the wall, and he watched.

And it was funny how you could always tell, even if you were fifty fucking feet from the table. You didn't have to hear the numbers, you didn't have to see the table, you didn't have to see the guy's chips in the well. All you had to do was watch him sweat, watch his face, watch him order too many drinks, smoke too many cigarettes, get his mind all fucked up.

When the shift ended, Nick walked over to the table—slowly, to draw it out.

And he had to smile. Greshner had a fucking five-dollar chip in the well. A five-dollar chip.

Fifty

"You look so beautiful tonight, he said, his chin in one hand.

Richard was gazing across the table at her, and she was glad she had gotten to Dr. Weinstein on the phone. It was the last prescription he'd give without seeing her, he had said, but at least she had gotten it. And she felt good—relaxed even though today on the set had been rough. She had forgotten a couple of lines, and Monica had gotten really upset. Peter, too, which had hurt. He had forgotten lines, too, hadn't he?

"When are you going to tell me why you haven't been able to see me?" Richard asked. The waiter set down their salads, and he moved his aside. "Hm?"

She finished her wine and poured another glass. "Oh. God. Let's wait, all right?"

He tilted his head. "Is it that bad?"

"No. It's not bad at all. I just feel like waiting."

Now he smiled wanly. "Waiting for good news? Are you sure it's good for both of us?"

"Richard, I might as well tell you if you're going to ask all these questions." She took a deep breath. "Actually, it really is good. I've been working."

He blinked. "At a job? Do you mean at another modeling job?"

"No, no. Acting. On a soap."

He was staring. "For how long?"

"This week. I got it on Monday, and I started on Wednesday."

He was silent. Then: "And you didn't tell me? I don't understand."

She sighed. She had been afraid he wouldn't. "Look," she said. "It has nothing to do with you. I had to get used to it, and—"

"Nothing to do with me?" he asked. "You've had one of your dreams come true—unless that's another thing you haven't told me about—and you didn't tell me? I still don't understand."

"There's nothing to understand," she said, but he was still staring at her as if she were crazy.

"You say you got the job on Monday," he said. "You must have been thrilled. I presume you celebrated?"

"Not really. Sort of."

"With whom?"

She sighed. "Come on. Cut the cross-examination."

He laughed. "Ah. I like that. Now I'm cross-examining you, when all I'm trying to find out is the broadest details of your *life*. Tell me *something*, Larkin. Did you celebrate with another man? What is going on?"

"I was with my roommates," she said. "And actually, they're the only people I've told. I haven't told my family yet, either."

"Ah. Well. *That* makes me feel better, knowing how close you are to your family. You might *never* tell them. But we're talking about us. I'm the man you're involved with, the man you've thought about—or at least you've *said* you've thought about—marrying. And you haven't told me about one of the major events of your life. It would be like me not telling you about being made a partner at my firm."

"I really wouldn't go that far."

"*I* would."

"Well, I wouldn't. And stop staring at me as if you think I'm crazy. I'm not." She started to pour another glass of wine, and he took the bottle.

"You've had enough," he said.

"What? What are you doing?"

"You've had enough. Trust me. This is serious, and I don't want to discuss it if you're going to get drunk."

"I'm not getting drunk. Give me the bottle."

"Not until we discuss this. What kind of relationship do we have if you keep things that are this important from me? What else haven't you told me?"

She sighed. "Nothing. I promise. Now will you give me the bottle?"

He handed it over and looked into her eyes. "Are you seeing another man?"

"No." She poured another glass and took a long sip.

"Are you sure? What about one of your costars? Your leading men. Christ, Larkin, I don't even know what *show* you're on, what *role* you play."

"So watch. 'Coronado' on CTC at two-thirty every day. I have a big part—your basic soap opera vixen role, Serena Blake. And my leading man is as gay as the day is long, so you can forget about that."

"You're not taking this very seriously."

She didn't know how much more she could stand. And actually, she *was* beginning to feel a bit fuzzy around the edges, past the point she liked. But it was harder and harder these days to stay at that point, she had discovered. One second and then she seemed to be over the top.

"Larkin."

"What?"

"I said, you're not taking this very seriously."

She looked into his eyes. She didn't want to hear any more of it. "All right. Maybe you're right. Maybe it did mean something that I didn't tell you about it. All I know is that this isn't the way I want to spend my time." She reached for her glass and finished what was in it.

"You're leaving?"

"Let's take a rest, all right? We won't see each other for a while, and then we'll see how we feel."

"That never happens, you know. When people say they're going to take a rest, that means they're breaking up. Is that what you want?"

She was looking at two of him now, two Richards she really didn't want to be with anymore. "I don't know," she said, but by the time she said it, she couldn't remember what the question had been. "I have to go."

Hailing a cab was a nightmare—too many people, too few cabs, lights that were too bright shining into her eyes. She had thought Richard might follow her out, but he didn't, and in the cab she tried to remember what they had fought about—dinner? another man? Oh, the show. Not telling him.

Well, Christ—maybe he was right. He was so *needy*. She didn't need someone like that now, with the pressure of the show.

When she got home, only Danielle was there, getting ready for bed.

"Where's Maura?" Larkin asked. She swayed as she stood in the doorway to Danielle's bedroom, and somehow she hit her head.

"God. Are you okay?"

"I'm fine. Did I ask you, though, where Maura is?"

"Um, she had some late meeting with Terence and Alexandra, and then she was going to see a play. Um, are you sure you're okay?"

"I'm fine. I just—" She didn't want to say she had had one too many, because it would sound wrong. She really meant just one too many, as in just one. Too complicated, though. "Good night," she said, and she went down the hall to her bedroom.

When she got undressed, she couldn't remember what the really bad thing was that had happened—oh yes, Richard. Well, it was time. Or meant to be, Danielle would probably say. Something like that. Too much nagging. Taking the bottle away from her. Ridiculous. She was well rid of him.

"Larkin?"

The voice was coming through too many layers. Danielle. Hadn't she just talked to Danielle?

She tried to open her eyes, to open her mouth, to say, "I'm asleep" or something, anything, but she couldn't move. A voice inside said, This is wrong, but before she could think anything more about it, she was asleep.

Fifty-one

Danielle couldn't believe she was doing it, but she had made up her mind. Plus she had the feeling that if she thought about it for a million days, she might change her mind, so it was important to "act now," the way they said to.

Except that she couldn't stop thinking about Larkin, the way she had been so super-drunk last night. Plus it was weird, too, because it was so much like Cleve. Highs and lows, except the lows were extra-low. And the thing was, it seemed unhealthy, the way she kept going into those deep sleeps. Last night she hadn't even woken up when Danielle shook her a million times—like maybe she was taking something else. Because actually, Cleve had done the same thing, even though she couldn't remember too well, because she was so young. But her mother talked about it sometimes, and the truth was her mother did it sometimes, too, Valium or whatever, sometimes Percodans, and wine. So Danielle kind of knew the symptoms.

The thing was to talk to Maura, she guessed. Maura always knew what to do. And right now, God—she had to think about something else.

Al-Sadir was at one of the tables playing baccarat, which was a super-hard game to interrupt. The whole place was roped off and down some steps, because it was only for the really rich customers to play, and the club didn't want just anyone hanging over their shoulders and watching. It was that way at the Atlantic City casinos, too, and at first Danielle had thought it was a gyp and kind of unfair, but when you thought about the amounts, you could kind of understand. Sometimes fifty thousand dollars in a game, sometimes even more.

He was actually kind of a good-looking man if you thought about it kind of the way Maura would, maybe if you were looking for a star of some kind of desert picture, with robes and all that. Not that he was wearing robes, but he probably wore them when he went back to wherever he came from. And she guessed he was nice, the way he had promised her all those things. He didn't seem like the kind of guy who'd be really rude or anything, anyway.

And she wasn't going to let herself get "cold feet." This was something a million people in history had done, even if she couldn't think of their names. But in movies about the Depression and even modern times, women made sacrifices for their men.

He looked up and saw her, and she waved.

He nodded and went back to watching the play, and she thought, What if he isn't interested anymore? But a few seconds later, when the round was over, he cashed out and stood up.

"What a pleasant surprise," he said, walking up the steps from the baccarat pit and taking her hand. "To what do I owe this pleasure?"

"Um, I thought I'd say hi."

His eyes were totally dark and intense. "That is not all." He was squeezing her hand.

"Well, I thought maybe you wanted to go have a drink." *You have to do it.* "Somewhere else."

He made some kind of signal with his hand, and Danielle followed where he was looking. A man she had seen around but didn't know who he was, was leaving.

"My chauffeur will bring the car around," he said. He still hadn't let go of her hand. "Then we will be on our way."

In a way she felt like backing out, or more than in a way. It had seemed like such a good idea when she'd thought of it. She'd ask him to lend her the money, she'd sleep with him, and it wouldn't be any different from the past, when she had slept with guys on the beach and stuff back in Venice even when she hadn't liked them. Except that they hadn't even had any money, and it was a long time ago, when you didn't have to worry so much. But she'd make him "take precautions," the way they said. And it was honorable, because she was doing it for someone else. Kind of like a sacrifice. Only now, she was beginning to wonder. He seemed so steamed up, it was kind of scary.

When they were in the limo she realized she hadn't rehearsed how to ask for the money, plus when she was supposed to ask. If she did it now, it would seem totally weird, as if she were a hooker or something. Plus maybe he would get really mad. Maybe afterward would be better. But were those the only two choices? She couldn't even really think straight, because Al-Sadir was talking about his house back home, and what he had left, and she was pretending to be listening, saying "Uh-huh" and "Really?" and things like that. Luckily, he hadn't hardly touched her, but she guessed that would change.

The limo whooshed them along through the streets, and she wondered if people were cursing them the way she always saw people on the street, yelling, "Goddamn limos" and things like that. There *were* a lot of them in New York, you couldn't help noticing no matter who you were.

They didn't go far—when they got out, she recognized the street, because it was near a boutique she had stolen a watch from, in the east Seventies. The surprise was that they went down some steps, and then into a house, not even an apartment building. It was kind of like the club—super-fancy, with big, wide stairs and fancy wallpaper and old, antique furniture and paintings.

But there was nobody else there—no butler, no maids, nobody.

Al-Sadir had just opened the door, and boom, there they were, alone in an echoy foyer. The door slammed shut, and Al-Sadir looked into her eyes. "So. We are finally alone," he said, and his voice bounced off the walls. "As I knew," he added. He was half smiling, and she didn't know what to say. "Nobody to disturb, no one to interrupt. No one but you and me. To experience everything," he said, and he put his hands at her waist. "Such a beauty," he whispered. "Such a lovely thing, so young." He was almost singing, like he was in some kind of weird trance, and she wished like crazy that someone else was around. Or that maybe she hadn't thought of the idea in the first place. "You come and you follow me," he said, and he took her hand and led her up this giant staircase right out of the movies.

The bedroom he took her to had all kinds of tent-type things over the bed, but super-see-through, kind of like mosquito netting except it probably cost a jillion times more. Maybe silk.

She could hear him breathing behind her, and then he turned her around and kissed her, and she closed her eyes and said to herself, Just pretend it's the beach and you never met Allan. Close your eyes and keep pretending.

When it was over she opened her eyes and felt like she was in a dream—not that she had forgotten who she was with, even for one tiny second. But to see the room, to see Al-Sadir and feel him sweating and super-heavy on top of her, it was like something she'd only dream. And she had to admit that technically, it hadn't been the worst thing in the world: it hadn't hurt, and it didn't take that long, and he didn't smell or anything like that. And there wasn't any sand or broken bottles or the kind of thing you sometimes had in Venice. Plus he had used a condom, so that was good.

But she still felt bad. And she hadn't even asked him anything. Plus now he seemed to practically be a log.

"Al-Sadir?" she said.

"Mm." So he was almost asleep. And his teeth were kind of biting into her shoulder.

"Um, I think I should go pretty soon. It's getting kind of late."

"Mm" was all he said.

She tried to move, but she couldn't, really. And then he started to snore.

She sighed and looked around the room. It *was* pretty nice, she had to admit. And the cloth that covered the chairs kind of reminded her of when she had been in this play in sixth grade, all about a princess from the Middle Ages. She had been the star, and the only bad part was that her father was in town and he had promised to come and then he hadn't.

Al-Sadir groaned and moved, luckily onto the mattress, and Danielle sat up and got out of bed. It looked like there was a bathroom through a door, and it turned out there was, along with a giant bathtub with a Jacuzzi and everything. But she wasn't going to take a shower. What if he was like *Psycho*? Not that she thought he was—he had everything he wanted in the world, anyway—but she could never understand these people who took showers with strangers around. You had to be crazy.

She washed her face and heard a sound, and it turned out Al-Sadir was getting up and putting on a bathrobe. When he saw her, his eyes lit up and he said, "Ah, more beautiful each time I see you. Perhaps you would like to take a Jacuzzi."

"No, thanks," she said. She started to pull on her underpants and kind of wished he wasn't watching, but there wasn't anything she could do. "The thing is, I kind of have to go." And maybe you could lend me thirteen thousand dollars.

She thought maybe he would say something—"Now let me give you a token of my appreciation" or something like that. Like, what had happened to being draped with jewels? Back at the club that time, he had said he'd drape her with jewels. But he wasn't draping her in anything, and he wasn't talking about any kind of tiny little gift, even.

"Um, I have a question," she said.

"Yes?" Suddenly he seemed kind of distant.

"Um, I was just wondering." But she looked into his eyes, and she couldn't say anything. She just couldn't ask.

"Yes? What is it?"

"Um, don't say anything to anyone at the club, okay?" So she had chickened out. But at least she was following an instinct. She had learned a million years ago that it was super-important.

"I would not dream of betraying this night," he said. "I hope to have so many more, to show you the pleasures, to show you the finest things; we have not even eaten, Danielle. You come downstairs with me and we eat, we drink—"

"I just can't," she said. "I really have to go." And she waited. But he wasn't saying anything about a gift.

"Then I see you again," he said when he took her to the door.

"Of course," she said.

He took her hand and kissed it, and then that was it, out into the night with nothing.

Fifty-two

The apartment was dark, and at first Danielle didn't think anyone was home—Maura went to plays almost every night to try to find new clients, and Larkin would have the lights on if she were home.

But then Danielle heard the TV and walked down the hall to the living room, and in the dark, lying on the couch with the TV flickering, was Larkin. There was a blanket over her back even though it felt boiling to Danielle, and she was breathing like she had a cold.

"Larkin?"

Larkin turned over and wrapped the blanket higher around her neck. God, maybe she was sick and it wasn't what Danielle had thought. She turned the TV off and picked up some dishes off the coffee table, and Larkin sat up.

"Mm. Hi," she said, rubbing her eyes. "Shit, what time is it?"

"Um, nine-twenty."

Larkin let her head fall back against the cushions. "I dreamt I overslept and forgot to go in to the show." She put her hand on her chest. "I'm sweating from it. Do you ever have dreams that are so realistic, you still can't believe they were dreams even when you're wide-awake?"

"Sure," Danielle said. She sat down in the butterfly chair next to the couch. "Um, so are you feeling okay?" Larkin didn't look drunk or anything, or sound it, but she looked so pale. "You look really pale."

"I'm fine," Larkin said. "I couldn't get sick even if I wanted to; I can't miss any days from the show—at this point, anyway." She took a deep breath. "I never knew how tough it was going to be."

"Are you sorry you're doing it? I mean, do you wish you hadn't gotten the part?"

"Not at all," Larkin said—and quickly, like she meant it. "I love doing it when it's going well. And it *is* great exposure. I just wish I knew it was going to be all right—that I wasn't going to screw up in some extremely major way."

"But we can help you—like with lines and everything. I had fun doing it, pretending to be that guy. And remember the pact? We're always supposed to help each other, no matter what."

Larkin smiled. "Tom List. You're almost as good as Peter is."

"But we don't get why you're so *worried*," Danielle said. "I mean I know there are a million lines to learn, but you're so *great*. I look at the tapes, and all I can be is super-proud. You look like a real star."

Larkin looked real pleased, and Danielle was glad she had said it. It was the truth, too. "Well, thanks," Larkin said. "But let's not talk about it anymore. How was the club?" She lit a cigarette and leaned back into the couch.

Danielle didn't know where to start. It was a super-good time to talk about it, since Maura wasn't there and she had the secret feeling Maura wouldn't understand about Al-Sadir. "Um, actually, I have kind of a question."

"Shoot," Larkin said.

But she didn't know how to start. She guessed the truth was that when it came to something important, like asking Al-Sadir for money or asking Larkin how to do it, she never really could come up with the right words. "Well, actually, I kind of have a question, but it's kind of a long story."

"Tell me," Larkin said, settling back into the couch and pulling another blanket over her knees.

Danielle told Larkin as much as she could, about the money Allan owed and Al-Sadir and how he had said he'd give her so much. And then nothing. "And it was weird," Danielle said, "because when I thought about it before I did it, I kind of pictured being in bed with him and then all these jewel boxes around the room, and he'd say, 'Take your pick, Danielle; I want you to look beautiful.' But he didn't even offer me cab fare."

Larkin took a deep breath and then coughed. "I don't know," she finally said. "It's tough if they don't offer it. At the showroom the men supposedly always knew exactly what you were doing and why, that you weren't with them because you were in love with them. But even then you could get ripped off. I mean look at me, the one time I did it."

"God, I know. I kind of felt just like that. Except different, because he probably has no idea. He probably just thinks I have the hots for him or something. But what do you think I should do? Do you think I should bring it up, or wait for him to hand something over to me, or what?''

"I don't know. Bring it up next time. It's just a loan you want, isn't it?''

"Definitely. But what if I'm crazy, asking for that much money? I don't know; maybe I have rocks in my head. It's just that I know he's super-wealthy.''

"Then ask. Men like that love to help women like you. Just ask. You have nothing to lose.''

Danielle bit her lip. She guessed Larkin was right. "You know, it's weird. When I came home and you were the only person here, I was kind of glad Maura wasn't home. Because there are certain questions I'd ask her and certain questions I'd ask you, and I'd never even tell her I was doing this. I mean, I told her about Allan and the money, and she was totally shocked.''

Larkin smiled. "That doesn't surprise me.''

"But why? I mean, why is she like that? I've never been friends with someone like that before, someone who has this big—I don't know, like a code or something. Like some kind of knight in the olden days except that she's a girl.''

Larkin laughed, and Danielle wondered if she had said something dumb. But then Larkin said: "She'd probably like that, that image. The thing about Maura is that if she likes you—and she does like you a lot, by the way—you can't ever do anything that would make her stop liking you. I remember at Yale . . . well, the hundreds of things I did that alienated everybody else—my family, my professors, people in my classes. They were things I did mostly because I was scared—drinking too much, basically self-destructive things. And everyone else just jumped ship as quickly as they could. Not that I blame them. But Maura never did.''

"But the way she never talks about herself. Like you never know is she going out with anyone, what she's thinking, that kind of thing. And when I told her about Allan, all she could say was, 'That's very serious, Danielle.' It made me feel bad.''

"Well, she's probably worried, but for your sake. She cares more about you than she does about Allan. As well she should.''

Danielle shrugged. She guessed. "But do you think she's happy? I mean, you know, in general?''

"Oh, I don't know,'' Larkin said. She lit another cigarette. "Maura's better at being happy for other people, if you know what I mean. So are you going to tell her about this business with Al-Sadir or not?''

"Uh-uh, definitely not. I know everything you said is probably true, but I still feel bad about it, like . . . I just feel bad. So don't tell her, okay?"

Larkin shrugged. "Suit yourself."

Danielle felt cloudy and bad, and she didn't know why—she had started to feel bad a few minutes ago, but she couldn't put her finger on it. But suddenly she could. What she was doing with Al-Sadir —she was still going to do it, definitely a hundred percent. But she suddenly knew who it reminded her of, and it was the worst. Her mother, because what had her mother done? Borrowed from about ten thousand men and never paid them back, and she couldn't believe she hadn't even thought of that before. God. Victoria Austin, the most giant borrower in California. And now her daughter.

But it was dumb to worry about things like that. She had to do it for Allan.

Fifty-three

"Maura?" Danielle whispered from the other side of the door. Maura pulled on her bathrobe, looked at the clock—it was almost midnight—and opened the door.

"Hi. You weren't asleep, were you?" Danielle asked.

"No, I just got in."

Danielle rubbed her eyes. "I thought I heard you. I was asleep, but I thought I'd better wake up."

"What's the matter?"

Danielle looked around. "Um, can I shut the door?"

"Of course. What is it?"

Danielle sat down on the bed. "I think you'd better kind of talk to Larkin." She was looking down at her hands. "I mean, I feel bad 'cause I talked to her for a long time tonight about something else, and I never even said one word about this, but I couldn't do it. And you're a better friend of hers."

"But what is it?" Maura asked, sitting down.

Danielle swallowed. "I think she has a super-serious problem with drinking. And I know, like, you said she got drunk when you guys were at Yale, and you didn't make a giant deal of it or anything, but she reminds me a lot of my father, and it's bad.''

Maura swallowed. ''Is there something special, something you've seen, or just a feeling?''

Danielle shrugged. ''I think it isn't even just drinking, to tell you the truth. I think she's taking something else. I mean, I was worried about her the other night, and I tried to wake her up and I couldn't, just like when we tried when we wanted to have the party for her. And I know I don't exactly walk around acting like some kind of doctor, and I might not be the one everyone goes to for advice, but I know about this because of both my parents, not just my father. My mother took tons of things, and she acted just like Larkin.''

Maura didn't say anything. She had never seen anyone get as seriously drunk in her life. But it didn't happen that often. Larkin went on binges, but then they were over.

''I just thought you—I don't know, maybe you could say something. 'Cause it would be really bad if she went to work drunk or anything like that. That's how my father screwed up a thousand times.''

''I have to think about it,'' Maura said. ''I don't want to say anything that's going to upset her right now.''

Danielle looked uncertain. ''You think? I mean—''

''I have to think about it. I'll ask her about it,'' Maura said.

Danielle stood up. ''Okay. Whatever, I guess.''

Danielle left and shut the door, and Maura turned out the light. But she couldn't sleep. What if Danielle was right? She knew that, to an extent, it was obvious. The other night, Larkin had been in bad shape, and it could have been from something more than drinking. No question about it.

She'd mention it tomorrow morning; she'd get up early and talk to Larkin. At night she wouldn't be able to, because these days she worked late every single night. So she'd get up early and do it. As a friend, it was her duty.

''I'm fine,'' Larkin said. ''Really. I promise. Aren't you *tired*? I can't believe you got up this early.''

''It was the only time I could talk to you today.''

''But why today? Why would you even bring it up?'' She put three teaspoons of instant coffee in her cup and poured boiling water in.

"Well, the other night," Maura said, "Danielle and I were both worried. And—"

"Danielle's father is an alcoholic," Larkin cut in. "She has her own thoughts about it that aren't necessarily very accurate. Have you thought of that?"

"But we're not talking about Danielle."

Larkin held out her hands, palms down. "Are my hands shaking?"

"I didn't ask you to perform a test, Larkin."

"But look at them. Are my hands shaking?"

"No."

"Richard was the same way the other night. Did I tell you? We're not going to see each other for a while."

"What happened?"

"Too needy," Larkin said with a shrug. "I'm tired of him."

"Are you sure that now is the time? With so much else going on—"

"That's why I did it," Larkin said, flipping back her hair. "Too much else is going on. I don't have time for him. But anyway, to get back to your question: I'm absolutely fine, and I promise I'd tell you if I weren't." She touched Maura's shoulder. "I promise. Really."

It was impossible to tell. Was it true or was Larkin acting? God knows she could pull it off.

But what was the choice, anyway? People always said you couldn't help someone who didn't want to be helped, and she knew it was true. No one could force her to go on a diet, and no one could stop someone else from drinking—or doing anything—if that person wasn't ready.

Still, she hoped for Larkin's sake that Danielle was wrong.

Larkin got into the limo and slammed the door.

"How's it going?" the driver said—Zeke. He said the same thing every morning.

"Fine," she said, moving against the right door. It was the only place he couldn't see her, she had discovered, without turning around.

"Nice day," he said.

"Beautiful."

She opened her purse and shook out a pill and chewed it up, then shook out another and broke it in half.

Then she swallowed and looked out the window.

She felt horrible. She hated lying. She had lied to Maura, she had lied to Danielle, and she hated it. And it amazed her that Maura believed her. Danielle she could understand—Danielle didn't know her that well. But Maura?

She closed her eyes and tried to forget about the conversation. She had done the right thing. They didn't understand she wasn't really taking a lot or drinking a lot. They wouldn't understand that for her, the amounts were different. They were necessary, and they didn't mean anything at all.

Fifty-four

It sounded like a party coming from behind Terence's door—loud laughter, glasses clinking, music in the background—and Maura didn't understand. Terence had said they'd meet late at his place to discuss "something important," but there was definitely music coming from inside. And she didn't feel like having some sort of party with Terence and Alexandra. The day had been tough—she hadn't been able to stop thinking about Larkin, and everyone who had called had been on a short fuse today. And three times in less than an hour at the end of the day, a man had called and refused to leave a message, something she had to ask Terence about, because he had sounded very insistent and slightly crazy. But not at a party. She rang the doorbell and braced herself for the worst.

Terence opened the door and immediately danced away, beckoning Maura into the room, and Maura saw it was more noise than people, really only Terence and Alexandra (over in the kitchen) so far. "Come in, come in, come in!" Terence called out. "So much to celebrate, so little time!"

It smelled like roast lamb coming from the kitchen, and Maura was famished. But she was going to try not to eat any of it. It was a matter of principle with her (although it was almost impossible to stick to) never to eat in front of Alexandra, particularly since Alexandra had started losing weight. But she looked over to the kitchen, and Alexandra was pigging out, hunched over the counter with a big bowl of potato chips all to herself, so that was one plus. Alexandra gave a perfunctory wave and went back to eating, and Maura followed Terence to the living room. "Is it just us?" she asked. "What are we celebrating?"

"Ah, 'just us,' " he said, still dancing as he poured her a glass of wine. "They could be taken somewhat metaphysically, your words, couldn't they? Just us, as in the more cosmic meaning, or just us, meaning, Is that all there is? Or just us, meaning—"

"Meaning is anyone else coming?" She hated not knowing that kind of thing.

"Well, actually, Max is in his room, but Vanessa is coming. Part of the reason for the celebration, actually."

"How long have you been planning this?"

"Hm? Why do you ask?"

"I don't know," she said. "I could have brought something. And you're all dressed up. I thought we were having a meeting."

"Ah, don't be so *literal*, Maura. We do this all the time. Any excuse to celebrate. It keeps us positive. Sit down. Relax. You're making me nervous."

He was making *her* nervous. He was too up, too talkative.

"Listen," she said. "After you two left, a man called three times and refused to leave a message."

At first Terence didn't say anything. Then: "Don't worry about it."

"You know who it was?"

"No—I don't think so. But don't worry about it." He looked around. "Get yourself a drink or something. I have to baste the lamb."

He walked away, and she had the feeling he was upset.

The record ended, and Maura heard the clicking of dog nails and then human footsteps coming from the other end of the loft, and Sophie came out of Max's room, followed by Max, putting on a coat. "Maura, hi," he said, coming over. He kissed her on the cheek. "How's it going? Glad you're here. I'll be back in two minutes, all right?"

"Sure."

"Sophie," he called.

Sophie was sniffing Maura's feet.

"Sophie," Max called again.

He came over and gently pulled on her collar. "I keep forgetting she can't always hear anymore," he said, leading her away.

Maura watched them leave, Sophie walking more slowly than she'd walked the last time.

Terence came back in, and he looked like silly Terence again, wired up and jittery.

"Max looked so sad when Sophie couldn't hear him," she said. "How is she doing these days, anyway?"

Terence shrugged. "She's fourteen. What can he expect?"

The music blared on again, and Maura looked over to Alexandra standing at the record player, dancing with a piece of bread in her hand.

She wanted to leave.

She leaned close to Terence. "So what are we celebrating?" she yelled.

He looked at her. "Why do you keep *asking* me that? We have all *kinds* of things to celebrate. Vanessa and I are flying to the Coast next week to meet with Duane Haskins, for one thing. And Larkin's part on 'Coronado'—that's something to celebrate."

"Why didn't you invite her?"

"This isn't a *client* party," he said. "We have those at Christmas. This is just us. Why are you so *nervous*?"

The downstairs buzzer rang, and Terence got up. "That's probably Vanessa," he said. "And Max doesn't know, by the way."

"Doesn't know what?"

"That she's meeting with *Haskins*. That this is her big chance. So don't say anything. She wants to surprise him."

Vanessa rang, and Terence gave her another Terence-style greeting, complete with hugs and screams and compliments. More screams and hugs with Alexandra, and then she came around to Maura.

Maura shook her hand. "Congratulations," she said.

Vanessa looked worried. "You haven't told Max, have you—?"

"Certainly not. I only heard about it ten seconds ago myself."

Vanessa was looking around. "Where *is* Max?"

"Out with Sophie," Maura said.

"Oh. Terence, get me a glass of red wine?"

"Anything, my dear," he said, bowing. "Oh. Maura? Anything to drink? I thought you were going to get yourself something."

"Red wine would be fine," she said.

Vanessa sat down and let her head fall back with a theatrical groan. "No one ever *told* me success would be so *exhausting*." She ran her fingers through her hair and looked at Maura. "I heard *you* have something to celebrate, too. A part for your first client?"

"That's right. On 'Coronado.' "

"That's wonderful. The money on those shows is terrific. Your friend—Larkin, right?" Maura nodded. "Your friend must be thrilled."

"She is."

"Isn't it hard to learn all those lines, though?"

"She seems to be managing," Maura said.

"What I'd give for a part on one of those shows. Terence, dear, why didn't you and Alexandra send me up for that role?"

"Yours not to question, my dear," he said, handing the drinks out. "And anyway, look at you now. The way Duane Haskins works, if he doesn't use you in 'Jake's People,' he'll use you in 'Pete & Charlie' or 'Echo Bay' or all three. Once you're in with him, you end up on all his shows. You couldn't ask for better."

The door opened, and Max and Sophie came in, and Vanessa jumped up and kissed Max. "Mm," she said. "Long time."

Maura felt a pang. She had never seen Max embracing her, kissing her. Why *were* all the good ones taken?

"I've got a surprise," she said, following him to the kitchen. He handed a biscuit to Sophie and refilled her water bowl. "Are you listening?" Vanessa said.

"Of course. Let me just set Sophie up." He poured out some food in a bowl and then stood up. "So. What's the surprise?"

"Well. In exactly three days, Terence and I are flying out to L.A. to meet with Duane Haskins, who wants to meet with us to discuss a *definite* future commitment!"

"Vanessa, that's great! Congratulations!" He kissed her again. "Do you know which show he wants to see you for?"

"He's not sure yet."

Max was smiling. "That's great. Really."

"*And,*" Vanessa said, taking his arm in hers and starting to stroll back to the living room area, "it's on the Friday of Columbus Day weekend, so you can come, too."

"What?"

"It's all on Haskins. He's booking us two rooms—one for me and one for Terence—so you could come with us for free. All you'd have to pay would be the plane fare, and I'm sure you could get a deal through work—and we'd have four or five days out in L.A.!"

"Vanessa, I can't go away for five days." They had reached where everyone else was sitting—and everyone was listening—but Max turned around and started back for the kitchen.

Vanessa followed. "What do you mean? You can't have anything planned, because we were going to go up to Vermont."

"That was different."

"Why?"

"Sophie," he said. "We were going to bring her to Vermont. She needs her medicine four times a day. And we couldn't bring her to L.A."

"That's right—we couldn't."

For a few seconds Vanessa just looked at Max, and he just looked at her. Then she said, "Never mind. Forget I asked." And she came back to the group and refilled her glass with wine. "I forgot about Saint Sophie," she said. She walked over to the record player and turned the music up, and came back and pulled Terence out of his chair. "Dance with me," she said.

Maura looked over at Max. He was crouching on the floor patting the dog.

"He should marry *her*," Vanessa said to Terence, swinging past Maura in some half version of the fox-trot.

"Does that mean you set a date?" Terence yelled over the music.

"We *had*," she said, and then Maura couldn't hear anything more.

She couldn't stop looking at Max. It was hard to figure him out, to understand what his relationship with Vanessa was. All through dinner he had barely said a word. Yet it was clear that when he looked at Vanessa, and especially when she looked at him, there was a lot going on, despite their fight. Vanessa couldn't say two sentences without glancing at Max, even though she hadn't spoken directly to him at all since before dinner.

And Maura was trying not to get all caught up again in the way she had felt when she had first met him. He was taken. And she had also learned a long time ago that people also ran true to their tastes. You didn't go out with tall, skinny blondes and then switch to overweight brunettes. It just didn't happen.

"Well, everybody," Vanessa said, standing up. "It's been lovely, but I have to get home. Beauty sleep and all that. Max?"

Max got up, and Vanessa got her coat, and they walked to the door together.

Out of the corner of her eye, Maura watched: They were talking quietly, then Max was touching her elbow, then her waist, and then he kissed her, and she threw her arms around him, and the kiss seemed to go on forever.

Maura looked away, and Terence smiled at her. "Getting any ideas?"

She didn't say anything.

Max came back and they all had coffee, and then Max stood up from the table. "Anyone want to come out for a walk?" He seemed to be looking at Maura.

"Actually, I'd love to," Maura said. She could feel Terence watching her as she stood up and put on her coat.

Sophie seemed glad to get out, wagging her tail and nosing Maura's knees in the elevator. "How is she feeling?" Maura asked, patting her behind the ears.

"It's up and down," he said. "All those tests took something out of her." He paused. "When I picked her up at the hospital, she suddenly looked so old. Her muzzle looked so white. I had never seen it so clearly, and it broke my heart."

"I can imagine," Maura said. A blast of cold hit as they left the building, and Maura pulled her coat shut more tightly. But Sophie seemed to need the cold air: she immediately broke into a trot and raised her tail. "But look at her now," Maura said. "She looks good. She must have been hot."

"I know. She belongs in the country," he said. "I've been thinking about it a lot."

"You mean thinking of moving? Where are you from, anyway?"

"New Hampshire, originally, but all over the place. My family traveled every couple of years. And I miss it."

"Do you think you could find work outside of the city?"

"I could be a country lawyer," he said. "It sounds kind of nice, doesn't it?"

"It does," Maura said. "What does Vanessa think of the idea?"

He smiled. "What do you think? We haven't discussed it much, but it's obvious what she thinks." He paused. "It just wasn't obvious to her what *I* thought until we talked about it—that I've been getting more and more disenchanted with New York, that even my career means nothing to me if I can't be happy in other ways."

She was almost afraid to ask. "Ways such as—?"

He was hesitating, walking along in the wind. "Relationships," he finally said. "I suppose that's the most important. Building something. And since Sophie isn't going to be around forever, giving her someplace great to live out her last year or two." He reached down and scratched the dog behind the ears and then looked at Maura. "What did you think of the L.A. thing?"

"You mean your not going?" She paused. "I don't really know the circumstances."

"You know all there is to know except that Sophie isn't in the best shape and I'd have to leave her in a kennel. And going out to L.A. to hang around some producer's pool just isn't worth it to me."

"Then it's obvious you did the right thing."

He sighed. "I wonder."

"When's the big date?"

"The what?" he asked.

"I heard Vanessa say you guys had set a date—?"

"Oh. April." He looked into her eyes. "Sounds like a long way off, doesn't it?"

She couldn't say anything. All she could do was look into his eyes and think, If only he were with me.

Fifty-five

"So, um, do you know what you're going to do?" Danielle asked.

Allan looked into her eyes—they were so damn trusting. "I don't know," he said. "I'll work it out, though."

"But what if you get caught?"

"I won't get caught—not for a while, anyway. Murray doesn't bring in an accountant until January."

"But what if he does? How do you *know* he won't? And what if you still owe all that money? What are you going to do?"

He brushed her hair back from her face and kissed her forehead. "I'll work it out."

She was frowning. "But what if—what if I could come up with the money?"

"What are you talking about? Where would you get that kind of money?"

"I don't know. But what *if*? It's still thirteen thousand, right?"

He sighed. Well, twenty if you were counting. "I don't want you to even *consider* helping. All right? Because I know and you know

there's no way you could do that without doing something crazy."
She didn't say anything. "Do you promise me? I'd rather go to jail
than involve you in this. I wish I had never told you about it."

She snuggled up against his cheek. "But you kept *me* from getting into trouble. Think about that. Think about Mr. Minsky."

"That was different," he said. "Now, promise me."

"Okay. I promise," she said.

He looked up at the ceiling. Twenty thousand dollars, and January wasn't that far away. How *was* he going to get out of it?

Danielle counted her tips and put them back in her purse. It
hadn't been that great a night, and now that thirteen thousand dollars was the only thing she thought about, everything else seemed
tiny. The thing was that she *knew* she could get Allan out of trouble,
even if he didn't want her to. She still didn't understand why he
seemed so relaxed about it. Maybe just so she didn't worry? She
didn't know, but she knew it was super-serious even if he was
pretending it wasn't. And it was worth sleeping with Al-Sadir,
maybe, if it meant keeping the man she loved from getting into
horrible trouble.

Suddenly she saw him, Al-Sadir, going down to the baccarat pit,
and she figured, Might as well get it over with.

She kind of rushed across the casino floor so she was standing
at the ropes just as he was sitting down. Right away his face lit up,
and he made some kind of gesture to the dealer and stood up.

So we can get this over with, Danielle was thinking. But when
Al-Sadir came up to her, he said, "What a pleasure to see you
again, Danielle. We can meet when I finish?"

"Um, actually, I was hoping we could go now, since my shift's
over."

He gave a funny smile. "In one hour," he said. And she couldn't
believe it. He would rather play baccarat than be with her? It would
have been funny if she weren't in such a hurry. "You might care
to watch the game?"

She figured she "might care to," since if she didn't, maybe she
would run into Nick, which was the last thing she wanted to do.
So she went into the pit (her first time, actually) and sat next to
him, and she couldn't believe how comfortable they made things
for the super-rich players at the casino. The chair she was sitting in
had to be more comfortable than the most giant bed on earth. It
was hard to imagine what it was stuffed with, but whatever it was,
was the greatest. And it was super-quiet, muffled in some crazy way

so you couldn't hardly hear the casino. Just chink chink, click click of cards and chips. And she had to admit it was kind of exciting, the amounts. Al-Sadir bet five hundred at first, then a thousand, and then two thousand, the club's top limit. It seemed crazy, and she kept thinking, How could I be upset about Allan when people at this table are betting ten times what he lost??? And they didn't even care about the money—they probably hadn't even had to work for any of it. And Al-Sadir didn't seem nervous at all. He wasn't even sweating.

And after almost an hour, she couldn't believe it, but he had won more than twenty thousand dollars.

"God, Al-Sadir, you won more than I've made the whole time I've worked here," she said.

He stood up. "And I leave a winner," he said, holding out his elbow. "With good luck from a beautiful young woman."

She walked out with him, and all she could think about was the money. He had won *so much*! He *had* to be willing to lend her some money now that he had won so much. That was all she wanted anyway, was a loan. And think when Allan had won that night: he hadn't won even nearly that much, and he had given her seven hundred dollars, so what was Al-Sadir going to give her, or lend her? Tons, she hoped.

The cab ride was a little weird. She didn't know where the chauffeur was, but all they took was a regular horrible New York City cab, which had some disgusting slime on the seat, and then all Al-Sadir wanted to do was make out, which she just couldn't believe: for one thing, the driver kept looking in the rearview mirror, and he had been a terrible driver to *begin* with, even before Al-Sadir had started his funny stuff. And then forget it—he was practically hitting every car.

Plus what was Al-Sadir in such a *hurry* for? They were going to be alone in that giant house anyway.

They got there, *finally*, and Danielle jumped out of the cab and ran to the door just so Al-Sadir wouldn't try to grab her on the sidewalk. And she bet the driver would watch if it happened. Some people were just sick.

"Tonight I cannot wait to touch you," Al-Sadir said as he started opening the door. "Tonight I am like an animal."

He opened the door, and she thought he would grab her—what about the cab ride over?—but the door slammed shut and Al-Sadir walked straight past her, into one of the side rooms that kind of looked like a study.

"Now I must ask you to turn your back," he said, moving across the room.

"Why?"

"Because I am opening my safe."

"I won't look." Except she already had. He was near a fireplace, and she bet the safe was under the painting.

"You will not look because you will turn your back. Now."

She didn't like his tone of voice, but she figured she didn't have a choice. But in a couple of seconds she heard sounds, click click click, just like on "Columbo," and she was dying to turn around, plus she wished she had those glasses they advertised in the back pages of comic books, where there was a little tiny mirror on the earpiece. The people always looked totally shocked in the drawings, when the guy saw what they were doing with his back turned, and she had always wondered if they worked as well as they looked.

She heard some rustling, and then the door shut, and she turned around.

But Al-Sadir looked furious. "Who told you to turn around?" he shouted. Plus his accent had gotten super-thick all of a sudden.

"I heard you shut the safe," she said.

He narrowed his eyes. "You turn when I tell you to turn."

She shrugged. "Sorry. I didn't know it was such a giant deal." Except she had been right—the safe was under the painting. Didn't people ever put them anywhere else?

He looked like he was fuming and thinking, and she suddenly wondered if he was going to kick her out. But instead he came striding across the room, like in three giant steps, and he swooped her into his arms. "You excite me when you argue," he said. His lips were almost touching hers. "Now I take you upstairs, and you fight me some more." And he picked her up and put her over his shoulder.

It was different and it was weird, but it turned out to be okay, since she kind of felt she was just acting, saying no and running around upstairs as he chased after her. It was kind of like the super-old sitcoms her mother used to watch during the day, when the boss would be running around the desk after his secretary, but a little different, because they were in a giant, fancy house. She ran along the staircase and opened a door of a room she had never seen, and she screamed, because Al-Sadir had caught her just when she got inside. But she also screamed because of the room. It looked like a palace in "Cinderella," all what did you call it? Brocade, maybe, that gold cloth, and things draped everywhere, and gold-edged boxes on glass tables.

"What's this *room*?"

He didn't say anything.

"Al-Sadir, what's this *room*?"

"You like it?"

"Of course. What is it, though?"

He was smiling. "It is the favorite of all the women," he said, walking in slowly, kind of as if it was a museum or something. And it looked like a museum. He faced her. "Perhaps this is where you would like to make love."

She nodded. "But the way you said that time at the club," she said. She didn't want to be too obvious. "You know, draping me in cloth. And jewels."

He did it super-slowly, undressing her and putting the things on her one by one, first a drapey silk cloth, then a bracelet that looked kind of plain, then a necklace he said was rubies and emeralds, and she started to get excited. It felt good, like a really great lover (she didn't want to think about Allan), just knowing it was worth so much money. Earrings that weren't pierced. A long band of gold around her waist. Bands of gold around her thighs. He smiled. "The jewels feel good, do they not?"

And he was super-gentle, and she really couldn't complain, even though she felt extra-bad about Allan. When she was with another guy, it always happened like this; it always made her miss him more. But she had to remember, this was all for a reason, and she had to ask or it would just be bad, period.

"That was great," she said, running her fingers through his hair.

He sat up and ran a hand along one of the gold bands that was around her thigh. "It is always good when you have the right surroundings, the things that add to the beauty. Though you need so little, you are so young."

She bit her lip. It was time. "Al-Sadir, I have a question," she said.

"Ask me anything, my little beauty."

"Um, I have a small problem."

He looked upset already, and kind of irritated even though she hadn't said hardly anything. Maybe he was just worried about something in his own life. "What is it?" he asked.

"My father is kind of in trouble," she said. "He's not that responsible a person. I mean, he's *going* to be, he's turning over a new leaf and everything, but he kind of got into some debt."

At first he didn't say anything. Then he said: "And why do you tell me?"

It wasn't what she had expected him to say, but maybe he didn't know what she was leading up to. "Well, actually, I was hoping that maybe you could lend me some money. I mean, since you won so much and everything tonight, and you seem to have so much." She shrugged. "It would just be kind of a loan. I mean, it *would* be a loan. Definitely."

He smiled. "You give yourself away without realizing it, Danielle." It was the first time he had ever called her "Danielle" instead of "my peach" or "my beauty," and she didn't like it. It seemed too close. And she didn't like what he was saying, either. "You say a 'loan.' Why do I know it will be a loan? How do I know such a thing? How can you assure me? And even if I take the assurance, people default on loans all the time."

Default. She didn't even know he'd know the word. She hardly even knew it herself, except that her mother had defaulted on about a million and one loans. "I wouldn't default. I'd pay you back."

"You are talking about how much money? Not that I am saying yes, of course."

She swallowed. She didn't even want to say it now.

"How much? If you cannot say, it must be quite a large amount."

"Not really," she said quickly, and she shrugged so she would seem casual. "Thirteen thousand."

"Dollars?" He looked totally shocked.

"Al-Sadir, you *won* twenty thousand dollars tonight."

"You are right. *I* won. Not your father. I earned it."

"You won it at a game."

"What do you think this is?" he demanded. His accent had gotten thick again. "Since when do you work at the fifth floor of King's club?"

"Al-Sadir, I was just asking you to *help* me. To lend me some money. But if you can't, just forget it. I just don't see why you think it's that giant a thing if you can win that much in one *night* at baccarat."

"That is not for you to think about," he said. "Now get dressed. Take off these things." He pulled at one of the necklaces.

She shrugged. "Fine." But she hated him.

"And out of this room when you finish."

She looked into his eyes. He thought he was so smart. "Let me get dressed in privacy," she said.

"Do not hold your breath. I would not leave you in here with these possessions."

Just what she wanted him to say, and to do. She shrugged again. "Fine," she said. Super-calmly, but also like she was disappointed.

And her heart started to pound. What she was about to do was maybe the craziest thing she had ever done, definitely crazier than stealing the cashmere scarf from Bloomingdale's. But she didn't feel crazy. She felt right, the way those pioneer ladies had probably felt right when they sometimes had to shoot intruders and do crazy things to protect their land and their children. Well, she wanted to protect Allan. And she could do it.

Al-Sadir was watching her, but she was taking the things off super-slowly, gathering her clothes super-slowly, and maybe he'd get bored. Even if he didn't, he wouldn't suspect, because she was putting each thing back in the box it came from. The first necklace in the gold box, the thigh things in a greenishy-gold box. "I feel you let me down," she said, looking at him.

He just glared back at her.

"You promised me so much. What's the difference whether I'm here with you or in a hotel room with some guy who doesn't have anything? You said you would do so much for me." She pulled on her underpants and then her bra. She still had the ruby and emerald necklace on, and it was totally noticeable, the way she wanted it. Then she pulled on her shirt—

"The necklace," he said.

She narrowed her eyes. "Come on. What did you think? I was going to try to *steal* from you?" She unlatched the necklace, threw it in the box, and snapped the box shut. "There," she said. "Everything accounted for, okay?"

He turned to pull up a chair, and the moment had come—with one hand she pushed the top of the box up and slipped the necklace up her shirt sleeve. Al-Sadir had already sat down and was just turning back, and her heart was pounding so hard, she thought she would choke. "I mean, *really*," she said. "You know, I was really getting to like you."

He didn't say anything, and she started to get scared. He *had* to stay distracted!

She walked up to him and brushed his knee with hers. "We had some fun," she said. "Remember, *I'm* the one who came up to *you*. Way before I needed money."

"I do not know that," he said.

"*I* do," she said, and she sank to her knees and made her eyes go all heavy-lidded. "So let's be friends?" She kissed his thigh—super-hairy, when you came to think of it—and pulled his robe back. The next part would be kind of tricky, because she had to make sure her right sleeve didn't go anywhere near his body, or he'd hear something.

But she could tell he was already thinking about other things.

Fifty-six

Don't panic when you see the set, Larkin told herself. There was something about the soundstage that made her feel as if every line she had learned had suddenly drained from her mind. And at this point it was almost a conditioned response: walk in, and she'd forget her lines.

"Larkin!"

She turned around. Peter was coming toward her. "Whew. We're starting late. Nice break, isn't it?"

She looked at her watch. Peter was right. How had she lost ten minutes?

"Come on," he said, grabbing her elbow. "And tell them to put some extra rouge on your cheeks. You look like death."

"Thanks," she said. "Now I'm *really* confident."

"Oh, you'll do okay. You always do with a little help, right?" He winked.

"What?"

"You know. Whatever it is you're taking. That 'serene bitchiness' *Soap Opera Digest* wrote about."

"I don't—"

"Don't *worry* about it," he said. "I think it's fine. We all do what we have to. Now, come on. Get into Makeup, and I'll see you out on the set."

She walked into the dressing room in shock. So Peter knew, and maybe everyone did. But what was there to know? One, two, maybe three pills every so often. Why was everyone making such a major case about it?

"Jesus *Christ!*" Monica Morgan yelled. "Get it *right*, Larkin."

"I will. Sorry." She couldn't concentrate. And Peter was trying to help, which was making it worse, nudging her when she was supposed to speak, as if she were deaf and didn't know her cue. "I'm ready," she said.

"Christ, I hope so. ACTION!"

"I didn't—I didn't think Allison would be so observant," she said. "How did she know we were together that day?"

"It was obvious," Peter said. "For one thing, that perfume you wear. She can smell it on you, and she can smell it on me. You have to stop wearing it."

"CUT!"

Larkin turned to look at Monica. What was wrong? She hadn't even said anything!

"You want to wake up, Larkin?"

"Sorry," she said.

She looked at Peter. Even he looked annoyed. So maybe . . . well, maybe it was time to cut down a tiny bit.

"Danielle? Maura?" Larkin let the door slam shut and knew there was nobody home. The apartment was pitch-black. Silence. And she couldn't stand it. She had made the simplest of plans: Go home, settle down with the script, do some talking. No drinking, no Valium. But now that she was alone, it seemed impossible.

What if Maura was right?

She didn't want to be alone.

It was all she could think about.

But who could she call? She tried Maura's office, but she got the machine, and if Danielle was out . . . well, she could be anywhere.

She went into the kitchen and put the water on to boil, and sat down and opened the script to where her lines began. "SERENA (gently): But, Tom, how could you ever think that? I would *never* betray you. *Never.* I *love* you."

She thought she heard something at the front door, but it was from the next apartment.

"TOM: But, Serena, what about the phone call? What about all those letters? Did you honestly think Allison wouldn't find them?"

She didn't want to call her mother or her sister. But she had to talk to someone, a friendly voice, someone who wouldn't scream at her over her lines or tell her to wake up.

She put down the script, picked up the phone, and dialed Richard's number—he always wanted to see her, no matter what—and she let it ring six, seven, eight times.

She hung up and called his office, but there was no answer there. Which meant he was out, too. The whole world was out.

She picked up her purse to get her cigarettes, and the bottle of Valium fell against her hand.

And she thought about Maura, and Peter. What was it Peter had said? "You always do with a little help."

But Peter had his bitchy side—everyone knew that; he wasn't the most popular person on the set. And Maura was a worrier, and Danielle had her own issues about drinking. Why had she thought they were right, just by making certain pronouncements? Everyone needed to calm down from time to time, to loosen up so they could concentrate. Everyone.

Fifty-seven

"Fielding-White Agency; may I help you?"

"Yeah. Alexandra, please."

"Is this Jim Gray again?" Maura asked. She knew the answer—he was an actor who had called twice today—but she had to be sure.

"Sure is," he said. She could picture him, too, because his eight-by-ten hung on the wall right across from her desk. Handsome, sandy blond hair, nice smile.

"Hold on, please," she said. She looked up as the outer door opened. It was Vanessa, followed a couple of seconds later by Max.

She buzzed Alexandra and got the same answer she had gotten the other two times: "Tell him I'll call him back," Alexandra said.

Maura hesitated. "This is the third time he's called," she said, motioning to Max and Vanessa to sit down. Max sat down, but Vanessa stood over the desk, looking at her picture on the wall.

"He's not going to be particularly inclined to believe you, I don't think."

"Tell him I'll call him back," Alexandra said again, and hung up.

Maura sighed. "Hello?" she said into the phone.

"She'll call me back," Jim Gray said.

"That's what the lady said."

"All right," he said. "You give Alexandra a message for me. Will you do that?" He sounded furious.

"Of course," she said.

"Tell her I'm going to call SAG tomorrow morning unless I hear from her this afternoon. Will you tell her that?"

Maura wanted to ask what it was about, but she knew she couldn't. "I will definitely tell her that, Jim. Anything else?"

"That should be enough," he said, and hung up.

"Hello there," she said, putting down the phone. Her voice had come out oddly, like someone else's—but she was nervous with Vanessa around. She couldn't quite look directly at Max. "Vanessa, you're here to see Alexandra or Terence?"

"Either or both," she said, pulling her hair back as she looked at another actress's picture. "We're just here for a moment. Are they both in?"

"Yup. I'll tell them you're here."

She could have buzzed, but she wanted to give Alexandra Jim Gray's message face-to-face and see what her reaction was.

She knocked, went in, and said it straight out, to Alexandra, although Terence was listening. "Jim Gray says that if you don't call him back this afternoon, he'll call SAG in the morning." She paused. "Does that mean you'll talk to him the next time he calls?"

Alexandra's face didn't move—not a muscle, not an eyelash. Then she looked at Terence. "Maybe you should call him, Terence."

Terence nodded.

"If he calls again, though—" Maura said.

"We will call him," Alexandra said in a falsely calm voice. "Thank you for delivering the message. It is being taken care of," she said slowly.

Odd. "Well, Vanessa's out in the waiting room and wants to see either or both of you. Should I send her in?"

"Yes. Please," Alexandra said in the same odd, slow way.

Maura went out to the waiting room and told Vanessa she could go in, and Vanessa murmured something to Max and walked in. A few seconds later the door closed.

"So. How's it going?" Max asked. Now he was looking into her eyes.

"Oh, it's crazy, as usual. How's Sophie?"

He smiled. "You always ask, don't you?"

"Well, why not?"

"She's okay. What was that phone call about?"

Maura shook her head. "I wish I knew. A client—this guy right here, on the wall above you. He called three times today, and three times Alexandra refused to talk to him. He said to say he'd call SAG if she didn't get back to him, which is what I just told her." She paused. "Now Terence is calling him."

Max raised a brow. "Interesting."

"Isn't it," she said. "I wish I knew what it was about."

"Did you ask them?"

Maura laughed. "You jest, sir." He laughed, too. "What are you two doing here, anyway?"

"Oh, Vanessa has to work out some trip details with them. I'm just along for the ride." He was looking at her too carefully. It made her nervous. "So what else?" he said. He looked past her, up at the wall. "Is that your roommate? Larkin James?"

She turned around. "Yup. I put her in the best spot, so everyone could see her. She looks good, doesn't she—?"

He nodded. "How's it going with her? How does she like being an in-the-flesh TV star?"

"Oh, she's having some trouble." She looked into his eyes. *He* was the one she could talk to about this. "And you're a good person to ask, maybe." She paused. "If you had a friend who was having a hard time, maybe drinking too much, maybe taking something else, but you weren't completely sure. You would talk to them and then what?"

"What do you mean, then what? You're talking about Larkin?"

She nodded. "She says she's fine. But I don't know if she's all right or not."

He raised a brow. "That's a tough one, if she says she's fine. You think it's serious?"

"I don't know. It's just—well, you know what the pressures of the business are like."

"Everyone handles them differently," he said. "Some people thrive on them. It's all a challenge to Vanessa. She loves every minute." He didn't sound as if *he* loved every minute, though. "I don't know what to tell you about Larkin," he said. "But I know you can't do anything about it unless she does, unless she's ready."

"I guess."

Silence. She didn't know what to say, because she didn't know when Vanessa would come back in and her time would be up. She wondered if Max felt the same way or if that was taking much too big a leap.

"So do you have any other clients yet?" he asked.

"Not yet, but I'm looking. See all these cards here?" She nodded at a basket of postcards, all with hopeful messages from actors and actresses. "Every one of these is an invitation: 'I'm leaving two tickets at the door in your name; hope you can come.' All for Terence and Alexandra, of course, but they never go to any of these things. So I go to as many as I can."

He was smiling. "You're kidding. How many can you see in a week?"

"Ten, fifteen, sometimes more if I really work it out well."

"I don't understand. How can you see that many plays in a week?"

She smiled and held up her chart. She hadn't showed it to anyone except Terence, and he hadn't been particularly impressed. "Usually the people who write to Terence and Alexandra will say what scenes they're in, since they know agents and casting directors aren't going to sit through an entire play. So I try to work it out so I can see as many as I can. One at the end of the evening, another one in a first act. It doesn't work out too well all the time, but my all-time haul was five in one night. And then, of course, once I missed absolutely everybody I was trying to see that night. No cabs, huge rainstorm; it was a mess."

He laughed. "I'm impressed. Then do you contact them afterward? The actors who've written the cards, I mean?"

"I haven't, yet. I don't want to get their hopes up. But I will. I'll find one one of these days."

He smiled. "I bet you will."

The outer door opened, and a young, scruffy-looking guy came in, out of breath and jumpy. "Terence or Alexandra?" he said.

She knew they didn't have any appointments, and the guy looked odd; right away she felt uneasy around him, and she was glad Max was there. "Uh, they're in a meeting right now, and—they're not expecting you, are they? Your name is—?"

"Jack," he said, "and you tell them I'm here."

"Uh, Jack—?" He didn't say anything. "Jack what?" she finally said.

"Jack. They know me." He nodded at the phone. "Tell them."

She had the feeling it wasn't a good idea to argue with him, and she buzzed Terence.

He came on the line right away. "What is it?"

"Uh, there's someone named Jack here to see you. He said—"

"Tell him two minutes," Terence said. "Tell him not to leave."

Hm. She hung up and gave the guy the message, and a second later the inner door opened and Terence was showing Vanessa out.

Without a word, he motioned to Jack and he went in, and Terence shut the door.

Max was looking questioningly at Maura. "A client?"

"I really don't know. I've never seen him before."

Vanessa laced her arm under Max's. "Darling, I'm starved. Let's get a cab and have Thai?"

"Sure. Maura, good to see you again." He said it formally, which made her feel good. Didn't it mean he felt awkward with Vanessa right there? Or was she just dreaming, making much too much of nothing?

Fifty-eight

Danielle's heart was pounding more than ever in all the times she had shoplifted. She had never been to a jewelry store like this, and she had *certainly* never been to the back room of a jewelry store, but Larkin had called the guy, and then she had told Danielle exactly what to do. Say it was her mother's, use Larkin's name a lot, be super-calm. Because no one wanted to jump to any conclusions, and they wouldn't if she seemed relaxed.

But it was almost too hard, even though she had had a ton of training. For one thing, this was a part of Madison Avenue she had been just a little too close to with Al-Sadir—on Sixty-third, and his house was super-close by. Plus the store was tiny and *filled* with jewelry, and it just felt weird: the fanciest jewels she had ever felt, before Al-Sadir's house, were the Monet earring stands at the Beverly Center.

Plus the man, a super-old white-haired man, all stooped over and hunchy-looking, hadn't said a word except a few grunts. He had led her to the room, sat down on one side of the table, and she had sat down on the other, and now he was holding out his hand. He was a little bit like Mr. Minsky, now that she came to think of it. "The necklace?" he said.

"Um, okay. Here it is." She pulled it out of her purse and then unwrapped the toilet paper. She still couldn't get over how beautiful it was, so gleaming and bright.

She put it into his hand, and he right away made his hand go up and down, as if he were weighing it or something just by feel. Then he took out one of those magnifying-type things and snapped it into his eye. His lips went in and out, in and out, and he started breathing kind of hard, as if he had a cold. Then he flipped the magnifier out of his eye and set everything down.

"Excellent paste," he said. "*Excellent* paste."

She swallowed. She knew what he meant. Paste meant fake. "Um, are you sure?"

He smiled, but it wasn't that nice a smile. "After fifty-one years in the business, I'm sure. But it's *excellent* paste."

"But, um, how much does paste cost? I mean, how much are these worth?"

He shrugged. "I'd give you four hundred."

She picked up the necklace and looked at it, and it didn't look that gleaming anymore. Some jewels. Al-Sadir had draped her in paste!

"I'm going to get a second opinion," she said. Because maybe he was lying, trying to trick her out of valuable jewels. And what about Allan?

He shrugged. "You won't do better than here; I can promise you that."

She wrapped the necklace in the toilet paper again and put it in her purse. "I'll just have to take that chance, won't I?" she said, and she had the feeling the words were from some movie or something. What chance was *she* taking? But it felt right, to be kind of huffy, because she was a hundred percent sure, totally definitely, that he was making it up. Maybe *Larkin* had gotten an honest deal from him, but that didn't mean he was honest with everyone. Plus what if she had gotten gypped and didn't even know it?

But the rest of the afternoon felt like it was lasting a hundred years, and each time she went to a jewelry place—there were a ton on Madison—the answer was the same: paste. So Al-Sadir had lied. And Allan: what was he going to do?

Fifty-nine

Allan put his head in his hands and closed his eyes.

Seven days. Murray was going to start looking at the books in seven days. It was one of those fluke things, the way the cops sometimes caught murderers because of parking violations. Or running a red light, having one of their taillights out. And then it turned out the guy had a sheet a mile long and was on the ten-most-wanted list.

But he wasn't a murderer. He had made a mistake. He hadn't meant to hurt anybody. He hadn't meant to lose.

And he couldn't stop thinking of his father. It had been years since he'd dreamt about him, and now it was every night, awful dreams that took place in the office or up in the mountains, fishing, his father looking happy till he heard the news. He had never had realistic dreams in his life, but suddenly they were like goddamn documentaries: "How could you *do* it, Allan? Murray was like a *brother* to me. Why didn't you *stop*? Such shame, such humiliation."

And he didn't know what the hell he was supposed to do. Sometimes you read about people killing themselves, usually the father of a family with overwhelming debt, sometimes a single mother. And he had always thought, How could they do such a thing over money? Money was paper, paper with green ink on it. To kill yourself over that—

And he had never even had a family, never had the chance. He *wanted* the chance now. He wanted what Danielle had been talking about. He knew he'd make a great father. Now that it was too late. He was ready to quit gambling, finally. The thrill was gone. But it was too late. Now he'd be fired, maybe sent to jail; Danielle would be crazy not to break up with him.

He had blown it completely.

Sixty

Don't look at the clock, Larkin said to herself. Finding out what time it was would only make it worse. She had been tossing and turning for ages trying to get to sleep. And knowing how many hours—

She turned and looked. Christ. It was two-fifteen. And she had to be up at five, which meant at the most she'd have two and a half hours of sleep.

She covered her eyes and tried to think, tried to make her mind blank. But every time she closed her eyes, she saw the script—words she hadn't learned, feelings she wouldn't be able to express.

At least today she had done all right, at the doctor's. It was important to keep the stories straight, she had discovered. You couldn't just march in and say, "Please write me a prescription for Valium." You had to finesse it; saying she had some other problem—a pain in her side, which was vague but believable—distracted them. Then, "And by the way, I've been feeling a little anxious these days" sounded much more casual. And there was nothing to make them suspect she was going to other doctors, too.

So she had learned *those* lines well.

She opened her eyes and stared at the ceiling. One thousand, nine hundred ninety-nine . . . It wasn't going to work. People said to stop trying to go to sleep, to get up and read or cook or watch television. But she had *done* those things the past two nights, and they hadn't done anything but wake Danielle and Maura up. And what about the Valiums? And the drinking, which she hadn't done much of, but some. Weren't they all supposed to make you sleep? What was happening to her?

* * *

There was a sound—a buzzing—over and over again, and it became part of the dream, a buzzing coming from a building.

"Larkin!"

She opened her eyes.

Maura was shaking her.

Oh God. She sat up. "The show," she said.

"That's right, the show. The chauffeur's downstairs. I thought you were *up*."

She threw the covers back and staggered out into the hall. Her head was killing her, and her knees hurt—why did her *knees* hurt?—but God, what had she done?

Maura was following her. "Are you all right? I told him to wait, but are you all right?"

"I'm fine," she said. She shut the bathroom door and started to run the water. Maybe if she rinsed her face, she'd wake up?

"But what happened?" Maura called through the door. "Didn't your alarm go off?"

She had a vague memory of another buzzing she had incorporated into a dream. Too easy to reach over and hit the button. "I don't know," she said.

"Well, I left a message down on the soundstage that you'd be about fifteen minutes late," Maura said. Silence. Then: "I don't think it should be too big a deal."

Shit. She was already letting Maura down. She opened the door and looked in the mirror. "But look at me. I look like hell."

Maura looked at her and took a deep breath. "So you don't look your best this morning. They'll help you in Makeup. Just do the best you can."

It was like too many things she had thought about when she was growing up, too many times she had screwed up and wanted someone to say, "It's all right. Just do the best you can." That was what parents were supposed to say, weren't they? Only, hers never had said that. Only Geoffrey had, but then, he had expected too much. He had always wanted her to do more, to do better, at everything she did.

Maura was saying, "Do your best" as sincerely as anyone ever had. Only, what if she wasn't up to it anymore? Something was happening, and she didn't seem to be able to do her best anymore, at anything.

Sixty-one

Maura stood up and moved through the crowd. This is your chance, she said to herself. What she had just seen was the performance she had been waiting for. "Steve Cressman," the program had said. He'd performed in summer stock and about ten off-off-Broadway plays.

And he didn't have an agent.

She made her way through the crowd backstage, and some of the cast members were already disappearing into the dressing rooms, sweating and tired and obviously not waiting to see anybody. It was a tiny, unknown production, and most of the people who were milling around either had something to do with the production or were friends with people in the cast. Not a lot of expectations on anyone's part.

Almost everybody was in black, and Maura was starting to feel self-conscious—like some sort of gigantic pink potato, completely out of place.

And then she saw him, wiping his face with the back of his sleeve, coming straight toward her.

"Hi. Steve?" she said.

He nodded and kept moving. "Hi. How're you doing?"

"Uh, can I talk to you?"

He stopped. "Sure. What can I do for you?"

She looked around. Suddenly she was too aware of everyone else, of how close people were. "Uh, could we go somewhere slightly more private?"

He was smiling. "What did you have in mind?" But he was already leading her back toward the stage.

"I'm with the Fielding-White agency—"

"You're kidding." Still smiling, only he seemed to be in some sort of shock.

"Nope. Not a joke," she said. "I got your flier, and I thought

I'd come see the play tonight, and I'm glad I did. You were wonderful.''

He was just staring at her.

"Anyway, I thought if you could come in tomorrow and meet Terence and Alexandra, we could talk about my representing you.''

"You're kidding.''

She smiled. "Great. My first discovery, and he only speaks two words.''

"No, no. I'm just so shocked. It's just been so many years—although I probably shouldn't say that.''

"Don't be silly. I know it usually takes years. But I should tell you—I'm new at Fielding-White, and I'm new in the business. If you came in, you'd be my client, but first you'd have to be approved by Terence or Alexandra, and . . . well, you'd have to realize you'd be getting a very new agent. You'd be my second client.''

"Is your first client working?''

"She's on 'Coronado.' ''

He was beaming. He held out his hand. "To our brilliant careers,'' he said. "When can I come in?''

Maura felt like singing. She had thought it would be a horrible, humiliating, uphill, and ultimately losing battle, trying to get Alexandra and Terence to agree on a new client. She had thought she'd watch him turn into another Keefe before her very eyes. She had thought Alexandra would be her usual bitchy self, that she wouldn't even want to meet with Steve. But they were meeting with him, he was charming and lively and smart-sounding and cute, and they obviously liked him.

And the idea of trying to find him parts, fighting for him, sending him out with ideas and encouragement and the best hopes in the world—it was so exciting.

"I think we're all in agreement,'' Alexandra said, standing up and holding out her hand. "Welcome to Fielding-White.''

Steve was beaming again, and he still looked as happy five minutes later when Maura met with him alone in the outer office. "There are just a few things I want to go over with you before you leave,'' she said, pulling out his eight-by-tens and résumé. "I think you need some new pictures.'' She looked down at the top one, which showed a handsome guy but made his face go bland—there were none of the great angles his face had, none of the shadows. "In fact, you definitely do. Let me show you what I'm talking about.'' She pulled out folders for four of the actors they handled and showed him the different looks each actor had in each picture. "See, all of yours look the same, Steve, and basically not all that great. You look good, but it's not eye-catching, and you don't look like any particular type. But look at these—in this one Hugh Randall looks like he could play a young cowhand, and in this he looks much older and much more worldly."

"That was what I was trying to do," he said. "These are all *supposed* to look very different from each other."

"Well, if you go to Mario Simonetti, the photographer a lot of our clients have used, he'll know what to do. So much of it has to do with the lighting that if you don't go to someone incredibly experienced, you're just not going to get what you need. Anyway, see him this week, and we can have new pictures by next." She picked up his résumé. "Now, on the résumé. You list karate and diving as your sports skills. Are you *great* at both of them?"

"Well—" his face started to redden—"I can *do* them."

Maura took a pencil and crossed them off the list. "Forget it. Everyone can do them a little bit, or thinks they can. If you list it, it means you're an expert and that you can do it enough to look expert, even if that means after a hundred takes. It's better not to list anything at all. And what about this 'Fluent in French' under skills? Are you really?"

He smiled. "Really. I spent four summers there with my parents when I was young enough not to mind learning another language."

"Okay, good. It's good to have. You never know. Let's see . . . on the rest of it, all the plays you've listed here. You really have been in all of them, playing the parts you've listed, right?"

He was smiling again. "Do people really lie on that part of the résumé?"

She nodded. "You wouldn't believe how often. And they always get caught, which is really embarrassing if it's gotten past the agency. We had one actress go to a casting call for a television show, and she had put that she was the understudy for the lead role in a tour of *Hello, Dolly!*, figuring there was no way anyone would know she was lying. It turned out the casting director had also cast the touring show. Very embarrassing. And it happens all the time."

He glanced at his résumé. "If I had decided to lie, Maura, I would have made it a lot more impressive than what you've got in your hand."

She laughed. "All right. As long as you understand."

She told him the other things she wanted him to do—cut his hair, look into getting caps for his teeth, clothes she wanted him to be sure to have on hand—and then he signed the contract, good for a year but escapable if either one was unhappy.

"Now, do you have a way of making a living at the moment? Are you solvent and all that?"

He shrugged. "I'm doing the usual waiter routine."

"But it's working out—?"

"It's fine as long as I can act, too. That's why I jumped at this play."

She nodded. "Okay. So there's just one more thing, then," she said, writing down her home phone number and giving him the piece of paper. "Call me anytime, if you're worried about anything or just want to talk, if you've heard of something you think I should know about—anything at all. Even if you want my opinion on what color shirt you should buy for an audition. Even if you *don't* want my opinion. Whatever. I'll always talk to you, no matter what, anytime, day or night." She stood up. "So that's it, then, unless you can think of anything else."

He smiled. "Sounds great so far," he said. He shook her hand, thanked her, and left, and as soon as the door was shut, Alexandra called her name.

"Just a second," Maura said, putting back the eight-by-tens. She didn't care about the pictures or cleaning up. But she wanted the moment to last. *This* was why she had stayed at Fielding-White. She had actually found someone, someone Alexandra and Terence could even agree on. And it felt magnificent to start him on his way. Because she knew, the same way she had known with Larkin—she just knew he was going to make it.

"Maura?" Terence called.

She took a deep breath and went in.

"Congratulations," Alexandra said.

"Absolutely," Terence said. "Well done, my dear. Very well done."

"Thank you. It didn't seem to take you very long to make up your minds. I had thought you might want to see a performance."

Alexandra shook her head. "Not with directors like these," she said, picking up Steve's résumé and letting it fall to her desk. "He hasn't worked with all that many, but the ones he's been with are the best. You don't question someone when he's worked with Angus Jorgenson and Jason Wilentz."

"And being cute doesn't hurt," Terence said. "Any designs, Maura?"

She just looked at him and didn't say anything. "Well," she

finally said, "I have a lot to do, so . . ." And then she remembered something. "But actually, there is one more thing. I need my check before lunch today, so I can deposit it at at the bank. Do you want to give it to me now?" She looked at Terence, and he looked blank, so she turned to Alexandra.

Alexandra let out a stream of smoke and leaned back in her chair. "That might be a problem," she said.

"Why? What do you mean?"

"We're running rather short this month. We were hoping you could defer your salary."

Her heart was already pounding. "The answer is no," she said, and she tried to keep her voice in check. "I would if I could, but I can't. At all."

Alexandra was looking across the room at Terence, and Maura turned to face him. He wasn't meeting her eyes.

"Terence, what?" she said. "One of you had better tell me what's going on."

"Don't get so *upset*," Terence said.

"Why not? I've worked my ass off, and now you tell me I'm not getting paid."

"You're getting paid," Terence said. "Just not right away."

"What does that mean, 'not right away'? Not that I accept it; I just want to know what you're talking about. And how long you've known I wouldn't get paid. I *do* have to pay the rent, you know. And eat. Minor things like that."

Terence sighed. "I thought I told you not to get upset."

"And I told you I wanted to get paid. So we're even. Now tell me."

He held up his hands. "A few days. A week at the most."

"Why?"

"Maura, we have tremendous overhead."

"The rent is eighteen hundred a month," Alexandra said, stubbing out her cigarette.

"And? So? Has it gone up in the past week? What are you two talking about? My client, my first client, happens to be bringing in a *lot* of money. And I don't get paid? That doesn't make a hell of a lot of sense."

Alexandra moved in her chair, but she didn't look uncomfortable, even slightly bothered by the conversation. "You've taken on some risk by participating as an agent," she said calmly. "Terence discussed that with you in advance. Neither of us is drawing a salary this week. And Terence is going to incur tremendous expenses when he takes Vanessa to L.A.''

"Look," Maura said. "We never discussed this situation. I brought in a client who's making money. It's payday. Time to get paid. Case closed.''

Alexandra sighed. "All right. To tide you over, we can give you a week's pay. How would that be? And next week, on Wednesday, you'll get the rest. Now, be reasonable. That isn't so much to ask.''

Maura hesitated. Saying yes would go against every one of her instincts. But it wasn't *that* unreasonable a request, what they were asking. "All right," she said. "As long as it's only till next week.''

Sixty-two

Richard was gazing at her, his chin in his hand. "I can't stop looking at you," he said softly.

Larkin closed her eyes and leaned back against the pillows.

"Does that bother you?" he said.

She opened her eyes and looked at him. Did it bother her? She didn't know. Months ago it would have, and did. But there was something easy about it. He didn't hammer away at her; he didn't ask her question after question; he hadn't even noticed the Valium or the drinking. "No," she said, and she touched his cheek. She *did* like him. He was never cruel.

"So would you like to go out, or eat in?" he asked. "What do you want to do? It's completely up to you.''

She sat up and stretched. "I wish it *were* up to me. I do the same thing every night, Richard. It's called memorizing lines.''

He was shaking his head. "But it's worth it. Every show has been better than the last. I've taped them all. You can see for yourself.''

She smiled. "Have you really?''

"Of course. And I mean it: You get better and better.''

"Well, thanks.''

He took her hand and brushed it against his lips. "I missed you.''

She didn't say anything. She knew what she was supposed to say, but she couldn't get herself to say it.

"Larkin?"

"Mm."

"This isn't for one night."

"No, no. Of course not."

He was hesitating, looking into her eyes. "I have to ask," he said quietly. Then he said, "Never mind."

"Richard, what?"

He paused. "What happened? Why the call? Why are you here?"

"What do you mean, why am I here? Because I wanted to see you, obviously." She touched his shoulder, his chest. She didn't want to get any more complicated than that.

She could feel him watching her, and she could remember how irritated she had always gotten in the past: Why was he so *fascinated* with her? Didn't he ever get tired of watching her, looking at her?

But now it didn't bother her. The irritation was only a memory, half felt. The important thing was that she felt safe.

Sixty-three

Danielle tucked the five-dollar bill into the little tip sack attached to her belt and looked around.

What a night. The club was dead, D-E-A-D, and no one knew why. Usually weekends were super-crowded, plus with a million out-of-town friends of the members, and you could count on a ton of money if the people were from faraway lands. But hardly anyone was here, and the people who were, were the worst tippers she had ever seen.

And she felt bad anyway. Not that it was her fault that Allan had gotten in trouble, because she knew that wasn't true at all. But still, it was kind of like: if the club didn't exist, he wouldn't be in trouble. So it kind of made her hate the club. What if he had to go to jail?

She just couldn't get over it. And the way he had saved her—it was weird.

"Danielle!"

Uh-oh. She turned around, and Al-Sadir was coming straight toward her.

"Hi," she said.

"Hi," he said, in a weird way, as if he was imitating her.

She just kind of stood there. The last she had seen of him, he had seemed pretty happy to have her around, because of the blow job, she guessed. But maybe he had had time to think about the money again. Or maybe he had discovered that the "jewels" were gone. So she didn't know.

"You are working late tonight?"

"Um, till ten."

His eyes were shining. Super-dark. "I can hardly keep from touching you," he whispered. "But I know it gets you in trouble if I do."

"You're right," she said. "It would." Plus what if Allan ever saw? Not that he was going to come in, but still!

"I feel I have an apology to make." He took a deep breath. "I spoke very soon, very quickly," he said. "Perhaps too soon, without thinking."

"You mean the other night."

"Yes, the night, the other night." He took a deep breath. "I won very well tonight at baccarat, Danielle."

She didn't say anything, but her heart was speeding up.

"And I have done much thinking. Perhaps I was wrong. I could help you."

She let out her breath. "Do you mean it? Really?"

"You come to my house tonight. Then we talk."

"Um, so . . . okay, I could do that. But are you going to wait here, or should I meet you?"

"You meet me at the house. You have the address. Just ring the bell."

"Okay. Like, probably at ten-fifteen. Okay? 'Cause I'll have to change."

He shook his head. "Do not change the clothes. Put on a coat and come over."

Well, she didn't know about that. But she guessed it didn't make a giant difference. So she said okay, and he left, and she couldn't believe it. He had changed his mind. She felt like calling Allan that second, but something said, "Wait," and she had to listen to that voice. But she felt a ton better about even the waitressing already. The rest of the night was going to fly by.

There was no answer, and she started to wonder. Here she was, standing out in what had turned out to be the super-cold, with her stupid waitressing outfit on and a coat that let tons of wind in, and there was no answer. Was it a joke? Maybe it was some kind of trick? But why would he do that? He had invited her over.

Suddenly she saw the light flick on in the window, and a second later the door opened, and it was Al-Sadir, dressed in some kind of thing she had the feeling was called a smoking jacket, or maybe a smoking outfit, black pants and a gray silk jacket. It looked kind of nice. "Welcome," he said, in a sort of extra-formal way.

"Whew," she said when he shut the door and she was inside. "It's freezing out there."

He was reaching for her bag and coat, and she felt a little weird dressed the way she was. But she guessed if he had seen her nude, there was no big deal. Plus in the paste.

"You look so lovely," he said.

"Thanks."

"Would you care for a drink? A soda, perhaps?"

"Sure," she said, and she followed him into the kitchen. It was the first time she had ever seen the room, and it looked just like on an ad, all gleaming and with one coat of paint instead of the nine million in her apartment. Plus drawers that actually shut.

"For you," he said, handing her a glass. And then he poured some for himself, which was weird, because he was a liquor drinker, not a soda drinker. It was one of the first things she had ever noticed about him.

"Come," he said, taking her hand.

They went into the study, the room where the safe was. There was music on, kind of like some kind of wailing, only pretty, and he said it was music from home.

"Sit," he said.

She sat down on the couch, and he sat down next to her. Then he reached into his jacket, pulled out his wallet, and pulled out what looked like a million dollars. "So you see," he said.

"Al-Sadir, I can't *believe* it. How much did you win tonight?"

He smiled and put the wallet back in his jacket. "Quite one bit," he said. "Quite one bit. And naturally, when that occurred, I thought of you."

"I'm glad," she said.

"So the other night, you felt quite free when you asked me for that money."

She didn't know exactly what he meant. Was it an insult? "Um, well, you know. Between friends."

"Exactly. Between friends. And between friends: Do you steal?"

She wasn't sure she had heard him right, and she took another sip of Coke. "What?"

"Do you steal from your friends?"

Uh-oh. "Of course not."

"Am I your friend, Danielle?"

She didn't like his voice. It had gotten all creepy and foreign. "Of course," she said.

"And yet you take from me."

"I only asked to borrow the money. It was just a question."

"But we are not talking about the money. We are talking about the necklace. That you stole. You STOLE!" He screamed it out.

"I didn't. I don't know what you're talking about," she said.

He stood up and walked to the door and locked it.

"The door is locked," he said. "And it will stay locked until you admit the truth."

She looked over at the door, and she bit her lip. God, what could she say? Maybe that she wanted to leave. She would just stay totally calm, because what if he was crazy?

She put her hand on her forehead and closed her eyes. "Ohh," she moaned, and she let her head sink to her knees.

"What? What? What are you doing?" He had come back to the couch again.

She put her hands at her temples. "Oh God. I don't feel so good." Then she covered her mouth and looked up at him. "I think I'm going to throw up." That would probably be good, because someone like him wouldn't want someone vomiting all over the carpet.

But he just looked at her. "I tell you again: You are here until you admit the truth. You think I am a *fool*? You think after you leave, I don't check every box? You think you are the first to think of such a thing?"

"But I didn't *take* anything," she said.

He wrenched her up and brought his hand back, and she saw it coming, but she still couldn't believe it until it hit, right in her eye and against her nose.

The pain was unbelievable, and she screamed, only the scream came out like a tiny sound. She tried to cover her face, but he grabbed her wrists and held them down. Her nose was killing her.

"Do you know what they do in my country to men who steal?"

She realized she was crying, that her throat was aching and she couldn't say anything even if she wanted to.

"I will tell you what they do to men who steal. They cut off their hands. They *chop* off their hands in the public square. And you *steal* from me?" She tried to move her hands, but he had them too tight, her wrists.

And she couldn't believe what was happening. All those years in California, where all the crazy people were supposed to be. She had hitchhiked with a thousand people at least, slept with guys she had never even met except right then, and nothing had happened to her. Nothing. And now she was looking into the eyes of someone who was crazy.

"Listen," she said, only her voice came out tiny. What was happening? "You have to let me go, okay? Because I told someone to meet me here—"

He was smiling.

"Okay, it isn't true," she said, sniffling against something that was dripping on her face. She licked her lips and tasted blood. "Al-Sadir, I'm *bleeding*."

He just looked at her.

"I tell you what they do to men in my country who steal. And who are caught. Now I tell you what they do to the women." He forced her down, back into the couch, and he moved on top of her. "It is not that they 'sleep with them,' as you would say in America." He was ripping her leotard, and she felt like he was ripping her skin. And she remembered how when she was little the doctor had said the shot wouldn't hurt, and she had *known* that it would, and when it hurt more than anything she had ever felt, she hated him and her mother and everybody right then. Only, she knew it was going to be nothing compared to this.

What if she never left? What if he had some horrible hiding place, or he sent her back to where he came from? She had seen a whole TV movie about it. What if he killed her and threw her in the river?

What did they tell you to do if you were trapped? Why hadn't she ever read any of those pamphlets those women on the beach handed out?

Already she missed everybody like crazy, all the people she loved. Cleve she hadn't spoken to in so long, and Allan, and Maura and Larkin, and even her mother if it meant this was the end. What if they never ever found her?

"I tell you the difference," he said. "They take the women to the square, like the men, but then they tie them—as I will tie you. The man, the victim, is the first to rape her." He drew back and looked into her eyes. "Then the others, whoever he names." His hands were between her legs, and she tried to squeeze them shut. "In one hour I have friends to come," he said. "And in one hour you will be tied for each of them."

She jammed her knee into him, and he yelled, and she bit him as hard as she could in the shoulder, and he yelled again and jumped back. "You little bitch," he said.

But she was already at the door—it stuck and then she got it, and she grabbed her coat off the floor and ran as fast as she could even though she heard him coming and maybe she wouldn't make it—but she knew she could if she could get to the outside, if she could get the outer lock undone—

She raced out into the cold, and it hit her like crazy—all she had on was shreds plus her coat. But for the first time in her life, the cold felt like the greatest, even on her crazy bare feet.

The street was dark—probably a streetlight was out, because she couldn't remember it being so dark ever before—and she ran to the corner and it was freezing and her feet hurt.

There was a cab stopped at the light, and she jumped in and slammed the door, and she gave her address in this breathy voice that wasn't even hers, but at least a sound had come out.

Except that the driver was looking at her real funnily. "You want a Kleenex?" he finally said.

She moved over on the seat so she could look in his rearview mirror. There was blood all around her nose and mouth. "Um, sure, if you have one."

He handed one through the thing you put money in—she guessed a bullet-proof shield—and she wiped at her face, but the blood had kind of dried.

And she knew she was in some kind of a state of shock or something, because now her knees were shaking like crazy. But at least she had made it out of there alive.

Sixty-four

George Falcone flicked off the TV with his remote and leaned back in his recliner. "I don't like it," he said to Maura.

"They said to wait a week," she said. "They gave me half my salary. But there was something . . . I didn't like the way they had discussed it without me. If I'm some sort of partner and sharing in the risk, then I should know when something's wrong the minute it happens. Not days afterward."

"No kidding," he said. "But I don't like it anyway. They—"

"Oh, and another thing. One of the actors called today, someone who worked weeks ago, and asked where his check was. Alexandra took the call, so I didn't hear the answer, but I'm sure he should have gotten paid already."

"What about Larkin? Has she been getting paid?" He reached for a Kleenex and winced at the movement.

"Can I help?"

"Nah, I've got to get used to it. So what? Is she getting paid or not?"

"She is. But they wouldn't dare not pay her, because that would get right back to the producers, and they'd be on top of the situation so fast, Alexandra wouldn't know what had hit her. Or Alexandra and Terence, I should say."

"You seem to think it's Alexandra's fault."

"I don't know. I just don't know what's going on. But Terence is away in L.A. right now anyway, and Alexandra just keeps saying, over and over, that it's the overhead and it's temporary."

George was shaking his head. "I don't like it. One thing about my place, my girls *always* got paid. My girls and my office girls, the dancers and the office people. Before me, sometimes. I paid out of my own pocket lots of times."

"I know," she said. "I know."

The door opened and Vince came in, bringing the cold air with him.

"Hey," George called out. "Shut that door."

"Whew," Vince said. "It's fucking freezing out there."

"Hey. Watch the language. What are you, nuts? Look who's here."

"I know who's here," Vince said, coming over to where Maura was sitting. He leaned down and kissed the top of her head. "Maura doesn't mind. She likes that kind of talk. Don't you, Maura?"

She didn't say anything. He had his hand on her shoulder, and it was burning into her.

"So what'd I miss?" Vince said, sitting on the arm of her chair. "Everything going okay in the big bad world of show business?"

"It's fine," she said.

"Yeah? Still at it?"

"I signed up a new client just yesterday," she said.

"You dating him?"

"No. Why would I be?"

He shrugged. "Just curious. So what's he do? Act, sing, dance?"

"He's an actor."

"Yeah? He find you or you find him?" he asked.

"Why are you asking me so many questions?"

"Hey, I'm curious. Since when is that a crime?"

"I found him, all right? I went to a play—I go to a few plays a night, sometimes just for half an hour each play, to see people who send me cards hoping I'll come. Or who send cards to Alexandra and Terence, actually."

"Yeah? They do that, too?"

"Not much," she said. "They're kind of busy for that."

"Ah, Maura," George said, adjusting himself in his chair. "I always knew you'd make it. Always."

She smiled until she saw Vince's face. He looked furious.

"Yeah, well," he said. "I still say it's a shitty world out there. They'll eat you for breakfast, Maura."

"We'll see," she said. She stood up. "George, do you need anything from the store? I have to go, but I can go around the corner for you if you want."

"What am I? Nothing?" Vince said. "I can go to the store for him. What do you want? Soda? What? *TV Guide*?"

"Yeah, some ginger ale and a TV dinner would be good," George said. "Turkey. Hungry-Man, all right? You got the money?"

"Yeah, yeah," Vince said. But he was staring at Maura—she could feel him looking at her, not taking his eyes off her. "So I'll be back," Vince said.

"Yeah. Take your time. Maura, thanks, honey. And next time you bring me some better news."

She kissed him on the cheek and walked to the door, Vince right behind her.

When they were out on the landing, Vince took her arm. "What'd he mean, better news?"

"Nothing," she said, moving toward the stairs.

He followed her down. "Come on. What was it about?"

"I said nothing. It's unimportant."

He put a hand on her shoulder and came up even with her on the stairs. "Hey. Nothing's unimportant when it comes to you. Now, what was it?"

"Just a mix-up with my paycheck, that's all," she said, *knowing* it was a mistake to tell him. But she didn't want to prolong the conversation either. "They said they don't have enough to pay me this week."

He looked disgusted. "What'd I tell you? You're working for a couple of lowlifes, Maura. I saw that girl, she looks like a nut case to me. And the guy's a faggot. You're working for lowlifes."

"What do you mean, you saw them?" They were on the third-floor landing, and she stopped. "Where did you see them?"

"One day last week. I was in your neighborhood, what can I say? On my route. And I saw them, leaving the office together. And they look like thieves, let me tell you. Real lowlifes."

She started walking down the stairs again, and her knees felt a little shaky. She didn't like the fact that Vince had been around the office, "route" or nothing.

"Listen, Maura." They were on the second-floor landing.

"What is it?"

"I'm going to do some checking around for you, okay? No charge."

"Vince, what are you talking about?"

He held up his hands. "Listen, don't get so touchy. I'm not talking about *us* or nothing. I'm talking about you. Not getting ripped off. I'll check it out. Look around. Let you know if I find anything out."

"You're not going to find anything out because there's nothing to find out. And I *don't* want you sneaking around my office. I don't want you anywhere *near* there."

She had raised her voice too much, and his eyes had changed. He looked furious again, that fury that appeared with him out of nowhere.

"Oh. Right," he said sarcastically. "You don't want. The way you don't want this." He took her in his arms and kissed her.

Then he let go of her, and she fell back against the wall. "So I'll see you," he said, and he raced down the last flight of steps and let the outside door slam in the wind.

Sixty-five

Larkin looked in the mirror and pulled her hair back from her face. The day had gone well. She hadn't missed one of her cues, and she hadn't forgotten a single word. She was even getting to like the character she was playing, someone she had thought of as merely a silly caricature of a typical soap opera villainess at the beginning. But she felt she had added shadings to Serena's character, that she had deepened her. Things were working out.

"Larkin?"

She looked up. "Hi, Felicia," she said, pinning her hair back so she could rinse off her makeup.

Felicia came in and sat down in front of the dressing table. "We have a problem," she said. It was her producer's voice, the one she used when she cut people's lines.

Larkin looked at Felicia in the mirror and then turned to face her. "What is it?"

"I'm afraid we're going to have to let you go."

She hadn't heard right; that was it. "I'm sorry," she said. "What—?"

"I'm afraid we're going to have to let you go," Felicia said, leaning forward slightly. "I'm so sorry, Larkin. But it just isn't working out."

Larkin couldn't see her completely clearly. Her voice sounded far away. But what she had said . . . Maybe it wasn't definite? "I don't understand," she said. "I didn't miss one cue today. I thought it was such a good day."

Felicia was looking down at her hands. "I'm sorry," she said softly. "I've already told your agent—"

"Maura? You told Maura?"

"Well, of course. We always speak to the agent first."

"Oh *no*. I wish you hadn't."

Felicia was looking into her eyes. "I wish it could have worked out." She stood up. "But I'm afraid there's no chance."

"But I still don't understand. What did I do? What did I do wrong?"

"We felt there was no feeling in the last few days. The emotions have to be *strong* on a show like 'Coronado.' You seemed to be drifting."

"I was tired," Larkin said. "I haven't been able to sleep."

"I'm sorry," Felicia said. "Today was your last day, Larkin. I *am* sorry."

"But my part was being *enlarged*. You *told* me that."

"I did, and I'm afraid we spoke too soon. Serena will leave town suddenly. We haven't worked beyond that point."

Suddenly Larkin felt as if she were talking to her mother. No. The answer was no again, for the thousandth time. And what was she supposed to do about money? "Well, that's just great," she said, standing up. Why bother washing off her makeup? Why even bother changing clothes? "Thanks a fuck of a lot, Felicia. You've been incredibly loyal."

She was shaking when she got out to the street, shaking as she ran across Eleventh Avenue to the gas station, where it was usually easy to get a cab.

But there was nothing except two women in fur coats—where had *they* come from?—who were obviously waiting for one of the taxis at the station to pick them up.

A driver was paying for his gas, and Larkin walked across to it, through the puddles, and opened the door.

"That's *our* taxi!" one of the women said.

"Go fuck yourselves," Larkin said, and she slammed the door. She gave the only address she could think of going—home, even though she couldn't bear the idea: Danielle would be at the club, and Maura was at work. But she couldn't barge in on either of them; she'd have to weather it out, get through the afternoon—somehow.

She found the bottle of Valium in her purse and shook two out, and then she stopped. Maybe it was time—really—to quit. She had lied to Danielle and Maura, but the truth . . .

She took a deep breath, unrolled the window, opened the bottle, and turned it upside down, and the pills sailed and then dropped. The end. They were gone. Her heart was pounding, but she wasn't going to think about that. She was going to relax, breathe deeply . . .

The cab stopped for a light, and Larkin looked in the rearview mirror. The driver was staring at her.

"What are you staring at?" she said.

"Huh?"

"You. What are you staring at?"

"Hey, lady, I'm trying to drive. I ain't staring at nothing."

She moved to the right side of the seat. He was lying, of course. Probably recognized her from the show, although she didn't suppose many men watched. But then, what was it she had read? That 'Coronado' was the top-rated daytime show in prisons across the country. Number one on the prison Nielsen list.

She started to laugh, and the driver turned to look at her, and she stopped and opened her purse for a cigarette. But there was a sign—three signs, she realized—that said NO SMOKING—DRIVER ALLERGIC, and she put the cigarette back. The man was obviously crazy, and it was no time to start a fight.

But when he stopped for a light and she looked up, he was adjusting his mirror.

"I want you to stop that or I'm getting out of this cab," she said. Why were people *like* that? Why did they make her so angry, she was shaking? She felt as if she were about to burst.

"Lady, I ain't doing nothing," the driver said. "You crazy or what?"

She opened the door and she ran.

"Hey!" she heard. She heard a door slam shut and she ran faster, she heard some kind of commotion behind her and she kept running, and she ran until her face hurt and it felt as if her knees would break and her lungs would burst. But when she finally turned around—at Ninety-sixth and Broadway, which meant she could walk the rest of the way—it was quiet, and no one was chasing her.

Sixty-six

Maura took a deep breath and opened the door. Larkin had sounded fine on the phone: Yes, she felt bad, but she understood it happened all the time. Yes, she understood it didn't mean anything in terms of her career. Yes, she could go out to dinner with Maura and Danielle.

But that was one of the things that worried Maura. Larkin was too calm. And it pointed more than ever to what had to be done: Someone had to really talk to her about the drinking and the drugs or whatever she was taking, even if it was an awful time for her and even if she didn't want to listen. It couldn't go on forever.

"Hello?" Maura called.

"We're in here," Danielle called out.

They were in the living room, both drinking beer, and Maura had the impression she was interrupting something. Danielle looked embarrassed.

"So," Maura said. "How's it going?"

"Everything's great," Larkin said. "I got fired, Danielle was almost raped by one of her casino customers—"

"What?" Maura said.

"Larkin," Danielle said. "I told you not to say anything." Her face was bright red.

"What happened?" Maura asked, sitting down. "Are you all right?"

She nodded. "I'm fine. Thanks."

But Maura remembered—it hadn't registered before: Danielle didn't want to talk about it. At least to her.

"Well," she said, trying not to feel like an outsider. "Are you guys ready?"

"Of course," Larkin said, standing up. "We've been waiting for *you*. We thought the Greek place on Broadway."

"Fine," Maura said.

No one said anything in the elevator, and Maura didn't understand. Was it that Danielle was upset about whatever had happened, and Larkin was upset about being fired?

Luckily, the restaurant wasn't too crowded, and they got seated right away. The idea of standing around with everyone in such a bad mood was awful.

"So," Larkin said when they sat down. "I've decided. Richard and I are going down to the islands—the Bahamas if we can get a reservation at the place Richard wants."

"That's great," Danielle said.

Larkin was looking at Maura. "What's the matter with you?"

"With me? Nothing. Why?"

"You're not saying very much," Larkin said.

"What do you want me to say?"

"Never mind," Larkin said, looking around. "Where are the goddamn waiters in this place?"

A waiter appeared, and Larkin ordered a drink while he handed out the menus.

"Um, I'll have a beer," Danielle said.

"So will I," Maura said. She had never seen Danielle drink more than half a beer before.

When he left, Larkin lit a cigarette. "If he keeps staring at me like that, we're leaving," she said, throwing the match past the ashtray.

"Who are you talking about?" Danielle asked.

"The waiter. Didn't you see? It was disgusting. And he was leaning against me, too."

Maura didn't say anything. She had been watching—casually, and for no reason. But she was sure the waiter hadn't been staring at Larkin, and he certainly hadn't been leaning against her or touching her.

He came back, handed out the drinks, and took their orders. When he left, Larkin shook her head. "He should be fired. That was disgusting."

"Larkin, what are you talking about?" Maura asked.

"You saw him. Staring at me. It was disgusting."

"He wasn't staring. I checked."

"Oh. You checked. Really. Why would you check on something like that?"

"Because you mentioned it before, obviously."

"And that means you have to check on it? You really see that as your role, don't you? Smoothing things out, making sure everything's wonderful for everyone else. Why do we have to go out to *dinner* on the day I get fired? What is that all about?''

"I thought it would be nice to all be together tonight. You were the one who said you wanted to get out of the house." Which was true. But Larkin looked surprised, and she narrowed her eyes.

"It just all goes together, doesn't it?" she said. "I had never realized how perfectly you worked out your career until today. Plan everyone else's life for them, because that's what you do anyway, isn't it?''

Maura hesitated. "I hadn't realized it bothered you that much. You didn't have to go along with it. I didn't have to become your agent.''

Larkin turned away. "Forget it," she said quietly.

"No. Tell me what you really think," Maura said. "It's important.''

Larkin shook her head. "Forget it. It's over.''

"All right. I'll tell *you* something," she said. She took a deep breath. "You think I interfere too much. You'll think so even more after I tell you this, but I don't care. A lot of what's been going on is because you've been drinking too much. And maybe doing other things; I don't know. Now that you have some time off, it's something you should really think about.''

"I see," Larkin snapped. "That makes a lot of sense. It's all my fault.''

"I didn't say anything was your fault. I told you today on the phone that everyone gets fired from soaps every week of the year. That in itself means nothing. I didn't give it a thought in terms of your career. But in terms of why it *might* have happened—"

The waiter came back with some bread, and Maura stopped talking.

When he was gone, Larkin shook her head. "I can't stand it anymore," she said. "I think we should leave.''

"He wasn't doing anything," Maura said.

Larkin blinked. "Did I ask you?''

"I'm telling you," Maura said.

Larkin started to light a cigarette, but her hands were shaking. "What would you know about it? You don't have men *staring* at you all day. You don't know what it's like. But then, that's why your job is so perfect, because you get to live through everybody else. Since your life will never be interesting enough on its own. Everything will be ordinary for you, always. Forever.''

Maura swallowed and looked past Larkin. *It's whatever she's taking, whatever she's been drinking or not drinking or not taking,* she told herself. But the words didn't make her feel any better. "Look," she said, and she stood up. "Finish the dinner on your own, the two of you. I really don't feel like staying anymore."

"Wait," Larkin said. "Maura, I'm sorry. I didn't mean it."

"Don't say that," Maura said. "I think you did mean it."

"But I didn't. I don't know what I'm saying anymore. It's everything that's happened, it's—you're right, I've been drinking too much, taking too many pills. But I'll stop."

"That's great," Maura said. "But I'm going to go home now." She was surprised at herself, surprised she was actually leaving, but it was all she wanted to do. She'd never forget what Larkin had said. Ever.

Larkin closed her eyes. "Shit," she said. She looked at Danielle. "Damn. I can't believe I said those things."

"I can't believe it either," Danielle said. "You really shouldn't've."

Larkin tried not to think about Maura's face, the hurt and surprise in her eyes. But who wouldn't have been hurt? "I must be losing my mind," she said. "She's my best friend in the world."

Danielle was picking at a hangnail. "But don't you two have fights a lot?" she asked. "Maura made it sound like you did, especially that summer."

"They've always been about me," she said. "They've always been about what's right for me, what's best for me—we've spent our entire friendship talking about *me*. They've been fights that didn't matter. This one does."

And she had already decided: When she went away with Richard, she'd kick the Valium and the drinking, away from everyone and everything. She'd write Maura a long letter, and she'd come back to New York her old self—or a better self, if she was lucky.

Sixty-seven

Maura looked at herself in the mirror and swallowed. An ordinary face. The face of someone who nobody stared at.

She hated what she saw.

The door opened, and Maura watched in the mirror as one of the women from an office down the hall went into a stall. She was an unnoticeable, too. Did she also wonder what she had to do to make people look at her? And what Larkin had said—it wasn't that Maura had never thought it. But it hurt. Her best friend.

And afterward, after Danielle and Larkin had come home—they hadn't stayed to eat either—Larkin had insisted on coming in, insisted on explaining it was tension talking, that she was wound up from not having had any pills, that she was falling apart.

But it didn't make a difference, because Maura kept thinking, No matter how crazy I ever got, I would never say those things to Larkin. Partly because she would never want to hurt her, and partly because they wouldn't be true.

"Yes. Fielding-White. May I help you?"

"Maura."

"Vince?"

"Listen, I gotta talk to you."

"What's the matter? Is George all right?"

"Dad? Yeah, he's fine. It's you I'm talking about." He paused. "Your bosses, Maura."

"What are you talking about?"

"Listen. I told you I was going to look into that shit, and I did."

"What do you mean?"

"Come over after work and I'll tell you about it. George wants to see you, too."

She sighed. Hadn't she just seen them both? "All right," she said.

Alexandra was in a foul mood and Terence was still in L.A., and

Maura was tempted not to even bring up the subject of money. But she had to. They had said Wednesday, it was Wednesday, and she still hadn't gotten paid. So at the end of the day, when she was getting ready to leave, she knocked on Alexandra's closed door.

"Yes?" Alexandra called.

"I need to talk to you," Maura said through the door.

Silence. Then: "Can't it wait? I'm working out a contract."

"Actually, it can't," Maura said. And she opened the door.

Alexandra *was* at least looking at a contract—Maura had pictured her just sitting and smoking—but she looked annoyed. "Yes? What is it?"

"Well, it *is* Wednesday," Maura said.

"And?"

"And you said today I'd get paid. And I'm leaving for the afternoon."

Alexandra sighed and leaned back in her chair. "Well, it's going to have to wait."

"What are you talking about? You told me to wait last week, and I did."

"I'm sorry," she said. "Really, Maura. The money isn't here. And now that Larkin isn't producing for you . . ."

"That doesn't affect last week's pay."

"But you won't be bringing that much in—"

"As I said," Maura cut in. "It doesn't affect the past week. And you don't know what might come up with Steve or anyone else I might find."

Alexandra smiled. "Deals don't generally go through as quickly as Larkin's did. Beginner's luck and all that."

"Evidently my 'beginner's luck' doesn't end up in any kind of compensation, though."

"Maura, we're talking a *few days*."

"If that were true, it would be fine. But you've broken one promise—"

Alexandra spread her hands. "What do you suggest?"

It was a good question, and she didn't know the answer. "I'll talk to Terence when he gets back," she said, and she walked out.

She didn't like it. She didn't like the fact that Vince was helping her in some way she didn't even understand, she didn't like Alexandra's attitude, she didn't like Terence's silence, even if he was in California.

* * *

She knocked on George's door—the bell didn't work—and she heard a TV get louder and then go off. Then the door opened, and Vince said, "Hey. Come on in."

She looked past him into the living room—the whole apartment was only two small rooms—but she didn't see George. "Where is he?" she asked.

"Ah, he had to go to the therapist. Come on in. Sit down." He sat on a broken recliner, and she sat down on the couch. "So, Maura." He steepled his fingers between his knees. "Maura, Maura, Maura. You sure got yourself into some kind of a mess. You didn't sign no papers, did you?"

"Do you mean with Alexandra and Terence? No, not yet. Why?"

He let out an exaggerated sigh. "Whew. Smart girl. Because they're in a shitload of trouble, both of them. Starting with this." He put a knuckle up to his nose and inhaled.

"You mean coke?"

"Coke is just the beginning," he said. He was shaking his head, and she had the distinct feeling he was trying to drag it out. "Coke was what got them into trouble, and *they're* what's going to get *you* in trouble unless you bail out, and I mean now."

"Vince, tell me."

"All right. First of all, the way I got on to this, you know I was hanging around, trying to see where you work and all that, just friendly. And I see a guy I know, only he never had any money and now he drives a Mercedes. I already know what he's doing— everyone does; he's a dealer—and I see this heavyset chick—Alexandra, right?—she's meeting him. So from there it's not such a big jump; I talk to him since I know him, what? Fifteen, twenty years. And she's in trouble."

"You keep saying that, but you haven't told me anything. A lot of people buy coke, and a *lot* of coke."

"But they're in deep, Maura—both of them. And my friend Mike, he says they've been spending the clients' money."

"How would Mike know?"

"He knows, okay? He doesn't even want to deal with them anymore, but they got someone else, he said. So you get out while the getting out's good."

She knew it was probably true. It fit, for one thing. The business was successful enough, yet they never had any money. There had been those odd phone calls, the visit from the guy she'd never seen before. Alexandra had lost all that weight, Terence was always so energetic, they both had incredible mood swings. Damn it, it fit.

"Shit," she said.

"Hey, why the long face? You can get out and walk away from it."

She looked around George's apartment, at the cracked walls and the cracking Naugahyde furniture. So much like her father's house. And she had thought she would get away from it all. "I liked the job," she said. "I really think I was good at it."

"Maura, it wasn't for you."

She could just hear her father saying those same words. He probably would, when she called and told him she had quit. He'd think she was fired, and he'd try to make her feel better by saying, "It's not for you. It's too fast out there, Maura. You don't belong." It's not for you, Maura. None of the good things are.

"Look on the bright side," Vince said, moving to the couch. "It brought us together." He was touching her wrist, moving his hand up her arm.

She moved her arm away. "It didn't bring us anywhere," she said, standing up.

He stood up. "Hey, now," he said. "That isn't playing fair, Maur."

"Why is that?"

"I done something for you." He put his hand at her waist.

"Leave me alone," she said, but she didn't move away from him. At first she didn't know why. But it was the feeling of his hand—anyone's hand, she realized. Any man's hand. It had been so long.

"You know you want me," he said. "You always have, Maur. Since we met. Since before."

He leaned down and kissed her, and she opened her mouth, let him in, started melting into the kiss.

And then she realized. This was Vince. Not Max, not some great guy, not anyone she could face having slept with.

She pulled away.

"What?" he said.

"Sorry. I can't."

"What—what's the problem, Maura?"

"Nothing. I just—I'm not going to sleep with you. That's all."

"What—I'm not good enough for you?"

"Don't be ridiculous." She moved away from him—at first she had thought he might fight, but he didn't. And she picked up her purse. "Tell George I said hello. I have to leave."

"Hey—you thought I was serious, I'm not good enough for you? I was doing you a *favor*, Maura."

"Go to hell," she said, and she walked out.

Sixty-eight

"Mm. Great food, isn't it?"

Larkin wished she hadn't come. What was wrong with her, thinking she could spend day after day with Richard? He was sweet and wonderful—there was no one in the world who would do what he had done for her, was there?—but he was making her crazy.

The sun and the ocean were nice—she loved the Bahamas—but all Richard had done for the past four days was *stare* at her.

"You have a piece of shrimp in your beard," she said.

He picked up a napkin and brushed it off, and it fell into his wine.

There was a man across the room, and he was watching her—he had been watching her all during lunch—and she looked at him and raised her wineglass. Richard didn't notice—he didn't notice anything when he was eating. But the man did. He raised his glass and made a little nod with his head.

He was good-looking and rich-looking and with his wife, and she had first noticed him on the beach, great legs and a magnificent chest. Dark eyes, dark hair, the middle-aged age that always seemed to appreciate her most.

"So I thought this evening we'd go into town," Richard was saying. "Hear that band Elizabeth and George said was so good, down at the pier. Are you up for it?"

"Sure." And why had she done something as crazy as throwing all her pills out the window of that cab? Why hadn't she kept even *one*?

"You look so beautiful," he said, reaching across the table and covering her hand with his.

She forced a smile and looked across the room at the man. He turned as if he could feel her.

"Larkin?"

She was pouring more wine into her glass. "Mm?"

He covered her glass with his hand. "I thought you were going to stop."

"This is just *wine*, Richard. You've had two glasses. That was only my first." Which was true.

He sat back in his chair. "I just like to see you when you haven't had any at all," he said.

"Well, it's too late for that, isn't it?"

He was still gazing at her. "I've been thinking," he said.

"Mm?"

"Now that you're not working . . ." He stopped.

"Yes?" Bitch.

He shook his head. "Never mind," he said quietly.

"Richard, what is it? If you have something to say, say it."

"I said never mind."

"All right. If that's the way you want to be." She pushed her chair back. "I'm going out to the beach again."

"Do you want to get married?"

He had blurted it out, but she knew she had heard him right—for four days she had had the feeling he was going to ask her. And how much of a bitch could she be? She looked down at him and put a hand on his shoulder. "You'd be crazy to marry me, Richard. Let's try to keep things simple, all right?"

His face fell, and she walked away—would he really want her to see him like that? He fell apart so *easily*—and she walked past the glass doors to the patio and out into the sun.

Normally she hated the sun—it was every redhead's nemesis, of course, something that had prevented her all her life from being where she wanted to be. All those ridiculous vacations her family had taken, and she had spent half of them indoors. But the sun felt wonderful, and she had put an enormous amount of the strongest suntan lotion the hotel drugstore sold all over her body.

She hadn't looked at the man as she had left the restaurant. She wanted to pace it, not to rush it, to see if anything or nothing at all would happen. Half the fun was the suspense, wondering how far he'd come along, and she lay down on a chaise by the pool where she'd be able to see him leaving the restaurant if he came outside.

What about Richard?

She wasn't going to think about Richard. Thinking about Richard made her think about her life—how she had screwed up, what she had fucked up. How had she thrown so much away? Maura—her best friend in the world. And the job, something she had always wanted.

She closed her eyes and tried to think of something else. What had she *done*? She was down here with someone she didn't love, she had alienated everybody she *did* love—

"Hello there."

She opened her eyes. He was standing in her sun, so she didn't even have to shade her eyes.

"Finished so soon? Where's your wife?"

"She has a headache. Where's your husband?"

"Oh, he's not my husband." She sat up and pulled her robe off. "Would you get my suntan lotion out of my bag?"

"Sure." He reached in and tossed it to her, and she poured some out into her palm and started putting it on her legs. He was watching every move, of course, which was the general idea. She moved her hands slowly, up her calves to her thighs, and then she brought one knee up and looked at him. "So," she said.

He looked thoroughly hypnotized. "So," he said. His voice had gotten husky.

"We could go somewhere," she said.

He inhaled slowly and deeply. "Name the place."

"Hm. Not your room, later, after your wife leaves? Doesn't she shop?"

He shook his head. "Not for a long enough time," he said. "And some things can't be rushed."

She let her knee flop to the side, and the man stared. "We should make it soon, though, don't you think?" She put some more lotion on her hands and rubbed it along the edge of her bikini.

"What about your room?" he asked.

Something made her look off to the left, and she saw Richard coming. "I'll talk to you later. My friend is coming, so you'd better go."

He took off quickly but calmly—a man with experience—and she took a long, deep breath. God, how she wanted him now.

"Who was that man?" Richard asked, sitting down on the next chaise.

She shrugged. "Someone who thought he knew me."

"Huh. But you don't know him?"

"Nope," she said, turning over onto her stomach. But she was going to get to know him soon. She closed her eyes and pictured him and the way he had just been staring at her.

It would have to be soon, the get-together. She sat up and pulled her hair back from her face. "Richard, I wonder if you could get something for me in town today."

Sixty-nine

"Yeah. Give me Alexandra."

"Who's calling, please?"

"Lew Burnham."

"Oh, hi, Lew, it's Maura." He was one of their clients, someone she had met last week when he had come in to sign a contract for a commercial.

"Hi, Maura. Is she there?" He sounded upset.

"Yes. Just a minute."

She buzzed Alexandra and told her who was on the line.

"Tell him I'll call him back."

Great. "Alexandra, I told him you were in."

"Why did you do that?"

"Because he's a client, a working client, and I couldn't conceive of a reason you wouldn't be free to speak to him, to tell you the truth."

Alexandra sighed. "All right. But I'm reading a script. I don't want to be disturbed after this, by anyone or for anyone except Terence if he calls from L.A."

"Fine."

And she wondered. Was Lew Burnham one of the clients they had taken payments from? It was hard to believe anyone would stand for it. But then, she could imagine how Alexandra would put it—that their accountant had screwed up, that it would be a few days, nothing to worry about. And even if the person *was* worried, he probably wouldn't do anything about it, because if there was one thing she had learned working here, it was that actors were incredibly superstitious and insecure. If they got a job wearing a certain shirt or pair of underpants or socks, they'd probably wear those things to every audition from then on. And if they had a certain agent . . . Well, everyone knew how impossible it was to find an agent, and a good one who found you work. Maybe there wasn't *really* anything to worry about. Was there?

Maura looked at her watch. Steve Cressman was supposed to come in to talk about a part he was going to be trying for tomorrow, and he was late. Fifteen minutes, which was bad. What if he was late for the audition? It was one of the things that you had to drum in, that acting wasn't just some sort of fun thing to do, that it was a business. Larkin—damn. It was hard to think about. But Larkin had taken it seriously, to the extent that she had done it. Never late once, which was amazing.

The outer door opened and Steve came in, red-cheeked and breathless. "Whew. Those trains are crazy. How're you doing?"

She had forgotten how cute he was in addition to being a great actor. Really sweet face, with soft, doglike brown eyes. "I'm fine, but you're late," she said as he sat down.

He nodded. "The trains are crazy. We stopped for ten minutes in some tunnel, so—" He looked at his watch. "Ten minutes is about how late I am, right?"

"That's right. But you have to leave enough time for things like that to happen. You can't be late for the kind of audition you're going on tomorrow. Leave twice the time."

He nodded. "Okay. Will do."

"Okay. As long as we understand each other. Let's talk about the part." She pulled out the breakdown sheet. "Okay. What they need is 'a young man 22–27, handsome but doesn't necessarily know it, naive in many ways, especially when it comes to relationships. Physically strong, must look good in scenes at gym but not *too* good. No Tom Sellecks, please.' "

He nodded. "I can do that."

The outer door opened, and the guy who had said he was Jack the other day breezed in and walked past her desk.

"Uh, excuse me," she called.

"Alexandra's in," he said, and he opened Alexandra's door, walked in, and shut it.

Steve looked at Maura and said the same thing Max had said that day: "Client?"

"I don't think so," Maura said. Dealer was more like it. And she wondered. If she confronted Alexandra after the guy left, what would Alexandra say? Would she deny it? She could say it was none of Maura's business, but of course, it was, since money was disappearing—and from so many quarters, it seemed.

Steve was looking at the paper on her desk, and she saw it was the list of actors whose pictures she had submitted for the role. "Here," she said, handing it to him. "Unless you can read upside down."

He smiled. "Thanks. So these are the ones from this agency who are reading for the role?"

"Not at all," she said. "Those are the ones whose pictures we submitted. Out of all of those—we sent in sixteen, right?"

"Fifteen . . . right, sixteen."

"They asked to see you and one other."

"Which one?"

She smiled. "Does it matter?"

"I just want to know."

She handed him the eight-by-ten. "This one. Dennis Kincaid."

"Oh, great. He looks perfect," Steve said.

"He could play the role," she said. "But you'd be better."

The inner door opened and Jack came out, shut the door, and walked past without even looking at Maura.

And she decided something on the spot. "Listen," she said, coming around to Steve's side of the desk. "I have to talk to you about something completely confidential."

"What is it?"

"If there were something funny going on here at the agency—something shifty—"

"Like what?"

"I don't know. Maybe nothing. I don't want to say yet—"

"Something to do with that guy who just left?"

"Maybe," she said.

"Go on."

"As I said, I don't know. But if there were, and I decided to quit. Or if I were fired. Would you, uh . . ." She didn't know how to put it.

"You're asking if I would stay with them or go with you?"

"Well, yes."

He laughed. "Are you kidding? I don't even *know* those two. Of course I'd go with you."

"There's a chance you'd be my only client for a while."

He spread his hands. "Hey. You're my only agent. You took a chance. I could take a chance."

She felt like hugging him. "Okay. Good. It might not even happen. But if it does—"

"I'm with you all the way," he said.

"Good. That helps." And it did. But it was easier to talk about than to actually do it. She wanted what Vince had said not to be true. But she'd have to face facts, sooner or later, and sooner if they continued not to pay her. Maybe she could talk to Max. Maybe he'd know what to do. Maybe.

Seventy

"Your girlfriend's been trying something," the voice over the phone said.

Allan kicked the office door shut. "What did you say? And who is this?"

"Huh. You don't recognize my voice? It's Nick. From the club. How've you been? Long time no see."

"Right," Allan said. "What are you talking about?"

"Your girlfriend, Danielle. Tried to shake one of our customers down for thirteen G's. I put two and two together, thought I'd give you a call."

Christ. Danielle—! What had she been *doing*?

"Anyway, I came up with the idea you got some trouble, maybe with another lender, maybe at work. With a Mr. Murray Bauman, 555-4676, is what I have on your card. Might need to make a couple of deposits, am I right? Mr. Business Manager?"

"Nope," Allan said, but he was starting to sweat. "Not even close."

"Not even close, huh? Is that right? So if I was to call this Mr. Murray Bauman, you wouldn't mind? Like if I was to say I thought his business manager was having some trouble, *I* don't know if he has sticky fingers, but Mr. Murray Bauman better check the books because Mr. Allan Greshner owes somebody twenty, thirty G's, you wouldn't mind?"

"I don't care what you do."

"Okay, then. Is that what you want? 'Cause I got another idea."

"What's that?"

"You need how much? I've seen you lose twenty G's at King's alone; maybe there's more. So let's say twenty, thirty G's. I lend it to you, you're clean with your boss, whoever, no fuss no muss, case closed."

"Except with you," Allan said. "Then I owe you twenty thousand plus how much interest?"

"Well, the way I look at it, you don't have such a bad deal with me, seeing as how the other deal means I make some phone calls. This way you got a few interest payments, but maybe you make some money at the club, and like that."

Christ. "Tell me about Danielle."

"Danielle, ah, Danielle can take care of herself, you know what I mean? You know Danielle. She sleeps with me, she sleeps with you, she sleeps with the guy she tried to shake down, she does what she has to do."

Allan's head was pounding. Danielle sleeping around?

"I don't have to tell *you*," Nick said. "So listen. We got a deal or what?"

"What? Oh." Christ, what to do? It was a chance, much as he didn't want to admit it. If he could say to Murray, "Look, I had some trouble, but it's all here, every cent," Murray was the kind of guy who'd maybe understand, at least with the son of Julius Greshner. It was possible, a better chance than having a big red twenty-thousand-dollar hole in the books.

He sighed. He didn't want to deal with Dotson, but here he was. "All right," he said. "I guess. Yeah, sure. What the hell." Sound casual. Make it sound like not a big deal, even though he was sweating like a pig.

"Smart man," Nick said. "Smart man, Greshner. Okay, so we meet tonight, okay? At the club, only you don't tell *no one* why we're meeting, you got that? This is a side deal, just you and me. Fifth floor, you got that?"

"Fifth floor," Allan said. He felt like he was dreaming. "What time?"

"Nine-fifteen," Nick said. "Sharp, Greshner."

It seemed like an odd time, but he said all right and hung up. Danielle sleeping around. Had she done it all for him, trying to get the money? He couldn't stand to think about it.

He picked up the phone and started dialing her number, but then he put the receiver down. He had to let it settle, to figure out what he was going to say. His little baby seal. He couldn't stand it.

Nick put the receiver down and lit a cigar. He felt like a king that had just gotten laid. He was at the top of the world and going even higher. This was what life was all about.

Seventy-one

Danielle bit her lip and looked at the doctor again. She couldn't believe what he had said, and the number of weeks. "Um, are you sure?" she asked.

"You're definitely pregnant, yes, Danielle."

She closed her eyes. "Um, so it wouldn't be sooner, right? I mean, like, if I had slept with someone last week, it wouldn't be theirs."

"No," he said. "You can get dressed now."

"But, um, if I wanted to know—I mean, can you tell who the father is, like from a blood test or something?"

"Only after the baby is born," he said.

She hopped off the table and felt dizzy. What had she done? What if the baby was Nick's? One second she had been so happy—maybe not even for one whole second. And then after—uh-oh.

She went home, but it felt totally empty since Larkin was in the islands and Maura was at work. She wondered about calling Allan, but she couldn't do it. What could she say, anyway? She felt all teary and scared, and there was no one.

Out on the street she just felt like going home to Venice, to where at least it was warm. Up till now it had seemed like a horrible idea, because she'd have to be with her mother, but maybe she could go home and just not call, or call some of the time, and start her own new family. Because the thing was that she really wanted a baby, even no matter whose it was.

A lady on the street passed, on Broadway, wheeling a baby carriage, and Danielle felt like saying, "Hey, me, too! What's it like?" Except that the woman probably (almost definitely, like 99 percent definitely) had a husband and would probably look at her like she was crazy if she said she didn't even know who the father was.

God. What a gyp. The thing she had wanted most in the whole world.

But maybe Allan would be totally great about it. Maybe he would say, "Darling, I love you, it doesn't matter whose baby you're carrying." There had to be *some* men who would feel that way, right? And Allan was the greatest guy she had ever met. So maybe it would be true. She could talk to him tonight after her shift, and kind of "test" him out. And then she'd see. The main thing was that she loved him, so she had to have faith. It was the most important thing in the whole world.

Seventy-two

"Whew. I knew you were going to be something," he said, stroking her back.

"Mm," Larkin said. She felt so good, she didn't even want to speak. It had been ages since she had been so thoroughly sated that she couldn't even move, didn't even want to speak. "What's your name, anyway?" she suddenly asked, rubbing her lips against his wet chest.

"Povarich," he said. "Michael Povarich."

She sat up. "The Dr. Povarich they've been paging for days?"

"The one and only," he said, spreading his palms.

"So does that mean you have medications with you? Pills, that sort of thing? What sort of doctor are you?"

"Internal medicine, family practice. What kind of pills?"

She had to be careful. He sounded cautious all of a sudden. "Oh, I don't really know. Do they still make Valium or is there something new on the market?"

He laughed. "Hoffmann-LaRoche would be very upset if they

284 / Janet Kotselas Clarke

heard that someone didn't know whether Valium was still on the market. It is still, rather. Why? Do you need something?"

She hesitated. "Well, I don't know. I hate to take any sort of pill. But I've just been so jumpy down here. Not exactly the way you're supposed to feel on a vacation." Already she could taste the bitterness, that flavor that tasted yellow now and meant she'd be feeling good. She had forgotten how much she missed it. "I don't know. Maybe it's not such a great idea. It's just that I haven't slept more than two hours a night since I've come down here."

He sat up and stretched. "Well, a couple of Valium wouldn't hurt. I wouldn't want you to take more than two a day, though." He stood up and went to his beach bag.

"You carry them with you?" she asked. Maybe he was more interesting than she had thought.

"For my wife," he said. "She's on quite a bit of medication. Here," he said, tossing her the bottle. "Take out what you need and give the bottle back."

She opened the bottle and poured them out into her palm. There had to be thirty pills. "Uh . . ." She had to stay calm. "I guess five? Or six?"

"That would be fine," he said.

She poured ten out and slipped them into the night table drawer, and took two right away. She chewed them and then swallowed as he came back to the bed.

He lay down beside her and then moved on top of her. "Always happy to help a damsel in distress," he said, looking into her eyes. "As long as you don't get *too* relaxed." He reached between her legs, and she wrapped her knees around him.

"Never," she whispered, and then she heard a sound.

It was a sound as if in a dream, so precise it was like a dream detail that would never be forgotten.

The door was opening, and she opened her eyes.

Richard.

"Oh God," she heard herself say.

The door closed, and Michael raised his head. "What was that?"

She moved out from under him. "God. I can't believe it. *Shit.* I can't *believe* it."

"What happened? I—"

"Richard. He just came in. He—"

"Oh Christ," he said, and he jumped off the bed and started grabbing his clothes.

"What are you doing?" she said. "He's not going to come *back*."

"I have to get to my wife. Does he know who I am?"

"I don't think so."

He was cursing and jumping and getting dressed faster than anyone she had ever seen.

"I don't know you," he said, coming to the bed. He kissed her and raced to the door, and then turned back. "My wife is in a *very* fragile condition. If she hears anything about this—"

"She's not going to," she said. "I know Richard. He would never say anything. And I certainly wouldn't."

He still looked panic-stricken. "We'll see," he said, and he left and shut the door.

The Valium was beginning to work. She knew it because she had that dreamy feeling. But it wasn't a good feeling. Everything was going sour. What had she done, picking up a stranger? When was she going to learn that it felt wonderful for a short time and then it was over? She didn't know if she'd ever be able to forget Richard's face.

And whose was the other face, the one that had burned in her mind?

She slid open the night table drawer and took out two more Valiums and swallowed them.

It was Maura's face she had tried to forget.

God. Who else would she hurt this year, or next? How many people was she going to treat so badly?

She felt sick all of a sudden, dizzy and lonesome, and she had to get out of the room.

Find Richard. That's what she'd do. Make up with him, somehow.

She put her bathing suit back on, sandals; her robe was somewhere. . . .

The sun felt horribly bright, and she couldn't remember—

Oh. Richard. She had to find Richard.

But why was she so dizzy?

Maybe three pills had been too much, on top of the wine at lunch? Or was it four? It felt as if the sun were cooking her. Had she put on suntan lotion? She couldn't even remember. She could remember screaming on St. Kitts as a child after she had stayed in the sun too long, and her mother saying, "It was your own fault, Larkin. Why do you expect all of us to take the blame?"

She saw Richard out in the water—she had always been able to recognize him from the way he moved, even the shape of his head from far away.

She'd make up with him, tell him it would never happen again. They could get married. Even down here, if he wanted. Some sort of ship's captain could marry them. Join them forever.

The water was freezing against her toes, lapping up against her ankles—it was painful, a cutting cold closing off her veins.

But she had to start making sacrifices. Doing the right thing. She'd make her way through the water, through the waves, prove him wrong. Prove . . . What was she trying to prove? Oh yes, that she loved him. Or that he was wrong. That was it. He was wrong because she really was a good person, she could be if he gave her a chance.

She saw him bobbing there in the waves, and a wave slapped her knees and she heard herself cry out—it was so *cold*—but she had to do it. The waves slapped her stomach, and she couldn't stand it—the cold was almost killing—but she let her knees buckle and she plunged in—that was the way Geoffrey had always done it— and she started to swim.

She had always been a strong swimmer. At camp, the one summer she had been allowed to go ("We feel your daughter is a bit more mature than our other campers, Mr. and Mrs. James. We feel quite sure she'd be happier elsewhere")—that summer she had won medals in swimming. Geoffrey had been so proud.

But the waves were strong, swimming against them and diving in; each one sounded so *loud*—but she dove down, under the rushing water, and pushed herself up, once and then again and again, and Richard—

He was getting closer, wasn't he?

The water felt good now at least, but the sun was so hot . . . And why was he swimming out so *far*? She took a deep breath and pushed her face into the water and forced her arms to go full speed. Ten more strokes and she'd be there, and she'd rest against his shoulders, rest her chin on his head . . .

She had to gasp for air—suddenly she was exhausted, and her arms felt like lead, and they ached, and the first panic came: she was exhausted, completely.

"Richard?" she called. Her voice died on the water. And why did he keep *swimming*? Where was he *going*? Was he trying to teach her some sort of lesson? "Richard, wait. I can't go any farther. Richard!"

He was still moving, still swimming, and for the first time she felt she wouldn't be able to catch him. He wasn't going to turn around and he wasn't going to stop. She'd have to swim back to shore by herself.

She turned around to see how far she had come, and her heart almost stopped: She could barely see the shoreline. It was far away, shimmering in the heat, an unswimmable distance.

"Rich—" She was turning around and she had seen—

It was a jug, a floating jug of some sort, with a tan wrapping, a yellow—

How had she thought it was him?

She was out here *alone*.

She heard a sound. It had come from her, but she didn't know what it was—a cry, maybe because she knew—

It was too far.

Swim!

But she couldn't. She was trying, but her arms ached, and her lungs hurt, and the sun was melting her scalp, blinding her. . . .

She saw something moving from shore—a boat? Was someone coming for her?—and she tried to raise her arm, but she sank. She had never sunk in her life; what was happening? And suddenly there was water; she tried to take a breath, but she had taken a gulp instead, and she gasped and tried to make a sound—a sound that someone would hear, maybe? Her thoughts felt small, like a child's. The water caught in her mouth and she coughed, and suddenly she couldn't stop coughing, and her breath—it was water coming in now, into her nose and her mouth, and she tried to get it out, to cough and make her nose come up over the waves, to breathe *something*.

But then she knew, and she thought, Please, no, but she couldn't fight anymore, and she closed her eyes and felt the water come up over the top of her head.

Seventy-three

Allan pocketed the money and shook Nick's hand. Why was it that money had suddenly become so easy to take when it wasn't his? He felt as if he were pocketing a present, a dollar bill from his Uncle Morris or a piece of candy from his Aunt May.

Twenty G's. What had happened to him?

"So hey," Nick said, jumping up. "I got a girl you wouldn't believe, and she's been asking for you, Greshner."

"What? What girl?"

"You wouldn't believe her." Nick was pacing now, and Allan realized he was wired, probably on some kind of drug. Coke? He didn't know. He knew about as much about drugs as his father had. "And she's been asking, Greshner. *Asking.* 'When's that *guy* coming back?' " he mimicked in a high, sick-sounding voice. " 'He was so *cute*.' What'd she say? 'Like some kind of teddy bear,' that's what she said."

Allan didn't like it. Sure he was flattered, if it was true, but it sounded kind of fishy. And tonight was one of Danielle's nights. "I'll take a rain check on that, okay?"

Nick suddenly looked furious. "What? You're too good for me and my friends all of a sudden? You sit down, we have a drink, and like that."

Allan suddenly remembered where he had heard "and like that" before. "Kojak." So this was an insecure guy he was dealing with, taking mannerisms from tough-guy TV characters.

"Nah," Allan said, starting to move to the door.

Nick's eyes were shining. "Hey. One drink. She'll be here any minute. What's your hurry?" There was a knock at the door. "Too late, huh? You can't back out now. Come on in," he called.

The door opened, and a girl who looked startlingly like Danielle, only brunette—Allan had never seen her before, that he could remember—came in. "Oh. Hi," she said shyly. "Hi, Nick. Hi, Al-

288

lan.'' She held out her hand, and Allan shook it. ''Um, glad we could finally meet.''

''Oh. Thanks,'' he said. Christ, what was he saying? ''I don't remember seeing you here ever.''

She was blushing. ''Well, I've been kind of in the background. I'm training in a couple of areas. Um, what are you drinking?''

''Nothing,'' he said. ''I've got to get going, actually.''

Her face fell. ''Oh. Um . . . oh.'' She bit her lip. ''God. But we just met.'' Her eyes were huge—blue and confused and innocent-looking. ''I guess, then, maybe I'll see you?'' She looked so sad. ''Gee . . .'' Her voice had trailed off.

''Well, I guess we could have a drink,'' he said.

Danielle looked around the club and felt sick. Now that she knew she was pregnant, suddenly everything she could breathe or eat or drink seemed dangerous. How come everybody had a cigarette in their hands? Didn't they know sometimes people were pregnant, and there were babies trying to breathe inside? Not that she guessed they actually *breathed*, but still.

The truth was it probably wasn't the greatest place in the world to work if you were pregnant. So that was one of the things she had thought about, when she wasn't thinking about The Giant Question. God. Sometimes she forgot, and she started thinking about how great everything was going to be, how Allan would be the father (he automatically was in the thoughts), and they'd be up in the country, maybe, or at a theme park, like even Disney World, where she had never even been, so they could make it a ''first'' for everyone in the family, since probably Allan had never been either. And they'd all be having such a great time in the dream, or the thought.

And then the truth. How could she have been so DUMB? And what did other people do in her situation, other women? She had the feeling there were two sets of people. There were the ones who told the truth, and the ones who pretended nothing ''strange'' had ever happened. What *could* you do, if you were married? What could you say? ''Honey, I had an affair, and this isn't your baby, necessarily.'' Really, what could they say? But what did you do about telling yourself, knowing in your heart?

The thing was, she knew it was Allan's. She just knew, in her heart. So didn't that count? She wished she knew at least that, but who could you ask? The doctor said that if they were about the right ''time of the month,'' it was impossible to say. And he didn't even seem that concerned, like it wasn't even that giant an issue. She couldn't believe it.

"Miss!"

She turned around. This super-snooty woman—she had seen her a jillion times, always with a rich guy everyone hated to serve because he never tipped—was calling her from a couch.

"Yes?" One of her last nights as a waitress, thank God.

"I'd like a Scotch and soda, light, on the rocks, and some cigarettes—Camel filters."

"Okay," Danielle said, and she started to walk away.

But suddenly she saw Nick—something had told her to look at the double doors that led to the stairway, and there he was. And she wanted to avoid him, but he was already coming her way and making a sign for her to come over.

"Um, I have to get that woman's order," she said when he came up to her and touched her on the elbow.

"Forget it," he said, and he snapped his fingers for Michelle, another waitress, to come over. "Tell Michelle what the lady wants."

She did, but she didn't know what was going on.

"I have to talk to you," Nick said, and it sounded serious. "You're going to have to come with me, Danielle."

She didn't know what was going on. She hadn't even had a fight with any of the customers, so it couldn't be that. No one could have complained.

She followed him up the stairs to the fifth floor and followed him down the carpeting. It felt like a million years ago that she had slept with him. And now . . . she just couldn't believe it. He was maybe the father. But it didn't feel like it could be true.

They went into the same room she had slept with him in—the den-type room—and he shut the door.

"There are a couple of things," he said, putting his hands on her shoulders. "One's not so good; the other I don't know."

She couldn't even begin to think what he was talking about.

"You'd better sit down," he said, and she did, but on a chair—not on the couch like the last time. "So listen," he said, sitting down across from her. "You're going to be taken off the dealership for a few weeks—"

"What?"

"Now, don't get upset; I swung things for you pretty good. King wanted you out, but I told him you were too good to lose."

"What are you talking about? I haven't done anything wrong."

"Not at the club," Nick said, and he looked down at his hands. He looked like he was thinking how to put his next words. Then he looked into her eyes. "Al-Sadir," he said. "He lodged a complaint against you, and King was pretty upset. Danielle, you can't shake the customers down for money. Not like you did, anyway."

"But—"

"Now, let me finish. It didn't look so good at first. He's a good customer, Danielle, and with a guy like that—especially these Arab guys, where everyone thinks they're worth millions—they expect results, you know? 'I want that girl fired,' and the girl gets fired. But I put in a good word for you, and King likes you, so he agreed. But it means no dealing for a month."

She didn't know what to say. She wanted to know everything Al-Sadir had said, but she also didn't want to hear any of it. He couldn't have told Nick everything, and she didn't want to tell him, either. She didn't want to see the look in his eyes. "Um, what's the other thing?"

"That's it? What's the other thing? No, 'Thanks, Nick; you saved my job'?"

She shrugged. "Of course thanks. You should know . . . It's just that you said there were two things."

He was hesitating, and he looked again like he was thinking of exactly what to say. "I wish I knew how to tell you this other thing. It isn't even any of my business, I know that, you don't have to tell me that, but I like you—you know that—and I've kind of always watched over you, you know?"

He seemed to be waiting for an answer, so she nodded. But she just wished he'd *tell* her. "What is it?" she finally said.

He took a deep breath. "I know you were involved with Allan Greshner," he said. What did he mean by 'were'? "And I know you didn't want to go out with me anymore—you know, whatever." *What did he mean by 'were'?*

"Did something happen to Allan?" Her voice had come out like a whisper, and she had suddenly had a horrible picture of Allan lying shot in some alleyway, all because she hadn't been able to get him the money.

"To Greshner? Nah. Nothing like that." His eyes looked super-blue and shiny all of a sudden.

"Then what are you saying? Allan—"

"Greshner's been seeing another waitress," he said, super-quickly, kind of like a blurt. "He got the money he needed from another source, one thing led to another, and like that. And I wanted you to know so you'd be let down gently, not see something you don't want to see.''

She didn't believe him. It wasn't true. Allan—"I don't believe you," she said. "You're just saying that, for some reason I don't know. To upset me, maybe."

He was smiling. "Why would I want to upset you? I'm trying to let you down *easy*." He held up his palms. "But hey—you want to see it that way, I can't do anything about that. I saved your job, but you want to be accusing me of things—"

"I'm not accusing you. I just—you have to be wrong, that's all."

"Hey, you want to see who's wrong? You can—" He stopped. "Nah. Forget it. I'm not that cruel."

"What? What were you going to say?"

"Nothing."

"Nick, tell me."

He sighed. "Okay," he said quietly. "You want to see you're not wrong? Go down—nah, never mind."

"I don't believe you. Go down where? And who is she? How come I've never seen her?"

"You work different times, different places, and her name is Valerie. But forget it, Danielle."

"Where are they, if they're here?"

"Forget it."

She stood up and opened the door. "Come over here and tell me where they are or I'm going to start opening doors, Nick."

"Hey, you want to get fired for real, Danielle? That's the way to do it."

She walked out and started down the stairs. He had said, "Go down," so they were probably on the first floor. But she didn't believe him. He couldn't be telling the truth. She was just going to check to be a thousand percent positive.

The first floor was extra-crazy for some reason, nine thousand people, it looked like, all jammed around the craps tables and roulette, the fancy ones with a twenty-dollar minimum. And Allan never hung out on the first floor, he never had ever, so there, she felt like saying.

Except that then she saw him, walking through the crowd down one of the aisles. And this girl, a dark-haired girl who was holding on to his arm and laughing—her hip was touching his hip, and she was laughing. Danielle swallowed, but her throat was dry.

Allan didn't see her, and she was just turning away—her knees felt like jelly—but the girl saw her, and her hand kind of went up to her mouth, like "Oops."

Danielle turned and ran.

Seventy-four

Maura took a deep breath and rang the bell. She had called Max earlier, and he had said sure, he'd be free tonight to talk, but she still felt odd about the whole thing.

The door opened, and Max and Sophie were standing there.

Maura laughed. "One smiling and one wagging. Nice way to open the door."

"She insists," he said, following her back into the loft. "Can I get you a drink? Coffee or anything?"

"A beer would be great," she said, walking into the living room area. She looked around to see if there were any signs, but signs of what? That Terence snorted a lot of coke? That he was stealing money from people? What sort of signs would those things leave?

"How's Sophie feeling?" She stooped down and scratched her behind the ears, and Sophie wagged her tail harder.

"She's good," he called as he brought the beers in. He set the tray down on the table and knocked on the wood. "Just a little insurance," he said, smiling. "So sit down. Relax."

She was more nervous than when she had come in. She loved the way Max's face looked; she liked him so much.

"So tell me what's up," he said. "Tell me *something*, Maura. You're making me nervous."

"This isn't going to be easy," she said. She took a sip of beer. Where was she going to start? "I think—" She took a deep breath. "I think Terence is having some problems, and I think they're affecting the business."

He looked interested but unenlightened. So he probably had no idea. "What sort of problems?"

She told him what Vince had told her—about the coke, the debts, the money that belonged to clients.

"How do you know all this?" he asked.

It was a question she had anticipated, but not one she had been looking forward to answering. "There's this guy. And he's . . . I don't know how to put it—he used to go to school with someone who's a drug dealer; he runs in a similar crowd. He's the son of the guy I used to work for, George Falcone. Anyway, he was kind of looking into the situation."

"Looking into it? Why?"

"Why are you turning into a lawyer all of a sudden?"

"Because I *am* a lawyer. And you're making some pretty serious charges."

"I'm not making *charges*. I'm trying to figure out what's going on. You were there that day I got the call from the actor threatening to go to SAG. There've been a lot more of those—at least calls that seem like that. And you saw the guy who came in that day. If that wasn't a dealer, I don't know what is. And I haven't gotten paid." She paused. "I have every right to look into this, Max."

"I know, I know. I just don't understand. This person you're getting the information from. Would he have any reason to lie?"

"No. Absolutely not."

"Are you sure? I mean, what is he doing? What made him look into this? Did you ask him?"

"I don't—no, not exactly. I told him I wasn't getting paid—Terence and Alexandra kept asking me to defer my salary, and he looked into the situation, and he told me what he found." She paused. "All right, look. He *is* a little odd, maybe he does have reason to lie—"

"Why?"

"Well, he—I don't know, he likes me, and maybe—" She shrugged. "Maybe he would exaggerate a little. But I really don't think he'd make it up."

He was looking into her eyes. "I see," he said quietly. For a while he didn't say anything. Then he shook his head. "I've been wondering about Terence, and I've been wondering about their business. I haven't been able to put my finger on anything specific, and I haven't even had any reason to think about it beyond my own curiosity. But it makes sense, what you've told me. . . ." He paused. "What do you think you're going to do?"

"I guess wait for Terence to get back. The thing that bothers me most, though, is that I really was good at what I did for them, and I thought they were giving me a chance because they thought so, too."

"Maybe they did."

She shook her head. "I don't know. This whole thing makes me feel as if it was all unreal, as if Terence and Alexandra weren't even taking the business seriously."

"I'm sure you're wrong there," he said. "Terence takes the business completely seriously. Maybe too seriously. He's always told me—and I believe him on this—that he hired you because he thought you'd be great at it."

"Maybe," she said.

"If what you say is true, I'm much more worried about him than about you—I know you can land on your feet. But he's been driving himself to this for a long time. He's constantly pushing himself." He sighed. "Every time I see people like that, I wonder what it is that makes them do it."

"You mean what makes them so driven."

"Sure. Vanessa—" He sighed. "There's nothing she wouldn't do for a great part. Nothing. And I know that. I'd be a fool if I didn't know it. She's out there with Terence right now, and they're both selling everything they've got." He reached for his beer and took a long swig.

"How can you live with that?" she asked. She knew it was a destructive question, the kind no one likes to hear. But she wanted to ask it, and she wanted him to think about it. Decide Vanessa wasn't for him.

"I don't know," he said, looking into her eyes.

"Did you resolve the issue of your not going with her out to L.A.? I mean, was that still a problem? Am I asking too many questions?"

"You could never ask too many questions," he said. He was looking at her in the oddest way. "And the answer is yes, it's still a problem. And you know they've stayed longer than they had thought they were going to."

She wanted him to kiss her. She wanted something great to happen, and she almost felt it was going to. There had been a moment there, so much tension.

He stood up. "Want another beer?"

"No, thanks."

But it was silly to hope, another pathetic wish. The only people she could attract were weirdos.

Seventy-five

The phone rang, and Danielle bit her lip. She knew it was Allan. He always called around now, after she was home from her shift. So did that mean he hadn't hardly stayed at the club with that girl, Valerie? God. She couldn't believe she had even gotten through her shift.

It rang and rang, and she didn't know what to do. If she didn't answer it, maybe it would all turn out to be a horrible dream; if she didn't talk to him, maybe everything would change. Saying she knew, saying the truth—she just couldn't face it.

But it kept *ringing*.

"Hello?" she finally said.

"Hi, honey."

She closed her eyes. But when they were closed, all she could see was Allan with that girl on his arm.

"Danielle?"

"I'm here," she said.

"What's the matter?" he asked. "Is everything all right?"

"Everything's fine," she said, but she knew she sounded dead. "There were a couple of things that happened, but they don't really matter anymore."

"What? What happened, honey?"

"You can stop calling me that, because it's all over, the thing between us. The relationship."

"Danielle, what happened? What are you talking about?"

"I don't want to talk about it. Accept it gracefully, Allan. It's over. I don't want to see you anymore."

"But, Danielle . . ." There was a silence. Then he said, "I can't believe you really feel that way. But if you do . . ."

She closed her eyes. *Picture him with that girl Valerie*. She had to, to stay mad.

"I don't want to lose you," he said. "I love you. But I never thought I could hold you forever.'' Then silence. So he was so ready to give up. And why not, now that he had a new girl?

"Good-bye, Allan," she said, and she hung up.

The tears started, and they felt like they were burning her cheeks, and she lay down on the bed and cried into her pillow. She was all alone, and why did that feel so bad? She had always been alone, there had never been anyone to depend on, never. Definitely not her mother, definitely not Cleve, not even Allan, even though she loved him more than anyone in the whole world. And she missed him already.

Think of that girl. And the truth was that she had even still, even after seeing him with the girl, she had thought maybe it was some kind of lie. But not when she was talking to him. Because he could have said, "I'll never give you up, I'll love you forever," and he hadn't.

And she had to face it: she had been trying to force him with things like the baby, always asking, asking, asking. The articles said people always tried to make their "mates" into people they weren't, and maybe she had done it with Allan. Only, she had been so sure he'd love it if only he'd let it happen. And it was such a gyp, because when she left Venice she had thought, I'll go to New York, and I'll become rich and famous. It's all I want in the whole world. But then she had fallen in love with Allan, and she had realized that was what she wanted more than anything. To be in love. Except now she had nothing.

She wiped away the tears and looked in the mirror across the room. She looked streaky and horrible. Maybe the baby would love her, when it was born, and she'd love it more than anything in the world. But except for him (she just knew it was going to be a boy), she was going to be all alone, forever.

Seventy-six

Maura heard crying the minute she opened the door, and she knew it was Danielle. So much sobbing! She ran down the hall and knocked softly on the half-open door. Danielle was curled up with her face down in her pillow, but she waved her in and then sat up and wiped her face.

"What happened?" Maura asked. "What's the matter?"

"Everything. I broke up with Allan. I found out I'm pregnant." She sniffled. "And I don't even know who the father is, and the *doctor* says there's no way to know till the baby's born. Maybe not even then."

"Wait a minute. Slow down. Why did you break up with Allan?"

Danielle told her a teary, confused story she could only understand every other word of, but the gist of it, she guessed, was that she had seen Allan with another woman.

"And it wasn't just 'with' like the way we're together, talking," Danielle said, wiping at new tears that kept coming. "He was really with her. She looked super-happy, and she was all over him."

Maura had never seen so many tears in her life. "But Danielle—"

"And another thing," Danielle said, her voice rising. "Why was he so happy to break up? He said okay, and that was almost it. That he always knew he wouldn't be able to hold on to me. That's what he *said*, anyway."

"But did you tell him why? What did you say?"

Danielle shrugged. "It doesn't matter why. Everything's a mess." She bit her lip. "And I couldn't exactly scream at him for being with another woman and then say I didn't know if he was the father." She was looking down at her hands.

"That's it, isn't it? You didn't want to tell him you don't know?"

The tears were starting again, and she covered her eyes. "I can't," she said. "It would be better for him not to know anything than to know I slept with Nick and—that's the thing. One second I feel so bad, I love him so much and I don't want him to know I was with someone else, and the next second, I remember he was with *Valerie*. Bitch. I don't even know her, but I know she's a bitch. I can tell."

"But Valerie isn't the problem, Danielle. You have to think about yourself. How you're going to have a baby all on your own. It isn't going to be easy."

"I'm not having an abortion," Danielle said, pressing her fist to her mouth. "I'm not against it or anything like that, but I don't want to have one. I'd never get rid of this baby."

"But what will you do?"

She shrugged. "I can take care of myself." She looked as if she knew she had made a mistake. "And the baby," she said quickly. "I can do lots of things. I can maybe deal out in Atlantic City. At a real casino."

Maura didn't say anything. What could she say that wouldn't be cruel? She didn't know how Danielle had been managing to take care of herself since she had left home. How was she going to take care of *two* people?

The phone rang, and Maura got up. "I'll get it," she said. She didn't want to be too critical. Other people did manage their lives, in ways she could never imagine. They saw possibilities in things she saw nothing in; they tried things for themselves she'd never try on her own.

"Hello?"

There was a tone, something that sounded underwater, and then a crackling. "Hello?" a voice said. "Maura Cassidy or Danielle Austin?"

She could still hardly hear, but she had a horrible feeling. Why would someone be calling for one or the other? "This is Maura, but I can hardly hear you," she yelled.

There was another crackling, and then she could only hear every other word—"Inform, Larkin James, accident"—she felt the room swim, and the line suddenly went clear: "Mr. Richard Smythe asked that we call, and we haven't been able to reach you until now. Can you hear me?"

"Yes," she said.

"Naturally, her family has been informed. We at the hotel extend our deepest sympathies."

She hung up.

She closed her eyes and put her fist against her lips.

Book Five

Seventy-seven

Danielle followed Maura back into the apartment, but it felt so creepy, so quiet.

"I can't believe it," she said, following Maura into the kitchen. She didn't want to be alone. "There were so many people there, Maura."

Maura nodded, but her back was turned. Danielle had never seen anybody cry so much in the past few days, and it was weird since she had never seen Maura cry, ever, before this. Was she crying now? "Did you notice, though, we were her only friends there except for Richard?" Maura asked.

Danielle hadn't thought of it. But now that she did, it was true: everyone else at the funeral had looked super-snooty and super–Park Avenue.

"Maura?"

"Mm." Maura was fiddling with the stove, and her back was still turned.

"Are you okay?"

She didn't say anything. She was fiddling with the knobs and cursing.

"Maura?"

She finally turned, and her face was all twisted. Danielle jumped up and put her arm around Maura's shoulder. "Come on. Sit down. You've been standing all day."

Maura sat down and she started to cry, and Danielle felt so bad. She didn't know what to say.

"I just feel . . ." Maura sobbed. "Just that it's all . . . It was such a short time; she had such a short life . . . and I always felt she'd be the one to make it."

"I kind of did, too," Danielle said. "I mean, with her acting and everything."

Maura closed her eyes. "I pushed her too hard. If everyone hadn't *ridden* her so much—"

"But you did it because you knew she really wanted to be an actress. She wanted to succeed, Maura."

"But she didn't have to do it so *fast*. She wanted to quit the show, and I wouldn't let her. She probably got fired on purpose, even if she didn't actively try to."

"But then that's what she wanted. You couldn't do everything for her. You couldn't live her life."

Maura stood up. "I'm sorry. I have to get out of here. I'll be back later."

"But where are you going? Are you okay?"

"I'll be fine," she said, but she walked out without looking back. Danielle looked around. It did feel creepy in the apartment, and sad. In a way, she guessed it hadn't really hit. She *knew* it hadn't hit, that Larkin was actually dead. How could someone just be gone like that, and she'd never see them again? She had never had anyone die in her whole life.

And it made her scared. What if Allan died? What if she never saw him again? It was easy to go around saying, "I'm mad at him" or whatever, but what if something giant happened to him? She had never wondered about Larkin, but now Larkin was gone, and who would have suspected?

Suddenly she didn't feel too great, and she turned off the water. Coffee was a horrible idea, and the thought of tea made her want to vomit, and all she wanted to do all of a sudden was lie down.

When had everything gotten so scary?

Danielle woke up and all the lights were on, and she didn't know if it was the day or the night. What week was it? Did she have to go to work? And then she remembered: Larkin. And she had felt sick and gone to lie down on the couch.

She got up and felt something funny, and she looked down at the couch. Blood.

"What?" she heard herself say, and she stood up and blood came pouring out from between her legs. "Oh God."

She put her hand there and ran to the bathroom, but she was trying to keep her knees together, so it took a super-long time, and she finally got there, but it took forever and she knew there was blood everywhere and she sat down on the toilet and pulled out a whole bunch of toilet paper. But she heard sounds in the toilet, something dropping, and she was afraid to look, but she looked down and she almost passed out: clots the size of her fist, clots of blood that were purple and some were red. "Oh God," she said, and she saw some Stayfrees on the floor across the bathroom. Maybe if she just held one there? But she tried to get up and heard another plop and it was more, and there was blood on the seat now, and she started to cry.

Seventy-eight

Max opened the door, and Maura took a deep breath. "I know I should have called," she said. "Do you have company? Am I barging in?"

"Of course not. Come on in. How was it?"

"Let's not talk about it, okay?"

He shut the door and looked into her eyes.

Let him do it, she thought. *Let me not be making a complete fool of myself.*

He cupped her face in his hands. "This is crazy," he said softly.

"I know," she said.

He kissed her and kissed her again, and they walked toward the bedroom with their arms around each other.

"Shit," she said, wiping her hair back from her face. "Nothing should ever be that great."

He was running his fingers through her hair. "I couldn't agree less. Why do you feel that way?"

She closed her eyes. She was so sad all of a sudden that she didn't even know if she could speak, if she could find the words. "Because you wake up, or come out of it, whatever it is after making love like that, and you remember what led you to it." She sat up and looked down at him. "You were the only person I wanted to see in the world after that funeral," she said. "I just wanted to talk to you; I knew you'd be the only person who'd know how I felt. So it was nice. You were home, you were great, we did what I had been hoping we'd do for a long time."

He was rubbing his eyes.

"You look like you know what I'm about to say," she said.

He shook his head. "Tell me."

"Oh." She looked down at the covers, the rumpled bed she'd probably never see again. "Everything's such a mess," she said, and she felt her throat start closing over her words. All she had done for days was *cry*. When was it going to stop?

And what had she done, sleeping with Max? It had ruined everything. She had always been able to tell herself that she couldn't make it work with someone wonderful, that she had been made for sick, Patrick-type relationships. Now Max would go back with Vanessa, she'd be alone again, and she'd know—for the first time—what she was missing.

She looked down at him. "When's Vanessa coming back?"

"Tomorrow."

She wanted him to say more. She wanted him to say, "And I'm going to tell her it's over, of course." She wanted him to say, "But you should stay here, Maura. I don't want to hide anything from her. She'll have to know." She wanted him to say something like that—anything—but he wasn't even meeting her eyes.

Seventy-nine

"I'm afraid we can't admit you without some sort of identification or someone else to vouch for you," the nurse was saying.

"But I'm twenty years old," Danielle said.

The lady shook her head. "With no insurance, no name, I'm sorry, we have rules."

"But I'll *sign*."

She sighed. "Isn't there someone else you can call?"

Danielle couldn't believe it. She was still bleeding and she hurt now, and they were telling her she had to go someplace else to *find* someone.

And the only other person she could think of was the person she had thought of first, before all the others. Allan.

But she didn't think of him with love, or wistfulness, any of the ways she had thought about him lately, wishing everything could be okay. She didn't even like him right now. She just wanted to be okay.

"Okay," she said. "Um, he might not be home, since no one else in the whole world seems to be, but his name is Allan Greshner." She gave the lady his number and waited, the way she had waited when the lady tried Maura.

But in two seconds the lady was talking, explaining—"Yes, she'll be fine, but we need *someone* blah, blah, blah"—and she almost felt good, like he was going to come, and she'd be maybe looking like she was dying or something, and she could say, "See?"

Because that was the problem. One minute she didn't like him, and the next she wanted to hurt him because she missed him. She just didn't know how she felt.

It seemed like hours till he came, and she started to get scared again; they gave her more Kotex, these giant diaper-type ones, and the blood was still coming, and she felt like, Why didn't they start doing something? How did they know she wouldn't bleed to death?

Plus she knew she hadn't even begun to think about the truth. Just the same as with Larkin. These things hit, but they didn't *really* hit for a long time.

The baby. She had lost it. And she knew what other people would say: "Don't you see? This is the way it was meant to be, Danielle. You didn't know whose baby it was, and now . . ." And then what would they say? God took it? She didn't believe it for a minute, and she wanted the baby back.

She heard footsteps on the echoy floor, and she looked up and it was Allan, and he came up to her and hugged her, but she held back. She didn't want to be so close to him.

"Are you all right?" he asked.

"Just help me get out of here, okay? You have to talk to that nurse over there."

He went, and she could hear him say, "I'm Allan Greshner,"

and then they talked for a while, and then finally, even though there were about nineteen people ahead of her, but she had been waiting so long that it didn't really count, a guy who was an orderly came, and he made her get into a wheelchair and they wheeled her away. She was in a panic—where were they taking her?—and she forgot to look at Allan, and when she finally turned around, she had been whipped around a corner down the hall, and it was too late.

"So how are you feeling now?" she heard. She had opened her eyes, but they had closed right away again, and she tried to open them.

Allan, sitting by the bed. And a whole roomful of women in white. God. Talk about not a private room!

"Mm," was all she could say.

"They said you'll be feeling better in a few hours. It's just Valium, but a lot of it."

She bit her lip. Larkin. Was this how she felt?

Allan reached out and took her hand. "I'm so sorry, honey," he said. "Why didn't you tell me?"

She didn't want to talk to him, and she didn't want to talk to him with so many people in the room. One of the women across from her, an old lady, was watching and not even pretending to do something else. Almost like she was about to say, "So go on. Tell him, honey."

"Danielle? Why didn't you tell me?"

"I can't talk about it," she said. "Okay? We can talk about it another time, but not now, Allan."

There were tears in his eyes, she thought for a second. "You know, I had been thinking about what we had decided," he said. "And maybe this isn't the best time to talk about it, but I think we should try again, Danielle, when you're feeling better."

She couldn't believe he was saying it. What about *Valerie*? What about his secret life, the things he did that he never told her about?

"Forget it," she said. "It's all over."

"But why? It doesn't have to be."

He was rubbing her hand, but she yanked it away. "You don't know what you're talking about," she said.

"Then tell me."

She felt like being mean. He had hurt her, hadn't he? "It wasn't even necessarily yours," she said. *There*, she felt like saying. Only, he didn't look that shocked. She looked over at the busybody woman, and *she* looked shocked. "So so much for that idea, huh?

Starting over. It sounds really easy, but it wouldn't be, Allan. Because I'm not the only one with secrets, am I?''

"What secrets are you talking about?'' he asked, super-calmly. Why was he so relaxed about everything? She had just told him he wasn't necessarily the father of her baby, and he was acting like she had just told him what time it was or something. ''Tell me what secrets,'' he said.

She shrugged. ''Valerie, for a start. Maybe that's why you're so relaxed about the baby. Because you know I'm not the only one who's been unfaithful.''

He was looking at her in a funny way. ''Valerie? You mean Valerie up at the club Valerie?''

''No, Valerie Bertinelli. Of course Valerie at the club. I'm not dumb.''

''Danielle, I hardly know her.''

''Oh. Right. Tell it to someone else, Allan. I have eyes. I can see.''

''But there was nothing you could have seen. Nothing to see. I met her once and spent a few minutes with her. Nick Dotson said she had seen me—some story—'' He stopped. ''You must have seen me that day,'' he said.

''Maybe,'' she said, shrugging. ''How would I know what you mean by 'that day'? There could have been lots.''

He was looking at her super-carefully. ''But there weren't,'' he said.

She picked at a hangnail, and the blood came shooting out onto the sheet. Whoops.

''Danielle, I barely know her. Look at me.''

''That isn't what I heard,'' she said.

He was starting to look real pissed off. ''Tell me what you heard, and tell me who you heard it from.''

''Nick said. He warned me.''

''Oh Christ.'' He stood up. ''That guy is going to be sorry he ever spoke to either one of us. Honey, don't you know he'll tell you anything to upset you? Just to split us up?''

She liked the way it sounded, like they had to work against the odds to be together. But was it true? ''I don't know,'' she said. ''Maybe.''

He looked super-sad and serious all of a sudden. ''If he was with you, he has to be in love with you. How can he lose by lying?''

She was already thinking about something else. ''He lent you money, didn't he?''

Allan sighed. "I wish I could say no, but he did. Look. Is he on tonight? As pit boss?"

"Um, I don't think so," she said. "Actually, I know he isn't, 'cause it's one of his days off."

"Do you know where he lives?"

"Allan, what are you talking about? You can't just go *after* him. Anyway, what did he do?"

"You were here tonight, alone, because he lied to you. I almost lost you because you believed him."

"But what about the other stuff? What I told you?" She looked across the room at the old woman. Hanging on every word. "You know, about . . . you know."

"When you're better, we're going to get married. We're going to start over, and we're going to start fresh. How does that sound?"

She couldn't believe it. She was so happy. "It sounds great," she said.

He leaned down and kissed her. "So you rest up, all right?"

She pulled him down to kiss her again. "I love you," she said.

"I love you, too." He hesitated. "Nick's coming to the apartment tomorrow morning at ten for our, uh, arrangement. I'll call you after he leaves."

"But you're not going to do anything crazy—?"

"I'll call you as soon as he's gone," he said.

"Promise?"

He said okay, and she watched him walk out of the room, the man she really loved.

Eighty

Nick rang the doorbell and smoothed his hair back. Shit, he felt great. Greshner was *such* an asshole. Giving him his home address, and here he was ringing the doorbell like some kind of fucking old woman coming to tea.

He rang again. What was the asshole doing? Getting dolled up?

It made him sick just to think of the guy with Danielle, that smug, asshole smile wiped across his face. Talk about shit-eating grins.

And where the fuck was he?

The door opened, and Greshner stepped back into the apartment.

"What'd you, fly in the fucking window? What took you so long?"

"I was in the bathroom," Greshner said.

Christ. Probably having the shits, the asshole. Talk about cracking under pressure. What a fucking *victim*.

"Yeah, so, I've been thinking," Nick said. Apartment wasn't too bad. Not bad at all. Greshner was watching him like some kind of nervous dog. Asshole. And following him, too.

Hm. Nice view, the bastard. "Nice view," he said.

Greshner looked pissed and scared. "Yeah, it's the best thing about this apartment."

Nick smiled. Do I care? "So I've been thinking," he said.

"So you said," Greshner said.

Nick took out a cigarette, lit it, and threw the match on the floor. Pick it up and you're a real asshole, he was thinking, but Greshner was pretending he hadn't seen a thing.

So now was the time. It made his heart go faster just to think about it. Who would have guessed this could be so much fun? Torture. It was so easy. And what did he have to lose? Zip. "The thing we agreed to. The price." Greshner was going pale already, and he was sitting down slowly, like his ass couldn't remember where the fucking couch was. Nick put his feet up on the coffee table. "Methinks I spoke too soon. Shakespeare, right? We had to read that shit in school."

Greshner had gone fucking mute.

"So the thing is, I have some new expenses I gotta meet, so we're going to change the rate, like the banks, you know?"

"To what?" Greshner asked, only it had come out like a fucking croak.

"Say from seven-fifty a week to a thousand." He watched Greshner's face—more pissed than scared now—and he decided to do it again. What the fuck. "Or shit—did I say a thousand? I meant twelve-fifty. My old lady needs some new clothes, you know? And—" He put his hand to his mouth. "Oh. Sorry. Your ex, I guess."

Greshner was just looking at him. Blinking like a fucking doll or something.

"Or *is* she your ex? We sharing her or what?"

He hadn't expected it, and it caught him off guard. Greshner was up off the couch and at his neck like a fucking animal.

"Hey—what the fuck—"

But Greshner—when the fuck had he gotten so strong? He had his hands on his neck, on his fucking Adam's apple—and Nick couldn't make a sound.

He went for Greshner's eyes, but Greshner moved his head back and there was nothing—the groin? He kneed him but missed, and he suddenly realized Greshner was trying to kill him. So Christ—he had his gun, but what the fuck good was it? Everything was going dark around the edges, and it was hard to breathe; he heard a horrible wheezing, and it was coming from his windpipe. He kneed Greshner again, and Greshner made some kind of sound and he was off him, and Nick—it was like slow motion, and it was beautiful—he reached behind his pants . . . How many times had he done it at home? Thousands, and it had been worth it, because he reached behind his pants like a fucking cowboy, drew out the gun and said, "Last wish, brother," aimed for Greshner's heart, and pulled the trigger.

Greshner looked like he was going to shit—maybe he was. His mouth was open, but he didn't make a fucking sound—his mouth was just a big O—and then the blood came out, and the sounds . . . Nick didn't want to hear; it was like some kind of fucking animal reaction; he took off and was gone in a flash. The door slammed and he heard the sounds, and he took the stairs to get away and to get away from the sounds. What was he, some kind of fucking pansy? But the sounds; he had never thought they'd be like that.

There were a million fucking stairs—nineteenth floor, the asshole lived on—but finally he was out in the street. Cars honking, people screaming, New York. The kind of quiet he needed to hear, because it wasn't screaming.

Eighty-one

Danielle nodded at the doctor and tried to concentrate on what he was saying. No sex for a couple of weeks; don't get pregnant for a couple of months. And she'd be okay. So that was great. But she wanted him to leave so she could call Allan and find out what had happened with

Nick. She had had such a really bad feeling all night, like that Allan was going to do something crazy, and now it was time that Nick would have come and gone, and he had promised to call, so where was he?

The doctor was sticking out his hand. "So I expect to hear from you in two weeks, Danielle, all right? You know that health care means calling your doctor for regular checkups."

"Uh-huh."

"So you'll start doing something you've never done before. It's a different way of thinking."

"Okay," she said. "I promise."

God, when was he going to *leave*? He gave her a little bit more of a lecture, all about poor people and how they didn't take care of themselves, how she didn't have to pay for things if she got Medicare or something, Medicaid, and then *finally* he left.

She dialed Allan's number, and it rang, rang, rang, so maybe he had gone out? Nick had come and gone?

It rang and rang and rang, and every time it rang, her heart skipped another beat. He had *promised* he'd call after Nick came.

She flipped off the covers and got out of bed. She had the most horrible feeling that something really awful had happened.

Eighty-two

"Fuck you," Nick said. Fucking asshole tourists in New York. If they couldn't figure out how to fucking walk fast, what were they here for? They needed laws in this city. Keep people like that out. And in their cars, too. Fucking tourists couldn't drive to save their lives.

But he had to think, that's what he had to do. He had been a fucking fool to leave the goddamn apartment. What the fuck had he been thinking? Dead was what you wanted. Not moaning. Not screaming.

But it was too late to go back. And what did he have? Zip. Christ. What to do?

There was his grandfather's place, always, out on the Island. And Vegas. Or Florida. He had more friends there, in Florida. And he could use the sun. Christ, New York was a fucking sewer when it got cold. A deep-freeze sewer. *That* was what hell was. None of this heat shit. Flames weren't so bad. It was the cold that killed you.

But what the fuck to do? He wanted to *know*, goddammit, one way or the other.

Leave, stay, what? He knew it would be crazy to go back. Only idiots went back to the fucking scene. But he was streetwise; he could go back and not let *them* know he was back. Just check it out. But shit—was it crazy or not? For the first time in his life, he didn't know what to do.

Eighty-three

Danielle jumped out of the cab at the red light, but right away she got a huge pain and she pressed her hand against her stomach. And she couldn't believe it: down at Allan's building the sidewalk was swarming with cops. There had to be a million. So God, what did that mean?

She started walking super-quickly—she didn't think she could run—and suddenly something caught her eye, a shape that was familiar, the way he moved. It was Nick moving through the crowd, and he looked like he was trying not to be noticed. But then he looked up and he saw her, their eyes met like in some kind of a movie, and her mouth dropped open. She wanted to scream—it had to mean the worst thing in the world that he was here—but in two seconds he was right next to her, and there was something sharp sticking into her side.

"It's what you think it is," he said. "And if you fucking scream, you get your pretty little ribs blown to bits, all right?"

Her heart was pounding. Cops all over the place, Nick; did it mean Allan was dead?

"Now, we're going to move out of here slow, and you don't make a sound, you understand?"

She screamed as loud as she could, and they came from everywhere.

Eighty-four

Maura opened the door to the office and tried to stay calm. After she spoke to Terence and Alexandra this morning, would it all be over? She hated the thought. It felt corny to think about, but this place had been the source for so many hopes. She had finally found something she was good at, something she really enjoyed. But she wasn't going to be part of a scam. No way. If they could tell her and prove to her that none of it was true, that she had come to a series of wrong conclusions, great. But she doubted they would.

And Max. She couldn't bear to think about it. Why had she tortured herself by sleeping with him? It was something she had known she'd regret—what had she said to Larkin all these years? Getting involved with people who were already involved—married or engaged, what difference did it make?—was asking to make yourself miserable. The difference was that Larkin had always wanted to be with men she couldn't have, with men she didn't, in fact, even want. But she wanted Max. And she wanted a life. And soon she wasn't going to have either one. And Larkin—she still had to wonder if she had pushed her too hard.

She heard voices and went and sat down at her desk, and she hoped it was just Terence or Alexandra talking to someone from one of the other offices—not both of them together.

The door opened and Terence and Alexandra came in, smiling and flushed and looking pleased with themselves.

Terence came over and kissed her on the cheek. "Sorry to hear about Larkin. How awful for you."

She tried to read his eyes, to see if the old Terence, the one who *had* cared—even if he sometimes showed it in odd ways—was still there. But he just seemed tanned and satisfied.

"Yes," Alexandra said, picking up the stack of mail at the corner of Maura's desk. "Sorry to hear about it." She tossed the eight-by-tens back on Maura's desk and tucked the rest of her mail under her arm.

"That's all it is to you, isn't it?" Maura suddenly said. "Another eight-by-ten, one less 'difficult' actress to worry about. You two are incredible."

Alexandra blinked. "I don't feel we've done anything to deserve that—either one of us. And if anyone hounded her about her work, it was you, I would think. We didn't even want to *handle* her."

"Right," Maura said. Her voice was shaking. "No doubt. Since you weren't going to be able to keep more than your share of her money."

Alexandra stared. "What are you talking about?"

"Well, *my* money, to start with. But I'm talking about actors' money. Jim Gray, Lew Burnham—"

"What about them?" Alexandra asked.

"Tell me I'm wrong," Maura said, looking at Terence. "Tell me you two aren't in way over your heads. With Jack and whoever else you owe."

Terence swallowed. "It shouldn't concern you."

"Shouldn't concern me? First of all, it concerns me because you two owe me money. It also concerns me because I work for you, and if you're doing something odd, I want to know about it. And as a friend, Terence, it concerns me if you're in way over your head with coke or whatever it is you're using."

Alexandra threw up her hands. "Oh, honestly. What *business* do you think you're working in? If you're going to get upset every time anyone snorts a little coke—"

"I'm not upset over 'anyone' snorting coke. I couldn't care less if you do it until it kills you, Alexandra. Terence is something else. And the business is what I'm talking about. Tell me I'm wrong about the money."

"You're wrong about the money," Alexandra said, "and you don't know what you're talking about."

"Then why did Jim Gray threaten to go to SAG?"

"It had nothing to do with money."

"So if I called and asked him—"

"It would be very unprofessional of you," Alexandra said.

"But he would tell me I was wrong?"

Alexandra turned and opened the door to the inner office. "I've had enough of this ridiculous nonsense. She's your friend, Terence. Do something." She went in and slammed the door behind her.

Maura looked at Terence. She couldn't read his eyes. "You could get in a lot of trouble for this," she said. "Serious, serious trouble."

"We're handling it," he said. "Vanessa made an incredible deal with Duane Haskins out in L.A."

"She's going to move out there?"

"Nope. That's the best part. For a show he'll be shooting in New York."

"Oh."

"But it means a tremendous amount of money for all of us," he said.

"Great," she said. "Just tell me, Terence. For old times' sake and all that. Am I wrong about what I said?"

He sighed. "There's something you're going to have to learn about this business, Maura. There is no 'for old times' sake.' I'd be crazy to even discuss the allegations you've made."

"Ah. I see. Allegations. Goddamn you, Terence, why did you have to screw this up? I can't work for you anymore."

"But why not? We'll pay you. Everything will be all right."

She shook her head. "I can't trust you, I can't trust that you won't do it again, I can't even trust you now when you say everything will be all right. I'm sorry, Terence."

She told herself to walk, to walk out before she changed her mind. It was too important.

She walked out and her knees almost buckled, and—God, not again—she started to cry. Thirteen years of not crying. She was certainly making up for it now.

She walked out into the street, into the clear, cold wind, and her tears dried, but she felt worse than ever. Everything was falling apart. Everything. And other people might not have quit under the circumstances. Was she crazy to have done it?

She could call Max. He would tell her she had done the right thing.

Don't go looking to get hurt.

But she had an excuse. Really.

You'll hear that horrible coldness. He slept with you, and now it's over. Face the fact that it was a onetime thing. You were upset; he felt sorry for you.

But she wanted to call. She wanted to hear one way or the other—

She ducked into a coffee shop and dialed his office number. He would have to be there; he always got there early, just the way she did.

He answered on the first ring: "Max Epstein."

"Hi. It's Maura."

"Maura, hi." Warm, not unfriendly.

"Uh, listen. I thought I should tell you, since you were certainly in on all of this. I just quit."

"Really." Less interested now.

She felt she was skidding. "Uh, should I call you back? Is this a bad time?" *Say yes, that someone's in your office, that that's why you sound so neutral and cool.*

"No, no. This is fine." Silence. "So what did they say?"

He didn't even sound interested. "Actually, not that much. The expected denials, that sort of thing." She hated the false casualness of her voice, but she was trying to keep her voice even, trying not to cry. Why did he sound so cool?

"Oh," he said.

God. So her most neurotic thoughts had been accurate. "Well," she said. "Congratulations on Vanessa's deal."

"Yeah. It's pretty impressive," he said. "She's very pleased."

The natural next question was, "And are you?" But she didn't want to ask. It was too intimate all of a sudden; he was obviously keeping their conversation as impersonal as he possibly could.

Silence.

"Well, I just thought I'd let you know," she said.

"Right," he said.

"So." So nothing. It's over, Maura, because it never was. "Well, I guess I'll talk to you."

"Right, Maura. Good-bye."

" 'Bye," she said. She hung up and closed her eyes.

Book Six

Eighty-five

"So who are you going to see today?" Danielle asked, putting down her hot chocolate.

"Another agency," Maura said. "But I don't have any expectations at this point. Three solid weeks of looking—I don't even know how many I've talked to, except it's a lot."

"But *one* of them's got to want to hire you, Maura. I mean, you've got the experience, even if it isn't a super-long time."

"It's true, but unfortunately, experience doesn't count for that much—at least the amount I have. A lot of them hire college kids to be interns for the secretarial parts, and for the agents, they want people with years of experience."

Danielle looked down into her coffee, and her face started to redden. "It kind of makes me feel bad, how you were the one who started me out and now you don't even have a job. I mean, who knows where I'd even be living if it wasn't for you? And I learned so much from you guys." She bit her lip.

Maura sighed. "Listen to me. Don't ever—for a minute—get into that trap of feeling guilty because you have something and other people don't. We all rooted for each other. I want you to be happy, and Larkin certainly would have wanted it. After Larkin died, I couldn't imagine doing anything—least of all what I had been doing, since I kept thinking I had pushed her too hard and made things worse for her—''

"But you didn't."

"I know. It took a while, but I finally realized that if I pushed her, it was in the only direction she ever wanted to go. The only time she was *ever* happy was when she was acting. I was good at helping her, and I think I'd be good at helping other people.'' She sighed. "But being good at something doesn't mean you'll necessarily get to do it.''

"But it does,'' Danielle said. "Or maybe it doesn't all the time, but you can't give up, Maura. Look how much you did. And look at the guy Steve. You found him, so it wasn't just Larkin. And *he* said he'd stick with you no matter what.''

"That's true,'' Maura said. But she was sick of talking about jobs, sick of thinking about jobs. Max hadn't called her since the day she had quit, and she couldn't stop thinking about him. How could she have been so wrong about him? "So what are your plans for today?'' she asked.

Danielle shrugged. "Allan still hasn't decided if he's going to stay at his job or not. I mean, his boss said he could, now that Allan's out of the hospital and everything, but Allan kind of feels it's all 'cause of his father, that his boss said he could come back to the job and just pay him back. And he's thinking, I mean since I quit at the club, and we don't have to testify for a while, maybe we should start real fresh, like somewhere totally new.''

"You mean out of the city—? Not just new jobs."

Danielle nodded. "I would've told you last night, but you were asleep. But I wouldn't screw you up with the lease, I mean I would stay as long as you needed, till you could find another roommate and everything.''

"Right,'' Maura said. Although it was two new roommates she'd need, and she couldn't bear to even think about showing Larkin's room yet. Her things were still everywhere. Anne James had said she or Fernanda would come pick them up, but they never would, Maura knew. It would be up to her and Danielle to do something with all the clothes.

"Well,'' Danielle said, standing up. "I'd better get going. I said I'd meet Allan for breakfast so we can talk a little more about his job and everything.''

Maura forced herself to smile. "Okay. Have a good time. See you later.''

Danielle was frowning. "I know you'll get something,'' she said.

"I just know it. And I know you and Larkin never believed in any of that psychic stuff or the numerology I did for you guys, but I tried it again last night with your birthday, and it really did say you'd succeed."

Maura smiled again, but she meant it this time. "Okay. Thanks," she said. Because strangely, it made her feel better.

Danielle left, and Maura went back to what she had been doing before Danielle had come in: reading the ads. There were never any ads for the kind of job she wanted. But she was trying to prepare herself for the worst, to gird herself if she had to start all over.

She opened the page and started at the top: "Admin Assts! Dozens of hi-pay jobs, you choose fave profession. Fashion, film, cosmetics." "Non-profit! Enjoy helping people? Come see us about fab jobs, MUST BE PEOPLE-ORIENTED." "Workaholics only. Do you give your *all* when you believe in a job? Come talk if you want to get ahead. Nine-to-fivers need *not* apply. MUST BE AMBITIOUS."

She threw the paper across the room. Square one.

The phone rang, and she was tempted not to answer it. No one on any of her interviews had even said they'd call. She had had to force her way into each of the agencies she'd seen, and at the end, all they had said, at best, was that they'd keep her in mind. Most hadn't even let her come in; they didn't need any new agents, and that was that.

The phone kept ringing, and she finally answered it.

"Maura," the voice said.

She sighed. "Hello, Vince."

"So how's it going? I haven't heard from you in a while. I called you last night."

"Obviously I was out."

"Oh yeah? Anybody I know?"

"What difference does it make?" Since she had just been getting the paper anyway.

"Hey, just asking. What got you so pissed off?"

"I'm just not in the mood, all right?"

Silence.

"I'll talk to you another time," she said.

"Not in the mood for what, Maura?" he said in a smooth, silky voice.

"Good-bye," she said, and she hung up.

So she was a bitch. She didn't care anymore.

The phone rang again. "Yes," she said.

"Yes what? Yes you want to fuck?"

"Go to hell." She slammed the phone down.

She went into the living room and flicked on the TV with the remote control, but she turned it off right away. She missed Larkin.

She looked across the room past the TV, and the first thing she saw was a sweater of Larkin's, and she had to close her eyes for a second.

And she wished they had had a chance to make up to each other. Because now, if she had known, would she have taken it so hard, been so stubborn? The point was the friendship, not the pain.

Shit.

She got up and got the classifieds from the kitchen and brought them back to the living room couch. Maybe if she was more comfortable while she read them—? But just looking at them made her head swim. What a botched-up part of her life.

She heard a sound, and she lowered the volume on the set.

There it was again, a knocking down the hall. So the doorbell was broken again.

She got up and went down the hall, and she had already decided: if it was Vince, she was going to tell him to go away. Maybe some of the good parts of her life were over, but some of the bad parts were going to be, too.

She looked through the peephole. Max?

She opened the door, and he was smiling his great, Max-style crooked smile. "So," he said. "Can I come in?"

"Of course. Shouldn't you be at the office?"

He was looking into her eyes. "I'm taking the next couple of days off. Going up to the country to look around." He was hesitating. "I was hoping you'd come with me."

She didn't know what to say.

"Just to look around," he said. "See if you like it."

She couldn't help it: her guard was up. "See if I like it as what? I'm out of work, in case you forgot. And looking for a job as an agent, not as a farmer."

"It's been rough, huh?"

"Very."

"You'll find something."

"Christ, I wish everyone would stop saying that. How does anyone know I'm going to find anything? *I* certainly don't know that; I don't know how everyone *else* is so sure."

"Because you're you," he said. "Because you will."

She sighed and shook her head. "Sorry, it's not you. It's just that it gets a little monotonous when everyone keeps telling you how great you are but they're not the people you want to hear that from.''

"But sometimes that's necessary," he said. "It's a necessary step. The same way you had to tell Larkin over and over even though no one else did. You believed in her because she was great. And I believe in you; I know you can do it." He smiled. "And I won't stop telling you that even if you want me to. So there." He took a deep breath. "But listen—that isn't why I came." He paused. "And I'm not very good at this, so I'm just going to spill it out. I'm sorry about the other afternoon, when you called."

"That's all right."

"It isn't all right. It isn't at all all right. It's just that I've been confused." He paused and put his hand on her cheek. "Since the first night I met you, actually."

She didn't know what to say. It was too good; it was coming too easily.

"Okay, this is it." He took another deep breath. "Vanessa and I called off the wedding. It will be the right thing to have done no matter what. But I was hoping . . ." He stopped. "Well, to me the idea is, we drive up to the country, give Sophie a run around some fields, look at some houses, try to make life here a little easier by getting a place to get away on the weekends. Make life in the city bearable till we're ready to give it up." He paused. "Is any of this appealing to you in any way, or have I made a huge and horrible and embarrassing miscalculation?"

She laughed. "I can't believe you feel you have to ask."

His mouth had dropped open. "Meaning it appeals to you."

She laughed again. "Of course it does, Max."

"This feels too easy," he said, taking her in his arms. "It was so wrong for such a long time with Vanessa, and I just couldn't admit it to myself. And I couldn't let myself think about you at all."

"I know what you mean," she said, looking into his eyes. "But maybe—well, maybe it's time to have things be easy for a change. I'm willing to try it if you are."

He kissed her and she closed her eyes, taking him more deeply into her arms.

Book Seven

Eighty-six

"Just a minute, please. I'll see if he's in."

Danielle punched the hold button and buzzed her boss, and he took the call after she told him who it was: Arlen Victor, a super-important lady at MGM.

And she felt like a million dollars. Today was the beginning of her third week on the job, and Mr. Hartell had told her yesterday that she was doing really well. "I'm very pleased, Danielle. Very pleased." Which was a miracle, because who would have thought she'd ever be able to type well enough to get a real job? But she had practiced like crazy—it was one of Maura's conditions—and she had actually gotten it.

And the great part was that Maura had found it for her, and *that* was great because it showed how successful Maura had gotten in only a few months at the agency where she was working. Four, if you counted. Maura knew people in L.A., she had come out twice, she even had three clients who basically lived here. And she and Max had stayed with them, which was fun. Maura Cassidy, agent. And now you could say Danielle Austin, secretary to a super-important West Coast agent, because that was what she was. Plus one more thing, but it was a secret.

And the thing was, Cleve had come back from Paris and he had started going to AA, and he was totally serious now, and he had said to her, "Danielle, you know, Allan has a similar problem. Maybe you should reconsider." And she had to tell him he was wrong, because maybe Cleve had needed help, but it didn't mean Allan did. He had quit the gambling a hundred percent, and he didn't even want her to play the lottery anymore (which she did anyway—and he didn't *really* mind, but he wasn't interested for himself at all). And it kind of made her mad at Cleve, like that *now*, now that she didn't really need him anymore, all of a sudden he was Mr. Attention.

But the most important thing was Allan, and he really had changed. Coming to California had maybe helped, because he had never even been, so it was like: A Whole New Life. And he had started in a whole new area, real estate, and she couldn't even complain about him being gone a lot, because when she got home from work, he brought her with him on his calls, which was fun. Giant mansions, sometimes.

Plus seeing her mother had been okay. Victoria had been totally shocked to meet Allan, and it was kind of like, "Well, you must be grown-up now" to Danielle. And the thing was, Victoria was the one who was still a kid. It really made Danielle realize how much *she* had grown up.

So everything was great, especially the secret. She didn't even hardly want to admit it to herself. She wanted to call Maura and tell her, but Allan deserved to know first, to be the first. So lunch with Allan would be the test, even though her horoscope had said, "Don't reveal any important pieces of information today." But she was trying not to believe a hundred percent of what she read these days, because maybe it *wasn't* all true. It was like, when she looked back at when she had moved in with Maura and Larkin, she had really been a baby. She didn't really know anything except how to be a super-great shoplifter, and even that had gotten a little rusty.

She looked at her watch, and her stomach flipped. Twelve-fifteen, so it was time to go. Her heart was pounding. Allan would be at the restaurant, and then—

"So I've got something to tell you," she said. He looked great. They went to the beach all the time on the weekends, and he looked great with a tan, just like a real beach guy.

He put his hand over hers and looked super-concerned. "What happened? What is it?"

She had to laugh. "It's not anything bad. It's good. At least, *I* think it's good." She bit her lip. She didn't know what to say. She looked into his eyes. "Um, Allan, are you pretty happy now?"

He smiled. "You mean now, in California and with you? That kind of now?"

She nodded.

Now he looked serious, and she got nervous for a second. But then he said, "I never thought I could be this happy. Really."

"So like, we said we'd get married, but you know, it's so in the future. But if we had a reason . . ."

He was smiling. "A reason like a baby? That kind of reason?"

She nodded again. "We're going to have a Libra baby," she said, and then she put her hand over her mouth. "God, I didn't mean to say that. I'm not going to read the horoscopes anymore. Because *they* said you'd be mad, that it wasn't a good day to tell you. So it means November. Forget the Libra part."

He laughed and he hugged her, and she knew deep down that the happiness was finally real, not like before, with dreams of becoming super-rich and famous. Maybe she'd never *be* those things. But she didn't care. Love was the most important thing in the world, and she had found it.

About the Author

Janet Kotselas Clarke grew up in New York City, where she still lives part-time. As research for NICE GIRLS, she worked in a casting office and as a hostess in a private club.

When not in the city, she enjoys working in the garden of her country house in upstate New York.

She is also the author of CHASING FAME and the forthcoming SMALL TOWN.